SHADOWS OF THE NIGHT

SHADOWS OF THE NIGHT

SONGS OF THE ASCENDANT - VOLUME I

DARIN KENNEDY

To Isaac —
Rock On!

Darin Kennedy

64 SQUARE
PUBLISHING

SHADOWS OF THE NIGHT
SONGS OF THE ASCENDANT – VOLUME I

Copyright © 2024 by Darin Kennedy

Cover art Copyright © 2024 Paul Maitland
Acrylic ink, acrylic gouache,
and coloring pencil on Bristol paper
Cover design by Natania Barron
Book design - Vellum Edgewood
Printed in the United States of America

ebook ISBN: 978-1-943748-03-7
paperback ISBN: 978-1-943748-04-4
hardcover ISBN: 978-1-943748-05-1

Charlotte, NC

To Pat Benatar,
Midnight Angel and Muse of this book and series
Thank you for the music

It's disgraceful how these humans blame the gods. They say their tribulations come from us, when they themselves, through their own foolishness, bring hardships which are not decreed by Fate.

— HOMER, THE ODYSSEY

CHAPTER I

WORKIN' FOR A LIVIN'

Jackson Browne had it right.

These towns do all look the same.

Always one of Dad's favorite tunes, anytime "The Load Out" came on the radio, we'd sit right there in his Ford F-150 until the song transitioned into Maurice Williams' 1960 hit, "Stay," the two of us singing along falsetto until the piano, guitar, and drum outro faded into Seger or Mellencamp or one of the other rock gods who haunted his favorite classic rock station. The anthem of the working man behind the scenes, the song is a love letter to all the people who make sure the show goes on night after night.

Funny. At the time, I never dreamed I'd be one of them, playing real world Tetris every night hauling speakers in and out of trucks, setting up the lights and equipment that turns an empty stage into an unforgettable evening, and tuning the instruments for this generation of music royalty. At twenty-three, I was supposed to be in grad school putting a couple extra letters behind my name, not crisscrossing the continent every other month with a job that requires as much brawn as brains.

But hey, it's a living. The pay is decent, the only roof I need for most of the year sits on four wheels, and we get most of our meals catered or on the bus. Not to mention that as much as the loading docks of the gazillion outdoor amphitheaters and indoor arenas coast-to-coast all look alike, whether you happen to be in New York or New Mexico, it doesn't change the fact that I've seen more of this country in the last year than dear old Dad saw in his fifty-two spins around the sun. Though it's mostly been from the window of a big silver tour bus, as Mom never stops reminding me, it's still been a good run.

"Hey, Ethan." My supervisor, Jerry, popped around the corner of the dock where I'd been enjoying a quick moment alone after me and the guys finished loading the last truck. His grey dreadlocks coursed down from his aged scalp and onto his shoulders, the color a stark contrast to his mahogany skin. "Why're you sitting by yourself in the dark? You want to get left here in Albuquerque?" His words, flavored Jamaican with a hint of Deep South, harbored more concern than rebuke.

"Sorry." I pulled myself up from the discarded milk crate that had served as a stool while I was taking a load off after a long night working in the sweltering mid-August heat. "Long night. Let my mind get away from me."

"Seems to be happening a lot lately." He raised an eyebrow. "Everything okay with you? Family stuff again?"

"I'm fine." I took the last slug of my soda and flung the can into the darkness by the dock. "Same shit, different night."

"Can't let guilt rule your life, kid." Jerry shook his head. "I know stuff back home ain't great, but your mom's a big girl. She can take care of herself."

Jerry always tries to come across as a badass when he's in front of the boys, but the truth is he's a big softie. Unless you cross him, of course. That never ends well. With thirty years in the business, Jerry Reid doesn't suffer fools for a minute.

"I just worry about her, you know." I let out a quiet sigh. "She's all alone."

Jerry raised a grey eyebrow. "Didn't you tell me you have a sister?"

"Emma?" My sister's crooked grin flashed across my memory. "She got her law degree and headed straight for Seattle. She makes it back to Knoxville for holidays when she can, but as far as she's concerned, Tennessee is strictly rearview mirror."

"So, it's all on you, then?"

"Losing Dad and Grandma back-to-back last year did a real number on her, and she's never been the same since Jacob died in Afghanistan three years ago." Not that any of us were ever the same after we lost my big brother in a war our country should never have started. "I want to help, but to be honest, it's hard to see her this way." My voice cracked a bit. "It's easier to just stay away." I let my gaze drop to the floor, too ashamed to meet another person's eyes in that moment.

"Don't go beating yourself up." Jerry cleared his throat and hawked a wad of spit onto the asphalt. "Wanna know the truth? You didn't bail on your mom. Hell, you've been on my crew for three years now, long before any of that bullshit happened—except your brother dying in Bush's war, of course. Truth is, we all have our own lives to live. You're just living yours, like your sister." He glanced up at the twinkling stars overhead. "I get that you love your family, but if you were the kind of guy to settle down in your hometown and grow roots, I don't think we'd be hanging out behind a loading dock in Albuquerque at one a.m. shooting the breeze."

"I know." My gaze wandered the parking lot, my eyes stinging with tears. "Doesn't mean I don't feel crappy about it."

"Then let me give you something different to feel crappy about," Jerry said with a chuckle.

"Good lord, what now?" I wiped the moisture from my eyes and forced a smile. "I was basically sitting back here waiting for y'all to start warming up the trucks. What's tonight's disaster?" Before he could answer, I spotted the one vehicle in the long line of trucks and buses with dark headlights. "You've got to be kidding. Her Majesty's tour bus?"

"Dead as a doornail. Mr. Shepherd and a couple of mechanics have been working on it since the encore. The lighting out here sucks, and they can't quite figure out what's wrong." He pushed a stray lock from his sweat-drenched face. "Anyway, the engine won't turn over, and Miss Snow has refused to leave her dressing room until there's a nice air-conditioned bus set at seventy-two degrees waiting for her."

Persephone Snow, tween television star turned singer and self-proclaimed Princess of Pop, waylaid most likely by either a dead battery or bad alternator. The enormous "SPARKLE" tour logo barely visible along the bus's side hit me as almost poetic.

"Can't she ride with the band?" My brain performed some quick calculations. "Or maybe the backup dancers?"

Jerry answered with the most withering look I'd ever seen in those kind brown eyes.

I raised my hands before me, palms up in a quick shrug. "So we're stuck here until her bus gets fixed?"

"They've got another bus on its way. All of her big stuff is already loaded onto one of the trucks, but Miss Snow has requested that all of her personal belongings be transferred to the new ride before she comes out."

"You're kidding, right? She's got a metric ton of crap."

"A metric ton of crap that you are now officially in charge of." Jerry chuckled.

"Is Gus sticking around to help?" Miss Snow's taciturn bus driver, Gus Shepherd, rarely moved from his seat, routinely leaving the heavy lifting to the crew. To be fair, our current situation notwithstanding, he kept the bus's motor purring with a near arcane knowledge of combustion engines. He'd even managed to get a couple of the trucks up and running two stops back, saving us a day. Still, if it didn't involve getting the talent from Point A to Point B, he typically wasn't interested.

"Mr. Shepherd is pushing sixty and his back just isn't what it used to be." He motioned in the direction of the highway. "No need to keep him out here in the dark all night. We'll put him up in a hotel in town. In the morning, he and his crew will get the bus back in shape, and then he'll catch up to us." Jerry's mouth quirked to one side. "But don't worry. You won't be stuck out here by yourself. I'm leaving you some help."

"Wait. You guys are moving on?"

"Denver is six or seven hours away. We'll get everybody else there by early morning, and you guys can follow later tonight or tomorrow."

I sucked air through my teeth. "And who exactly is it you're leaving with me?"

Jerry paused, a half-guilty expression crossing his features. "Dino."

The laugh was out of my mouth before I could stop it. "Seriously? You're going to leave me here alone with Dino?" I fought to hold back an annoyed sigh.

"Hey, Dino works as hard as any of us." A quiet chuckle passed his lips. "More importantly, he volunteered." His head tilted to one side. "Anyway, I made it worth his while just like I plan to make it worth yours."

"All right, but exactly how are the two of us supposed to get to Denver?" I motioned to the dead tour bus. "Her Majesty may allow us onto her golden chariot long enough to move her things, but you're crazy if you think she's going to let a couple of roadies hitch a ride north with her."

"You've got that right," came a feminine voice from above our heads, "especially if they're calling me names behind my back."

Against my better judgment, I turned my head toward the voice and found a seriously pissed pop star staring down at me from the loading dock above our heads.

Persephone Snow's crystal blue eyes shone despite the low light, her waist-length platinum-blonde locks framing anything but her usual effortless smile. Changed out of her final costume for the night —an ensemble that required as much double-sided tape as it did fabric—she stood, arms crossed, in a pink crop top, skin-tight jeans, and a pair of wedge sandals. Despite the furrowed brow, squinted eyes, and pursed lips, she was still the most beautiful woman I'd ever seen.

"Miss Snow," I stammered, my cheeks hot with embarrassment. "I'm so sorry. I didn't know you were there."

"Clearly." She pulled in a breath through her flared nostrils and let it out with a huff. "I take it you're this Harkreader person who's going to be taking care of all my things?"

"Yes, ma'am."

"Ma'am?" Her voice shot up an octave and a few decibels as well. "Do I *look* like a ma'am to you, Mr. Harkreader?"

"No, ma'am." I almost caught the word before it escaped my lips. "I mean, Miss Snow." I lowered my head in deference, my flushed face burning with a potent mix of anger, embarrassment, and attraction.

"Better." She shifted her attention to Jerry. "I hear the trucks are moving out in five, Mr. Reid. I trust you've left your best man to get me situated on whatever passes for a tour bus at midnight in Albuquerque, New Mexico?"

"Of course, Miss Snow."

Her gaze darted briefly to me and then back to Jerry. "And you'll let him know he can keep his smart mouth and any little nicknames to himself?"

Jerry sighed. "Of course, Miss Snow."

"Splendid." She spun on one heel and headed back into the arena. "I'll be in my dressing room. Have Mr. Harkreader come get me when everything is ready."

As the distant sound of a slamming door echoed from the open dock, Jerry laughed and shook his head. "At least she won't forget you, Ethan."

I pinched the bridge of my nose. "I'm just glad she didn't fire me on the spot."

As we walked down the line of trucks and buses for Miss Snow's defunct Shangri La on wheels, the lone vehicle among our convoy that always raised the hairs on my neck came into view.

The chief of security for the tour, an imposing Frenchman named Luc Delacroix, traveled from city to city in a modified Commander 8X8, the biggest, baddest RV I'd ever seen. Matte black from headlight to exhaust, the Australian behemoth had been upfitted with every piece of communication equipment imaginable and appeared as well-armored as an M1 Abrams. The man clearly took his job seriously, though I had trouble imagining the war zone that would make necessary driving what was effectively an urban tank. Not to mention, I checked the price tag for such a ride. I'm sure the glorified bodyguards for the rich and famous were paid well, but damn, I still wasn't over the sticker shock of that particular Google search.

Who knows? Maybe it was a gift from one of his favorite clients.

Rarely seen except when he was directing the security team at the various venues or accompanying Miss Snow on her frequent errands, Mr. Delacroix had maintained a pretty low profile for the entire tour, an impressive feat for a six-foot-four mountain of muscle. Even more rare had been sightings of his wife and daughter who traveled with him in his hotel-on-wheels. I didn't even know their names, but I had spotted the pair a few times sharing a meal with Mr. Delacroix in various hotel restaurants and once ended up sharing an early-morning workout with them in a hotel gym three stops back. Both Middle Eastern beauties, the mother could easily pass for her daughter's older sister, though I put the woman somewhere in her forties.

The one time I'd caught Delacroix's daughter's gaze for half a second, she'd answered with a curious smile, but her mother had put the kibosh on any further communication, unspoken or otherwise, with a glare like a pair of black suns that bored straight through to my soul.

I may not always be the quickest on the uptake, but even I can take a hint.

I turned to Jerry as we arrived at his bus. "So, you guys are seriously taking off?"

"It's what makes the most sense, Ethan. I promise to make it up to you."

"Any idea where Dino is? I don't want to be out here lugging a whole bus worth of crap by myself."

"Right here!" Dino appeared around the front corner of the lead bus. "Hi, Ethan!"

Perky and unflappable twenty-four/seven, Dino never seemed to be without a smile. Eighteen years old and fresh out of high school, he was more than just an employee of the tour; he was a fan. Like, a serious fan. Being a part of this tour, even on the most grueling nights, was his wildest dream come true, and nothing yet had been able to dampen his mood. Most of the time, his constant positivity was a welcome change from the more jaded attitude common among the rest of the crew. Occasionally, though, it made me want to kill him.

Guess which side was winning out tonight.

"Hey, Dino." I pulled in a deep cleansing breath and let out a half-amused sigh. "Looks like it's you and me."

"Can't wait." Dino drew close. "Once we get the new bus loaded, do you think Miss Snow will let us ride along?"

"Only if there's room after the Easter Bunny and the Tooth Fairy get on." I kept my voice low, not wanting to get burned twice the same night. "Just saying."

"Tooth Fairy?" Dino stared at me quizzically. "I don't understand."

"You two will be riding with me." Dressed impeccably in his black suit, starched white dress shirt, and narrow black tie, Mr. Delacroix approached from his imposing road machine, as silent as the night despite his massive frame. "Plenty of room up in the cab." His eyes shifted from Dino to me. "Good evening, Mr. Harkreader. I trust you and your associate can make the transition to Miss Snow's new transportation go smoothly, and more importantly, quickly."

Holy shit. He knows my name.

"Yes, sir."

He turned to Jerry. "In that case, Mr. Reid, I suggest you all get on the road. I will stay here with Miss Snow, Mr. Harkreader, and..." His gaze, like a hawk's, shot to the fourth man in our circle.

"Dino, sir." He trembled at the man's deep baritone. "My name is Dino."

"Dino it is, then." Delacroix returned his attention to Jerry. "I'll be in contact once we're on the road."

Jerry answered with a quick nod and headed for his ride. Within minutes, the massive convoy of buses, trucks, and other vehicles vacated the lot, leaving the three of us alone.

Of course, no time passed before the replacement bus arrived. The vehicle in question, a repurposed commercial tour bus for seniors with the previous logo painted over but still visible even in the low light, was anything but what I'd expected.

Miss Snow was not going to be happy.

"You can't be serious." For the second time that evening, Persephone Snow's voice caught me by surprise. "You expect me to travel in *that*?"

"Miss Snow." Delacroix strode over to the unhappy pop star as she appeared from the shadows. "I thought I asked you to remain inside."

"And I thought I told you to find me a decent replacement for the *very* expensive bus you people can't seem to get running." She crinkled her nose in disgust. "Or do you want me to go onstage in Denver smelling like Ben Gay and cat pee?"

"It's the middle of the night, Miss Snow." Delacroix somehow maintained a cool monotone despite his charge's tirade. "Beggars can't be choosers."

"I am not a beggar, Mr. Delacroix." Her crystal blue eyes flared in the dim light. "I am Persephone Fucking Snow. When I ask for something, I expect it to be done and done properly. Now, I'm stuck standing behind a loading dock in the hottest spot in the entire country sweating like a pig, the sushi dinner in my mini-fridge I'd been looking forward to all day has spoiled, and I'm starving because the only food you've been able to obtain for me is some pizza, and you know I'm not doing gluten these days." She cast a derisive look at the replacement vehicle. "What, an old school bus wasn't available? Or maybe a dump truck full of manure? And if anybody says the words 'dry heat,' they're fired on the spot."

"Miss Snow." Delacroix inhaled, maintaining his clearly practiced calm. "I offered to let you travel with us, but you declined. This transportation is the best we could find on such short notice. Now, would you prefer to be stuck in this parking lot for another couple of hours waiting for what will inevitably be an even less desirable solution, or do you want to go check out your new set of wheels?"

"Fear not, Miss Snow," came an indistinct whisper from the shadows, the accent Australian and the tone guttural. "My employer has arranged for more than adequate transportation to your next destination."

From the still-running replacement bus stepped a slim man dressed all in black. A full-length duster stretched from the asphalt beneath his dark boots to his tightly collared neck. He studied us from beneath the wide brim of his hat through the smoky lenses of a birdlike mask reminiscent of those worn by doctors during the Black Plague.

"Who the hell is that?" Miss Snow took a step back. "Mr. Delacroix?"

"Get behind me, Miss Snow." Delacroix stepped in front of his client without a moment's hesitation, her slender form disappearing behind his massive frame. "Let me handle this."

"What are you supposed to be? Some kind of freaky cosplayer?" Dino took a single step forward and was immediately flung to the ground as if an unseen person had swept his feet from beneath him. The swift fall drove the wind from his lungs, though good fortune had his shoulder take the brunt of the fall rather than his skull. Still, the impact left him down for the count, leaving only me and Mr. Delacroix to protect Miss Snow and deal with whoever or whatever this creep purported to be.

"Stay back!" I raised my fists and stepped into the space between Delacroix and the mysterious figure in black. Adrenalin surged through my body with fight beating flight by a narrow margin. "I don't know who you are or what you want, but if you think you're taking Miss Snow anywhere, you've got another thing coming."

"Two against one," came the muffled voice from behind the bird-like mask. "However shall I win against such odds?" With the cryptic statement, the man lifted one hand before him as if he were commanding an army to rise.

And rise an army did.

An army of shadows.

CHAPTER 2

THE WARRIOR

L ike some *Twilight Zone* version of *Peter Pan*, the mysterious
figure's dozen or so shadows sprang to life. Each cast by one
of the loading dock's various halogen lights and radiating out
from the man's body like the hands of a schizophrenic clock, the
shades leaped up from the asphalt as one and formed on either side
of their master like a platoon of soldiers ready for battle. As the line
of dark silhouettes advanced, the target of their attack took off in the
opposite direction.

"Leave her alone." Ignoring my racing heart, I moved to engage
our strange assailant, hoping I could occupy him long enough for
Miss Snow to get to safety.

A strong hand at my shoulder halted my forward movement.

"So," Delacroix whispered as the indistinct forms moved to
surround us both, "our unseen enemy has employed the Midnight
Angel and her Ravens."

"Midnight Angel?" I glanced across my shoulder at Delacroix, keeping the weirdo in black and his platoon of shadows in my peripheral vision. "Ravens?"

"More later, if we survive. For now, know this: before you stands a skiomancer. Darkness dances at his delight, and shadows fight at his command."

The man in black tilted his head forward in an almost polite bow.

Delacroix pulled close to my side, keeping himself positioned between the fleeing Miss Snow and her would-be kidnapper. "While I appreciate your bravery, Mr. Harkreader, there would be no shame in stepping aside." He trained his laser-like gaze on the skiomancer before us. "This is not your fight."

"No way." I spread my feet shoulder-width apart like I learned in a tae kwon do class a million years ago and dropped into my most comfortable fighting stance. "You think I'm leaving you to fight this freak alone?"

"Whoever said he would be alone?" A lithe figure in a red tank top, black yoga pants, and sneakers somersaulted from atop the dead tour bus and landed before the mysterious man in black. The woman whose platinum wedding band matched the one on Delacroix's left hand now stood between us and darkness, her hair pulled back into a long ponytail, with a long, curved sword in one hand and a matching shorter blade in the other.

"Dearest," she said, her delivery deliberate and her accent marking her as Middle Eastern, "get Snow and this boy to safety. I'll handle the skiomancer."

"Who's she calling 'boy'?" I muttered.

"Like hell," Delacroix grunted, ignoring me. "I'm not leaving you alone with this animal."

"We all have our roles, darling," the woman said. "Fulfill yours while I fulfill mine." Dropping into a low martial stance that made mine look like something off an action movie's blooper reel, she returned her full attention to the dark stranger. "Hello, Raven."

"Daughter of Neith." He offered her a subtle bow. "And here I thought I'd be facing only your lover and the hired help."

"Ah, Rupert. I was wondering which of her minions the Angel sent on this errand." She stepped forward with authority, her two blades crossed before her. Her bearing left little doubt that she knew exactly how to use both to lethal effect. "As I recall, I last encountered you in Marrakesh during that whole affair with the Redstarts." She directed her curved sword at his raised arm. "I trust your shoulder has recovered appropriately?"

The man she called Rupert balled his gloved fingers into a fist before his hidden face. "Your blade may have cut deeply, but my mistress's skills were more than adequate to repair the damage."

"Excellent." Delacroix's wife pulled her blades close to her body and returned her enemy's bow. "I'd hate to lower myself to battling a bird with a broken wing."

"Enough talk." The man in black dropped into a fighting stance, and though his face remained obscured behind the creepy leather bird mask, I could almost feel the wicked smile spreading across his face. "Shall we dance?"

"As if any other outcome were in the cards." She murmured an unintelligible phrase, and as if in answer, both her blades began to glow from within. "Come, skiomancer, and face my steel."

The words were barely out of her mouth when the Raven directed his gloved finger at Delacroix's wife. From every direction, shadows flew at her, the dark silhouettes descending upon her like a pack of rabid dogs. My heart pounded with the cold certainty that I was about to witness a woman being ripped limb from limb by forces I couldn't begin to comprehend.

My morbid prediction could not have fallen further from the truth.

With a grace I've only ever seen on TV watching Olympic gymnasts compete for the gold, she leaped backward, the shorter blade clenched between her teeth, and curled her compact form into a one-handed backflip. As the various shades arrived at the spot she'd just vacated, she spun like a whirling dervish, her shimmering sword passing through the convergence of shadows and dissipating them all with a single slash. The Raven howled as if struck himself, the remaining shadows surrounding us growing hazy and indistinct in his pain.

"Your kind never learn, skiomancer," the woman whispered after retrieving the shorter blade from her teeth. "As with our encounter in Morocco, I will allow you the opportunity to leave with your life." She pointed the longer blade at his chest. "With the understanding, of course, that you and yours will not return or bother Persephone Snow again." Her head tilted to one side. "I'd hate for your mistress to have to train another in your stead."

In the distance, a scream split the night from the direction of Delacroix's black monster of an RV, a scream I'd already heard once that evening.

"Miss Snow." I narrowed my eyes at our bizarre opponent. "What have you done to her?"

"Me? Nothing." He looked past me in the direction of the shrill cry. "But if the Daughter of Neith travels with an entourage"—his invisible glare burned through me despite the obscuring mask—"why would any of you assume I came alone?"

"Dearest," the woman whispered to her husband, "take the boy and attend to your charge while I deal with this Raven."

"But, Danielle—"

"*Names*, darling." She stepped toward the Raven, her shining sword brandished before her and directed at her enemy's heart. "Now, go. I'll join you when I can."

Delacroix hesitated, then turned in the direction of his dark home on wheels. "Come on. Miss Snow needs us."

He took off at a dead run, and I followed without question, not that I'd even know what to ask. The two of us arrived at the Commander in seconds, and any questions regarding the cause of Miss Snow's bloodcurdling cry were immediately laid to rest.

Lying flat on her back on the still-warm asphalt, she stared up in terror at a second Raven, this one a hulking form in his black duster, wide-brimmed hat, and dark avian mask. A pair of shadows cast by the Commander's bright headlights swirled about her, pulling at her clothes, her hair, her flesh. As her screams diminished to a quiet whimper, adrenalin sent my pulse soaring. My vision went red as I rushed Miss Snow's tormentor.

"Get off her, you bastard!" I swung my right fist in a wild haymaker and caught the Raven's chin through his leather mask. The blow knocked him back a few inches, which was good because I was pretty sure I'd just broken my hand. As I followed with a left, however, he was more than ready for me. He caught my fist like an errant fastball and dug his gloved fingers into my knuckles. The pain sent me to my knees.

"I'm impressed, boy," he murmured in a Scandinavian accent as he stared at me through the translucent lenses of his mask. "No one's landed a blow on me in years." He doubled the intensity of his grip, sending my entire arm into spasm. "That being said, no one touches me without my permission."

"My apologies, then, Raven." Delacroix stepped across my crouched form and sent his foot flying at the Raven's head. The roundhouse kick landed with a satisfying thud that sent our shared enemy to the unforgiving asphalt, freeing me from his cruel grip. "Stay down or, shadows or not, I will pound you into oblivion."

The Raven glared up at Delacroix. "I've often wondered what kind of man could tame a Daughter of Neith. You do not disappoint." The pair of shadows attacking Miss Snow leaped from her suddenly still form and flanked Delacroix on either side. Far more solid than they appeared, one grabbed his left arm and the other his right. As they held him in place, the Raven rose from the ground and pulled a long, twisted dagger from his belt. "What a shame to end a man such as you so unceremoniously." He lumbered forward, his cruel blade held in the same gloved hand that had crushed mine moments before. "First you, then your little friend."

As the Raven raised the dagger above his head to make good on his threat, a shouted voice came from above.

"Father, avert your eyes."

A quick glance up revealed a glimpse of a female form hurling something from atop the massive RV before instinct forced my eyes closed. Half a second later, a flash filled my vision despite my clenched eyelids, and a thunderclap buffeted my ears from just a few feet away.

Deafened and half-blind from the explosion, I could see nothing but a blur of olive skin, billowing dark hair, and flashing steel. I rubbed at my eyes in an effort to bring the world back into focus and fought to hear anything besides the high-pitched ringing that filled both my ears.

And then, a pair of sounds: a body hitting the ground like a bag of golf clubs followed by Delacroix's voice.

"Don't kill this one," he grunted, his blurred outline pointing a finger in my direction. "He's with us."

I shook my head once more in an attempt to clear my senses, and when I again opened my eyes, before me awaited a sight that would be forever burned into my memory.

Triumphant over the massive crumpled form of the second Raven, Delacroix's daughter stood like an avenging archangel. A sword like the samurai carried in the old Kurosawa films I loved as a kid rested lightly in her right hand while some kind of grenade dangled from the fingers of her left. Glistening in sweat, she sported a white T-shirt that featured Sarah Michelle Gellar's no-nonsense stare and three simple words down one side.

Eat.

Slay.

Love.

A girl after my own heart. Though technically before my time, I'd seen every episode of everyone's favorite vampire slayer at least twice. Hell, I even liked Season 6.

And...I'm staring at her chest.

My gaze rose from Buffy's grim visage and met the perturbed stare of a young woman I'd only seen in passing a few times since the beginning of the tour and locked eyes with but once. Those same eyes now stated in no uncertain terms that they were "up here."

"Sorry," I stammered, "my vision is still clearing."

"One down, Father." Ignoring my failed attempt at an apology, she turned her head in the direction of the battle between her mother and her vanquished foe's partner-in-crime. "One to go."

"One?" A wheezy laugh sounded from the mammoth tangle of arms and legs at her feet. "You've clearly never crossed paths with a Conspiracy of Ravens before."

Delacroix's daughter dropped to one knee and brought the pommel of her sword down on his temple, rendering her foe unconscious and sending his hat flipping into the now-still shadows that had threatened us all moments before.

His taunt, however, proved prophetic.

Delacroix and I turned in the direction of the dead tour bus where we'd left his wife—he'd called her Danielle—and found the woman her enemies called "Daughter of Neith" facing not one but three of the dark-garbed skiomancers.

Not to mention more of the living shadows than I could possibly count.

From every direction—left and right, above and below—they flew at her, ephemeral as wind until it was their turn to strike. Each slash of her gleaming blades dispatched the menacing shades a handful at a time back to whatever hell spawned them, but like the Hydra of myth, every shadow destroyed was replaced a moment later by two or three more. Delacroix's wife showed no sign of slowing as she continued to battle against the encroaching darkness, but the night was long, and her enemies were growing in both number and power.

One lucky strike and the multitude of shadows would overtake her.

"Mother!"

Delacroix's daughter was gone in a blink, racing for her embattled mother as if the Devil himself nipped at her heels.

Delacroix stopped long enough to peer down at Miss Snow's unmoving form. "Keep her safe," he grunted before taking off as well.

And there I was, standing next to an idling RV that likely cost more than I'd make in the next twenty years, a down-for-the-count assassin in black at my left foot and a dazed pop superstar flirting with unconsciousness at my right.

Unsure whether I was more likely to end up in prison or sued for every penny I had—important safety tip for the lawyers: that's not a very high number—I scooped up Miss Snow and took her to the back of the RV to see if there was any way inside the fortress on wheels.

"Mr. Harkreader..." she said just before passing out in my arms. "You stopped them."

Yeah. That was totally me.

As we came around to the side door of Delacroix's vehicle, I caught movement out of the corner of my eye coming from the direction of the downed tour bus.

"Stay back!" I shouted. "I'm not playing games here."

"Ethan?" came a thankfully familiar voice. "It's me, Dino."

"Dino?"

"Yep." My friend materialized from the darkness massaging the shoulder he'd fallen onto earlier. Other than that and a slight limp, however, he appeared none the worse for wear. "Whoa. Is that who I think it is?"

"I don't believe it either." I carried Miss Snow's unconscious form to the RV's side door. "Listen, Dino," I whispered. "Take Miss Snow inside, lock the door behind you, and don't make a sound. You hear me?"

"What's going on, Ethan?" Dino's worried gaze danced back and forth between the downed Raven at the other end of the RV and Miss Snow's unconscious form draped across my arms, his usual bulletproof smile replaced with a grimace of pain. "Why are these people attacking us?"

"I have no idea, but what I do know is that Miss Snow is counting on us to get her through the night alive, and the only people who can do that need my help." I gestured for him to open the door to Delacroix's Commander. "Now, like I said, inside, lock it up tight, and not a sound. You understand?"

He gave me a silent nod and then took the dazed pop star from my arms.

"I'll be back for you soon." I helped him get her into the rear of the RV and locked gazes with him just before I closed the door behind them. "Not a peep, got it?"

As the lock clacked on the door, a sound I was actually surprised I could hear after the flashbang grenade, I turned toward the battle in progress. The Delacroix family fought valiantly—husband, wife, and daughter—against the trio of Ravens surrounding them, but as the number of shadows continued to grow exponentially as the battle wore on, the outcome became clearer and clearer. Despite their best efforts, it was only a matter of time.

But what could I do? Scant yards away, a family of what were basically superheroes fought for their lives against the literal forces of darkness. Meanwhile, I was nothing but a college dropout with a brain like a steel trap for song lyrics and an apparently useful talent at fitting sound equipment in a standard truck trailer.

The Commander's idling engine shifted tone, creating a dissonance with the ringing already going on in my head. And that's when it hit me.

I may not be much use in a fight, but my driver's license was up to date, and it just so happened I was standing next to what was basically a street-legal tank.

I circled around to the driver's side, climbed up, and tried the handle.

Thank God, the door opened.

"All right, Ravens." I muttered as I pulled myself behind the wheel and dropped the gearshift into drive. "Let's see how well you fare against a few tons of Australian steel."

CHAPTER 3

HEARTBREAK BEAT

The tires barked as I jammed my full weight down onto the gas pedal and yanked the wheel in the direction of the dead tour bus. There, Delacroix, wife, and daughter continued their valiant struggle against the trio of Ravens and their two-dimensional army of shadows. The twin LED headlights lit up the skirmish like an arena spotlight, creating as many shadows as they destroyed. I sent the twenty-ton RV rocketing for the nearest figure in black, sending him scampering to one side. I caught a glimpse of Ms. Delacroix as I barreled past, her head dropping in a curt nod as her eyes and mine briefly met.

My initial gambit over, the shadows came for me. Flying at the cab of the massive RV like a flock of insubstantial birds, they quickly obscured every bit of visibility, leaving me no choice but to slam on the brakes and bring the enormous battering ram to a halt.

My only play rendered useless after a single run. Now, what the hell was I supposed to do? Other than get out of there, of course, as the countless shades began to pass through the glass, the door, the roof, and the floor, filling the cab like poisonous gas from a James Bond film.

I yanked the handle, but the driver's door didn't budge. The shadows, exactly as solid as they needed to be to kick my ass, held it fast as dozens more continued to come. I scooted across the cab, pulled the opposite handle, and again met resistance. With everything I had, I put my shoulder into it and forced open the only viable avenue of escape.

The swirling shadows pulled at my hair, my clothes, and my very flesh with fingers of ice, their darkness obscuring my vision as I fought to free myself from Delacroix's vehicle. With a bellow from the bottom of my soul, I willed every ounce of strength I had into my legs and leaped out into oblivion. Passing through the cloud of shades was like diving through black oil, arctic cold, and mind-numbing depression all at once. Though the experience lasted but a second, I feared the moment would haunt me for the rest of my days: the unbelievable chill, the despair, the utter hopelessness.

As my eyes readjusted to the halogen light of the parking lot, my heart froze.

Only two of the Delacroix family remained standing.

Danielle Delacroix, embroiled in battle with the first Raven, still brandished her pair of glowing blades as she dispatched shadow after shadow in an effort to get to their dark master just feet away. Mr. Delacroix, conversely, had somehow fought through the river of darkness and now traded blows with a second Raven, this one nearly as massive as the one that had tormented Miss Snow minutes before at the other end of the lot.

Their daughter, however, had apparently fallen to shadow at the feet of the third Raven. This one a female, she stood imperious over a sphere of darkness that I guessed contained the missing member of the Delacroix clan.

Before I could talk myself out of the most suicidal thing I'd ever done—at least in the last couple minutes—I rushed the Raven tormenting the youngest Delacroix. Vaulting over shadow after living shadow, I came face to obscured face with the malevolent woman in black.

"Well, well, well," the lone female Raven said with a cackle, "what do we have here?" Her more familiar midwestern American accent did little to stop the chill creeping up my spine. "A hero?"

"What are you doing to her?" I shouted, dodging to avoid a vicious shade's ephemeral talons going for my throat. "Let her go."

"You insert yourself into affairs that are none of your business, boy."

Again with the *boy*.

"Look, I don't know what you or these other 'Ravens' are supposed to be or why you're here, but I'm going to make you wish you'd never set foot in this place." I raised my fists before me and did my best not to tremble as my dark-clad adversary broke into laughter.

"You're an infant playing with matches," the Raven taunted, "and you're about to get burned."

My father taught me from an early age that a man should never hit a woman, but I was pretty sure his lesson didn't include superpowered kidnapper-assassins. I pulled back to throw the last punch I'd likely ever launch when a burst of light and sound erupted at my feet, dissipating the sphere of swarming shadows separating me and the no-longer-laughing Raven.

Having freed herself from her shadowy captivity with her remaining flashbang grenade, Delacroix's daughter rolled to one side in agony, holding her ears. I was half-surprised not to find blood seeping between her fingers. Though it was likely the only move she had left, I was pretty sure the instruction manual on those did not include setting them off when still on your person.

"Hey," I shouted, hoping she could hear me, "are you okay?"

Delacroix's daughter met my gaze, her look of utter resilience quickly shifting to cold fury as she focused on something or someone across my shoulder.

"Step aside, boy," came the Raven's muffled words, barely audible over the renewed ringing in both my ears. "I have work to finish."

"Yes, young man," came another voice, this one loud and clear despite my second flashbang grenade of the day. "Step aside." Her initial dance partner taken out of the fight—dead or alive, I wasn't sure—Ms. Delacroix stepped between me and the female skiomancer. "While your help is most appreciated, this fight is not yours."

Young man. I'll take it.

"Like I told your husband, ma'am, no way." I pulled myself up from the ground and stood shoulder to shoulder with Ms. Delacroix. "Time for Round 3?"

"Very well." The elder of the two Delacroix women gave me an appraising up and down and nodded. "You go high; I go low?"

I wasn't sure exactly what that meant, though I'd heard such words in more action movies than I cared to remember. In that moment, however, I refused to let down the most badass woman I'd ever met and answered with a simple nod.

In a blur of movement, Ms. Delacroix shot out a low sweeping kick at the Raven's knee. Desperate not to screw up her attack, I leaped at our shared enemy, shoulder forward, my teeth gritted as I braced for either impact or counterattack.

In the end, I met with neither as, atop a swirling mass of shadows, the female Raven retreated into the sky above our heads.

"You fight well, Daughter of Neith, and you, boy, are stupidly brave." She cast her masked gaze down at the fallen Raven. "You may have defeated one of us this evening—"

"Two, actually." Back on her feet, Delacroix's daughter joined her mother beneath the levitating Raven as her father continued his fight with the largest of our remaining enemies a few feet away. "Soon to be three."

"Brave words, little girl." The female Raven shifted in her direction atop her platform of shadow. "Careful, or they will be your—"

Ms. Delacroix sprinted toward the front of the downed tour bus, ran up the sloping grill and windshield, and leaped from the top in a twirling backflip. With a double slash like a giant pair of shears, she brought her still-glowing blades across the floating Raven's hamstrings, sending her falling from her shadowy perch to the cruel asphalt below.

The injured Raven howled curse after curse at the pair of Delacroix women as they approached from either side. I kept my distance, not sure what was about to happen, but quite sure I wanted no part of what was about to go down.

"Mother," the younger Delacroix woman asked, "shall we put this one out of her misery?"

"Mercy is a virtue, my dear," Ms. Delacroix answered. "But whether such mercy is ending both her pain and wretched life or leaving her alive to hopefully find a better path, I leave to your judgment." She gestured to her daughter's katana, held loosely in the younger woman's right hand. "I will abide by your decision, but for now, your father requires my assistance."

"More than you know," came a deep Russian voice, "Daughter of Neith."

Both Delacroix women and I turned as one to find the tables had turned in the fight between Mr. Delacroix and the last remaining Raven, though this time not to our advantage. Defeated and on his knees with his arms again stretched to either side by shadowy shackles, Luc Delacroix shook in anger. The lone remaining Raven stood behind him, his thin blade a millimeter from Delacroix's throat.

"Concede, woman, unless you wish to watch your husband's lifeblood spilled in such an ignoble place as this."

Ms. Delacroix directed the longer of her two blades at the remaining Raven. "Harm him in any way, and I will end you."

The Raven laughed. "You believe you still have the upper hand. How delectable." He pointed to the ground between us and his hostage. "On your knees, both of you." He didn't spare me so much as a glance.

"Don't do it, Danielle," came Delacroix's strangled croak. "I'm just a man, while you and Rosemary—"

"*Names*, darling," she repeated, though this time her voice was choked with emotion. "And you are anything but 'just a man.' I won't watch you die."

"So sentimental," the Raven rumbled triumphantly. "I'm surprised you've lasted this long, Daughter of Neith." Any remaining mirth left his voice as he again pointed to the asphalt between us. "Now, on your knees."

"We're not going to do what he says, are we?" The youngest Delacroix—Rosemary—searched her mother's eyes. "We can't give in to this *monster*."

"We must." Danielle Delacroix, the one the freaks in black called "Daughter of Neith"—whatever the hell that means—dropped to one knee, deposited her paired weapons on the asphalt at either side of her, and then brought her other knee beneath her. As she knelt in utter submission, she whispered, "Your father is counting on us."

"But—"

"Just do it."

With a pained grunt and obviously still reeling from the second flashbang, Rosemary knelt beside her mother, glaring at the menacing figure in black. "You'd best strike hard and fast, Raven, because if I get back on my feet, my face will be the last thing you ever see."

"Drop your sword, girl." His eyes, hidden behind his mask's dark lenses, shifted from daughter to mother and then to me. "In fact, why don't we have Miss Snow's little hero here take all your weapons and drop them at my feet?"

I looked to the older of the Delacroix women for guidance and at her quiet nod, stepped forward. I took both Rosemary's katana—I basically had to pry it from her fingers—as well as her mother's paired swords and carefully deposited them on the asphalt before the Raven. Our cloaked adversary in turn kicked each of the weapons under the darkened tour bus and out of sight, leaving father, mother, daughter, and me at the Raven's mercy.

"Now, at last, the time has come for—"

A loud metallic thunk split the night. The Raven holding Delacroix pitched forward, instinctively pulling the edge of his blade across his hostage's throat before he fell to the ground. Behind him, a panting Dino held a bright red fire extinguisher at the apex of its arc.

"Luc!" Ms. Delacroix cried out.

"Father!" her daughter simultaneously screamed.

Together they rushed to Delacroix's side. His hand, held to his neck, oozed dark blood from between the fingers. Despite the wound, however, the giant of a man remained upright, albeit on his knees.

"Luc," his wife asked, "are you all right?"

Delacroix's eyes shifted left and right as he cleared his throat. "Names, darling." His voice, though strained, remained full and strong. He pulled his hand away from his neck. Though blood trickled from a thin line just below the angle of his jaw, everything important appeared intact.

"Praise the gods." Ms. Delacroix breathed a sigh of relief. "A few stitches, and you should be fine."

"Yes, Father." For the first time that evening, the young woman called Rosemary actually smiled as a quiet laugh parted her lips. "You're going to be all right."

Meanwhile, I rushed to Dino's side as the eighteen-year-old hero of the night started to hyperventilate.

"Holy crap, Dino." I nodded in admiration. "You saved us all."

Between hyperventilating breaths, he answered, "I know you told me to stay with Miss Snow, but she's out cold. I heard what was going on and—"

"Stop." I rested a hand on his shoulder and offered him my biggest smile. "You did good, buddy. You did good."

"Thanks." He answered my grin with a nervous one of his own.

As Dino's gaze wandered past the trio of ninjas or superheroes or whatever the Delacroix family called themselves, his relieved expression quickly reverted back to one of terror.

"Oh my God," he gasped, "is that—"

I followed his horror-stricken gape to find swirling darkness flying silently at the Delacroix clan. Both mother and daughter remained distracted by the gash at Mr. Delacroix's neck while Delacroix himself was anything but ready for another round.

"Ms. Delacroix!" I screamed as a flash of silver shone from the center of the rushing shadow. "Look out!"

With nothing but flesh and bone with which to defend herself, the matriarch of the Delacroix clan spun around, fists raised and war chiseled into her features. The Raven we'd left unconscious at the other end of the parking lot materialized at the center of the mass of shadows and took full advantage of his turn with the element of surprise. Half a second after my shouted warning, he gutted Ms. Delacroix from hip to opposite shoulder with a vicious upward slash of his serpentine dagger before plowing into Mr. Delacroix, sending him flying into the family's armored RV.

This time, Delacroix didn't get up.

"Mother!" Rosemary screamed as the wounded woman sunk to the ground. "Father!"

"It's just us now, little girl." The Raven let fly a Nordic chuckle. "And this time, I'm the one that has the drop on you."

"You bastard!" Rosemary rushed at him. "I'll kill you for this."

"Not if I kill you first."

She flew at him, her footfalls fast and silent. In turn, he swung his blade at her as he had her mother, but that apparently was precisely what she was counting on. Diving past him like a professional baseball player sliding into home plate, she disappeared beneath the darkened bus only to reappear a moment later with her mother's blades in either hand.

"Let's see how brave you are now, you *bastard*."

As Rosemary and the last Raven began to circle, I pulled a terrified Dino close and whispered in his ear. "Go check on Mr. Delacroix and Miss Snow." I nodded in the direction of the big black RV. "I'll see about..." My eyes flicked in the direction of Danielle Delacroix's crumpled and bleeding form, my lips unable to speak her name.

With nothing but a curt nod, Dino crept off into the dimly-lit night, giving both Rosemary and her opponent a wide berth.

And that left me with...her.

I stole to Ms. Delacroix's side, steeling myself for whatever I might see.

Whatever I imagined, this was worse.

Blood pumped rhythmically from just above her left breast while parts of the human body people aren't meant to see peeked from behind her previously well-toned abdominal muscles.

"Rosemary." She looked up at me, the light quickly fading from her eyes. "Bring me..."

Her eyes slid shut as her words faded into a gurgling rhythm, her labored breathing growing faster with every blood-tinged gasp. I knelt by her shoulder and put two fingers over her carotid.

No pulse.

My mind flashed back to the week of EMT training I'd suffered through before deciding upon my current path as Roadie to the Stars. Dropping to both knees, I started chest compressions, trying my best to keep in time with a Bee Gees song that was already relegated to the oldie station the day I was born. Blood trickled from her mouth and her coughs became wetter and weaker when they came at all.

What the hell else was I supposed to do?

A quick glance around our asphalt battleground revealed Dino tending to a conscious but incapacitated Mr. Delacroix as Rosemary and her foe resumed their fight in earnest, steel clashing against steel in a sword fight ripped straight from the movies.

Meanwhile, nothing I did seemed to be having any effect. I pressed harder with each compression until I was pretty sure I felt a rib break beneath my palm. That's when Ms. Delacroix stopped breathing altogether.

Despite Barry Gibb's explicit instructions, Danielle Delacroix was dying, and there wasn't a damn thing I could do about it.

But it wasn't going to be for lack of trying.

I steeled my stomach as I lowered my mouth onto her bloodied lips and breathed a long, full lungful of air into her mouth. Her chest rose and fell, and she coughed once more.

I inhaled to give her a second breath, but as I bent forward to continue my losing battle with Death, Danielle Delacroix's eyes flew open, as aware and alive as when I first saw her. With blinding speed and inexorable strength, her hands flew to either side of my head, holding me as still as an animal in a trap. As her paired blades had glowed before, her previously fading eyes now shone with an inner light. I struggled to free myself, but like a fly caught in a spider's web, there was no escape.

And then, with a primal scream like you only imagine in your worst nightmares, the whole of Danielle Delacroix's essence flowed from her open mouth and into mine. Every inch of my body crackled with electricity, every hair stood on end, and my every molecule burned. All I'd ever been was washed away and replaced with something both new and yet very, very old.

Something powerful.

Something pure.

Something far beyond my understanding.

CHAPTER 4

HARD TO SAY I'M SORRY

"So, we have to kill him to fix this situation?"

I was just coming to when I caught the whispered words.

"No one is killing anyone, sweetie," came another quiet voice, this one a full octave deeper than the first, "but we do have an awful lot to sort out."

"I'm guessing you're talking about me." My voice, little better than a whisper, brought a quiet gasp of surprise. I forced my eyes open and found myself in a dazzlingly bright room filled with beeping machines. My nostrils flooded with the twin scents of bleach and fresh laundry while the blurred eye chart on the far wall confirmed I was in a hospital ER.

The IV sticking out of my arm and running up to a half-full bag of clear fluid removed any question.

Across from me in the tiny room sat Mr. Delacroix and Rosemary.

"So," I coughed, clearing both throat and lungs, "I'm not dead."

"No, Mr. Harkreader," came Delacroix's rumbling tones. "You, it would seem, are very much alive."

"For now," Rosemary added, her comment cut short by a stern glance from her father.

"What do you remember, Mr. Harkreader?" he asked. "Tell me in as much detail as you can muster."

I struggled not only to remember but to figure out the correct words that would keep the young woman whose eyes flung daggers with her every glance from killing me at the first opportunity.

"Ms. Delacroix. She was badly injured by the"—I dropped my voice to a low whisper—"man in black with the dagger. I was trying to save her, or at least keep her alive until an ambulance could arrive." I locked gazes with Delacroix. "Did she—"

He shook his head slowly from side to side, his only answer.

"That's what I was afraid you were going to say." My shoulders slumped as I filled with sadness at the loss of a woman I didn't even know. "I'm so sorry."

"What else do you remember?" This question came from Rosemary. "Did she say anything in the end? Do you remember what happened after she..." She looked away, her eyes welling with tears.

"She asked for you." Another peal of coughing took my breath. "She called for you by name."

"And then what, Mr. Harkreader?" Delacroix leaned forward, his eyes narrowed as if trying to peer into my soul. "What happened next?"

I hesitated, afraid that my memory of the following seconds represented either half-dreamed delirium, or worse, a truth so damning that Delacroix and his daughter would have no choice but to silence me to keep their secret safe.

"Her eyes. They glowed, like her swords did when she was fighting those freaks and their shadows."

"The Ravens." Rosemary ground her teeth in anger. "Murderers."

"Her eyes glowed indeed." Delacroix exhaled through his cavernous nostrils. "And then what? Tell me everything."

"She grabbed me." My entire body shook uncontrollably. "One

second she was too weak to move or speak and the next she had me in some kind of headlock. I couldn't escape her grip."

"Go on." Delacroix nodded solemnly. "This is the important part."

"It's crazy."

"I suspect it is," he said. "Tell us."

The scene played through my mind like a movie I'd seen a thousand times. Glowing eyes and swords. Bad guys in bird masks. An army of living shadows. And then, the part I had the most trouble believing.

"She breathed herself into me." It was my turn to look away. Even the slight movement of my head made the room spin. "I swear, she screamed her soul out of her body and into mine."

The man's solemn eyes slid shut. "And after that?"

"I woke up here. Heard you two talking." I again met Delacroix's gaze. "That's insanity, right? Just something I imagined before passing out? I mean, how could she have grabbed me, much less done any of the rest of it? She was barely breathing there at the end."

"To tell you the truth, Mr. Harkreader, the end of Danielle's life is the *only* time she could have done what you describe."

"My birthright, trapped in this foolish boy's body." Rosemary stormed out of the room. The door slammed shut behind her, leaving me and Delacroix alone.

"Please excuse Rosemary," he said. "She's understandably angry and frustrated, both at losing her mother and by what happened after. I know my daughter well, though. Given time, she'll come around."

"Unless I'm missing something, it sure seems like she hates my guts."

"At the moment, Mr. Harkreader, that is quite an accurate assessment."

Another cough racked my chest. "I'm not lying when I say I don't remember anything after that until waking up just now. What happened to your wife?" I swallowed back the bile in my throat. "What happened to me?"

Delacroix's gaze dropped to his lap. "In your much-appreciated efforts to save Danielle, you interfered with a process that has occurred for centuries, a process that occurs at the end of every Delacroix woman's life if she has not made earlier arrangements to pass on her inheritance to the next in line."

"Inheritance? Next in line?"

And did Mr. Delacroix take his wife's name? Not unheard of, but there was a story there.

"What you experienced last evening has been known by many names in many languages over the millennia, but since the Age of Reason, Danielle's family has referred to what happened between you and her as Transference."

"Like that stuff Freud talked about?" I may have only made it halfway through my sophomore year at Tennessee, but I really liked my psychology professor and still remembered a lot from the class. "I don't think Dr. Haskins ever said anything about glowing eyes or your soul leaving your body."

"Not that type of transference, Mr. Harkreader. What I refer to is a true movement of energies from one body to another, and not just life force, but power, skill, ability, knowledge."

"Life force?" A surprised laugh forced air out my nostrils. "You're talking like something out of a comic book or *Star Wars*."

"Says the man who just fought four figures in black who could control the very shadows." Mr. Delacroix pulled in a deep breath and again shook his head. "My apologies, Mr. Harkreader, but you have inadvertently become a part of a war that has raged for centuries, and I'm not certain anyone on this planet, much less Rosemary or me, knows how to extricate you from your new situation." His voice dropped to a whisper. "At least not while leaving you alive."

A chill ran up my spine as I inhaled to respond, but before I could say another word, a knock at the door to my room drew both our attention.

"Ethan!" Dino, his eyes still haunted but his general energy back to its normal level, burst into the room. "You're awake!"

"Hey, Dino." I attempted to keep the exasperation from my voice and failed miserably. Delacroix sat on the precipice of explaining what had happened to me and why my entire body vibrated like I held a live wire, but it seemed that discussion would have to be postponed, at least for the moment.

Honestly, a part of me was grateful for the interruption. I had a nasty feeling that nothing the widowed mountain of a bodyguard said was going to be good news nor any of the changes to my body and soul temporary.

"How are you feeling?" Dino asked. "Last night when the ambulance took you away, you looked pretty rough."

"I'm fine." At Delacroix's dropped chin, I added, "Though, not everyone can say the same."

Dino shot Delacroix a sheepish look. "I'm sorry about your wife, sir."

"Thank you."

I'd not often seen a man who could hold his own in an MMA cage match well up with tears, so I focused on Dino to give Delacroix what privacy I could.

"You really came through last night, Dino, and more than once." I gave him my best facsimile of a smile. "You feeling all right?"

"Just a few scrapes and bruises, but otherwise none the worse for wear."

"Good." For the first time since I'd awakened, another face loomed in my mind's eye. "What about Miss Snow? Is she okay?"

"She's fine." Delacroix stretched, clearly glad the subject had shifted from his recently deceased wife. "She's a couple doors down and recovering well from last night's attack. A little bump on the head and scared out of her mind, but otherwise physically intact."

"She's been asking for you," Dino added.

I swallowed back my surprise. "Persephone Snow asked for me?"

"The last thing she remembers is you slugging tall, dark, and ugly with a right cross and saving her life. She wants to thank you." Dino wriggled his eyebrows. "Personally."

My heart raced at the words, both at the prospect of warranting the attention of an international superstar as well as the guilt of feeling excitement at such a somber moment.

"Don't worry, Mr. Harkreader," Delacroix said, as if reading my mind. "You showed some real guts last night." A faint smile materialized on his face. "It would appear I'm not the only one who noticed."

I raised an eyebrow. "Do you think I should go see her?"

"I'll go ask the doctor if it's all right." Before I could say a word, Dino was out the door, leaving me again alone with Mr. Delacroix.

"I know this is a sensitive topic, but how is your daughter—Rosemary—dealing with her mother's death? I mean, aside from the whole 'Transference' thing."

"Not well." The two words banished any whimsy from his features. "She and her mother were close." He cleared his throat. "Thank you for asking."

"Not freaking out or anything, but as I was coming to, she said something about having to kill me to 'fix' this." I let out a nervous laugh. "I hope that isn't on the agenda for today."

"My apologies. You weren't meant to hear that." Delacroix sighed. "In any case, she was only speaking hypothetically." His voice dropped to a low mutter. "At least I hope she was."

I did my best to hide my shudder at that last bit. "She said something about her birthright. Said it was somehow 'trapped' inside me?"

"The Transference, Mr. Harkreader, was not meant for you."

"Understatement of the year." Rosemary strode back into the room, marginally more composed than when she'd left. "It was meant for me."

"Look, I'm sorry." I shot both hands up in self-defense. "I was only trying to—"

"Shut your mouth." She glared at me through squinted eyes. "You have taken something that wasn't yours to take, the very essence of my mother, and her mother before her."

"Rosemary," her father said.

"Generation upon generation of accumulated power and wisdom, neither of which you have the first idea how to apply. Do you plan to fight the Ravens when they inevitably return for Snow?"

"Rosemary—" Delacroix repeated.

"And what of the next crisis? Will you stand against the darkness, denying your own needs and wants in favor of the greater good? Do you have it in you to sacrifice everything, the way my mother did?"

"Rosemary!" Delacroix raised his voice and finally got his daughter's attention. "While your anger is more than understandable—"

"Understandable?"

Delacroix silenced her with a stern glance. "Mr. Harkreader was only trying to help your mother in her last moments. Nothing that has occurred is his fault, regardless of how unfortunate the current circumstances appear to be." His eyes locked with mine. "I'm sure he would gladly relinquish in an instant both the power and responsibility that have been thrust upon him, but harsh words and threats will accomplish nothing."

"But, Father..."

"Things are the way they are, Rosemary, and at least for the moment, Mr. Harkreader's fate and ours have become intertwined. Until such time as we can extricate ourselves from each other's lives, he will need to be brought into the fold." A quiet groan escaped the man's lips. "And trained."

"Brought into the fold?" I asked. "Trained?" I fidgeted with the IV in my arm and contemplated pulling it out and walking out of the hospital. "Look, I'm really sorry about what happened, Mr. Delacroix, but my brother Jacob was the soldier in the family. I'm just a guy who loads and unloads trucks for whatever tour is happening at the moment. No matter what you say has happened, I can't do the things you people do. Whatever this war is you all are fighting, it has nothing to do with me, and I want no part of it."

"To the contrary, I'm afraid to say." Delacroix rose from his seat and came to the bedside. "You, Mr. Harkreader, have basically become a nuclear warhead in a battle between light and darkness that has gone on for all of human history. Fortunately, you currently rest in the presence of two of the few on either side who consider a single innocent important enough to bother with helping." He glanced his daughter's way. "Rosemary's misplaced anger aside."

"Misplaced?" Rosemary hissed.

Delacroix again silenced his daughter with a furrowed brow

before returning his attention to me. "Trust that the opposition would love nothing more than to exploit your current status, and if that were to your detriment, they would likely consider that an added benefit."

I did my best to swallow back my fear. "You're talking about those 'Ravens' from last night?"

"The Midnight Angel and her Conspiracy of Ravens aren't the only ones I'm worried about," Rosemary muttered, her words calmer with each syllable.

"And, at least in the past, one of the more honorable," Delacroix added. "There are others who would end you without so much as a word, not necessarily to further their cause, but simply for the joy of watching you die."

"Your sales pitch for signing up needs some work." I dropped my gaze to the floor, unable to look either of them in the eye. "Not that it seems I have much choice in the matter."

"Will Mother's essence do anything in him beyond simply existing?" Rosemary studied me quizzically. "I mean, a *man* cannot be a Daughter of Neith."

"I have no idea, Rosemary." Delacroix wrapped an arm around his daughter's shoulders. "Not only is Mr. Harkreader a man, but he represents the first Transference ever outside your direct bloodline, at least to the best of my knowledge." His gaze flicked in my direction. "Frankly, I'm surprised he survived the process."

"So, what do we do now?" I stared, incredulous, at the remaining two Delacroixs. "Do we tell the tour managers, 'Sorry, but we have to cancel Miss Snow's multi-million-dollar tour because the shadowmancing supernatural terrorists in dusters and raven masks that attacked her are probably going to try again'? Because I can tell you exactly how that's going to go."

"Funny you should ask that," Dino said as he strode back into the room. "Miss Snow is down the hall raising hell and demanding that she be discharged immediately to head for Denver for her concert tomorrow night."

"Tomorrow night?" I sat up straight in the bed. "She can't go on a day after almost getting kidnapped or worse. That's ridiculous."

"*You* want to tell her that?" Dino's eyebrow shot up. "That there's something Persephone Snow wants that she can't have?"

"Yeah." My shoulders slumped. "Might as well try telling the sun not to rise."

"Indeed." Delacroix sat back down and patted the chair next to him for Rosemary to join. "We're going to have to handle this, and Miss Snow, delicately." He peered around at all of us. "The truth of the matter is that the Ravens can come for her at any time or place, be it onstage, her home, or otherwise. At least if the tour continues, we can keep the pretense of me as her personal security so I can watch over her."

"Pretense?" I asked. "I thought you were her bodyguard."

"A position I filled primarily so Danielle could keep close to Miss Snow while she was on the road and vulnerable. There have been rumblings on the dark web for months that someone was hoping to acquire our favorite pop starlet for reasons that unfortunately remain unclear."

"Someone?" I asked. "For ransom? Or something worse?"

Rosemary sighed. "If only this sort of people wanted something as innocuous as money."

I turned back to Delacroix. "If you knew this was coming, why didn't you notify the police?"

"The police?" Dino interjected. "Against people who can control shadows?"

Delacroix nodded. "Few exist who can fight against such as those who have targeted Miss Snow, and my wife felt that keeping civilians out of harm's way was likely the best strategy. Your current predicament, Mr. Harkreader, would suggest she was correct."

"And now that she's gone"—I swallowed back my fear—"you want me to fill her shoes?"

"No one can fill Mother's shoes," Rosemary answered, her voice quiet, "not me, not anyone."

"The big question is, if not money, what does whoever is behind all this want with someone like Miss Snow?"

"That is a question we'd all like answered." Delacroix rose from his seat and went to the door. "The level of chatter on the darkest corners of the internet regarding her has been unprecedented, and yet I've been around her daily for weeks and haven't seen or heard anything that would explain any of this." He studied me for a moment, his eyes keen and perceptive. "In fact, since she's asking for you, may I suggest you go visit her and see if she can shed any light on the subject?"

CHAPTER 5

SHE'S A BEAUTY

A pair of armed policemen in black uniforms flanked a door at the far end of the hospital hallway. One was busy talking on his radio while the other watched my every step like a cobra preparing to strike.

Funny, there were no guards outside *my* door.

The latter gave Delacroix a nod of recognition and waved him over as he kept one eye on me. I gave him a curt nod that remained unanswered as Delacroix knocked at the door with his massive fist, sending it ajar.

"Miss Snow?" he rumbled. "May I enter?"

"Mr. Delacroix?" she answered. "Of course. Come in."

"I've brought a guest." He gently pushed the door open, revealing me in all my hospital-gowned glory. "I believe you were asking for this young man?"

"I was." The faintest hint of color invaded her cheeks as she looked my way. "Hello again, Mr. Harkreader." Her tone harbored far less edge this time. "You're looking well."

"Miss Snow." I tilted my head forward in deference and immediately regretted it.

For God's sake, she's just a pop singer, not royalty.

"You can call me Persephone if you like." She bit her lip, thinking. "Seph, actually. 'Persephone' is a mouthful and 'Miss Snow' seems a bit formal."

"All right, Miss—I mean, umm, Seph."

"Better." She shifted her attention to Mr. Delacroix. "If you wouldn't mind, I'd like to have a moment alone with Mr. Harkreader."

Delacroix gave Seph a quick nod and stepped out of the room.

Her eyes returned to me. "Ethan, isn't it?"

"Yeah." I nodded. "Ethan."

"Are you feeling all right?" she asked. "You know, after everything that went down last night after the show?"

My deep breath elicited a fleeting pain in my chest I hoped wasn't a broken rib. "A little banged up, but nothing time can't heal."

She leaned forward and patted the corner of the bed by her feet. "Come here. Sit."

"Are you sure?" I stared at the starched hospital sheets. "You barely know me."

"Last thing I remember, you jumped into the line of fire and saved me from those awful people. I owe you my life, Mr. Harkreader." Her lips spread into the smile that graced the walls and phones of teens across the world. "Ethan."

She patted the bed again, and this time I complied. In that moment, it felt very much like I was a peasant being granted an audience with the Queen.

"Since the local police insisted on providing me with security until I leave town, I freed Mr. Delacroix up to keep an eye on you." Her mouth quirked to one side. "You know, he may come across as stern, but he's been in and out all evening checking on me. Best bodyguard I've ever had." She shook her head. "I was so sorry to hear about his wife."

"He told you?" I wasn't sure if I was more surprised that Delacroix had entrusted Seph with such knowledge or by Seph's blasé tone concerning the fact that a woman had died defending her life less than twenty-four hours earlier.

"She's been with us the entire tour." She raised an eyebrow. "Why wouldn't he tell me?"

Her confused stare brought back the last words Delacroix said to me before we left my room to venture down the hall to check on the target of last night's assault. He'd advised that I not tell Miss Snow—Seph—anything regarding the true nature of the events of the previous evening. Still, as I studied those crystal blue eyes full of questions, it dawned on me that I didn't know *what* he actually *had* told her. On a different day, I suspect he'd have been more on his game and briefed me before we went in, but the one-two punch of losing his wife and now comforting a doubly-grieving daughter would derail anyone's train of thought.

Fortunately, I think pretty quickly on my feet.

"I just mean, they usually keep to themselves, and he hasn't mentioned anything to me. What did he tell you?"

"That his wife's mother had fallen ill, and she had to fly home to care for her. He said she'll likely miss the rest of the tour."

"Wow, that's too bad." The lie felt slimy leaving my mouth. "Hope everything turns out okay."

"Talk about timing." Seph laughed ironically. "She missed all the excitement."

"Yeah." I worked to banish the image of Danielle Delacroix's gutted form lying on the Albuquerque asphalt, those glowing eyes staring straight into my soul, those inescapable hands holding my head as she relinquished all that she was to abide within the body of a man she'd known for all of five minutes. "*All* the excitement."

"Oh, don't get me wrong. I don't mean to make light of what happened. Last night was beyond terrifying. Just the thought of those freaks in black with their weirdo masks makes my heart race. Can't believe Mr. Delacroix isn't sending his daughter home after all that."

"His daughter?" I asked, attempting to play dumb.

"Yeah, a year or two older than me, olive skin, dark brown hair?"

"Oh, Rosemary." I kept as straight a face as I could. "I've seen her around on the tour."

"I'm sure you have," she said with a knowing smirk. "You're a red-blooded American male with functioning eyeballs."

"I suppose." I broke our locked gaze and massaged my neck in faux embarrassment. "I stay pretty busy." I looked back at her, pouring every bit of concern I could into my features. "Speaking of, are you serious about continuing the tour?"

"You know, last night I'd made plans to contact my manager and call off the whole thing as way too dangerous." Her mischievous smile returned. "At the moment, though, I'm under the protection of two armed guards, a trained security expert, and my own personal knight in shining armor." She shot me a wink. "What could I possibly have to worry about?"

"Knight in shining armor?" I asked dubiously. "You mean...me?"

"Of course I mean you, Ethan, unless you saw someone else leap to my defense last night and take down one of those creeps with a single punch."

I began to correct her, but better for her to think what she saw last evening was simply a gang of costumed weirdos we were somehow able to fight off. If she knew that she was nearly taken by a quartet of supernatural assassin-kidnappers who could command the very shadows, she'd likely lose her mind. And that didn't take into account the simple fact that they were almost certainly going to come for her again, which begged so many questions.

Rosemary stood alone against the last Raven as I lost consciousness, so what happened to the last of our enemy, not to mention the three we were able to stop?

What happened to Ms. Delacroix's body after she fell?

And what the hell did they tell the police?

"Anyway," she continued, jarring me out of my musing, "I'm ready to leave this hospital and get on with the tour. Like they say, the show must go on."

"Are you sure? I mean those people in black weren't joking around."

"Between you and Mr. Delacroix, I think I'll be all right." She extended a hand and patted my knee with her well-manicured fingers. "Quite all right."

My scalp tingled at her touch. "I don't know what Delacroix told you, but I'm no bodyguard. I'm just a tech who makes sure all the mics and amps work every night."

"I already have a bodyguard, Ethan." Her voice grew warm and husky. "What I don't have is someone to watch over me." Her lips curled into a mischievous smile. "You know, like the old Gershwin song?"

This time, it was my own cheeks that flushed with heat. "What about you and Mr. Cole?" Spencer Cole, a hip-hop star with more tattoos than I'd ever seen on a human being, had been a fixture on the tour for the first month and one of the only people allowed on Miss Snow's tour bus besides Gus, her driver. We'd crossed paths every so often as we made our way from city to city, but it occurred to me I hadn't seen him in weeks. "Until recently, it looked like you two were pretty tight."

"Well, someone's been watching their TMZ." Her shoulders dropped, deflated. "Spencer and I? We just weren't headed in the same direction. We kept up appearances as long as we could, but that's actually been over for a while."

"Good to know, I suppose." I dropped my gaze to my lap. "So, I've got to admit, I'm a bit confused. Last time we talked, I felt like I was gum stuck on your shoe."

"I'm sorry about that." Her cheeks flushed to match mine. "Look, I have to keep my walls up when I'm out and about, particularly on tour." She looked away. "This is only my second time out on the road, you know. First tour, I'd decided I wasn't going to be like all the other 'pop stars' you hear about on the entertainment shows. I made an effort to be nice to everyone, treat everyone with respect, and you know what happened? They walked all over me. Treated me like shit, all the while with a big fat grin on their faces. But it was my first time. What the hell was I going to do? Give back all the money? Cancel my big shot? No. I went with it, put up with the ridiculous hours, the horribly uncomfortable costumes, the hours in the makeup chair, the never-ending night after night." Her hands balled into fists. "Not this time."

"I don't know. It all looks pretty good from where I sit." I'd meant for the comment to be funny, but it came out way more biting than I'd intended. "I mean, you're the star, right?"

A quiet sigh parted those perfect lips. "I haven't always been—you know—*this*. I may be blessed with decent looks and a pretty awesome voice if I do say so myself, but that's it. All of this—the money, the clothes, the fame—it's all just temporary." Her eyes slid closed. "Truth? I just want to sing. That's all this has ever been for me."

"I'm curious," I asked, hoping to backpedal a bit from my caustic remark, "why 'Persephone Snow'?"

"Funny. Everything else may be smoke and mirrors, but that's actually my real name. My mom is half Greek and always wanted me to have something traditional and elegant, if not the easiest to spell."

"What did your dad have to say about that?"

"I wouldn't know." She looked away, her lips pressed tightly together.

"Wow. Sorry. Didn't mean to dig up anything to make you sad."

"Nothing to be sorry about." She breathed out a quiet chuckle, the cloud over her features breaking, allowing the sunshine to return. "Anyway, can you imagine showing up to first grade with a name like Persephone?"

"Thus, 'Seph,' I'm guessing." I raised an eyebrow and shot her my best smile. "Did being the prettiest girl in class hurt or help the situation?"

"Flatterer." She shook her head. "So, I definitely got a decent combo of genes from my parents, but having a personal style consultant, makeup artist, trainer, and hair professional at my beck and call goes a long way toward keeping up the 'Persephone Snow' the public has come to know." She crinkled her nose. "Hell, *expect*."

"That's got to be rough." As I studied her distant stare, a question that had been bugging me for a while pushed to the forefront of my thoughts. "Hey, you're usually three deep in cameras. Do the paparazzi know you're here?"

She laughed again. "Mr. Delacroix said they've got this place surrounded. Honestly, I'm impressed hospital security has kept them out of here so far."

"The armed policemen outside your door likely have a lot to do with that as well."

"Like I said," she smiled, "I'm perfectly safe."

If only that were true.

"So, what now?" I asked. "We both made it through last night's insanity. They said I'm pretty much cleared to go. Have they said when you get to leave?"

"She can leave any time she's ready." A young doctor who looked like he just walked off the set of *Grey's Anatomy* strode into the room wearing tailored scrubs, an immaculate white coat, and the requisite two-day stubble. "Your head CT is completely normal, Miss Snow, and your blood work doesn't show anything of concern. Other than a few minor abrasions and some muscle strains that will likely require some ibuprofen the next few days, you're fit as a fiddle and good to go."

"Thank you, Doctor." Seph shot the twenty-something-year-old who clearly had been a Men's Fitness cover model in another life a cursory glance and returned her gaze to me, the intensity of her stare even stronger than before. "Can't wait to get back on the road."

The young physician fidgeted with the chart in his hands, clearly unused to not being the center of attention. "Umm...a couple of the nurses were wondering if they could have your autograph. Would that be okay, Miss Snow?"

Seph blinked at me apologetically and returned her attention to the ER doctor. "Of course, Dr. Findlay," she said with a patient grin. "I appreciate everything you and everyone here have done to take such excellent care of me." She considered for a moment. "In fact, I'll have my manager get in touch and work something out to get a few comp tickets for you and anyone on your staff who can make the Denver show tomorrow night."

"That would be most appreciated." He retreated to the door. "I'll have my charge nurse get Mr. Delacroix our contact information."

"Perfect." She shot the young doctor her most radiant smile. "Thank you again for all that you did."

"It was my pleasure." He hovered by the door a moment longer.

Seph raised her eyebrows expectantly. "Was there anything else?"

The ER doc's cheeks flushed red. "No, Miss Snow." He turned and gripped the door handle. "Break a leg tomorrow night."

"Job security, Dr. Findlay?" she asked.

"No. Just..." A nervous titter escaped his lips. "Safe travels." And with that, he excused himself from the room.

"Now, Ethan," Seph said, her smile returning, "where were we?"

"Denver." Despite the heat she was giving off, I struggled to maintain at least a facade of professional detachment. "It's a little over six hours from here and it's already mid-morning. If we're going to get you there at a reasonable hour, we need to get moving. I'm just glad the show isn't tonight."

"All business, eh, Mr. Harkreader?" Her words were colored with a potent mix of frustration and intrigue. "That's fine, but I'm not getting on that ridiculous excuse for a tour bus from last night."

"Nothing to worry about there," I answered. "I was talking with Mr. Delacroix earlier. At least until we reach Denver, me, you, him, Dino, and Rosemary are all going to ride together in their big Commander RV, if that's okay."

I fully expected her to rail at the thought of sharing a vehicle with two lowly roadies, but instead, her only answer consisted of three quiet words that spoke volumes.

"So, Rosemary, huh?"

CHAPTER 6

MIDDLE OF THE ROAD

"So." Seph focused through the dim light of the Commander's spacious back area on the olive-skinned young woman sitting across from her. "Rosemary Delacroix." She put on the most beatific smile I suspect she could manage. "Simply rolls off the tongue."

"It's a family name, Miss Snow," Rosemary answered, teeth bared in an overly pleasant smile of her own. "Much like your own, I'm guessing."

"Please, call me Seph." She brushed a strand of platinum blonde hair from her face and shot me a knowing look. "Ethan speaks very highly of you, and any friend of his is a friend of mine."

"Seph it is, then." Rosemary looked my way as well, her exasperated stare a far cry from the smirk of shared secrets playing across Seph's features.

"Great, Rosie," Seph said. "Now, shall we—"

"Rosemary. My name is Rosemary."

"Oh, sorry. I just thought 'Rosie' sounded kind of cute." Seph studied Rosemary as if she'd never seen another human being before. "After all, if the three of us are going to be stuck together back here for the next six hours, chances are we're all going to be pretty familiar by the time we get to Denver."

"Agreed." The quietest grumble sounded over the twin roars of the road and the Commander's engine. "But my name is still Rosemary."

"And a lovely name it is." The six words were the first I'd spoken since making quick introductions back at the hospital. We'd snuck Seph out one of the loading docks to avoid the ever-vigilant paparazzi, and the tension between the two women had started as soon as we pulled closed the door of the Commander's rear compartment. Dino had opted to sit up front with Mr. Delacroix for the six-hour road trip, leaving me to play referee in the back.

"So, Rosemary, how did your family come by such a ride?" I motioned to the relatively opulent surroundings of the Commander's living compartment. "I mean, I know your dad works with some pretty high-profile folks..."

"Some more than others," Rosemary muttered, sending Seph's lips into a pensive purse.

"But this is one nice RV," I jumped in before Seph could speak. "I mean *really* nice."

Rosemary shot me a withering look. "Not that asking someone how they somehow managed to afford their possessions is considered appropriate in our culture," she breathed, "but if you must know, this vehicle is not just where we stay when we're on the road. It is our home."

"So, you, your mom, and your dad live life on the go, Rosemary?" Seph asked. "No roots, kind of like gypsies?"

"My family is not Romani, if that's what you're asking." Rosemary's eyes narrowed further until the brown of her irises were no longer visible amid her long, dark lashes.

Despite the perfectly functioning A/C, the temperature in the back of the Commander shot up a few degrees.

"You're speaking of your mom's family, I'm guessing?" Seph still wore her trademark smile, though the shine had tarnished a bit. "I mean, your father is a Frenchman, right?"

Rosemary again bared her teeth. "Do not speak of my mother."

"Whoa. Sorry." Seph looked at me, understandably confused at the continued hostility. "You're upset about your grandmother falling ill, and you're missing your mom. On that one, I can relate. Sometimes when I'm out on the road, I miss my own mom so much, I could just cry."

Rosemary's teeth ground together audibly. "That must be so difficult for you." Despite her best efforts, her stoic mask cracked just a bit, and my own heart broke knowing that she was not only grieving her mother's death but having to pretend that everything was hunky-dory while trapped in what she clearly perceived as the most vapid conversation of her life.

And we were only ten minutes into what promised to be the most excruciating six hours of any of our lives.

"Maybe a different topic." I continued to navigate the shark-infested waters of a conversation that had gone south pretty much from word one. "Tell us, Seph. What's the hardest part of being on the road for you?"

"No, Ethan." Seph reached across the table and delicately touched Rosemary's arm. "Clearly I've upset Rosemary. I want to know why."

Rosemary drew back from Seph's touch. "You wouldn't understand. My mother and I were—*are*—quite close."

Seph hesitated a moment before speaking again. "Sometimes my mouth engages half a second before my brain does. Truth is, I don't know how you feel, and I shouldn't be pushing my stuff on you. One thing that has always helped when I'm missing my mom or when we've had a fight or anything like that, though? I close my eyes and start naming the things I love about her. That always seems to bring her close, no matter how far apart we might be, physically, emotionally, or otherwise." She slipped her porcelain fingers around Rosemary's tawny wrist. "Tell me, Rosemary, what are the things that you love most about your mother?"

I tensed, fully expecting Rosemary to lunge across the table then and there and pummel senseless the biggest pop star in the country. My prediction could not have been more wrong.

Rosemary did not recoil from Seph's touch this time, but instead took a deep breath and allowed her eyes to slide closed, relaxing in an instant. Her breathing dropped into a slow in-and-out rhythm for several seconds before she finally spoke again.

"My mother, Danielle Delacroix, is the bravest woman I've ever known. I've seen her stare down the monsters in her life with a smile on her face and a spark in her eye. She's defended me when attacked, stood by me through every storm of life, and tolerated me when I was too young or stupid or headstrong to listen to her well-earned wisdom. And in every moment, every struggle, she's maintained such grace, poise, and elegance that I fear I will never measure up no matter how hard I try." She opened her eyes, the slightest hint of moisture playing at the corners of her twin pools of dark brown. "Everyone believes their mother is the best of them all, but I don't just believe it. I know it."

"OMG." Seph's eyes grew wide as both hers and Rosemary's welled with tears. "I don't believe I've ever heard more beautiful words spoken of another human being." Seph squeezed Rosemary's wrist. "You truly love your mother."

"I've barely scratched the surface." Rosemary's gaze focused on Seph's hand atop hers. "And the saddest part is she'll never know how much."

My eyes shot to Rosemary who immediately winced, realizing she'd said too much.

"I know what you mean," Seph said before either of us could utter another word. "It's difficult to say such things to a person's face, right?"

"Difficult, indeed." Rosemary dabbed at her eyes with her free hand. "And I would be remiss if I didn't ask you about your own mother, Miss Snow." She considered a moment. "I mean...Seph."

The tension in Seph's shoulders melted. "So, my mom's name is Wynter. Wynter, of course, with a Y." She smirked and fondly rolled her eyes. "What can I say? It was the 80s, and my grandpa is nothing if not the King of Puns."

"Wait," Rosemary asked, "Snow is your *mother's* surname?"

"What about it?" Seph pulled her hand away, her brow furrowed in indignance.

"I meant no offense." Rosemary raised a hand in quick apology. "You see, it's the same way in my family. Delacroix was—is my mother's name."

"Oh." Seph brought her hands together, interlacing her fingers. "So, yeah. No father in the picture. Just me and Mom." A mirthless chuckle left her lips. "You may find this hard to believe, but we didn't come from money. All of this..." She indicated her flawless manicure, platinum locks, and designer top, jeans, and shoes. "It's not me. Not that I'm complaining. I like nice things and pretty clothes as much as the next girl, but growing up, it was all hand-me-downs from cousins, and not all of them female." She quirked her mouth to one side. "I'm not trying to buy into the whole 'I grew up poor and just look at me now' thing, but it's the truth. Not that I knew it at the time."

"She shielded you from that." Rosemary nodded. "Allowed you to pick your own destiny."

"Exactly," Seph answered, "though your words are more eloquent than I could've ever put it." A dreamy smile filled her face. "Despite needing food stamps to eat, we never went hungry, and though my clothes didn't come from any of the fancy department stores, my mom worked magic with her sewing machine and a little embroidery, and I always went to school proud of what I was wearing." Clouds overtook the sunshine pouring from her face. "Not that the girls at school noticed or cared."

"And this is all before the show, right?" I asked. "Before your big break?"

"Show?" Rosemary looked at us both quizzically. "What show?"

Seph and I both turned to face her, dumbfounded.

"You know." I studied her features, trying to determine if she was joking. "Seph was Penny Sinclair on *Teen Spies.*"

Rosemary answered with nothing but a dumbfounded stare.

"Five seasons on the Disney Channel?" I continued. "Biggest show since *Hannah Montana*?"

"Why, Ethan," Seph said, almost purring, "you're quite the study."

"Pardon my ignorance." Strangely embarrassed, Rosemary's lips quirked to one side. "I didn't get to watch much television growing up."

My mind wandered a moment, imagining the kind of childhood a woman with the skills I witnessed the night before must have had. No time for television was likely the understatement of the century.

Seph returned her attention to Rosemary. "I don't fault you a bit for not knowing *Teen Spies*." She leaned in and added with a conspiratorial whisper, "I have kind of a love/hate relationship with the whole thing anyway."

"Mother always said time spent in front of the television could be better spent studying or training." Rosemary leaned back in her seat and peered out the window at the rushing landscape. "She wanted me to be the best I could be."

"In that, then," Seph added, "our moms have a lot in common."

I expected Rosemary to come back with venom. Wrong again.

"I suspect they do, Seph." Rosemary again tried on a smile, and this one actually seemed genuine. "I suspect they do."

A couple hours later, we sat at a Conoco service station near the Colorado border. Dino volunteered to top off the Commander's tank while Seph used the facilities. Mr. Delacroix had accompanied her to ensure that anyone who recognized Seph kept their distance, leaving me and Rosemary alone to chat.

"I'm so sorry about all of this." The two of us stood to the rear of the massive RV, and though Dino was the only person in earshot, I kept my voice low. "I can't imagine how much it sucks to not be able to talk about—you know."

"My mother's death?" Only a slight tremor betrayed the emotion in her strained whisper. "The truth is talking about it would just make it worse. More real." Her eyes wandered in the direction of the service station. "Honestly? Pretending she's still alive for the last couple of hours has, in a strange way, actually helped."

"Just curious." My eyes cut left and right. "When we were on the road, everything seemed safe, but right now, I'm feeling pretty exposed. Are we in any danger standing out here?"

Rosemary performed a quick scan of the area. "Skiomancers in general and the Midnight Angel's Ravens in particular act almost exclusively at night." She glanced upward at the cloud-filled sky. "And understandably so." She crinkled her nose. "However, there are far more threats in this world than mere dealers in shadow. Whether or not a different faction of Ascendant might be gunning for Seph, I have no idea."

Ascendant, huh? Filing that one away for later, the latest in a series of statements that twenty-four hours earlier would have sounded more like the ravings of a psychotic patient off their meds than anything resembling my actual life.

"So, you and your family just live like this, knowing that at any time, all hell could break loose?"

"Life, Ethan, is nothing but a long series of surprises, ending in what should be the least surprising event of all. Mother always taught me that death comes for each of us eventually and that our role is to not just survive but to strive each day to make life better for those around us and the world at large."

"Sounds like a good way to live." I peeked in Dino's direction and found him blissfully humming a tune as he continued to feed the gargantuan RV. "So, that's why you all do what you do? You sacrifice everything simply to make the world a better place?"

"It's far more than that, but yes." She offered me a rare half-smile. "One could almost say it's the family business."

The sun emerged from behind a cloud, bringing out the hazel flecks in Rosemary's dark brown irises.

"Speaking of business," I asked, doing my best to push away a deluge of confusing feelings, "whatever happened to the last Raven? You faced him alone while I was trying to help your mother there at the end. Did you stop him?" I surveyed her from head to toe, the brief look doing little to stem the tide of thoughts and emotions welling up within. "Were you hurt?"

"In the end, it seems, the Raven and I were pretty evenly matched. Whatever strength I gained from my rage at Mother's death was more than offset by my momentary lack of focus. We fought to a standstill, neither of us gaining the upper hand, that is, until..." She trailed off, her lower lip quivering with emotion.

"Until what?"

"The Transference." Her shoulders dropped. "It would seem the brilliance of my mother's essence leaving her body and entering yours banished the darkness and drove away the Raven."

"Okay." I worked to process the implications of what she'd said. "And what of the others, the ones we defeated?"

"Gone without a trace. We're not sure how many of them survived." She swallowed, her eyes shooting left and right as if scanning for eavesdroppers. "Much less, how many more of them there might be."

"But how could that be? You were right there. What were you doing when—"

I stopped mid-sentence, the tears welling anew in Rosemary's eyes answering my question better than anything she could have said. Last I'd seen, the remaining Raven had sent her already-wounded father flying into the vehicle I currently leaned against moments before her mother breathed her last. Between fighting for her life, keeping her father alive, and safeguarding her mother's body, she clearly hadn't had the bandwidth to keep tabs on our attackers.

"Wait." Something clicked in my head. "Not to be morbid, but I'm guessing if the cops had found your mother's body, we'd be anywhere but on the open road telling tales of sick grandmothers. What happened there?"

Rosemary studied the concrete at her feet. "Mother has been taken far from here. We prepared her body in the old ways, and then, as he always does, the Driver came and took her away."

"The Driver?" For such a simple word, the gravitas of the title hit me like a punch to the gut. "Is that supposed to mean something?"

"I thought Mr. Delacroix was going to be doing all the driving." Seph appeared around the far side of the Commander, shutting down the conversation immediately. "Unless he's going to let your buddy, Dino, take the wheel for the next few hours."

"Not likely." Delacroix appeared behind Seph, an apologetic half-smile plastered across his face. "I'm particular about who drives this thing, as you can imagine."

I shot Seph my most innocent smile and then peered around the corner of the RV again. There, Dino was checking his phone rather than standing lookout as I'd asked. So far, we'd managed to keep Seph in the dark regarding supernatural shadowmancing kidnappers, mostly for her own good, but that wouldn't hold up if we didn't all work together.

Though frustrated, I reminded myself that Dino saved all of our backsides back in Albuquerque. In any case, someone as intuitive as Persephone Snow would only be fooled for so long anyway, so there was no need to be mad at the poor guy.

"I bought refreshments." Seph held open a plastic bag filled with drinks. "Anyone thirsty?"

"Thanks." I grabbed the two Coke Zeros, handed one to Delacroix, and popped the other, leaving three bottles.

"Your turn, Rosemary." Seph held out the bag which now contained two Vitamin Waters and a bottle of Starbucks Mocha Frappuccino. "Take your pick."

Rosemary peered into the bag and pulled out the latter. "This is a coffee drink? It looks like chocolate milk."

Seph's brows bunched into an incredulous smirk. "You've never had a Frappuccino?"

Rosemary's face dropped into her default deadpan stare. "Water was always the standard with meals around our house." A wistful smile appeared on her face. "On weekends, though, Mother would sometimes serve us the juice of whatever fruit was in season."

"Freshly squeezed, eh?" Seph said with an admiring nod. "Only the best for Danielle Delacroix's daughter, I guess."

"Indeed." Mr. Delacroix nodded.

"Yes." Faint color rose in Rosemary's cheeks. "Only the best."

"So, to be clear," Seph said with an impish grin, "you've never tasted the goodness that is Starbucks?"

"No." Rosemary's chin dropped a millimeter, as if she were somehow ashamed at the revelation. "Caffeine and refined sugar are—"

"Blah blah blah." Seph swiped the glass bottle from Rosemary and unscrewed the lid. "Try it. I dare you."

Rosemary shot me a questioning look, and then, with the same courage she'd shown the night before, took the bottle of coffee, cream, and sugar from Seph and turned it up, draining half the bottle. Her eyes lit with a subtle glint as her lips spread in the first full smile I'd ever seen cross her face.

"*That* is delicious."

"Right?" Seph wrapped an arm around Rosemary as if they were besties and led her around to the Commander's side door, leaving me and Mr. Delacroix befuddled at the vehicle's rear. "Today, Starbucks," she declared, "tomorrow, the world."

CHAPTER 7

YOU'RE THE BEST

"Five a.m. and I aren't exactly strangers," I muttered as I sauntered up to Rosemary who was busy finishing what was likely her thousandth pushup of the morning. "It's just usually the end of my day, not the beginning."

Rosemary rolled to one side on her mat, the healthy sheen of sweat at her brow, chest, and arms reflecting the yellow halogen lights of the surrounding parking lot. "We may have made it to Denver without further drama, but we've got a lot of work to do if we want to —I believe your words were—get you whipped into shape?"

"We couldn't do this later?" I stretched, attempting to banish the crick left in my neck by the hotel pillow. "Like when the sun is actually up?"

I'd always ribbed my brother Jacob over the zero-dark-thirty physical training he had to do every morning during his early Army days. My words were coming back to haunt me.

Rosemary shot me a cross glance. "Unless I misread her offer, I

58

believe Seph has planned for you two to meet for brunch later this morning, correct?"

"Unbelievable, but true," I said with a goofy grin. Somehow, the universe had conspired to grant me an eleven a.m. date with the country's reigning princess of pop less than twenty-four hours after a meet-not-so-cute that had all the earmarks of me needing to find a new job. "What does that have to do with anything?"

"Your day is hers, and your night belongs to your employer." She sprang up from the ground and landed lightly before me in a low combat stance. "Your morning, however, is mine."

I gestured to the star-filled darkness where not even a hint of sunrise had yet to pinken the eastern sky. "You call this morning?"

"Complaining endlessly isn't going to help prepare you for anything, Ethan."

"Right." I stifled the smart remark that sprang to my lips and instead asked a question. "This is going to hurt, isn't it?"

Her eyebrows rose in amusement. "Pain is what lets you know you're alive."

"That's reassuring." I let out a nervous laugh. "Can I maybe pick a different drill sergeant?"

"I hate to be the bearer of bad news, Ethan," she answered with a quiet chuckle of her own, "but you're stuck with me." Her eyes searched the heavens as she considered her words. "As it stands, there is exactly one person on the planet with the requisite knowledge to help you through this transition in your life. Not surprisingly, it just happens to be the person who has prepared *her* entire life for that very transition since well before she took her first step or spoke her first syllable."

The lack of bitterness in her words impressed me as much as the words themselves.

"How do we start, then?" My mind ran through the training montages of a dozen movies and shows I'd seen over the years. "A gazillion pushups? Fifty laps of the hotel?" I inhaled sharply. "Or do we cut right to full-on Mortal Kombat?"

"Actually," she dropped into a yoga pose, "we're going to stretch."

"Stretch?" I asked. "Seriously?"

Her eyes cut in my direction. "For you to learn how to access and utilize the gift you've been given, we're going to need to stretch and strengthen both your body as well as your mind." She directed me to copy her pose, one called Warrior II.

I didn't even know there was a Warrior I.

I'd dated girls who were into yoga over the years and at some level understood it was harder than it looked, but I had no idea the degree to which holding what seemed relatively simple poses could cause me to hurt in places where I didn't even know I had places.

Rosemary walked me through half an hour of what seemed for her a simple succession of exercises she could have done in her sleep. By the end, however, I was drenched in sweat and couldn't identify a location in my body that didn't feel the burn.

"Wow," I whispered, "that was intense." I met her somewhat baffled gaze. "Will we be doing this every day?"

"More bad news, Ethan." She wiped her brow and took a swig of water. "That was just the warm-up."

The next ninety minutes consisted of every form of exercise/torture I'd ever done, seen, or imagined as the sun rose in the east Denver sky. I'd never been a slouch in the gym, and I worked out as much as the next guy, but this was next level. Still, through it all, I somehow kept up with Rosemary who seemed to run on sheer willpower alone. In the end, I wasn't sure what surprised me most: the indefatigable performance of my de facto workout partner; the strange new strength and endurance that flowed through my own body, knowing that a week before the same workout would have left me a puddle; or the fact that no matter what she threw at me, be it new or familiar, easy or difficult, my body somehow knew what to do as if she and I had been through it all a thousand times before.

"How in the hell am I keeping up with you?" I asked between sets of burpees. "You may be used to this level of punishment, but I'm basically a free weights and treadmill kind of guy."

"You now carry within you all that my mother was and all that she inherited from her own mother." Though only a hint of resentment came out in her tone and expression, that hint remained, just beneath the surface. "In your day-to-day interactions, you will likely notice little to no change, but when called upon, your mind and body can now tap into the centuries of training, experience, and muscle memory gifted you from the Delacroix line along with the strength, endurance, and fortitude afforded by the power my line has passed mother to daughter for over two millennia."

"Wait. Is this like *The Matrix*?" I dropped into a low fighting stance, the placement of my hands and feet simultaneously familiar and unfamiliar, and waved for her to come at me. "Do I suddenly know Kung Fu?"

"Something like that." In a blink, Rosemary swept out a leg and sent my feet from beneath me. In response, my arms shot out, my outstretched fingers catching cool asphalt a split second prior to my head hitting the ground. Before I knew what was happening, I finished a round off, landed on the balls of both feet, and resumed my previous fighting stance.

"It's amazing." I relaxed, though a part of me instinctively kept an eye on Rosemary, preparing for another attack. "My body just knows how to do this stuff now."

She huffed out a laugh and shook her head. "Imagine how effective you'd be if you'd trained for two decades on top of that."

She couldn't have taken the wind out of my sails faster if she'd tried.

"Look, this is not my fault. I'd give up this 'Light' in a hot second if I knew how to do it without croaking. I didn't ask for this, and yet I'm out here before sunup on my third hour of training preparing for a war that isn't mine to fight."

"Ethan—"

"First, you were all over Seph yesterday who has no idea that any of this is going on and is literally the person you're here to protect. Now, you've put me through the wringer with the workout from hell, all the while making sure I know exactly how much you resent being stuck training the guy who intercepted this gift meant for you."

"Ethan, wait—"

"I know you blame Seph for losing your mother and me for taking what was supposed to be yours, but neither of us did anything wrong, so—"

"You think I blame *you and Seph* for my mother and this colossal mess?" She glared at me with eyes like twin lasers.

I didn't see that one coming. "You don't?"

"Of course not." She ground her teeth, her gaze growing distant. "I showed mercy to that damned Raven and left him alive when I should have put him down like the rabid dog he is." Her head dropped. "Like Mother taught me." Her shoulders slumped in defeat. "Now she's gone, her essence lives in an unprepared vessel, and people are going to suffer because of my stupidity." She shook her head in frustration. "Yes, Ethan, I'm angry, and yes, some of that has been inappropriately directed at you and Seph. For that, I apologize, as there's only one person to blame for my Mother's death, the loss of my birthright, and your unfortunate current circumstances, and that's me."

"Because you chose not to kill?" I stepped closer to Rosemary and stretched out a hand, my every instinct demanding I comfort her in her moment of pain. "That's crazy. You're one of the good guys. You're only supposed to kill when the villain leaves you no other choice."

"This isn't a comic book, Ethan. You and I are now caught up in a war that has gone on for longer than recorded history. Mother was one of the few combatants struggling to hold back the darkness, and through my inaction, she is lost forever."

"But I'm right here." The words escaped my mouth before my mind registered I was going to say them. "I mean, she's here." Unbidden, my hand went to my heart.

Now that was strange.

"Somewhere inside me, all that your mother ever was—"

"Stop." Rosemary batted away my outstretched hand and turned away. "Don't do that."

"Don't do what?" I asked. "Be kind to someone who's hurting?"

She glanced back across her shoulder. "Why would you be kind to me? My failures are what left us both stuck in this terrible situation."

"And you could have skewered me on the spot and taken what was rightfully yours." I rested tenuous fingers on her shoulder and turned her to face me. "Instead, you brought me to the hospital, helped nurse me back to health, and agreed to train me so this war of yours doesn't end up killing me." I offered her a smile filled with gratitude. "Perhaps I'm simply answering kindness with kindness."

Another rare smile overtook her features. "Those are some pretty wise words from someone basically my age."

"I'm two years older than you, ninja girl." I grabbed a towel and dabbed at my face to get the salty sweat out of my eyes. "Seriously, I'd like to think that, in their own way, my parents raised me right. Not to mention I've learned a lot about how to treat and not treat people in my couple of years on the road."

"Apparently they did." She stepped closer. "And apparently you have."

"How goes the first training session, Rosemary?" Mr. Delacroix approached our little spot on the asphalt, freshly showered and dressed in his customary dark suit and tie. "Is it as we expected?"

Rosemary retreated a step and turned in her father's direction. "Yes, Father." She shot me a side-eye. "Though Ethan started out in reasonable shape, not many would have been able to keep up with the rigor of this morning's program."

"Reasonable shape?" I crinkled my nose and chuckled. "Thanks, I think."

Delacroix slapped my shoulder. "Don't take it personally, Harkreader. Rosemary has been training for as long as she's been alive. With a little specialization, she could compete in the Olympics in multiple events. 'Reasonable shape' is a pretty high compliment coming from her."

Rosemary raised an eyebrow. "Mother always taught me that idle praise accomplishes little."

"Speaking of your mother," I interjected, "now that I have the both of you alone, I have a question."

"I'm sure you have many."

"This power that now lives inside me. What is it? And what does it have to do with Ms. Delacroix being a 'Daughter of Neith'?"

"I'll explain it to you the way Mother explained it to me." Rosemary took a deep breath. "For twenty centuries, and possibly even further back in time, a single line of women has passed on power and knowledge and skill and wisdom from mother to daughter. My mother was the latest in the line to accept the Light, and I was to be the next."

"Always a daughter?"

"Women of the Delacroix line only have daughters, and even then, usually just the one."

"And your—their job is to police the world?" I asked. "Keep bad stuff from happening?"

"Among other duties and responsibilities." Delacroix answered before Rosemary could speak. "The conflict in which you now find yourself embroiled has gone on for all of human history, and the Daughter of Neith's role is to keep whatever peace is possible between those who walk the world with the powers of gods."

"And Neith is?"

"An ancient Egyptian goddess of hunting and war and death as well as an 'Opener of the Ways'. My family has carried her name for longer than anyone knows."

"How is it possible I've never heard of any of this before now?"

"Ascendant by necessity typically choose either a solitary life or remain in small clutches rather than live among the rest of the world," Rosemary answered. "Trying to assimilate into normal human society is difficult for such beings, regardless of the power they might possess."

Delacroix nodded. "And the relatively few times when humans bore witness to such beings in all their glory have been basically relegated to the stuff of myth and legend."

"For as long as there have been people, stories of those who could perform miracles have abounded, stories passed down from long before the first words were ever written." Rosemary cracked her neck, her gaze growing fierce as her eyes met mine. "For two thousand years, however, the Daughters of Neith have fought against the encroaching forces of darkness and chaos, bringing light and order and peace, however temporary, to the world."

"Much like the history that most of the human populace of this planet learns," Delacroix added, "there always seems to be a new threat to stop or evil to thwart, but our war is a hidden one, its scale much smaller and yet simultaneously much grander than the many wars of man."

"Most human conflict is resolved with human intervention." Rosemary followed on her father's explanation. "But when it comes to Ascendant, a different style of mediation is often required."

"And these Ascendant we keep talking about?" I asked. "You're talking about the Ravens that came for Seph last night and their boss?"

"Precisely, though shadow-dealers represent but a tiny fraction of Ascendant diversity," Delacroix answered. "The Midnight Angel is a skiomancer like those you faced last night, though her powers and abilities dwarf those of her followers. She retains her position by remaining the most powerful and skilled of them all, and her acolytes, the Conspiracy of Ravens, serve as her army. Trust that whoever has acquired the services of such a group, whatever they might want with Miss Snow, it's nothing you would wish upon your worst enemy, much less an innocent such as herself."

I considered his words. "But if you knew they were coming for Seph, why not have more than just the three of you present to defend her? I can't help but think that a few cops on the scene would have helped a lot two nights ago."

"Perhaps," he said, "though there are many variables to consider. We didn't know when along the tour, if ever, anyone might attack, nor did we know until they showed themselves who might have been sent to obtain Miss Snow. Bringing the police into Ascendant matters is generally frowned upon, not just because it exposes a war we have opted to keep clandestine for centuries, but also because such involvement of outsiders usually ends in unnecessary deaths."

"Mother entered every battle knowing the stakes that lay before her." Rosemary's head dropped. "And were she here, she would die all over again to prevent the loss of one innocent life."

A chill stole up my spine. "And you said there are more Ascendant out there than just the Midnight Angel and her Ravens?"

"More than anyone truly knows," Delacroix answered. "Skiomancy is but one of many manifestations of Ascendance. There are those who deal in the basic elements of earth, water, fire, and air;

some who walk the fine line between life and death; others whose abilities revolve around amplification or sublimation of the body, the mind, the soul; and even those whose vision can perceive other places, other times."

"So, what these people can do runs the gamut. Got it." I worked to keep all Delacroix and Rosemary said straight in my head. "And what about this Driver that Rosemary mentioned? The one who took away Ms. Delacroix. What can he do?"

"The Driver is simply the Driver." Delacroix's voice grew strangely quiet. "He's been an ally of the Daughters of Neith for as long as the Delacroix line has existed. He comes and goes without fanfare and typically only appears in moments of utmost need. If you ever find yourself gazing into *his* dark eyes, trust that whatever situation in which you find yourself entangled is as dire as they come."

"More than a small army of shadowmancers coming for an innocent woman to do God knows what unspeakable things?"

"That, Mr. Harkreader, is where you come in." Delacroix crossed his arms. "In a strange but fortunate turn, it appears that Miss Snow has taken quite a shine to you. This will put you, the first man in history to contain the essence of the Daughters of Neith, in a unique position to safeguard her until Rosemary and I can work out who wants her and for what reason. The three of us, along with your friend Dino, are the only ones who know any of this. We must keep her safe while maintaining an illusion of normalcy so that she may continue her tour as before. Do you think you can do that?"

"Yes, Ethan," Rosemary added, "can you do that?"

"Spend time with a beautiful, talented woman who looks at me the way Seph has the last twenty-four hours? No problem."

My answer simultaneously brought a pleased smile to Delacroix's face and a passing shadow of regret to Rosemary's.

"As long as you both keep me in the loop and train me so this war of yours doesn't end up killing me." I swallowed back the fear and bile at the back of my throat. "I may be a little cog in a big machine, but I've got a lot of years left to spin, and I'd like to keep it that way."

Delacroix laughed. "We'll protect you, Mr. Harkreader, as you protect Miss Snow." He checked his watch. "You can get started by heading upstairs and preparing for your brunch date with our shared charge." He motioned in the direction of the hotel main entrance. "I'll be along to collect you both at ten-thirty sharp."

"You're coming?" I tried to keep the disappointment out of my tone.

"You, Rosemary, and I are here to protect her from one threat, but I'm still the head of security for her tour." He gave me a frank look that said "no shenanigans." "Trust that I'll be protecting her from the more mundane dangers of the world as well."

"I guess that leaves just one question." My gaze danced between the father and daughter standing before me. "What does this mystery person who hired the Midnight Angel and her Ravens want with a teenage pop star in the first place?"

"God only knows," Delacroix answered, "but I have a sneaking suspicion we're not going to like the answer."

CHAPTER 8

TAKE MY BREATH AWAY

"Why, good morning, Mr. Harkreader." Seph gave me a frank up and down, her lips spread in a wide smile. "If you don't mind me saying, you clean up pretty nice."

"Thanks." My typical road togs aren't all that amenable to upscale dining, not even the midmorning variety, but a quick trip to a nearby J. Crew—first customer of the day, by the way—allowed me to trade out my vintage Counting Crows t-shirt, torn jeans, and sneakers for a polo and slacks. A new pair of Oxfords, some hair gel, and a fresh shave completed the look. "Right back at you, beautiful."

"And charming too." Her gaze dropped and a hint of color hit her cheeks.

As she stepped through the door in a pair of sandals that showed off what I guessed was quite the expensive pedicure, her denim miniskirt brushed my thigh. One of her loose-fitting tank top's spaghetti straps slid down her shoulder as she turned to face me. "So," she asked, "hungry?"

"Starving." Before I could stop myself, my hand slid the strap back up her arm to its rightful position. "Shall we?"

Starving was the understatement of the year. After a two-hour-plus workout, the requisite cool-down and clean-up time, my quick shopping expedition, and the rush back to the hotel, I hadn't even had time for coffee, much less a snack. I'd made sure to rehydrate as Rosemary's planned workout had left me parched, but beyond a sports drink and more water than I usually drink in a week, I was running on empty. I hoped my stomach wouldn't rumble on the way.

As we headed down the hall for the elevator, I considered taking Seph's hand but wasn't sure if that would be overstepping, even considering the events of the previous couple of days. Our knuckles brushed as we both reached for the down button, the brief contact sending an electric tingle up my arm. A few seconds later, the doors opened. Seph slid her sunglasses down over her eyes in response to the elevator full of tweens who greeted us, one of whom was wearing a Persephone Snow Sparkle Tour t-shirt. I studied their faces as we stepped inside, and at least two of the girls lit up like Christmas trees, recognizing the superstar in their midst.

The girls whispered behind their hands as Seph and I turned to face the closing doors. Neither ominous nor even particularly annoying but intrusive nonetheless, this was Seph's everyday existence. She stood stock-still, maintaining even breaths as the elevator descended. It had never occurred to me exactly how long twenty seconds could last.

As the doors opened, we stepped into the large open lobby, and the half-dozen girls spilled out behind us. Before we could take a step, the boldest among them spoke up.

"Miss Snow," said the lanky twelve-year-old in the tour t-shirt, orange shorts, and flip flops, "would it be okay if we got a picture?"

If I expected a sigh or groan from Seph, I was horribly disappointed. Instead, she slid into a practiced smile, stepped to the side of the hallway, and motioned for the tiny mob of excited tweens to join her.

"Ethan," she asked, "care to do the honors?"

"Of course."

I snagged a phone from the girl in the orange shorts, her braces gleaming in the bright lights of the hotel foyer. She rushed over to the gaggle of tweens surrounding Seph. I made sure to shoot a good dozen or so shots, not wanting to screw up the once-in-a-lifetime experience. As I returned the girl's phone, the youngest among them, a nine-year-old at best with freckled cheeks and strawberry curls, looked at me and then back at Seph.

"Is he your boyfriend?" she asked.

"Just heading out for a healthy brunch with a good friend." She gifted them all with her celebrity smile. "If I'm going to perform tonight, I need to keep my strength up, right?"

A series of quiet squeals erupted from the mini-mob as we turned and walked for the front of the hotel.

"You handled that well." I wasn't sure why I was so surprised. "A real pro."

"Thanks," she said. "Happens every day. I try to always have time for the fans, especially the young women, as long as they're polite."

"And when they aren't?" I asked.

"That's my job." Mr. Delacroix strode up in his standard business suit. "Your car is outside, Miss Snow. Are you and Mr. Harkreader ready to go?"

"I don't know." Seph studied me with those crystal blue eyes of hers. "Are you ready for this, Ethan?"

My stomach growled, bringing a grin to both our faces. "You have no idea."

We stepped out a side door and into a yellow cab, Seph and I in the back seat and Delacroix up front with the driver. Miraculously, not a single photographer lurked outside, or at least none I could see. On our road trip the day before, Seph had both regaled and horrified Rosemary and me with various tales of hotel balcony indiscretions, telephoto lenses, and tabloid embarrassment. Fortunately, most of her early rookie mistakes had occurred before she started dating anyone seriously, and the worst gaffes so far had been some unflattering bathing suit shots and a couple early morning photos taken before her "daily beauty routine."

"You mean you don't roll out of bed looking like this?" I'd joked at the time.

"It's hard to improve on perfection," she'd answered, batting her eyelashes, "but I do my best." Her sarcastic answer had brought a laugh from me while eliciting the eye roll of all eye rolls from Rosemary.

Speaking of Rosemary, I'd just experienced *her* grueling every morning regimen first hand and one thing suddenly became clear: though vastly different, both women's routines clearly paid off significant dividends.

I banished the memory of the streetlights' halogen glow playing off the sheen of Rosemary's tawny skin and brought myself back to the woman sitting next to me.

Conversation on the way to brunch remained limited to plans for the day and scheduling to ensure that Seph would be back in more than ample time to prepare for her concert that evening. Between flashes of nervousness over being the date of the one and only Persephone Snow, the intermittent glances from the cab driver in the rearview mirror, and the occasional grunt from Delacroix, I mostly kept quiet.

As we pulled up to the front of the restaurant, a pair of waitstaff stood outside, ready for our arrival: a woman with red curly hair and a man with dark hair and a beard, both all in black and competing to see who could smile the broadest.

"Miss Snow," the man said as Seph exited the cab with Delacroix, "we're so pleased you decided to grace us with your presence today."

"Yes," the woman added, "we have your table ready, and our chef has prepared the finest of breakfasts for you and your companion."

"That sounds delightful." She glanced in my direction and motioned for me to join her as I exited the cab streetside. "Doesn't it, Ethan?"

Both servers turned their megawatt smiles on me, and I fought the urge to get back in the cab. I'd always been more comfortable behind the scenes than in the spotlight. However, if I planned to enter the world of Persephone Snow in any capacity, the limelight was something I was going to have to get used to.

"Can't wait." I gave them both a polite nod as I took Seph's arm and led her inside with Delacroix close behind.

The pair of servers—their name tags read Allison and Matt—showed us to our table, placed cloth napkins in our laps, and then vanished briefly before returning with fresh coffee and orange juice. Delacroix, posted by the door, gladly accepted his own mug of coffee and sipped his dark roast black as he kept eyes on the street. Seph sampled her coffee, which was apparently doctored just the way she liked it as she shivered with delight at the first taste. Mine was perfect as well, no sugar with just a dash of cream.

"This is exactly right." I chuckled as I met the servers' shared gaze. "Her I get, but how could you possibly know how I take my coffee?"

"Mr. Delacroix wanted Miss Snow's brunch to go perfectly." Allison tilted her head forward in a pleased nod. "Now, if I may, avocado omelet with mozzarella for the lady and a waffle with blackberry compote for the gentleman?"

"That would be perfect," Seph gushed, "though I will take a side of grits if you have them." She shot me a wink. "They remind me of home."

"Make that two." I answered her wink with a broad grin.

"An excellent choice," Matt replied. "We have the best stone-ground grits in town."

"Buttered and salted to perfection," Allison added as the pair scurried off to the kitchen.

"This is amazing," I said as soon as we were alone. "Is it this way everywhere you go?"

"Celebrity has its perks." Her gaze dropped to a still healing bruise at her wrist. "As well as its pitfalls."

"Those freaks from Albuquerque aren't getting anywhere near you again. Mr. Delacroix and I will make sure of it."

"From your mouth to God's ears." She took a sip of her coffee. "Sorry. Not trying to be negative. It's just...this has been a lot, and I just want to get on with the tour and sing."

"Then let us worry about all the bad stuff. You just focus on giving it everything you've got tonight." I reached across the table and squeezed her hand. "Okay?"

"Okay."

"Good." I glanced in Delacroix's direction. The man continued to enjoy his coffee as he scanned the sun-drenched street outside for any sign of danger. "You think anyone is going to get through a mountain of muscle like that, you're crazy."

"To be honest, Ethan, it's you who has made me feel safe and protected the last couple of days." She followed my gaze to Delacroix. "It's his job to keep me safe, but with you, it feels personal."

"Personal?" I asked, my heart jumping a beat.

"Yes." My hand, still in hers, basked in the warmth of her touch. "Personal." An electric rush swept up my arm as she returned my fingers' gentle squeeze. "And after I was not so nice to you back in Albuquerque." Her cheeks again went pink. "Like I said before, sorry about that."

"All good." I pulled my hand away as Allison and Matt reappeared with our food in tow and set it on the table between us. "And already forgiven."

"Words that have never left the mouth of Spencer Cole." Her hand went to her mouth. "Sorry. I don't usually talk about exes on a first date."

"So." I took a bite of waffle, swallowed, and laid down my fork. "That's what this is? A date?"

She looked across the table at me quizzically. "Well, of course it is, silly. Why else would I have brought you here?"

"Oh, I don't know. Maybe out of a sense of gratitude or something?"

"Gratitude?" She crossed her arms. "I don't spend two hours getting ready to go for brunch out of a sense of gratitude, Ethan Harkreader."

"Whoa, sorry." I raised both hands before me in quick surrender. "I'm just saying that, well, you're you and I'm...me."

"What's that supposed to mean?" Her voice went up a few decibels. "I can't be attracted to a good-looking, age-appropriate guy who punched out some asshole that was trying to do me harm because I'm famous or something?" She shook her head, frustrated. "I'm just a girl, Ethan. Like I told you, the Persephone Snow the world sees is not reality." Her voice grew quiet. "And definitely not the one I want you to see."

"Everything okay, Miss Snow?" Delacroix pulled up by the table, giving Seph a caring fatherly look before fixing me with a "tread carefully" man-to-man stare.

"All is well, Mr. Delacroix." She sighed. "Just explaining to my date another of the many pitfalls of celebrity."

Ouch. That hurt.

As Delacroix returned to his post, I reached across the table and took both of Seph's hands in mine. "Look, I'm sorry. I get that you are just a person like the rest of us, but you have to understand that I feel like a little league player who just got called up to the Majors. Every time you look in the mirror, you see one of the most beautiful and talented women on the planet looking back, but it's all still a bit new to me. My apologies if I'm still a bit starstruck."

She studied me, her mouth quirked to one side, and then, with an arch of her eyebrow, asked, "*One* of the most beautiful and talented?"

Crap. Stepped in it again. "Wait. That's not what I—"

"Calm down, Ethan." She broke into laughter, and for a second I wasn't sure what was happening. "I'm just screwing with you." She ran her thumbs across my knuckles, the gesture endearing and a bit intoxicating. "That was sweet what you said. To quote a pretty cool friend of mine who I hope someday might be something more, 'already forgiven.'"

"So," I asked, my heart fluttering in my chest, "if this is an honest-to-God date, I'm more than happy to pick up the check."

"Oh, no, Boy Wonder," she said, her trademark grin back in place, "this one is on me." She leaned in and dropped her voice to a conspiratorial whisper. "And if you play your cards right, you might even get a first-date kiss."

"Oh, really?" I was glad my cheeks, burning in that moment, were clean-shaven. "And what if I told you I don't kiss on the first date?"

"I don't know, Ethan." She ran the tip of her tongue across her even teeth. "I can be pretty persuasive."

"I can only imagine."

"You won't have to for very much longer." Her eyes shot to a nearby stairwell leading up. "Meet me on the roof."

"Are you sure?"

"I was reading online. This place has the best view of the Denver skyline in town." She raised her eyebrows and inclined her head in Delacroix's direction. "Not to mention, I'd prefer not to have an audience for such an auspicious occasion."

Seph dabbed at the corner of her mouth and folded her napkin by her half-empty plate before excusing herself from the table. Delacroix glanced our way, but then a pair of cars on the street dueling with honking horns grabbed his attention, leaving me free to head for the stairs as well.

I imagined Seph waiting for me halfway up, her full lips pulled wide in an expectant grin. With neither of us able to wait until we got to the roof, we'd reenact the stairwell scenes from a dozen movies: impassioned lovers embroiled in a fevered kiss, ricocheting from wall to wall like battlefield shrapnel, proving the fine line between love and war.

The stairwell, however, was empty.

Though a bit disappointed, 'first kiss with a view' still sounded pretty good.

I stepped out into the cool Denver midmorning and was immediately awed by the beautiful Denver skyline. Doing the job we do, the guys and I rarely have an opportunity to get out and actually see the multitude of cities we visit each year. Both bigger and smaller than I expected, Denver's downtown area rested beneath a crystal blue sky the color of Seph's eyes.

"Seph?" Not too old for hide-and-seek, it seemed. She was making me work for it, and while I wasn't usually one for games, this one was punching all the right buttons. "Ready or not, here I come."

"Ethan!" Seph's voice from somewhere above hit my ears shrill and full of fear. "Help!"

I peered up into the sun's bright corona and found Seph's lithe form flying this way and that directly above my head as if she were being flung around by some giant invisible child. The gentle rooftop breeze quickly shifted into a full-on gale. That's when I put two and two together: the only thing holding Seph aloft was blast after blast of wind, coming in from every direction and leaving Seph spinning in the sky like clothes in a dryer.

"I'm here, Seph!" I shouted. "Hang on!"

An empty promise followed by an impossible request. Unless the Transference somehow included blue tights with an "S" on the chest and a big red cape, nothing I could do was going to help Seph in this situation.

And as far as hanging on? She was literally trapped in open air.

"So," came a booming voice from the opposite field of sky, the accent unmistakably German, "you must be this Harkreader everyone has been gossiping about." A deafening laugh pounded at my eardrums. "Not much to look at from where I'm standing." A whistling wind filled the brief pause. "So to speak."

I spun around, fully expecting to find a black-cloaked figure in a bird mask and wide-brimmed hat. Instead, the man floating on air some twenty feet from the edge of the building was dressed in a tailored ivory suit complete with a tie and a pair of spotless Chuck Taylors the color of driven snow. His long silver hair pulled back into a ponytail, he stared down at me through mirrored sunglasses.

"Leave her alone, you bastard."

"Or what, Mr. Harkreader? Even if you fully understood the power I've heard now runs through your veins, no Daughter of Neith has ever possessed the ability to fly."

"Come down here and—face me like a man and I'll—show you—exactly—what I'm—capable of." My every word came out quieter than the one before, and by the end of the sentence, I was gasping for air.

"Whatever is the matter, Mr. Harkreader?" The man smiled. "The view from this rooftop is indeed breathtaking, but you seem positively winded."

CHAPTER 9

SYSTEM OF SURVIVAL

I f there's a more terrifying sensation than the rush of air flowing out of your lungs and mouth while you're trying with all your might to inhale, I don't want to know what it is.

As everything began to go dark, my flailing thoughts latched onto something Delacroix had said regarding another group like the Midnight Angel's Ravens but who control the elements rather than shadows.

Fire burns, water drowns, and earth crushes, but air? I was getting my ass kicked by some kind of air elemental? And not with something flashy like a tornado or a hurricane, but simple asphyxiation?

Not too auspicious a first outing, Ethan.

Darkness continued to invade my vision from every side. My lungs burned for oxygen as I dropped to one knee and, for the first time in my life, wondered if I'd ever stand again.

"Now, boy," the man in the ivory suit taunted, "we shall be taking

Miss Snow from here. Unless you desire for me to finish collapsing your perfectly good pair of lungs, I suggest you stay down and don't try to stop us."

My panicked brain didn't bother looking for a retort. Instead, I stole a look up at Seph. Her form no longer jerking to and fro in midair, she was instead buffeted by blast after blast of air from below. The intermittent gusts launched her straight up again and again only for her to drop after every upward rush of air. Half her clothes torn from her, she dangled in the sky like a ragged feather trapped in a whirlwind. As I teetered on the edge of unconsciousness, one thing became very clear: neither Seph nor the universe had picked their latest champion very well.

The crack of gunfire sounded from somewhere far away, and a split second later, the oppressive pull of air from my lungs let up, allowing me to suck in one tiny but oh-so-sweet breath. Another gasp and the black at the edges of my vision retreated. A quick scan of the sky revealed that the man in the ivory suit responsible for all the chaos had vanished. Of more immediate concern, however, Seph's flailing form hurtled for the edge of the building like a marionette fired from a catapult, victim of a far more brutal and far less controlled gust of wind.

I rushed for the building's edge, my body moving before I had the chance to consider a plan. My lungs screamed for oxygen as my legs worked like pistons to reach Seph before it was too late. With scant feet between me and a three-story drop, I leaped into oblivion and snatched her from midair, pulling her close to my body. The paired momentum of her flight and my leap, however, sent us flying off the roof. Too winded to scream, her wide-eyed gaze locked with mine as gravity took hold and we plummeted. An image of Wile E. Coyote flashed across my mind's eye, though I was fairly certain the asphalt below would be far less forgiving than the desert floor of a *Looney Tunes* cartoon. I twisted our bodies around so that mine would take the brunt of the fall, not that a thirty-foot drop was going to leave either of us alive.

And then, the first bit of good luck that day.

A city garbage truck stopped at a red light on the opposite side of the street, the top of the immense vehicle just below our downward arc. As Seph and I swept past, I stretched out an arm and snagged one of the truck's hydraulic arms. The three fingers involved screamed as if they'd been yanked from their sockets and my shoulder flared with pain, but somehow I held on. The side of the truck clanged like a gong as Seph and I impacted the blue-painted steel. Fortunately, my left flank bore the brunt of the impact, leaving Seph breathless and terrified but conscious in the crook of my right arm.

"You okay?" I got out between gasps for air.

"I think so," she whispered, peering down at the road scant feet beneath us and then up at my straining arm. "What are you, Ethan? Spider-Man?"

"If only."

The garbage truck jolted into park and the irritated driver appeared on the street below us a moment later to see what had hit his truck.

"What are you two doing?" His accent marked him as a New Yorker in a previous life. "Get down from there."

"Just as quick as I can, trust me." I directed my gaze to the terrified woman held in my arm. "A little assist here?"

When he realized that Seph and I were literally hanging on by my fingertips, his expression shifted from annoyance to alarm. He rushed over and held up his grimy hands as I lowered a half-naked Seph into his waiting arms. As I released her, my throbbing fingers finally gave way. I'd fallen no more than a couple of inches, however, when both my feet kicked out instinctively as if I'd performed such a maneuver a thousand times. My toes found purchase along a horizontal seam of the truck's side, and then, using skills I hadn't possessed two days before, I pushed off into a tight backflip and landed on both feet none the worse for wear.

Besides, of course, my left shoulder and hand shrieking that they'd both been nearly pulled from my body and my lungs that still screamed for air.

"Wow, kid." The truck driver stared at me in disbelief. "You okay?"

"He's more than okay." Seph leaped out of his arms and rushed to my side, punch-drunk from her ordeal but unstoppable nonetheless. "He's magnificent."

Without another word, she curled into my aching form as if trying to bandage my wounds with her very essence and kissed me with a passion beyond anything I'd experienced in my twenty-three years on the planet. This was the stuff you read about in storybooks or watched unfold on the big screen: shared adrenalin, electricity, magic. Without a doubt, this was—

"Are you all right, Miss Snow?" Delacroix shouted as he sprinted down the sidewalk in our direction.

"I'm fine, I think." Shivering, Seph crossed her arms to cover herself. "Ethan saved me."

"You're not safe yet." Delacroix slipped off his suit jacket to cover Seph's half-naked form and turned to me. "Harkreader, we have to get Miss Snow out of sight before this guy comes back for round two."

"I can help." The truck driver's eyes shifted from me to Seph to Delacroix. "Just tell me what you need."

"The best thing you can do is get away from here as fast as you can," Delacroix rumbled. "You don't want any part of this." He leveled his most no-nonsense glare at the man. "Go."

"I heard gunfire," I said as the garbage truck pulled away and we all headed for the nearest corner. My gaze dropped to the smoking Glock in Delacroix's massive hand. The sulfur scent of an expended round left a distinct tang in the air. "I'm guessing that was you."

"Who else?" Delacroix's gaze went skyward. "Our friend the aeromancer wouldn't lower himself to using firearms." He let out an ironic chuckle. "And why would he? A tornado can send a straw straight through a hundred-year-old oak tree."

Or he could simply suck the air right out of your lungs from a block away without breaking a sweat.

"Hold on a sec." Winded and angry, Seph stepped into her bodyguard's space. "What the hell is an aeromancer?"

"There's no time, Miss Snow." Delacroix took her hand. "We've got to go."

Seph pulled her hand loose and crossed her arms. "You're going to make time. Now, what the hell is going on?"

I took Seph by the shoulders. "These people after you? They're not ordinary humans, but something more. They can control the elements, shadows—"

"Wait." She pulled away from me. "That shit the other night with the shadows wasn't just some kind of hallucination?" She glared at me as if I'd just slapped her. "You knew about all of this and didn't tell me?"

"I'm new to all this too, Seph." I shot a look at Delacroix. "And the secrets in question are not all mine to tell."

"My apologies, Miss Snow. We'd hoped to be able to protect you from all this madness without burdening you with unnecessary knowledge."

Her face flushed scarlet with anger. "That 'aeromancer' or whatever he is just hurled me off a three-story building. Burden me, please."

I took Seph's shoulders and pulled her to me. "You're right. You deserve to know it all, and we'll catch you up as soon as we get you away from this asshole."

"Careful with the name calling, Harkreader." The aeromancer descended from atop the bank across the street from the restaurant and levitated midair above us. "You never know who might be listening."

"What do you want from me?" Seph screamed.

"Our mistress has need of you, and fortunately for you, she needs you alive." The aeromancer winced, his hand going to his right shoulder where a splotch of red marred his otherwise pristine suit.

"Winged him." Delacroix raised his pistol. "Time to finish the job."

"You cretin." The aeromancer focused his furious gaze on Delacroix from twenty feet above our heads. "Do you have any idea what this jacket cost?" With a wave of his hand, the wind kicked up around us, and a microcosmic tornado sent Delacroix's weapon flying from his hand. "Whatever shall you do to stop me now, little man?"

From atop the roof of the bank, a streak of black and brown flew at the aeromancer like a dark meteor.

"He won't have to." Rosemary caught the man around the neck

with one arm to stop her fall, and with the other, plunged the shorter of the two blades her mother had wielded two nights before into his already wounded shoulder. The aeromancer cried out in pain, and the wind answered, hurling Rosemary headlong at the concrete sidewalk. The same instincts that had kicked in as I saved Seph activated again. I was halfway across the double lane of traffic before I realized I was moving. With my uninjured arm, I caught Rosemary's hurtling form and kicked off from the ground with all the strength remaining in my burning thighs and calves. The shift in momentum was all it took as Rosemary, in turn, twisted into an aerial flip and landed on the ball of one foot. Her paired blades held out to either side in a perfect T, she dropped to a low fighting stance and prepared for counterattack, her maneuver flawless.

My landing, it goes without saying, was nowhere near as graceful.

"Ethan!" Seph ran to my side despite me waving her off. "Are you all right?"

"I'm fine." I scanned my entire body for a square inch that didn't hurt. No such luck.

"Here." She reached down a hand. "Let me help you up."

My pride wounded a bit, I accepted her help. As Seph pulled me to my feet, I found the half-block tumble had left me in front of a coffee shop, the few late morning customers remaining rubbernecking from inside. Most of the block's foot traffic had fled, though more than one curious onlooker lurked at the various corners, cellphones in hand, likely recording the strangest thing many of them would ever see.

Rosemary and her father now stood back-to-back, his retrieved pistol and her mother's paired blades at the ready.

The aeromancer, however, was nowhere to be found.

I guided Seph to the bank's recessed entrance, and Rosemary and Delacroix followed. Not surprisingly, the door was locked. A peek through the glass doorway revealed that everyone had gone to ground.

"So, where'd our friend the chatty wind tunnel go?" I shot a quick glance upward and was glad to find only blue skies and the occasional cloud. "Off to lick his wounds, I guess?" I hoped my optimism didn't sound naive. "He who fights and runs away and all that?"

"The Ascendant all heal quickly," Rosemary answered. "That being said, I buried Mother's blade pretty deep in his shoulder." Her lips spread in a grim smile. "No way he's using that arm again today."

"Ascendant?" Seph asked. "Your mother's blade?" She turned to me. "Ethan, what is this? What have I gotten myself into?"

"Seph, please." Rosemary stepped between us. "Father and I will explain all of this in as much or little detail as you want once we are to safety, but for now just know this: there are people after you for reasons we don't know or understand, people who can do things that are beyond most people's comprehension. All of us, Father and Ethan and I, are doing everything in our power to protect you, but you have to trust us."

A bewildered Seph stared at each of us in turn.

"So, Ethan is some kind of superhero, you're a ninja or whatever, your dad is a secret agent bodyguard, and the three of you are here to protect me from a bunch of dark wizards straight out of Harry Potter?"

"Better than I could have explained it. Looks like you're up to speed." I took her hand and looked to Delacroix. "Now what do we do?"

Before he could answer, the ground beneath our feet began to rumble, the shaking of the concrete sidewalk sending all of us but Rosemary to our knees.

The last time I was in San Francisco, a tiny earthquake woke me from a dead sleep in the middle of the night, my first and only experience with seismic badness. I'd been sleeping off a night of after-show drinking in my hotel room and had no idea what was happening until the tremors flipped me off the edge of the bed and onto an unforgiving hardwood floor.

I could only imagine how worse it could be if the quake was actually gunning for you.

"What the hell was that?" Seph asked as she worked to rise from her awkward sprawl. "I didn't know Denver got earthquakes."

"Every place does, if you're patient enough," Delacroix answered, rising from a low crouch, "but you're correct, Miss Snow. Denver isn't particularly known for seismic activity."

"That's what I thought you were going to say." Seph yanked me to my feet and pulled me into a terrified embrace, the reality of our situation taking hold. "It's another one of these Ascendant people coming for me, isn't it, Ethan?"

A telltale word the aeromancer had spoken echoed in my mind, haughty German accent and all: *we*.

Before I could answer Seph's question, the heavens, previously bright turquoise and cloudless, went dark, purple, and overcast, the newly formed clouds spinning ominously in the sky above our heads.

"What if *all* of them are here?" Rosemary pulled close to Delacroix. "We need to get Seph out of here, Father. Ethan has barely begun to train, and even with all that Mother has taught me, I don't know if we can handle this."

"Agreed." Delacroix pointed to a corner opposite the direction from where we'd last seen the aeromancer. "That way," he whispered to Seph. "Don't let Rosemary out of your sight."

No sooner had Rosemary and Seph headed out than a gale force wind pushed them back into our tiny shelter.

A woman from inside the bank stared out at us, terrified, but mouthing the word "Sorry" before disappearing back to wherever she'd been hiding.

Truth be told, if I were in her shoes, I wouldn't open the door either.

"Dammit, they've got us pinned down," Delacroix groaned. "Rosemary, thoughts?"

"The very elements stand against us, Father." Her eyes cut to me, her face twisted with anger and frustration cut with cold acceptance. "And despite everything, I am but one woman."

"Then it's up to me." I met each of their gazes in turn: Seph's, Delacroix's, Rosemary's. "Your mother. She would have known what to do—"

"I know what to do." Rosemary's words, tinged with a hint of venom, stung. "But I can't. Not without—" She stared at me with sadness and fury and regret.

"Rosemary can't, Ethan, but you can." Seph, quiet for some time, spoke up, her voice filled with strained optimism. "The things you can do are miraculous." She took my hand in her trembling fingers. "You can get us out of this, can't you?"

I swallowed back my fear and looked to Rosemary. "May I borrow your mother's blades?"

Rosemary's eyebrows knitted together. "You can't go out there. You don't know what you're doing yet. It's suicide."

"The other option is all of us wait here to die." I held out my hands, palms up. "Your mother's blades, please, before I lose my nerve."

With one last moment of hesitation, Rosemary placed in my hands the weapons that she herself had trained countless hours to wield, the short sword in my left and the longer curved blade in my right. The leather-bound grip of each felt good in my clenched fists, but it was far more than that. I'd held those blades before on a thousand battlefields, wielded them in countless fights, and cleaned the gore from their razor edges time and again.

Impossible, and yet, the truth.

My eyelids slid shut as I soaked in the majesty of the moment, and when I again opened my eyes, the blades in my hands glowed with an inner light as they had two nights before.

As I stepped out of the shallow alcove and into the gathering storm, the wind and rain beating against my body and the ground quaking beneath my feet, I found cold comfort in one simple realization: either the powers and abilities that flowed into me at the moment of Danielle Delacroix's death would see me through the following moments and allow me to save us all, or those selfsame powers and abilities would soon reside in their rightful place, transferred to Rosemary at the moment of my own.

CHAPTER 10

DANCING IN THE STREET

"Are you done playing hide and seek," I shouted to the sky, "or can we go ahead and get this thing started?"

In answer, a wall of flames ten feet high rose from corner to corner at one end of the block followed by another linear inferno at the opposite end. Blast furnace heat struck me from either side as sulfur and acrid smoke filled my senses. I shook my head, realizing my baptism of fire was about to be just that: a lone novice hero with powers he doesn't begin to understand against all four elements in the hands of a quartet of experienced Ascendant mercenaries.

Awesome.

"This is your last chance, Harkreader." A woman's voice colored with a subtle accent of African origin emanated from the nearer wall of flame. "Hand over Persephone Snow, and you and the others may leave with your lives. Know that she will not be harmed, as our mistress needs her alive and well."

86

"I don't know," I shouted in no particular direction, "your cyclone ranger in the white suit and shades just chucked her off a building a few minutes ago after doing his best to suck my lungs straight out of my chest, so consider me a bit skeptical."

"You must excuse Dietrich," the voice continued. "He gets a bit overzealous at times."

"This is it, then?" I peered around the block. "You people are going to bring wind and rain, earthquakes and walls of flame, but none of you will so much as face me?"

"I will face you, Harkreader." Another woman's voice filled the air, the delivery rapid and the accent reminiscent of an old friend from college who hailed from Colombia. "Though you should be careful what you wish for."

A miniature storm of rain and hail swirled up the far sidewalk to its midpoint before dividing into twin storms, the parting cyclones revealing a woman in a skintight purple bodysuit, black leggings, and bright teal boots. Dark locks swept across her tawny forehead and down her back in a waist-length braid.

"A Daughter of Neith might command at least some level of respect," this newcomer to the fight boasted, "but a scared little boy who understands next to nothing of the power at his fingertips? I feel only pity."

Ouch. That was unnecessary.

"So, that's one of you." I forced every ounce of confidence I could muster into my voice as I glanced back at Seph, Rosemary, and Delacroix. "Anyone else brave enough to show their face?"

"You talk a big game, Harkreader." These words, more rumble than voice, came from beneath my feet. "But as Violeta said, you are nothing but a frightened child to us." The section of road where the garbage truck had saved Seph and me fractured upward as if a volcano were being born, the earth and clay and asphalt and stone all flowing up into a form that resembled a living statue with the dimensions of an enormous sumo wrestler. "Now, stand down, or you will force our hand."

"You've tasted but a sample of what I can do to you and your friends." The aeromancer—the voice from the fire called him

Dietrich—landed before me, the red stain at the right shoulder of his ivory suit larger than before.

I recoiled, my mind and body remembering all too well exactly what he was capable of.

"Ah," he continued, "the inescapable panic of having the very air stolen from your lungs. Truly terrifying, is it not?" He looked to the woman in purple and black. "Would you rather them filled with water, leaving you to drown in the middle of a city a mile above sea level?" His gaze shifted to the mountain of earth and clay staring at me from mid-street. "Or, perhaps, you'd prefer the unmatched horror of being buried alive?"

"Or the brief but exquisite agony of being immolated where you stand?" From the center of the nearer of the two walls of flame stepped a woman clothed in brightly colored textiles of crimson, orange, and gold. Though her robes and ornate matching hat were woven from colors of fire, the inferno that surrounded her didn't so much as singe a thread. "We'd hoped to take our leave and Miss Snow without such drama," she spoke, her African accent lending gravitas to her words, "but as you've insisted on meeting us all face to face, here we are."

Yes, Ethan. You asked for all four of the superpowered assassins to pop up out of their hidey-holes and face you as one unified front. Now what the hell are you going to do?

And yet, if I were just Ethan Harkreader, college dropout and roadie extraordinaire, such a quartet of godlike beings wouldn't have stopped long enough to give me the time of day. Their gathering before me represented a show of respect, and if there was one thing I'd learned as low man on the food chain over the preceding few years, it's that people with great power typically only respect one thing: equal or greater power.

If only Jacob could see me now.

"Before we begin, know one thing." I crossed the paired blades of Danielle Delacroix before me in a defensive posture and smiled, trying to remain cool and confident, though each droplet of sweat at my brow committed its own tiny betrayal of the abject terror at my core. "You will not be leaving here today with Persephone Snow. Let's be clear about that."

"Oh, you poor thing." The fire elementalist—pyromancer, I guess?—stepped forward. "You seem to suffer under the misunderstanding that our banter represents some form of negotiation."

"Your cause is lost, Harkreader," Violeta, the Latina woman in purple, added. "You are outnumbered and outclassed."

"We'd prefer if you'd simply give us the girl." Dietrich winced behind his mirrored sunglasses, his hand absently rubbing at the splotch of red at his right shoulder. "We have no problem with doing whatever it takes to achieve our goal, but as with anyone the least bit civilized, we all find unnecessary bloodshed rather gauche."

"Enough." The ground trembled as the sumo of earth and stone gave his decree. "Bring Snow to us. Now."

"Over our dead bodies." Rosemary appeared at my side. "As you all clearly are aware, my mother fell in defense of Miss Snow." She held her katana before her, defiant to the last. "I don't have the first inkling as to what your mistress wants with a fledgling celebrity, but if you value your continued existence, I recommend you all walk away."

After a brief pause, all four broke into open laughter.

"Skilled you may be, Baby Delacroix," Dietrich said through clenched teeth, "but our intelligence states that you have not an iota of your mother's power."

Rosemary raised an eyebrow. "I had more than enough skill to make you bleed like a stuck pig."

The aeromancer's nose crinkled as he turned his attention on me. "And this pathetic receptacle of all that your line has carried for centuries is laughable." The wind whipped around him as he raised his hands. "Last chance. Hand over the girl."

Before I could respond, a flash of movement from the corner of my eye pulled my attention. A hulking figure flew in a parabolic arc, clearing the ten feet of flame at the block's far end, only to land before me in a low crouch. Taller and more massive than Mr.

Delacroix as he rose to his full height, this new player to the game appeared like some sort of god of myth.

A gasp sounded from the line of elementalists as Violeta and the pyromancer together uttered two astonished words.

"The Greyhound."

"Who?" I asked Rosemary, and found similar bewilderment in her eyes as she studied this latest arrival to our impromptu battlefield.

At least six-foot-six, the powerful legs, muscular upper body, and broad shoulders of this newcomer led to a weathered face that had seen more than its share of decades on this planet. A grey mane of curly locks flowed into a thick salt-and-pepper beard. Every bit the personification of his namesake, no part of this man called Greyhound was greyer than his eyes filled with wisdom, their color reminiscent of the leaden heavens of a northwestern November.

"So, Ada, you've brought your entire brood to fetch one girl." The Greyhound locked gazes with the fire elementalist, the vaguely European accent delivered in a voice so deep, its rumble rivaled the tremors that had shaken the Denver street minutes before. "What, your fire not burning as brightly these days?"

"Sir Greyhound." The pyromancer inclined her head forward in a subtle bow. "With all due respect, I ask that you allow us to proceed without interference."

"Though the privilege of meeting such as you in combat would truly be an honor," Dietrich added, doing his best to hide the pain radiating from his wounded shoulder, "the mere thought of bringing a life such as yours to an end hurts my soul."

This time it was the Greyhound who laughed. "You think rather highly of your skills, Dietrich Falco." At the wounded man's raised eyebrows, just visible behind his mirrored shades, the giant before me added, "Yes, little aeromancer, I know your name."

"What now?" Violeta asked Ada. "He is legend."

"We have our assigned task." Ada's eyes narrowed at us. "Regardless of who they might be, anyone who stands between us and our goal is nothing but an obstacle." She let out a resigned sigh. "And you know what we do with obstacles."

"Remove them." The rumbling tones uttered by the sumo of earth and stone echoed off the buildings on either side as he raised his massive arms, sending a wave of asphalt as high as the wall of flame to our rear rippling down the street toward us.

"Move!" Rosemary shoved me to one side and then sprinted straight at the approaching breaker of broken road. Half a second later, the Greyhound leaped forward in another unbelievable bound, his inhuman speed, strength, and agility making short work of the hurtling wall of asphalt. As he vanished beyond the rolling wave of road, I returned my attention to Rosemary, whose methods in avoiding being taken down by a tidal wave of asphalt and earth were no less impressive. Sprinting up the side of the approaching wave as easily as I might run up a flight of stairs, she disappeared to the other side in a flying leap, drawing her katana from the scabbard hung across her back just before she dropped out of sight.

Unfortunately, that left me alone on a Denver two-lane street with tons of broken tar and gravel flying at me and a ten-foot wall of flame blocking my only escape.

Time, Ethan, to man up. Unless you want to end up a man down.

I was no slouch in the physical fitness department and was infused with the combined essences of two millennia of warrior women, not to mention I'd watched more than my fair share of *American Ninja Warrior* over the years.

How hard could this be?

Following Rosemary's lead, I raced toward the rushing tsunami of asphalt, the paired blades of the late Danielle Delacroix held out to either side like a set of eagle's wings, and put my faith in the instincts of a woman who I'd met minutes before those very instincts failed her, leaving her dead in an Albuquerque parking lot.

The wave of broken road crested before me, the center portion leading either side. My untrained eyes from days before would never have found the path across this latest danger. As the perceptions and reflexes that had miraculously saved me and Seph from our three-story fall kicked in, however, I saw the looming mass of black in a very different way.

A six-inch jutting clump of asphalt, just big enough to place a foot.

A narrow crevice in the rolling mass of earth, perfectly shaped for the toe of my shoe.

And another. And another. And another.

My body moved in perfect time with my mind, my feet finding foothold after foothold as I scaled the bulwark of tar and gravel hurtling toward the wall of flame to my rear. As I crested the top of the earthen wave, the various players came into view.

The grizzled mass of muscle known as the Greyhound battled with Dietrich and Violeta, their combined control over wind and rain buffeting him as he stalked step by painstaking step in their direction. Rosemary, on the other hand, struggled with the pyromancer the Greyhound had called Ada, as serpentine tendrils of fire came at her from every side.

Regardless of the steel or skill involved, a sword isn't much use against literal flames.

"Rosemary!" I shouted. "Hold on! I'm coming!"

"You're going nowhere, Harkreader."

The rumbling tones of the as-yet-unnamed earth elementalist had no sooner hit my eardrums than I fell flat on my face, my foot caught in a tentacle formed of crumbled road that ran up my leg like a fast-growing vine. The shorter of Danielle Delacroix's swords clattered across the asphalt between me and the monstrous form of gravel, tar, and dirt, but my faltering grip somehow held onto the longer curved blade, a blade that began to glow anew with no more effort than me willing it to do so.

I stabbed at the tentacle of asphalt that held my leg despite my mind screaming that I was more likely to hurt myself than do any damage to what had effectively been stone minutes before. I'm not certain which amazed me more: the glowing steel cutting through the hardened tar and gravel like a hot knife through butter or the deftness that my crude hands suddenly possessed.

In any case, I wasn't complaining.

Instinct, a few well-placed blows, and magic-infused steel soon made short work of my shackle, leaving me free to go after its originator—who had already grown to twice his original size. I sprinted at the twelve-foot giant of earth and gravel and tar. Instinct guided my every step even as I wondered who this strange new person was who charged into the maw of danger again and again.

"Eager to prove your worth, eh, Harkreader?" came a rumble from the earthen giant.

"Glutton for punishment, I guess." I swung on the earth elementalist's gigantic calf with the glowing sword. The blade again performed its magic, its razor edge taking off the colossal sumo's leg at the knee. "Though I've decided to take up spreading the love a bit."

A guttural laugh emanated from the sumo's lips. Not only did the titan of earth and asphalt not fall, but his severed extremity coiled like a snake on the ground only to leap from the shattered road and reattach to its previous home.

"If that's all you've got, Harkreader," came the sumo's rumbling tones, "then you are in way over your head."

"Perhaps, then," Rosemary appeared at my side and slid her katana back into the scabbard at her back, "we should exchange partners." Before I could respond, she was well above my head, scaling the now-fifteen-foot colossus like an expert rock climber on the easiest challenge at the local bouldering gym.

Damn, the woman could do anything.

"Ethan!" came Seph's voice, drawing me back to the problem at hand. "Help!"

I spun around just in time to see the cause of her alarm.

With Rosemary otherwise occupied, the pyromancer called Ada had been free to again pursue her team's target, and she hadn't wasted any time. Mere feet from the alcove leading to the bank's open doors, the woman dressed in colors of the flames that obeyed her beck and call strode forward, walking as if she had all the time in the world. I caught a glimpse of Seph as Delacroix pulled her through the door and into the temporary safety of the bank. Someone inside must have been watching and took pity on them, not that the gesture was going to do much good.

As Ada drew near to the bank entrance, the entire alcove, door, and facade burst into blue flame. Wood burned, stone scorched, and glass melted, all in a matter of seconds.

I could only imagine what would happen if she turned that power on me.

Or Delacroix.

Or Seph.

I scooped up the shorter of Danielle Delacroix's blades and had more than halved the distance between us when Ada stepped across the threshold and into the bank. Screams filled the air, followed by a pair of gunshots. A brief flash like a tiny meteor streaked past Ada's shoulder as one of the bullets disintegrated in the heat of the fire elementalist's aura.

Delacroix's gun wasn't going to help much in this situation.

By the time I stepped inside the seemingly deserted bank, Ada had already swept the right side of the lobby as evidenced by the sprinklers dousing that end of the building and was stalking in the direction of the offices at the other end. As her eyes met mine through the falling water, her face filled with cool dismissal.

"Mr. Harkreader, you got in one lucky strike against Daichi for all the good it did you before the Delacroix girl had to step in to save you." A circle of fire erupted around her feet, the flames rising and falling in time to the gentle swaying of their mistress's hips as she strode my way. Above her head, yet another sprinkler went off, the water instantly turning to steam, leaving the bank foyer a sauna. "Do you really wish to press your luck against one who can burn you to a crisp with but a thought?"

A big part of me agreed with her, a part of me that wanted to surrender, to lay down arms, and let her take whoever and whatever she wanted.

But if there's one thing I've learned in my few years on this earth, it's that you don't complain about what you lack but embrace what you are given.

The power meant for Rosemary lived within me, and barring some sort of miracle, would remain there until the day I died.

If that day was today, so be it.

CHAPTER 11

HOT HOT HOT

"I won't let you take her."

"You cannot stop me."

"I'll go down trying."

"That, Mr. Harkreader, is the least delusional thing you've said all day."

Ada studied me through the thick steam from across the shined tile of the bank's foyer while I scrutinized her every movement, ready to move the moment she attacked.

"What does this mistress of yours want with a pop star anyway?" I asked, buying Delacroix as much time as I could to get Seph to safety. "Do you even know?"

"It is not our business to inquire why our mistress wants something or someone, but simply to collect the object or person in question and deliver them in a timely manner, sometimes alive and sometimes...less so."

"As long as the check clears, it's all good then?" I wasn't sure if hitting the guilt button would accomplish much, but I gave it my best shot. "That's a pretty mercenary attitude, don't you think?"

"We are literal weapons for hire, Mr. Harkreader," she said without a moment's consideration. "Is there a better word to describe what we do?"

Good point. "You still haven't answered my question, though. Why her? Why Seph?"

"Seph? Ah, a diminutive. So, the starlet has taken a lover. How cute."

Dammit. Never was much of a poker player. "What are they paying you for this? I'm sure someone with connections like Persephone Snow's could easily—"

"Your understanding of the world around you is shockingly limited. We are Ascendant. Our requirements extend far beyond the currency to which you and your ilk cling as if imaginary numbers on a screen matter in the grand scheme of things."

"So...Bitcoin?"

Her eyes narrowed, my stupid joke distracting her for yet another few precious seconds.

Or so I thought.

"There's no other way out of this building, by the way." Her lips curled into a smug grin. "In case your stalling tactics are meant to help our quarry escape."

"Seph!" I shouted. "If you can hear me, stay with Mr. Delacroix and do what he says, no matter what!"

"No." Seph appeared from an adjoining hallway, an angelic apparition amid the obscuring steam and ensuing chaos. "She's here for me. No one else needs to suffer."

"Wise girl." Ada took a step in Seph's direction. "Come with me now, and I and the others will take our leave without any further property damage." Her eyes drifted to me. "Or loss of life."

"Not before we discuss terms." Seph crossed her arms and raised an eyebrow, affecting the attitude from our initial interaction when she and I were a little less friendly. "I have a few demands."

"Of course you do." The air about Ada's form shimmered with

heat and wisps of steam. "And what, pray tell, makes you think we care a whit about your wishes, little girl?"

"Because apparently you need me both alive and unharmed," Seph answered without a moment's hesitation.

"Alive, yes." The tile at Seph's feet began to smolder. "But unharmed?"

"Run, Seph!" I screamed as I raced at the pyromancer. "Get away from her!"

Seph turned and sprinted down the hall, the last thing I saw before the floor beneath me exploded upward in a blast of heat and countless razor bits of tile. The shockwave sent me flying into the ceiling where my upper back found one of the dozen or so sprinkler heads protruding from the grid of tile and metal. The searing pain just inside my right shoulder blade ripped a scream from the bottom of my soul just before everything went black.

My eyes opened on shattered faux marble tile obscured by dust, falling water, and billowing steam. A sound like twin police sirens rang in both ears, but otherwise, I couldn't hear a thing. My upper back burned in agony, the slow wet drip coursing down my right shoulder warm compared to the water coursing down from the broken sprinkler above my head.

"Seph." I pushed myself up from the floor, my back throbbing in time with my racing heartbeat. "Got to get to Seph."

I forced myself to my feet, the effort as taxing as if I fought Jupiter's gravity rather than that of good old terra firma. Fortunately, three of my four extremities seemed to be operating at nearly a hundred percent. My right arm, however, was going to need a few weeks of physical therapy, and that's if I was lucky.

I retrieved the longer of Danielle Delacroix's two blades with the hand that still worked and grabbed the other in my right—and usually dominant—hand, hoping against hope I could pull a Dread Pirate Roberts if I needed to. The grips of both swords were soaked, as were my hands, and as the shorter sword hung precariously from my injured right hand and arm, I prayed that such a minute detail wouldn't be the final nail in our collective coffin.

I charged down the steamy hall where Seph had disappeared God knows how long ago and the mysterious woman of fire had no doubt followed. The sprinkler heads along the hallway each rained upon the carpeted floor, confirming I was on the right track. I passed offices with closed doors on either side, each one locked and, I suspected, barricaded from inside, all leading to the rear of the bank.

I was quickly running out of hallway with no Seph, Delacroix, or Ada to be found when I came upon the answer to my search.

Standing open, an enormous steel door straight out of a heist movie led into a room filled with safe deposit boxes. Voices, shouted and echoing, hit my still-ringing ears from within.

Just the three voices I was looking for.

I peered into the bank vault, the scene within neither surprising nor reassuring.

Her back to me, Ada stood within the shimmer of her cocoon of heat, the water spitting down from the ceiling never reaching her dark skin but filling the space with thick, choking steam. Just past her in the tiny vault with their backs to the wall stood Seph and Delacroix, drenched by the sprinklers, the former barely visible behind her bodyguard's massive form.

"Finally," Ada's voice, just audible over the ringing in my ears, dripped with sarcasm, "as they say, the gang's all here." Though she didn't bother to look my way, her words and body language made two things perfectly clear: not only was she aware of my presence, but she couldn't have been less concerned. "Now, for the last time, Mr. Delacroix, hand over Snow unless you want me to flash fry you and Mr. Harkreader where you stand."

"Not happening." I stepped inside the vault, and despite the inch of water on the floor and the several feet that lay between Ada and me, the toes of my shoes began to smolder. "Stand down, Ada. This is your last chance."

Ada turned to face me, a sardonic smile across her lips. "You are quite bold, Mr. Harkreader, I will grant you that." Orange flames erupted at her feet despite the water. "Do you truly have such a profound death wish?"

"You're pretty brave, all untouchable surrounded by a million degrees Fahrenheit." At Ada's raised eyebrow, I proceeded with the gambit. "Care to drop the flames and see if you can take me in a fair fight?"

"First, boy, I know a dozen ways to end you without so much as striking a match, so don't believe for a moment that your bit of bravado means the first thing to me. That being said, unlike the idiots in the movies and television shows you're hoping I'll emulate, I understand that only a fool gives up a clear advantage in a fight." A maelstrom of fire swirled up her brightly clad form, culminating in an orb of flame that rested atop her outstretched hand. "Now, the time for talk is over."

With a crinkle of her nose, she flung the ball of fire at me. My body responded before I could think, sending me tumbling with unearned grace out of the vault and into an awkward back handspring. The fireball singed my hair as it flew by, missing my head by mere inches, and struck the wall behind me. This time, the resultant explosion sent me flying not upward but straight at the pyromancer herself.

My right shoulder cried out in agony as I brought up the shorter of Danielle Delacroix's paired blades, crossing the two lengths of razor-sharp steel before me as I hurtled like a meteor toward the woman clothed in fire. Time slowed to a crawl as I flew headlong at fiery death. Heat blasted my face, my hair and eyebrows singing despite the man-made deluge, under the fire of Ada's furious scowl.

And then, the latest in a succession of miracles.

The crossed blades before me flashed with renewed inner light a split second before impact, filling my vision with pure, blinding brilliance. Intense heat accompanied the bone-crunching collision with the angry pyromancer, leaving me blind, half-deaf, and with a barely functional arm.

But somehow, alive. I was in far too much pain to be dead.

As my eyes cleared, a flurry of movement, sounds, and sensations hit me from every side. Rough hands grabbed at my shirt and dragged me away, hands I hoped were friendly. Two voices alternated in my still-ringing ears, one shrill and the other a low rumble, as they laid me down on soaked carpet. The blurred features of the two figures standing over me slowly came into focus as if I were a patient coming out of anesthesia: Seph's crystal blue eyes staring down at me, full of fear and concern, and Delacroix's frantic frown as he shouted at me, his words slowly starting to make sense despite the intense ringing in my ears and the jumble of thoughts in my head.

"Get up, Ethan!" He pulled at my injured right arm in an effort to help me to my feet. He might as well have stabbed me in the back with an ice pick. "Help me with the door before it's too late."

Seph leaned in and grabbed my opposite wrist, her hands soft but her adrenalin-fueled grip strong as steel. Together, the two of them yanked me to my feet, and then Delacroix pulled me over to the large circle of steel that served as the door to the bank vault.

"She's getting up!" he shouted. "We've got seconds to get this thing closed."

Unclear how long even a bank vault door would last against someone I'd already seen melt steel with her mind, I put my good shoulder to the door and pushed with everything my tremulous legs had. Delacroix and Seph came up on either side as we worked to trap Ada in the safe. Though the explosion had left the door with some cosmetic damage, the massive hinges still seemed to work.

That was, until they didn't.

Still sufficiently ajar that I could see into the safe where Ada was gathering herself for another attack, the door wouldn't move another inch.

"Hold on, you two." Seph gestured to the bottom of the door. "Back off for a sec."

I followed her gaze to where a hunk of crumpled drywall blocked the door's seal. Delacroix and I pulled back on the door just long enough for Seph to rush forward and yank the rubble free, and then the three of us together put our shoulders to the door, sending it shut with a satisfying thunk. Seph grabbed the lock, a metallic version of the wheel from the deck of every pirate ship ever put to film, and gave it a spin.

"What the hell is that going to do?" I shouted over the ringing in my ears. "Slow her down for ten seconds?"

"More than that." Delacroix grabbed Seph and sprinted back up the hall for the exit. "Pyromancers may control fire and be able to withstand some serious heat, but they still have to breathe."

"She starts a fire in there," Seph added, "she'll suffocate." She looked on her mountain of a bodyguard with a proud grin. "Just like Mr. Delacroix planned."

"So, she'll have to be careful. Got it." Not Delacroix's first rodeo, I suppose. I did a quick calculation. "Still, my gut says she's coming straight through that door."

"And God willing," Delacroix said, "we'll be long gone before she makes it out."

We rounded the corner onto the bank's drowned and destroyed front foyer and headed for the gaping hole leading to the street left by Ada's dramatic entrance.

"Even if we get away from Ms. Matchstick," Seph said, "there's still the three outside."

"Make that two." Rosemary stepped through the demolished doorway. "Pardon the pun, but the Greyhound and I managed to knock the wind out of our favorite aeromancer, and our new friend is somehow currently keeping both earth and water at bay."

"What is he?" I asked. "All the elemental types freaked out when he showed up."

"Like they said, he's a legend," Rosemary answered, her voice filled with awe. "Been around for more years than anyone really knows. 'Strong, fast, and hits like a bus' is the joke, though no one knows exactly why he's called Greyhound other than the man himself."

"But he's right outside," I answered. "Aren't legends just that? Legends?"

"As you continue down this path, Ethan, a lot of people and things you've always considered make-believe are going to be proven all too real." Delacroix rested a hand on my uninjured shoulder. "You'd best get used to it."

"But why is he helping us? Where did he come from? And how did he know we'd even be in Denver today?"

Delacroix shook his head. "Other than rumors implicating Denver, Colorado as the Greyhound's main stomping grounds for the last few years, the answers to your questions remain no clearer than the reason why both the Midnight Angel's skiomancers and Ada's group both seem so hell bent on capturing Miss Snow."

Seph drew close and pulled me into a sidelong hug, the gesture unfortunately sending a knife-like pain lancinating through my injured right shoulder, "The way I see it, you're well on your way to becoming a legend yourself, Ethan."

Rosemary made a show of clearing her throat. "There'll be time later for patting each other's backs," she said with a scowl. "For the moment, Seph, we need to get you away from this place."

Delacroix stepped through the wrecked doorway with me and Seph close behind and Rosemary bringing up the rear. At the center of the destroyed street, the Greyhound continued to combat both earth and water at once. Crouched atop Daichi's enormous sumo form of asphalt and concrete, the grizzled Ascendant bludgeoned the earthen giant's head with what appeared to be the elementalist's own rocky arm. Violeta had opened a water main and sent thousands of gallons per minute flying at the Greyhound, all in an effort to dislodge the grey legend as Daichi swatted at him with his remaining arm, but neither seemed to have much effect.

Legendary, indeed.

Meanwhile, the aeromancer known as Dietrich Falco lay in the road writhing in pain, his right arm angled unnaturally just below the crimson splotch at his shoulder from Delacroix's bullet and Rosemary's katana. I made a mental note to ask later if the Greyhound or Rosemary had left him with that particular injury, but with Daichi and Violeta both occupied, Ada momentarily confined, and Falco out of commission, it was time for us to make our exit. For all his valiant efforts, the Greyhound would only be able to hold off the four elementalists for so long, and, as Rosemary had shared with me and Seph during our road trip from Albuquerque to Denver, Ascendant heal fast.

"The walls of fire are down," I noticed as we moved for the nearest corner. "Guess Ada has more pressing things on her mind at the moment."

"Wish we'd brought the Commander." Delacroix grunted through clenched teeth. "Don't think too many cabs are going to show up in a war zone.

"What about a limo?" Seph pointed to the far corner of the intersection where a black Mercedes limousine was parked.

Delacroix followed her gaze, his face breaking into a surprised smile. "Speaking of legends."

"The Driver?" Rosemary looked to her father. "I mean, I know he came for Mother two nights ago as a sign of respect." Her eyes cut left and right in disbelief. "But for the Driver and the Greyhound to both show up in one place on the same day seems a bit...beyond."

"Clearly," Delacroix added, with more than a hint of trepidation, "Miss Snow here is more important than either of us have been led to believe."

"The Driver, huh?" I asked. "The Greyhound I get, but what does this Driver person do? Tool around in a big black limo waiting for shit to hit the fan?"

"My place in the world is beyond your ken, Mr. Harkreader." This new voice, devoid of any appreciable accent, made Mr. Delacroix's baritone sound like a choir boy's soprano. "You have so much to learn."

I spun around to take a look at this Driver everyone spoke of with such reverence. No taller than me, the man's muscular frame filled out an impeccably maintained black suit complete with a starched white shirt, black silk tie, and shoes shined to a high luster. His skin was a dark umber, and his short-cropped hair, buzzed to the skin on the sides, led to a short, well-trimmed beard. The brown of his eyes registered so dark that he appeared to have no irises but only wide pupils that took in everything.

He studied me a moment longer and then shifted his attention to Seph. "Are you all right, Miss Snow?"

"I believe so, Mr...."

"I am the Driver." He offered what for him must pass for a smile. "Come with me, Miss Snow. Your ride awaits."

He took Seph by the hand and led her toward his black Mercedes limo as Violeta and Daichi continued to struggle with the Greyhound at the opposite end of the block. As they arrived at the car, the Driver opened the rear door and offered a subtle bow as he ushered Seph to her seat. Delacroix and Rosemary followed suit, leaving me momentarily alone with the mysterious stranger.

"What's wrong, Mr. Harkreader? I arrived in the nick of time to rescue Miss Snow and the rest of you from your botched efforts to keep her safe. Do you not trust me?"

"One thing my dad taught me." I pulled myself up to my full height and lowered my chin, speaking with as much gravitas as I could muster. "Trust is earned."

"Get in, Mr. Harkreader." The Driver gestured for me to join the others. "Though it has been some time since I've had to prove myself to anyone, I assure you that no harm will befall Miss Snow or the rest of you while you are under my watch."

CHAPTER 12

DRIVE

The four of us remained quiet for the first few minutes. Other than our breathing, only the well-tuned hum of the German engine and the muted whistle of air outside the car's windows filled the silence. I questioned whether our rescuer was going to be angry that I was bleeding all over the seat of his immaculately maintained vehicle. If scooping up eviscerated bodies to take them to their final rest and swooping into the heat of supernatural battles for last-minute rescues was his usual business, however, a little A positive on the fine leather likely represented the least of his worries.

Seph sat, her face buried in her hands, across from me with Delacroix on one side and Rosemary on the other. Delacroix held her tight in a fatherly embrace while Rosemary awkwardly patted her knee. I suppose being an only child raised to take over as the world's defender against all things bad and nasty likely didn't leave a lot of time for sleepovers and the like. Still, she was trying.

"What do these people want with me?" Seph asked, breaking the silence. "I've never hurt anyone, I don't owe anybody any money, and I've certainly never done anything to attract the attention of people who can do the things you people can." She looked up at me, her eyes a mix of hurt and embarrassment. "No offense, Ethan."

I attempted a smile. "Three days ago, I wasn't one of these people either."

"I wish I could tell you why these various factions of Ascendant have you in their sights, Miss Snow." Delacroix disengaged from Seph and pulled her around so he could look her in the eyes. "But for the time being, we need to protect you. Step one, we—"

"If you dare say one word about canceling my tour, I'll find another chief of security."

Rosemary pulled her hand back from Seph's knee as if struck. "These 'people,' as you call them, have almost succeeded in taking you twice in the last forty-eight hours and nearly killed us all in the process. You'd be a fool to dismiss Father and the protection we provide."

"I'd be a fool to call off this tour." She whipped her head around to look Rosemary square in the face. "Do you know how few people get this chance? The number of fans waiting to see me take the stage? How many millions of dollars are on the line?"

"Is any of that worth your life?" Rosemary asked.

"It *is* my life." She again withdrew into herself, crying into her palms. "My first tour was successful enough, but this one is my shot, my chance to make it big, to go down in history."

"If you're not careful, you'll be history far sooner than you'd like."

"What would you have me do? Tell my agents and producers and every promoter across the country that I can't take it? That I'm a bad bet? Because telling them I have shadow wizards and elemental freakeries after me isn't going to fly." She shook her head, the sobs choking out her words. "It'll be the end of me."

"None of us want that, Seph." I spoke up finally, hoping to bridge the gap between Seph's desire for life to return to her particular brand of normalcy and the clear reality that such a return was, for the moment, impossible. "But all of us in this car, you included, understand it's too dangerous for you to be out in the open where all these hired guns can get at you knowing exactly where and when you'll be."

"And where would you have me go, Ethan?" She glared at me through intertwined fingers, her eyes welling with angry tears. "Is there a cave in Montana where they might not find me? Maybe the middle of the Sahara? Or how about a monastery in Nepal? I could go hang with the Dalai Lama and eat berries or something."

"Miss Snow has a point." The Driver broke his silence with the first words he'd spoken since dropping his luxurious vehicle into gear. "While I agree with the general sentiment that her current course is clearly dangerous, unless you have an alternate plan that will guarantee her safety, at least her tour keeps her in a position where a lot of influential people have a vested interest in keeping her in one piece." A lone chuckle sounded from the front of the limo. "Not that any of them care one whit about her personally, of course. The money, though? They all care about that."

"After the first attack, I felt the same," Delacroix said, his tone even and measured, "but now, with at least two mercenary groups seeking to take her and possibly more waiting in the wings, dare we continue?"

"To be honest, Mr. Delacroix, any decision you make is likely irrelevant, as the entire world is game when it comes to the Ascendant." The Driver pulled his limo over at a busy street corner and peered into his rearview mirror to study the four of us. "Miss Snow, you have already faced skiomancers who deal in darkness as well as those with the ability to manipulate the four ancient elements. Others will come, as the bounty on your person is quite substantial. Some might consider continuing your current tour as brave, while others might judge such action as foolish."

"The bounty?" Seph stilled the tremor in her voice long enough to ask. "Sounds like something out of a movie." Seph's eyes dropped to her lap. "What do these people want with me?"

"I'm afraid I can't say, my dear." The Driver cleared his throat. "All I can tell you is they're going to keep coming."

"Of course." Seph considered for a moment. "Can you at least tell me what you think I should do, Mr. Driver?"

"I would argue that it doesn't matter what you choose. Regardless of whether you decide to hide or remain in the public eye, the forces seeking you will find you." His eyes met mine in the reflective glass. "But if you're asking what I'd do in your shoes, I'd say that now is not the time to cower and hide, but to fight and win."

"What if we're not good enough?" I asked as the Driver got back on the road and took a right at the next intersection. "If not for you and the Greyhound today, Seph would be at their mercy and the rest of us dead."

"Perhaps," the Driver intoned, "or perhaps you would have found a way."

"I trust you, Ethan." Seph turned to Delacroix. "And I'm sorry, Mr. Delacroix. I was just upset before. There's no one I'd rather have in my corner than you and your daughter." She laughed. "Not to mention, I'm guessing there's not another bodyguard on the planet who can spell skiomancer, much less know what to do when one shows up." She took his hand and again met my gaze. "Keep me safe, all of you, please?"

"I promise, Seph." I reached across and squeezed her knee. "You have my word."

"And mine," Delacroix gently squeezed Seph's fingers in his mammoth hand.

"And mine as well." Another of Rosemary's rare but worth-the-wait smiles.

That small reassurance dried Seph's tears, at least for the moment, and the conversation shifted from whether or not to continue with the tour to how to make such a path forward possible.

Delacroix interlaced his fingers and leaned forward as if in prayer. "Let's see, we've faced the Midnight Angel's Ravens and her Sister's quartet of—"

"Whoa, whoa, whoa," I interrupted. "The two factions of Ascendant gunning for Seph represent two sisters?"

"Of a sort," he answered. "Among Ascendant, family is often formed by circumstance and choice rather than by blood. There are three in that particular chosen Sisterhood. The Angels have been around longer than anyone can say. One calls herself Midnight and considers herself the patron saint of shadow-dealers the world over. The second, however, the one who sent her elementalists to retrieve you, prefers a brighter nom de guerre..."

"El Ángel del Alba." Rosemary's voice again took on a tone of reverence. "It is said that her beauty, power, and wisdom are matchless."

"Big fan, I'm guessing."

"I've never laid eyes on her." Rosemary deflated. "But if she's now sending her foot soldiers to kidnap innocent women, maybe not."

"Foot soldiers?" I asked with incredulity. "In the big chess game of life, I figured we were going up against rooks and bishops here." I shot a thumb toward the rear of the limo. "You're telling me that was just a bunch of pawns back there?"

The Driver laughed. "Do you not still live, Harkreader? Did you not notice that my old friend you all call Greyhound fought three of them to a standstill while you worked to briefly ensnare their fourth?"

"He did have a *little* help," Rosemary muttered under her breath.

"To the Ascendant, the world is nothing *but* pawns," the Driver continued, "but even among Ascendant there are the weak, the strong, and, of course, the—" He stopped as the limo came to halt back in front of our hotel. "And, we're here. Enough pontification for one day."

The Driver passed back a shopping bag from the front seat, the logo from one of those high-end stores everyday people never bothered even visiting. "Now, Miss Snow, let's get you cleaned up. Inside you'll find a full-length coat, wide-brimmed hat, fresh sandals, and a pair of dark shades." His polite smile filled the rearview mirror. "We can't have you entering the hotel in such a state, now can we?"

The Driver waited for Seph to quickly don the various accoutrements designed to avoid questions about her disheveled appearance, then opened his door, stepped out, and circled around the limo to the rear passenger side. Opening the door, he helped Seph out and onto the sidewalk where she was greeted by a small mass of fans and a collection of photographers. She shifted effortlessly into pop star mode, waving to the crowd and paparazzi as she quickly headed for the hotel's main entrance. I moved to join her, but the Driver blocked my way.

"Hold steady, Mr. Harkreader. Once I have ensured Miss Snow is safely inside, I shall deposit you and the others around back."

"Like hell you will." Delacroix attempted to leave out the other side of the limo only to find the door locked. "Let me out of here."

"Mr. Delacroix, Mr. Harkreader." The Driver's eyebrow arched conspiratorially. "We were able to get Miss Snow presentable without too much effort, but perhaps we don't have her try to explain to the press why her bodyguard looks like he just went ten rounds or why her brunch date is injured, bloodied, and carrying a pair of swords from a kung fu movie?"

"But she's all alone," I answered. "What if the bad guys—"

"Miss Snow is safe for the moment," he answered. "Skiomancers only attack by night, and Alba's little foursome remains miles away, not to mention neither group would dare interrupt me in the performance of my duties."

I wasn't sure who or what had assigned any sort of duty to the man before me, but I was relatively certain I didn't want to meet them.

"But there are others." I felt my ire begin to rise. "You said so yourself."

"If any other Ascendant were in the vicinity, do you think I'd have allowed her to set foot outside my limousine?" The Driver pulled himself to his full height and straightened his jacket. "I am not privy to every secret of this vast world, Mr. Harkreader, but you can rest assured that Miss Snow can make it the few steps to her hotel room without event." He closed the door without another word and returned to the driver's seat. "As for the remains of the day, that's up to you three. I hope for Miss Snow's sake your next showing is a bit more impressive."

∼

Dropped off as promised, Delacroix, Rosemary, and I made our way up the sidewalk, our war-torn clothes and various injuries leaving us resembling a trio of homeless vagrants.

"So, we're just going to let her go on like nothing happened?" I asked.

"As if that were a possibility," Delacroix answered. "I spied at least half a dozen folks with their phones up back at the restaurant. If Miss Snow's face isn't already plastered all over every social media and paparazzi site in existence, it soon will be."

"Not like the events of the last few hours aren't newsworthy." Rosemary adjusted the scabbarded katana at her back. "Biggest pop star in the country nearly gets kidnapped by a quartet straight out of Greek mythology, and one of the biggest banks in Denver gets trashed in the process. If this thing only ends up on the paparazzi sites, we'll be damn lucky. This is national news we're talking here."

I pulled out my phone and popped open NBC, ABC, CNN, Fox News, Inside Edition, and half a dozen other sites. There wasn't a single mention of Seph, aside from the concert that night in Denver, no tales of superhuman freaks downtown, and other than a couple reports of an "unfortunate gas main explosion," not much about Denver at all.

"It's like it didn't happen." I looked up from my phone at Rosemary and Delacroix. "How is that possible?"

"I have no idea, Harkreader." Delacroix halted us just before we rounded the corner, the sound of the waiting crowd raising the hairs on my neck.

I peered around the corner, keeping myself as out of sight as possible. The crowd had continued to grow after Seph's brief appearance, and now dozens of men, women, boys, and girls sat camped out in front of the hotel. Were they all fans, though? Could more Ascendant hunters be hiding among the mob? Or maybe a cadre of more garden-variety mercenaries there to simply make a buck? And if things went nuts again, how many innocents might be hurt?

"Someone or something is covering the Angels' tracks." Rosemary leaned against the brick of the hotel. "I know that Ascendant have a lot of influence, but who or what could have the kind of power to keep such a spectacle under wraps?"

"The same kind of people who can make shadows dance and bend the elements to their will, I guess." I looked to Delacroix. "A timelier question might be whether hotel management is going to let us set foot in the lobby looking like this?"

As if in answer, a bellhop rounded the corner bearing an armful of white terrycloth.

"Mr. Harkreader, Mr. Delacroix, Miss Delacroix." He handed each of us a robe and a pair of slippers. "Courtesy of Miss Snow. She asked that the three of you join her in her suite."

"We're supposed to wear these?" Rosemary asked.

The eldest of the bellhops, a grandfatherly man with bushy white eyebrows and a mischievous smile, raised an eyebrow at her. "I daresay, young lady, you will garner far fewer stares if you appear to be enjoying the luxury of our hotel than if you turn the corner with a sword strapped across your back."

Without another word, Rosemary lowered her head in not-quite-feigned disgust and held out her hand. "Fine."

Each of us slid into our makeshift disguises. I had little doubt the kind folks in the hotel laundry would have a few questions about the state of a certain trio of robes later, but for now, I was struck by not only Seph's thoughtful efforts, but the astounding discretion of the hotel staff.

The first thing I discovered? Hiding a sword inside a robe or long coat wasn't nearly as easy as some of my favorite movies growing up led me to believe.

And the second? When the adrenalin kick wears off, significant blood loss can leave you feeling like you're about to keel over.

"Whoa." Delacroix grasped my shoulder to steady me as I stumbled trying to navigate the hotel's massive revolving door, the small crowd of bellhops having already peeled off to deal with the mob of hopeful fans. "You going to make it?"

"I think so." My shoulder twinged in disagreement, and the gash in my back answered with stabbing pain of its own. "Curious. Rosemary said Ascendant heal quickly. With everything that's gone down, do I qualify for that upgrade as well?"

"If you are asking if the Transference made you Ascendant," Delacroix answered, "then no." He choked on the words. "That being said, Danielle, not to mention her mother before her, did bounce back pretty fast from anything that didn't..." He lost his words again, but this time didn't bother to complete the thought.

"What Father is trying to say," Rosemary pulled up on my other side, "is that if you're anything like my mother, just take it easy overnight, and you'll likely be back in fighting shape by morning."

"But the show is tonight." I met each of their gazes in turn. "Don't I need to be there in case the Shadow-Raven people or Earth, Wind, and Fire decide to perform an encore?"

"We'll have you there on standby," Delacroix whispered, "but event security with some tailored intel from me should be more than enough to keep both forces at bay for one night."

"The operative word there being 'should,' I'm guessing."

The elevator door opened and, thank God, sat empty. We boarded, and Delacroix hit the button for Seph's floor. None of us said another word as we waited for the elevator to reach its destination, each of us exhausted.

As we arrived at the top floor, Delacroix exited first, surveyed the situation, and motioned for us to join him. After a quick trek to the end of the long hallway, we stood outside Seph's door. Delacroix performed a prearranged knock, and a few seconds later, Seph's voice sounded from beyond the door.

"Who is it?"

"It's us, Seph." I tried to keep the pain from my voice. "Can we come in?"

The sound of turning locks and unfastening latches sounded, and the door opened on Seph, already changed out of her ruined clothes and wearing a pair of red sweatpants and a vintage Tiffany t-shirt from the pop star of yesteryear's 80s mall tour.

"Thank you, Mr. Delacroix and Rosemary, for everything today. I owe you both my life." Her gaze shifted to me. "And Ethan?" She grabbed me by the lapel of my white terrycloth robe, pulled me into the room, and looked back at Delacroix and Rosemary still standing in the hallway. "Please excuse my rudeness, but I need to have a word with Ethan, and it can't wait." At Delacroix's cross glance, she added. "Shouldn't take more than a few minutes, Mr. Delacroix, and then you and I can discuss logistics for tonight. Will that be okay?"

"Of course, Miss Snow." Delacroix forced a smile and stepped back from the open door. "You have my number." He turned to his daughter. "Come along, Rosemary."

"Yes, Father." She turned to leave and then glanced back, her lips pursed. "And remember what I said, Ethan. Don't do anything too strenuous."

CHAPTER 13

I THINK WE'RE ALONE NOW

"I hate to say it," Seph said as she fell back on the bed in exhausted frustration, "but I miss the days when the randos following me wanted nothing more than to take pictures to sell to the tabloids."

"I'm sorry, Seph." I sat next to her and reached to pat her knee, but backed off at the last second and rested my hand at the edge of the bed. "I know I'm new at all this, but I can't help but feel like I'm letting you down."

"Letting me down?" She sat up next to me. "You knocked out that shadow guy back in Albuquerque before he could get his hands on me, jumped off a building to keep me from splatting, and literally charged into a burning building to save me an hour ago." Her eyes dropped. "I owe you everything."

"If Rosemary's mother were still with us, you'd be safer."

"But she's not, Ethan." Her trembling fingers encircled my errant hand. "You're all I've got."

"And Rosemary," I whispered, "and Mr. Delacroix."

"Yes, yes," she answered, pulling away an inch, "them too."

"I don't get it. There are people with powers beyond comprehension blowing up entire city blocks trying to steal you away for God knows what reason." I turned to meet her blushing gaze, my brow furrowed. "Why don't I get the impression you're happy to have as many warm bodies as possible keeping you safe?"

"It's all very dangerous, Ethan. I'll grant you that." Her lips turned up at the corners, forming a wicked grin. "Is it wrong that the whole thing is a little exciting as well?"

"Exciting?" My eyes went wide with incredulity. "We have no idea what these people want with you beyond needing you alive. If you're lucky, all they want is to collect some insane ransom, though from what both Mr. Delacroix and that Ada woman said, they aren't after money." My heart pounded as her smile grew only wider. "Doesn't any of that freak you out?"

"Oh, it freaks me out big time," she answered, pulling close, "but you know what makes it all better?"

My neck and cheeks went red hot. "I'm guessing you're going to tell me."

"As far as I know, I'm the only woman on the planet that has my own private superhero looking out for me." She took a deep breath, the action expanding her chest against a t-shirt that was already a couple sizes too small. "I'm basically Lois Lane. Call me crazy, but it's kind of hot."

Despite Seph's closeness, I forced myself to look away. "So were Ada's magical flames."

She sighed, her shoulders and chest deflating. "You know, Ethan, you're kind of killing the mood."

"The mood?"

Seph shook her head, a soft chuckle parting her lips. "I know we were interrupted by that Falco creep and his own personal brand of hot air, but in case you've forgotten, we went up on that roof to get a little better acquainted."

"You mean you want to—" I'd have been lying if I said a part of me didn't want her in that moment, but I was more than a bit banged up and wasn't sure exactly how that was going to go. "I mean, you have to know by now that I'm way attracted to you, but I'm pretty sure I'm still bleeding here and—"

"Down, boy." She rolled her eyes with a smile. "While we're going to get you out of those clothes and get you all fixed up, don't forget that we just met two nights ago." She bit her lip. "And as much as I'm attracted to you as well, that's a little fast for me, so..." She led me to the bathroom, turned to face me, and stripped the terrycloth robe from my aching body. Spreading it on the floor to catch any blood, she gave me a quick up and down. "What say we get you out of those clothes and into the shower?"

"You're going to take care of me?" I wished my voice didn't sound so surprised.

"You dove off a building for me just a couple hours ago." She knelt before me, slid off one of my shoes, and then the other. "The least I can do is help you get cleaned up and bandaged."

"Okay." My cheeks continued to burn. "Thank you."

Rising before me like a battlefield angel, Seph reached for my waist and gently peeled away what was left of my ruined shirt.

"Look at you, all muscles," she said. "Did you look like this before everything with—you know—or is this all part of the upgrade?"

I gazed across the room at the mirror on the far wall. Other than the dried river of blood that had run from my injured shoulder and down my flank to soak the denim of my jeans, I looked the same as I had for years. I'd always been pretty lean, and the job, along with a few workouts a week, kept me in pretty decent shape.

"No major changes to the body of the car, just a few enhancements to the engine."

"Vroom, vroom, then." She turned on the shower, adjusted the temperature to get it just right, and handed me a pair of boxers covered in bright red hearts. "I bought these for Spencer." She shook off the momentary cloud that crossed her features and finished the thought. "They've never been worn."

"Thanks."

She stepped out of the bathroom to give me a moment of privacy to shed pants, socks, and underwear and slide into the boxers. Even that tiny effort left me aching from head to toe.

"Ready?" Seph stepped back into the bathroom dressed in only the Tiffany t-shirt and a pair of polka-dot cotton panties, sending the blood rushing to my ears, among other places.

She gave the boxers an appraising look. "Ah, good fit." She stepped into the shower and beckoned me to join her. "Now, let's see about getting you cleaned up and presentable."

"You're sure this is okay?" I stepped into the shower, the warm water running down my back both torture and relief. "I mean, I can —" I tried to reach up to touch my injured shoulder but my arm had other plans. A twinge of pain shot from the tips of fingers all the way up to my neck and scalp like an electric shock.

"Ethan, when a woman invites you to her hotel room, gets you out of your clothes, and hops in the shower with you, there's a reasonably good chance that you've already been identified as okay in her book." She twirled her finger as she stepped backward to give me some room. "Now, turn around and let me take care of my big, strong hero."

She grabbed one of the hotel's thick white washcloths, lathered it up with some sweet-smelling body wash, and set to work scrubbing the blood and soot and sweat from my body. My aching back, open shoulder, banged up chest, and throbbing arms all got attention in turn. Seph's gentle but firm touch explored every inch of my upper body. The gentle brush of her lips on my neck brought the expected response, but I remembered both Rosemary's admonition and Seph's own halfway clear boundary.

Today was not the day.

My upper body cleansed, Seph crouched to clean my thighs, my calves, and my feet. Her every soapy caress brought first pain, then peace to injured muscles and joints. Not since I was a child had someone taken such intimate care of me.

And then, she began to sing.

A melody seemingly both foreign and familiar, the wordless tune could have been a lullaby I'd half-forgotten from childhood, a power ballad an 80s hair band used to convince mothers of teenage boys to buy their albums, or a number one on the contemporary chart.

One thing was certain, though: be it the steaming hot water, the gentle caresses, or the almost motherly singing, my body was healing under the tender loving care of the most beautiful woman I'd ever seen. The pain, the aches, all of it, faded at her touch.

The strangest thing? Two nights before, I'd been a nothing in her book, at best an annoyance. Anything but kind at our first meeting, Seph now showed a tenderness I suspect she reserved only for the most special in her heart.

Which of the two women was the real Persephone Snow? The obvious answer: she was both. She wasn't feigning the care and consideration exuding from her every word and action now, but unless she was a far better actress than I gave her credit for, her chilly demeanor at our first encounter was genuine as well.

Kind and generous, but mercurial and cold when she needed to be. On brand, I suppose, for a woman named after a goddess who spends half the year in frigid Hades.

"You're quiet," she said as she moved around to face me and backed me again into the shower's soothing flow. "What are you thinking about?"

"I was just thinking how perfect this moment is," I sighed, "while at the same time griping with the powers that be about how the timing is all screwed up."

"The timing? Couldn't be better in my opinion." Seph pulled close to my nearly naked body. "Ethan Harkreader, you came into my life not a moment too soon and, as evidenced by the fact that I'm still here both alive and free, not a moment too late." She rested one hand at my hip and reached up with the other to run her fingers through the hair at the nape of my neck, pulling my lips to hers. "And now that we've got you all cleaned up..."

~

Still shirtless a pleasant few minutes later, I'd slid into fresh boxers and a new pair of jeans from the concierge while Seph changed out of her wet nothings in the bathroom. Back in her comfortable sweatpants and a striped hoodie, she looked more like a young woman fresh out of high school rather than the number one pop star in the United States.

"So," Seph knelt behind me on the bed and examined my right shoulder, "Rosemary said your body would be healing a bit faster than normal, right?"

"Something like that." I craned my neck around to look at her, a movement that would have hurt a hell of a lot more half an hour earlier. "Why?"

"Either all the blood made this look a lot worse than it was, or your body has basically hit the fast forward button on getting better." She ran her finger along the edge of my wound, her fingertip cool and smooth. "You're just one miracle after another today, Ethan."

With that, she crushed her chest into my upper back and ran a series of kisses down the side of my neck. Having this woman who so carefully guarded her public image with only the finest designer clothes, expensive haircuts, and flawless makeup actually let her hair down and take care of me despite the fact she didn't even know my name forty-eight hours ago was like something out of a movie I didn't want to end.

"So." She coiled around me like a spring, bringing her face to mine. "One last kiss before we start figuring out the rest of the day?"

No sooner had her lips brushed mine than a knock sounded at the door.

A very familiar knock.

"Miss Snow?"

Seph unleashed a quiet groan, planted one more rose-petal-soft kiss on my lips and went to the door.

"Come in, Mr. Delacroix," she said after undoing the various locks and latches again, and then added a quiet, "Rosemary."

Delacroix swept into the room, at least as much as a lumbering mountain with arms and legs like tree trunks can, his studied gaze taking in everything without a word. I'd never once seen him drop out of risk assessment mode, but in his line of work, that's likely a good thing.

Rosemary, on the other hand, crept into the room quietly, closing and locking the door behind her before setting a small backpack by the door. As she turned to join us, she didn't meet my gaze or Seph's, her eyes instead focused like laser beams on the center of the room's king-size bed.

"Everything okay?" I asked.

"I'm fine." She gave me a quick once over. "And you certainly look better." She stole closer and examined the wound on my upper back. "I've patched Mother up more times than I can remember. You're about as far along as I'd expect you to be at this point."

"Good to know." Though clothed from the waist down, I suddenly felt very naked. "Um, Seph, did the kind folks from downstairs send up a new shirt to go with the jeans?"

"First," she said, opening up a white box with a red cross decorating its lid, "a quick bandage so we don't mess up your new duds."

"I can do it." Rosemary stepped forward. "A nice pressure dressing will—"

"Thanks, Rosemary, but I've got this." Seph tore into a 4x4 pack of gauze and placed the squares of white cloth over the wound. As she fumbled with the tape, Rosemary mumbled something unintelligible under her breath, but everyone in the room more than understood the sentiment.

"You're not the only one who knows first aid, you know." A bit of the Seph I met that first night came out to say hi. "Back when I was doing cheering and gymnastics, people got hurt all the time, and I had to—"

"I doubt the girls and boys on your cheerleading squad typically got impaled on jagged sprinkler heads after nearly being blown up by an angry pyromancer, unless of course your school was far more interesting than most."

As relaxed as it had been moments before, the tension in the room went so thick you could cut it with a knife. Rosemary's specialty.

"You know what?" Seph threw up her hands, and my entire body tensed, preparing for the inevitable fight that would follow the next words out of her mouth.

Except those words were, "You're right."

Seph rose from the bed and motioned for Rosemary to help. "I care about Ethan and want him to get the best treatment possible. If you know a trick or two that gets him better faster, then so be it."

Both Rosemary and Delacroix looked on, each with their own personal brand of surprise.

"Thank you, Seph." Rosemary sat on the edge of the bed, her left hip brushing my right as she leaned in to take a closer look. "As I thought, this is healing, but Ethan will have a much better time with a non-stick gauze and a bit of antibiotic ointment." She retrieved the backpack she'd left by the room's entrance and brought it to the corner of the bed.

"Telfa, Kerlix, gauze, tape." She deposited each on the thick comforter and then went to work. With skill I would attribute to a battlefield medic, she had the wound dressed in no time.

"I suspect," Rosemary said as she applied the last piece of tape, "your wound will be closed by tomorrow." She looked to Seph. "Mom used to heal so fast that if we used something with an open weave like standard gauze, we'd end up picking little strings out of her skin for days." She lowered her head. "Thanks for letting me patch him up." She circled around before me so she could look me straight in the eye. "And thank *you* for trusting me, both before and just now."

"Trust you?" I raised my hands before me in disbelief, happy as hell that doing so no longer made my right arm feel like it was going to fall off. "All of this power and the responsibility that goes with it is supposed to be yours. I have a lot to learn and, my occasional groaning at two-hour workouts aside, know that I'm going to be following your lead every step of the way, both for my sake"—I looked to Seph—"and hers."

Rosemary swallowed. "As you said before, good to know." She, in turn, looked to Mr. Delacroix who had said nothing since announcing his and his daughter's presence outside the door. "Father, shall we begin?"

Delacroix's incredulous gaze passed from his daughter, to Seph, to me, and back to Rosemary. In continued silence, he went to the large circular table in the suite's kitchen area and pulled a folded document from inside his suit jacket. He opened his mouth to speak, but no words came as he continued to study the three of us.

Then, finally, he shook his head with a quiet chuckle and turned his attention to the paper, unfolding it until it covered most of the table. A schematic of the arena where Seph was to perform that night had been marked up the diagram in expert fashion with every possible entrance, exit, door, and window accounted for. Like I'd expect any less.

Delacroix jabbed a finger down on one corner of the detailed map next to the word "Buses" and locked gazes with me.

"So," he said, finally breaking his silence, "let's talk about tonight."

CHAPTER 14

TALK TALK

"You're sure she'll be all right?" I studied Rosemary across two steaming mugs, mine filled with the usual mix of black coffee with a hint of cream and hers an herbal tea. We sat in the back corner of the mostly abandoned hotel restaurant by a window overlooking an outdoor garden. "What if they come for her again, and I'm not there?"

"As I told you and the Driver confirmed, skiomancers rarely attack when the sun is up. For those who deal in shadow, daylight either diminishes or eradicates most of their abilities. Meanwhile, our friends from brunch are likely regrouping as we speak, but hopefully they won't try again until they've come up with what they believe to be a better plan. Both groups may have failed in their initial attempt to take Seph, but they'll be back, and next time, they'll be ready for you."

"Ready for me? If it wasn't for tall, grey, and mysterious and your friend with the limousine, we'd all be dead, and the bad guys would have Seph."

"But we're not," she said, her voice conciliatory, "and they don't."

"How can you be so calm?" I suddenly became aware of my leg pumping beneath the table with nervous energy. "All I want to do is drive to the arena and stand guard outside her dressing room. It's all I can think about."

"Father is watching Seph, along with the venue's security team. They and the local authorities have been notified of the recent attempt to take her, if not the supernatural circumstances surrounding the attempt, so there will likely be an increased police presence as well."

"So, all that stands between Seph and being taken is a bunch of mall cops with flashlights whose main job is to show people to their seats?"

"My father is one of those so-called mall cops, Ethan." Rosemary took a sip of her hot tea and placed the mug back on the table. "Please show some respect."

"Of course." I dropped my gaze, unable to meet the fire in Rosemary's eyes. "Sorry. I'm just a bit frazzled."

"It's all right." She reached across the table and patted my arm, her fingers warm on my skin. "You're just worried about her."

"Damn right, I am."

"You love deeply when you give someone your heart." A faint smile appeared on her face. "It's commendable."

"Well," I shifted a bit in my seat, "I don't know if we'd go so far as to start throwing around the L-word."

Rosemary raised an eyebrow. "Do you not love Seph?"

"Love is a big word. I don't say it until I'm sure I mean it."

"Commendable as well." Her lips shifted into a knowing grin. "Not to mention I'd argue that you're a man who lets his actions speak for him." She gulped down the last bit of her tea and motioned for the server to refresh her beverage. "I may not be all that experienced in matters of relationships, but I suspect I'd swoon a bit for a man who'd leap off a building for me."

"What else was I supposed to do? Let her fall?"

"Oh, she's fallen all right." Rosemary waved again at the server who was busy chatting up a young woman at the restaurant bar. "Don't you think?"

"It's weird, right? To think someone like Persephone Snow could want to be with someone like me?"

"Despite all the fame and money, at her heart, Seph is just like the rest of us, looking for her person." Rosemary's gaze meandered about the room. "As a specimen, you're relatively easy on the eyes, as they say, not to mention you possess a noble soul." Her gaze returned to mine. "She'd be a fool not to feel the way she very clearly feels."

"Wow." Crossing my arms, I leaned back in my chair and studied the woman who mere hours before had played drill sergeant as she put me through the most intense workout of my life. "You've given this a lot of thought."

Rosemary drew back from the table and looked away, abashed. "I'm a trained observer, Ethan, just as Mother taught me. That's all."

The server finally made it over to our table. A clearly interested young Latino man, his feeble attempt at banter as he refilled Rosemary's mug with hot water bounced off her like bullets off Superman's chest, sending him scurrying back to the kitchen with his tail between his legs.

Recognizing the shift in the tone of our conversation, I decided to let us both off the hook with a quick subject change.

"You mentioned your mother."

"I did." She dropped another tea bag from her tiny backpack into the water to steep. "What of it?"

"Not to be indelicate, but how are you doing?" When she didn't answer, I added, "I mean, I lost my dad last year and still haven't recovered."

"Mother taught me to always be strong regardless of the circumstance," she said with minimal emotion. "I would dishonor her were I to let her death affect me when another's life—particularly a life she was pledged to protect—is on the line." Her eyes remained riveted to the steaming mug before her. "There will be time to mourn at some point, but that time is not now."

"How do you do that?" I asked. "You know, compartmentalize away your feelings and just carry on?"

"Most people exist in a constant state of being ruled by their emotions, but both Mother and Father taught me that to survive, particularly in our line of work, that one must govern their feelings, not the other way around." Only a single tremor of her lower lip betrayed the slightest emotion. "I mean, look at Father. He has remained as strong as an oak throughout this storm of losing the woman he loves. It would be selfish of me to break down right now when he needs me the most."

"But she was your mother."

Her lips drew down to a line. "And when people's lives, one of which happens to be yours, are no longer in danger, trust that my father and I will grieve. I hope that is to your satisfaction."

Wow. Stepped in it twice in five minutes. A new record.

"Look, Rosemary, I'm sorry, and I'm definitely not trying to make you feel worse." I took a slug of my coffee and forced a smile. "Let's talk about something else."

She dabbed at the corner of one eye with her napkin. "What shall we discuss?"

"Maybe the elephant in the room? You know, the whole reason you and I are sitting here talking in the first place." I rested my forehead against interlaced fists. "This 'Transference' from your mother that lets me do all these amazing things. What has that turned me into? Your father said I'm not one of these Ascendant we keep running into, so what am I?"

Rosemary looked on me with a mix of concern and puzzlement. "I truly wish I could tell you. The powers, skills, and abilities you now possess have always simply been the reality for Delacroix women. From mother to daughter for longer than anyone truly knows, my line has been stronger, faster, more resilient; then there are the skills and knowledge that have been passed down for centuries via training and education in addition to the Transference." She lowered her head. "And then, there is the Light."

"You mentioned the Light before."

"You've seen the Light, or at least a small aspect of it, like when

Mother sent a part of her life force into her blades to make them more than simple steel." She sighed wistfully. "An ability you yourself have already demonstrated in battle, I might add."

"Good to know." The realization that Danielle Delacroix's paired blades lighting up in my grip represented my very life energy on display struck me deeply, and yet a part of me had understood all along exactly where the Light came from.

"All that being said," she continued, "Delacroix women have never identified as Ascendant, as the hallmark for such is rising above a normal parentage to become something more. The power passed down through my family for unknown generations represents something different altogether."

"And since I'm not a Daughter of anyone, much less Neith, I'm guessing that makes me even more of an anomaly."

"I'm glad you're able to keep a sense of humor about this. I admit that I was angry at first, furious that my long-awaited inheritance had passed into a vessel I deemed unworthy."

"Unworthy?" I asked, my cheeks and neck flushing with heat. "That's not very—"

She raised a hand. "Let me finish," she said, tilting her head forward in apology. "What I was going to say is that not only have you comported yourself with honor over the last two days, but you have shown true grit in the face of terror when others would have simply run." She shook her head and sighed. "And it goes without saying that having the responsibility of such power was likely the last thing you ever considered, much less desired."

I chuckled. "That's the understatement of the year."

Rosemary again rested her warm hand on my forearm. "Though I've danced around it before, please allow me to officially apologize for all of this. Understand that until such a time comes when we find a way to safely transfer all that is Delacroix out of you and into another vessel, I will help you, train you, and will always watch your back."

"Wow." To my recollection, it was the most thorough apology I'd ever received. "Thanks." I considered my next words carefully. "And let me just say that as long as this aspect of you and your family remains a part of me, I will continue to do whatever I can to prove myself worthy of the honor." I cracked a sarcastic smile. "I mean, the alternative plan was putting a pillow over my head when I was unconscious back at the hospital, right?"

Rosemary stared at me aghast for half a second before breaking into a quiet snicker. "Like I would grant you such a painless end."

I raised an eyebrow. "Dagger straight to the heart, then?"

"Something like that." Another quiet laugh. "Mother always taught me to play to my strengths." She drew in a deep breath. "In any case, that heart isn't exactly your own these days. I'd hate to bring the fury of a certain pop star down on my head."

I shook my head. "And we're back to this."

Rosemary studied me with a knowing grin. "I may be the trained-from-birth warrior or whatever of the two of us, but I get the feeling our little Persephone Snow is quite the fighter herself." She looked sidelong across the mostly empty restaurant. "She didn't get this far by letting people walk all over her."

"She is impressive, I'll give you that." I shot her my warmest smile. "But she's not the only incredible woman I've met in the last few days."

The color in Rosemary's cheeks rose, doubling a second later when a third voice entered our conversation.

"Nice to see you two getting along so well." Mr. Delacroix's deep baritone reverberated through the otherwise empty room. "Just not too well, Mr. Harkreader, if you know what's good for you."

"Don't worry, Mr. Delacroix. Rosemary and I were just talking."

Delacroix laughed. "Oh, it wasn't me I was warning you about."

Uncertain whether he was warning me of a certain temperamental pop star or a young woman who likely could eviscerate me in seconds with nothing but the silverware on the table, I answered with only a slight nod.

Rosemary squeezed my fingers gently and then retreated to her side of the table. "Father, shouldn't you be with Seph at the arena?"

"That's actually why I'm here." He glanced around the room to ensure no other ears were nearby. "I've briefed venue security with as much information as I can without them thinking I'm nuts, but that doesn't change the fact that we have both skiomancers and elementalists to worry about, not to mention whoever else might be gunning for Miss Snow." He looked to his daughter. "I want you to stick to her like glue, Rosemary."

"Of course, Father." Rosemary nodded. "Until we get all this sorted out and figure out what these various factions want with Seph, I will guard her life with my own."

"Just be careful. We've already lost so much. I couldn't bear to lose you as well." Delacroix's gaze shifted to me. "As for you, Mr. Harkreader, though you are still learning, we're going to need as much muscle as possible on site tonight in case things get interesting."

I smiled. "Nowhere else I'd rather be."

After we settled up with our server, Delacroix showed us to a sedan he'd borrowed from the arena. I'm guessing tooling around the streets of downtown Denver in the Commander was a bit over the top, though a part of me wished we were traveling in what was effectively an urban tank.

Rosemary sat up front with her father, leaving the entire back seat to me.

"So," I asked as we pulled out onto the road, "Seph is okay?"

"She's fine." Delacroix flipped his turn signal and made a sharp right. "If everything is on schedule, she and the band should be mid-sound-check right about now."

"And you're sure she's safe enough without you there?"

"Not to put too fine a point on it, but there's a reason I came to pick up you and Rosemary." He cleared his throat. "Hard to admit that just because I know what I'm dealing with doesn't necessarily mean I'm the best equipped to do so."

"Different subject, then?" I countered, refusing to hit Delacroix's pride with another body blow. "Something Rosemary and I were talking about."

"Sure," he muttered. "What do you want to know?"

"We were talking about the Ascendant, and how the Daughters of Neith and whatever I am now aren't the same thing."

"That's correct, at least as I understand it." Delacroix stopped at a red light and glanced my way via the rearview mirror. "Neither Danielle nor even her own mother ever fully understood the origins of their line nor the unique manner by which they passed on their powers and abilities from one generation to the next."

"As Mother explained it," Rosemary chimed in, "Ascendant are by definition different from their parents. Born to otherwise normal mothers, fathers, and families, they 'Ascend' at some point in their life, sometimes in their youth or adolescence and sometimes far later, and develop powers and abilities that set them apart."

"Whereas your family knows exactly where your power comes from."

Rosemary nodded. "The true origin of the Light of Neith is lost to history, but yes."

"Historically, some families who have borne Ascendant children welcome their strange abilities," Delacroix added. "Many, however, banish them from their lives."

"People often fear what they don't understand or cannot control, be they strangers, friends, or even family." Rosemary shook her head. "And what people fear, they destroy."

"Then there are those," Delacroix continued, "both Ascendant and otherwise, who seek to exploit the powers that set these individuals apart from the rest of humanity."

"So, death or slavery," I said, "unless they happen to have been born very lucky."

"There is one commonality," Rosemary whispered, "a strict rule among all Ascendant and any who know their truth, a law that must not be broken."

"Secrecy." Delacroix pulled through the newly green light and proceeded down the street. "Which makes today's attack in broad daylight all the odder."

"Maybe Ada and her peeps thought they'd be in and out so fast that they could get away with a quick extraction?" I considered the dearth of information on the internet over our fights in both Albuquerque and Denver. "Clearly, they've got the online part covered."

"Clearly," Delacroix agreed. "Still, they knew you and Rosemary would be there. They were ready for you, or at least thought they were."

"Not to beat a dead horse, but it wasn't exactly me who turned the tide today." The Greyhound's muscular form and the Driver's cool gaze both echoed across my mind's eye. "We can't be counting on divine intervention every time the bad guys show up."

"Which is why you and Rosemary must continue to train. The power granted you by our current circumstances is significant, but it must be honed if you are to be effective in holding back the tide."

"So, this is what the Daughters of Neith do?" I asked. "They keep the Ascendant in check?"

"We do what is right." Rosemary lowered her head as if in prayer. "My line has ever served as diplomat and warrior, leader and soldier, counsel and defender. Even assassin when necessary."

"Assassin?"

"Not Mother, at least not to my knowledge." Rosemary's voice grew quiet. "Every problem has a multitude of solutions, some better than others. There are times when the best solution is simply removing the problem altogether, would you not agree?"

"But you're the good guys, right? Isn't that murder?"

"Soldiers at war kill. Executioners. Officers of the law. Sometimes these actions are just, and sometimes they are not. I would argue that it is not the action, but the reason behind the action that makes it right or wrong."

Rosemary's monotone sent a chill up my spine.

"Back to the Ascendant, then," I muttered, desperate to change the subject. "What about their children? Do they end up—"

"Normal," Delacroix answered before I could finish. "Records only go back so far, but to our knowledge, no Ascendant has ever given birth to another."

"No measuring up to Mom or Dad, then, I suppose."

"Not in that way, at least, though many figures in history were in fact scions of various Ascendant, having inherited much if not all of their wealth and influence from those who walked the world as gods."

I met Rosemary's gaze. "Your family has had to keep its fair share of secrets as well." I recalled Danielle Delacroix's repeated insistence about the use of names on the battlefield. "That must have made growing up pretty rough."

"You have no idea," she answered, "and yet, I wouldn't choose another way."

I considered for a moment how generation after generation of Delacroix women, particularly in less-enlightened times, must have hidden the truth about their power, skill, and intelligence, all in a simple effort to survive and all the while fighting to protect a world that likely would have burned them at the stake at the first opportunity.

I swallowed back the lump in my throat. "You know, Rosemary, you said before that you would always have my back for as long as it took to sort out this mess with your inheritance."

"Yes?" she said. "What of it?"

"Just know that despite the fact I don't have the same two decades of training on how to survive this insanity that is your life, I promise with everything I have to always watch your back as well, whatever comes. Do you understand?"

She peered across her shoulder with those big brown eyes, the hazel flecks of her irises catching the sun like a miniature fireworks display as her full lips curled into a smile. "I do."

CHAPTER 15

RHYTHM OF THE NIGHT

"A re you sure this is a good idea?" I stood backstage with Seph as the preshow music drew to a close. "You know, after everything that's happened?"

Seph gestured to the infinitesimal crack between the curtains and laughed. "A little late to back out now, don't you think?"

"I can't believe you're not more freaked out." Not an ounce of fear showed in her radiant features. "I mean, anyone could be out there in the crowd waiting for you."

"You're just feeling the excitement, Ethan." She closed her eyes and let the adulation of the expectant multitude of fans wash over her like ocean waves of love. "It's like this every night. You know that."

"You're probably right." I forced a smile. "Still, all those people. It only takes one."

Seph shot me a cross glance. "All those people are here for me." She pulled in a deep breath and let it out in exultation, her ebullient smile returning. "And me for them."

A stray bit of laser light shot between the drawn curtains and hit Seph center chest. Harmless though it was, the moment sent a chill straight up my spine. The arena had metal detectors at every door, but how do you screen for people who can sic their own shadow on you or drown you with water from the pipes in the wall or simply command the earth beneath your feet to swallow you alive? I kept my fears to myself as hitting Seph with more worry just before she walked out to face the thousands beyond the stage wouldn't have accomplished a thing.

"We'll be right here," Rosemary said from her perch a few feet away, "along with Father and the rest of the arena's security detail." She motioned to the far corner of the backstage area. "If anything appears amiss, head for the exit, and we'll evacuate you to safety."

"And where is that exactly?" Seph said with a crooked smile. "You know, safety?"

Delacroix materialized from the shadows. "Everything backstage appears secure. Each individual has been positively identified as either our own crew, longstanding staff of the facility, or local police."

"I guess that just leaves the twenty thousand out there." I gestured to the curtain and waiting mob beyond. "So, now we just cross our fingers that neither our elementalist friends nor our skiomancer buddies decided to buy tickets for tonight's performance?"

"We've discussed this, Mr. Harkreader," Delacroix rumbled. "Unless you want us to cancel the rest of the tour and return Miss Snow to her home where she would be just as vulnerable to attack and without the requisite personnel to help keep her safe, the show must go on."

"I know." I locked gazes with Seph. "Doesn't mean I have to like it."

The booming music pumping up the crowd suddenly cut out as did the house lights. A breath later, the tinkling crystal that made up the first few measures of the title track from Seph's *Sparkle* album echoed down from every corner of the arena.

"Showtime." Seph gripped her rhinestone-studded microphone and moved to the glow-in-the-dark X taped at the center of the stage. All of us in the backstage crew had witnessed the opening moments of the show dozens of times over the preceding weeks, but this time was different, at least for me.

For the next three hours, Persephone Snow belonged to them, the faceless swarm of fans who had gathered in every city from San Diego to St. Pete for the last several months to revel in just a fleeting moment with the reigning Princess of Pop.

But after the show, when all the lights went down and all the microphones and speakers and instruments were put away, it was me she wanted to see.

A quick glance to my right down the long hallway leading to the loading dock revealed the outline of the man who ostensibly was still my boss: Jerry Reid, a man who didn't suffer fools or anyone who didn't live up to his expectations. He took me in, a college dropout from Knoxville, Tennessee, and gave me a job, a roof, and a family of sorts when every other employer had turned me away. I owed him big time, and it killed me a little having to lie to someone that was a bit of a father to me.

When I'd showed up mid-afternoon, several hours late for my shift, it was the first time we'd laid eyes on each other since Albuquerque. Delacroix, Dino, and I had all tried our hands at explaining what was going on without *really* explaining what was going on, and that had gone over about as well as I'd imagined it would. In any case, the news of my "promotion to temporary personal assistant" to Miss Snow crinkled Jerry's nose like someone who knew good and well they'd just stepped in dog excrement.

The war in his mind had played out subtly across his features. On the one hand, he could smell lies a mile away and usually didn't have an issue calling them out. On the other, however, and far more important, Jerry Reid moved through the world sporting hard won wisdom from a life spent on the road.

In the end, his simple "All right" freed me up to do what I needed to do, though I had little doubt he reserved judgment for another day.

A four-count drumbeat, Seph's cue to bring to life the current number one song in the United States, brought my attention back to the moment.

The curtains parted, and every spotlight in the place converged on Seph's lithe form. Dressed in a matching white tank and miniskirt that showed off her toned bare midriff, she strutted upstage in knee-high platform boots straight out of the 70s as if she were born wearing them. Her platinum locks, pulled back in a ponytail, held a tiara that reflected the dozens of lights like a miniature disco ball, each transient beam flying to meet one of Seph's thousands of screaming fans as she launched into the opening lines of her latest hit.

Reflected glory, shared with thousands. She wouldn't have it any other way.

As she wove her spell of melody and harmony and rhythm and dance, the crowd's excitement continued to grow, the just-visible thousands all moving in synchrony with the pulse-pounding beat of the still-hidden drums and keyboards. Guitar and bass kicked in from the wings as Seph dropped into the chorus, and twenty thousand voices joined in as she sang the words that had occupied the airwaves and screens of all types from coast to coast for well over a month.

"*The sparkle in your eyes...Cuts me down to size...Peels back my disguise...*"

In that moment, the world was Persephone Snow's to do with what she wanted.

And she knew it.

Seph's first album may have catapulted the woman before me into stardom after a particularly successful stint on tween television, but "Sparkle" had launched her career into the stratosphere, this time more rocket than catapult.

And sparkle she did, from the first note to the very last.

Every syllable sheer perfection, Seph's voice sliced through the roar of the crowd like a hot poker through the snow that was her namesake. Much of that could be attributed to the cutting-edge sound engineering and the walls of speakers on either side of the stage.

But most of it was simply her.

Persephone Snow, even among the others at her level, remained something special.

The teeming thousands beyond the stage hung on her every

word, movement, and breath. Some belted out the words along with Seph while others stood transfixed in the moment, silently allowing the waves of sound to wash over them. The rollercoaster of music and tone and rhythm and emotion led straight from the second chorus to the song's heart-wrenching bridge. Seph delivered the four simple lines chronicling the pain of love lost and never regained at tones just above a whisper, leaving the crowd silent as they hung on every beat, every note, every word, before returning for one last triumphant run though the song's catchy chorus.

As the last words left her lips and she dropped the microphone to her side, the myriad of lights that converged on her from every direction all went dark. The crowd erupted in applause, the cheers and whistles and clapping all coalescing into a deafening roar I'd heard several nights a week for years, but never truly appreciated until that moment.

The knowledge that the focus of all that adulation had just hours before showered me with her undivided attention and hopefully was looking as forward as I was to a more intimate rendezvous after the show was more intoxicating than I'd imagined.

The drummer dropped into a syncopated rhythm, kicking off the second song of the evening, a straight-ahead rocker appropriately titled "Kiss Me at Midnight" from Seph's first album. At the end of an impressive run across the toms, the massive curtain before the drum kit's raised platform fell to the stage to reveal the inimitable John Hart in all his two-stick glory as the band took the stage.

Jimmy Katz, six-foot-five with tanned skin and dark curls, stepped to stage right, a beautiful arpeggio from his Gibson launching the song from its rhythmic opening into full rock glory.

Peter Freund came up on Seph's other side, his long straight locks pulled back in a blond ponytail, and set his black bass guitar to a tooth-shaking counterpoint to Seph's clear vocals and Jimmy's intricate harmonics.

As the song dropped into its second verse, the lights came up on the keyboardist, a black woman with a foot-high afro named Missy MacArthur, the synthesized tones of her instrument filling the arena with chord after poignant chord, providing the mortar for the wall of rock being built by the rest of the band.

Finally, as the song hit the first chorus, Seph's two backup singers materialized beneath a green light opposite Missy. A strikingly tall woman with skin a deep ochre named Mandy King and a short, freckled blonde named Joelle Reece, the pair lent their voices to Seph's already powerful vocals, the triple harmony filling the arena with a sound comparable to how I used to imagine a chorus of angels would sound back in my Sunday school days.

Rosemary and I caught each other's gazes in the muted light. Our knees separated by no more than a few inches, she gave me a tight smile and a thumbs-up that seemed to say, "so far, so good" though a hint of worry paraded behind her dark eyes.

I pulled close and cupped my hand to her ear so we could communicate.

"Everything's going off without a hitch," I shouted. "Unless I'm missing something, tonight seems like every other show so far."

She brought her lips to my ear to answer. "The night is young, but everything does appear to be going well thus far." Her gaze followed Seph as she continued to enrapture the thousands under her spell. "Funny thing? Mother and I always stayed in the Commander on the nights of performances. Father would attend, as per his job responsibilities, but Mother and I would spend that time together, sometimes training, sometimes in meditation, but always in preparation."

"So, you've never actually been to a show before?"

"This is my first." Rosemary again looked out on the stage. "It is a thing of wonder. All these people, here for Seph." Her chin dropped, if but a millimeter. "Not hard to see why."

"Don't you worry." I tried to inject some levity into my tone, but I suspected any nuance was lost in the barrage of sound coming from every direction. "Seph may be blowing the doors off the place at the moment, but if anyone shows up that needs a flying roundhouse to the head, you'll be the one strutting your stuff."

"We all have our place, it would seem." Rosemary leaned back, her gaze drifting down to the guitar bag that contained our various blades and weaponry. "Is it possible the two factions vying for Seph have both decided to give her and us the night off?"

"I don't know." I pointed to another dark corner of the backstage area where Mr. Delacroix talked on his mobile with someone, his brow furrowed beneath the noise-canceling headphones he typically wore during Seph's live performances. "Who do you think your dad is talking to?"

"I have no doubt that it's important, but I know Father's face. He doesn't look any more worried than he does any other day." She chuckled in my ear. "He's heard for years about his 'Resting Bodyguard Face' and how he always looks like he's about to kill someone, whether he's defending a client or babysitting a kid's birthday party."

"I'm guessing that kid was you?"

She leaned back and raised her shoulders in a knowing shrug, and then cupped her hand to my ear again. "You're catching on."

"What do we do if nothing happens?" I asked. "Just sit here all night?"

"Welcome to the life, Ethan. This job is basically long periods of boredom punctuated by short periods of terror." Rosemary patted my knee before her hand retreated to her lap. "For now, I guess, sit back and enjoy the show."

By this point, Seph and her band had moved on to the third song of the evening, an upbeat number called "Dance 'Til Dawn." Jimmy retreated backstage with Seph's backup singers, leaving bass, keyboard and drums front and center as the tour's half-score of dancers hit the stage.

Six men and four women, I'd at least met if not shared a beer or a meal with most of them over the course of the tour. The tall redhead, Lexie, and I had flirted a bit at the beginning of the tour, but as far as I knew, she and one of the guys were shacking up these days.

If there's one thing I've learned over the years, it's how to gracefully bow out when the time is right.

While "Sparkle" showcased Seph's vocal range and "Midnight" her ability to belt out a rock tune that would make Joan Jett sit up and take notice, "Dance 'Til Dawn" proved beyond a shadow of a doubt that the woman could embody a song with such a title and yet continue to deliver lyric after lyric, somehow staying one breath ahead of the words no matter how aerobic the performance.

Funny thing? The main sound engineer and I were tight. I'd asked back at the beginning of the tour if any of the show was lip synched to allow for the dance numbers. He assured me that Seph's vocals for the entire show were completely live. The tour manager had of course demanded a backing track be prepared for every song and running in the background in case of disaster, but in typical fashion, Seph had made it very clear that the only vocals beyond her backup singers she wanted to hear each night were her own, thank you very much.

At the end of the four-point-five minutes of chest-thumping sound, pulse-pounding vocals, and mind-bending dance moves, the dancers retreated to the wings, leaving Seph centerstage and alone in the darkness. Lexie avoided my gaze as she slipped past, heading backstage for a quick costume change before the next song. A part of me had wished for weeks I'd pursued the beautiful dancer a little harder, but everything seemed to have worked out the best for everyone.

Another breath, and a lone spotlight from the back of the arena shone down on a completely still Seph, only the subtle heaving of her chest and shoulders from the previous number betraying her statuesque pose.

The first words of "Gray Haze, Sunny Daze" flowed from the dozens of speakers without accompaniment, Seph's voice again on point and as crystal clear as a cloudless blue sky. The arena immediately filled with lighters, or at least smartphone videos of a gazillion tiny flames. If someone told me that every single man, woman, and child in the space was singing right along, I'd have believed them.

Seph could sing her heart out, rock with the best of them, dance her ass off, and hold a room of thousands in the palm of her hand with only the sound of her voice.

And, at least for one sweet moment in time, she was into me, a fact I still half-expected to discover was nothing but a dream, or worse, some kind of cosmic joke.

In the midst of my contemplation, the twinned heat of Rosemary's brown eyes burned into me, bringing me back from my oblivious mental meandering. Her furtive stare discovered, she dropped her chin to her chest, kicked the guitar bag at our feet, and leaned forward to check for the dozenth time that her katana still rested inside.

Where it had been five minutes before.

And five minutes before that.

Was she angry? Hurt? Missing her mother? Simply focused on the matter at hand?

I wasn't sure what was going on in her head, but it appeared our conversation from before was only beginning.

Not that I had the first idea what more I could say.

Or why, in that moment of having captured both the eye and heart of one of the most beautiful, talented, and famous women on the planet, the tornado of excitement and anticipation at my core seemed undercut with such nagging doubt.

CHAPTER 16

MIXED EMOTIONS

"Ethan!" Dino popped around a corner. "You'd better come quick."

"What is it?" I rose from the box where I'd been taking a load off after inspecting Seph's revived tour bus top to bottom. A brief exchange with Gus had confirmed my suspicion that the engine had been tampered with by our shadow-dealing friends to keep Seph right where they wanted her, a darkened parking lot in the middle of the night. How they'd known it would go down the way they wanted, though, was beyond me. A few hours in the shop in Albuquerque, however, and the bus was apparently as good as new.

Still, I'd gone out to check on the bus immediately upon its arrival toward the end of the show, more to stand guard than anything else. I had no intention of letting us get caught with our pants down again, not to mention that Team Delacroix had things inside well in hand.

"Has there been another attack?" I perked up my senses for any hint of trouble. "Is Seph in danger?"

"Not exactly." Dino scurried away and motioned for me to follow. "Come on."

I'd barely spoken to Dino since my return as he apparently got stuck picking up my slack and, therefore, had stayed pretty busy. That being said, if he harbored one ounce of resentment about it, he didn't let it show. That's Dino, I guess. As easygoing as they come.

I heard it before either of them came into view. Seph's voice had that edge that let you know she was about to give it to you with both barrels, while Rosemary's had that cool indifference that said she was doing everything in her power not to gut you.

I doubled my pace, cutting Dino loose to get back to work just before I rounded the corner on an argument I can't believe I hadn't seen coming.

"I. Will. Be. Fine." Seph stood by the open door to the posh back section of her tour bus, dressed down for the evening in a graphic tee, ripped jeans, and Chucks, her hands on her hips. "Look, Rosemary, I appreciate your concern, truly, but—"

"The various factions of Ascendant hellbent on kidnapping you for who knows what reason have already come for you twice, once directly after a show and once when you were on a spontaneous outing. These people know your movements, Seph. I would be negligent if I left you alone with only—" Rosemary's gaze caught mine and she stopped herself before my name left her lips.

Seph's eyes followed Rosemary's, and as they landed on me, a self-satisfied smirk invaded her features.

"Look. Here's Ethan now. He'll tell you."

Great. Just the words I wanted to hear.

"What's going on?" I asked. "Is everything okay?"

Before Seph could say a word, Rosemary stepped into the space between us, turning her back on the woman of the hour.

However pissed Seph already was, that particular move multiplied it by a hundred.

"I was merely explaining to Seph that—"

"*Explaining*?" Seph interrupted. "Is that what you were doing?" Her eyes flashed with anger. "I am *not* a child."

"Fine," Rosemary whispered. "I was *communicating* to Seph that despite your newfound skills and abilities, were either the skiomancers or our elementalist friends to attack en route to the next city, that the two of you would still be quite vulnerable were you to be left on your own."

Seph stepped around Rosemary, lightly hip-checking her in the process. Rosemary didn't move a muscle, but if she had whipped out a dagger and plunged it into Seph's leg, I would barely have blinked.

"We are two grown adults, aren't we, Ethan?" Seph shot Rosemary an eyeful of daggers. "Rosemary here thinks we need a chaperone."

"As do I." Mr. Delacroix, who apparently had remained on the sidelines as his charge and his daughter each presented their arguments, entered the fray. "As much as I'd like to believe you're ready to protect Miss Snow on your own, Mr. Harkreader, you've only been in command of your abilities for two days. Someday, perhaps, you'll be more than up to such a challenge, but I'd really feel better if Rosemary and I were to keep close tabs on you both as we travel to Los Angeles, she from within Miss Snow's bus and me close behind you in the convoy."

Rosemary and her father's argument made perfect sense, but it was clear that Seph was hearing none of it.

"What if you and Rosemary were right behind Seph's bus in the Commander?" I asked. "That was the previous standard operating procedure, right?"

"Yes," Delacroix answered, "but that was before not one but two trained teams of supernatural assassins almost killed us all in their efforts to take Miss Snow."

"I'm afraid I don't understand." Rosemary turned to face Seph, her tone conciliatory and her hands raised before her chest. "I'm only trying to help keep you safe."

"Of course you are." Seph allowed her shoulders to drop. At least a bit. "And I'm telling you that Ethan has been the one to pull my can out of the fire every time so far, even before he could do all this... magical mumbo-jumbo." She waltzed over and linked arms with me. "I'm pretty sure I'll feel perfectly safe with him by my side en route to California."

Rosemary's lips thinned and her eyebrows threatened to leap off her face. "And I'm telling you that you'd both be better served if someone with more training and experience rode along with you."

"Tell her, Ethan. Tell her that you've got my back. That they can ride along behind and leave me with my own personal Clark Kent to keep me safe."

Clark Kent. Wow.

"First, Seph, as long as I'm still standing, no one will touch you." I dropped my hand to hers and encircled her trembling fingers with mine. "You have my word."

"See?" She returned my hand's gentle squeeze and smiled at both the Delacroixs. "There's my hero. Ethan's got this."

"That being said," I continued, "if either the skiomancers or elementalists attack again, that could potentially mean a quartet or more bad guys against just me. For all their skill, there's no way Rosemary and Mr. Delacroix would be able to get to us in time, and it's unlikely we can count on the Greyhound or the Driver to show up again if things go south."

She let go my hand and turned to face me. "What are you trying to say, Ethan?"

"That I think Mr. Delacroix and Rosemary are right." My hand went to my neck to massage the already tightening muscles there. "I mean, the most important thing right now is your safety, isn't it?"

"You're taking their side?" Her gaze leaped from me to Rosemary to Mr. Delacroix and then back to me. "Fine. Since everyone seems to be in agreement." And with that, she stepped aboard her bus, stalked straight to the private compartment in the back, and slammed the door.

"Well, that went about as well as expected." Delacroix rested a hand on Rosemary's shoulder. "Let's go get your things."

Left alone, I peered up through the passenger window at Gus Shepherd, a man I'd spoken maybe ten words to the entire tour and shot him a smile and a nod, a gesture he answered with only the subtlest of grins beneath his bushy white mustache as he started the bus, dropped it into gear, and prepared to head out.

~

The bus rocketed west toward Vegas, Seph's taciturn driver hidden behind a wall of faux paneling that transformed the vehicle's interior into what was effectively a studio apartment.

"Do you think she's going to come out?" Rosemary asked, her legs twisted into some kind of yoga pretzel in her seat opposite mine. "We've been on the road for an hour."

"Who knows?" I kept my voice low. "Back in Des Moines, she wouldn't come out of her dressing room for three straight hours because someone brought her a regular coffee instead of her usual fifteen-step latte from Starbucks."

"Though that seems a bit extreme," Rosemary eyed me with a faint grin, "I must admit that I respect a woman who knows what she wants and accepts no less than the best in her life."

"The best." I considered the words. "Do you think that's how she sees me?"

"I don't know. Why don't you ask her?"

Seph emerged from her vehicular cocoon, a seemingly genuine smile upon her face. "Hey, guys. Sorry about before. I was just disappointed." She hung her head slightly. "Not to mention, I guess I'm not used to being told 'no,' even when it's for my own good."

Rosemary and I shared a surprised glance and then both returned our attention to the astonishingly penitent pop star trudging toward us.

"Everything okay so far?" Seph asked.

"Smooth sailing." I patted the seat next to me and Seph scooted past my knees to take the window seat, her sweatpants-covered hip warm against mine. "We're an hour outside Denver, and we should likely hit Vegas by midmorning."

"Where we'll stop for brunch before we drive the last few hours to L.A.?" Seph asked. "I'm hoping we can spend at least a couple hours there. For all of this," she gestured around at the bus and all the trappings of her tour, "I've never once set foot in Sin City."

"Our time there will likely be minimal. With all the inherent distractions, it will be all we can handle to maintain your safety in such a place." Rosemary's eyes narrowed, the tactical wheels in her mind spinning visibly. "Can't give the opposition any sort of shot at you if we can help it."

"Of course not, *mon capitaine*," Seph said with a sarcastic snicker, "and I promise, I'll be good." Rosemary bristled at the snark, and Seph raised her hands before her in a gesture of truce. "Just kidding." She dropped one hand to rest atop my knee, her fingers warm through the dark denim of my jeans. "As always, thank you for all you and your father do to keep me safe."

I looked on, incredulous. A far cry from the spoiled star who'd berated me back in Albuquerque, the show of humility, apology, and gratitude left me wondering yet again which of the two sides represented the true Persephone Snow and which was the mask, though a part of me already recognized the truth was far more complex than that.

"So," I asked Seph, "you're okay?"

"Just needed a few minutes—sixty or so, I guess—to collect myself." She shrugged. "I have to admit I was really looking forward to having some alone time with my guy." She pulled close to me and encircled my arm with her own. "Still, in the end, you and Rosemary are right. My safety has to come first, and not just for me but for this gazillion dollar tour that's drawing to a close. Only one stop left stateside before we head to Europe in a month, and it's a big one."

"Los Angeles," I murmured. "As I recall, you didn't hit L.A. on the first tour?"

"Nope, just San Diego." Her head bobbed from side to side. "First time doing all this insanity, the tour was a lot smaller. Only twelve shows. Nothing like the monster this one has turned out to be."

"Monster?" Rosemary asked.

"I'm not talking about the last few days," Seph answered, "just the immensity of the tour." She cracked her neck and scrunched up her nose. "It's been crazy busy and exhausting beyond anything I've ever done, but I've loved every minute of it." She ran her hand down to my wrist and pulled my watch to her face. "What time is it, anyway?"

I tapped the screen and checked the digital readout. "A few minutes after one. Want to get some shuteye? Rosemary and I can stay up and keep watch."

"Nah." Seph's eyes slid half-closed. "I'll stay up with you two." She curled into my body like a content feline. "So what were you two talking about?"

"All the big Ws from my journalism class back at school." I took her hand and gave her fingers a gentle squeeze. "Who's after you? What do they want? Where and when are they going to strike next?"

"And the biggest mystery of all," Rosemary added, "why are they so interested in acquiring you?" She rose from her seat and slowly paced the aisle of the bus. "The elementalist group made it clear they're not doing this for money, but that doesn't tell us anything about their plans for you."

"Then there's the fact the two attacks were so close together," I added. "Less than a day apart."

"What about it?" Seph asked.

"That could suggest a couple of things, I guess. Either the people behind this are pulling out all the stops to obtain whatever they want from you—"

"Or worse," Rosemary added, "there are multiple interested parties after you at once, each hiring the mercenary group of their choice." She turned and studied Seph, her brown eyes filled with curiosity. "How in the world has someone of your stature in the world attracted the attention of Ascendants who typically shun the very spotlight that you inhabit?"

Seph's face twisted between irritation, confusion, and amusement as she pondered, as did I, whether Rosemary's words represented insult, compliment, joke, or simply a matter-of-fact question. In the end, we both had our answer when Rosemary's steely features broke into a broad smile.

"Perhaps they simply have good taste in music?" Rosemary uttered with a rare laugh and a wink.

We sat in stunned silence as Rosemary studied us both with a wry grin.

"You know what, Rosemary?" Seph answered with a laugh of her own. "I think you may be on to something."

∽

I started awake, my dreams filled with shadow and fire and suffocating pressure. In reality, the oppressive weight was nothing but Seph's head resting against my chest, her long platinum locks trailing down her back in a waterfall of blonde. I had no way of knowing how long we'd all been out, but a quick scan of the bus interior revealed Rosemary in the same relaxed yoga pose, either asleep or in some kind of meditative trance. Persephone's chest rose and fell against my belly, the soft warmth of her breasts against my body both comforting and exhilarating.

Everything was okay, or so it seemed.

My left arm had ended up trapped beneath Seph's ribcage, leaving my hand feeling like it was covered with ants. I worked to get my arm free without waking her so I could check the time, but failed. After a cute wriggle like a cat in a sunbeam, she lifted her head from my chest with a winsome smile.

"Just us," she whispered, her eyes flicking in Rosemary's direction, "at least for the moment."

"Sorry." I quietly cleared my throat. "I hadn't meant to fall asleep." I wrapped her in my arms. "I'm supposed to be awake and keeping you safe."

"You know, Ethan, despite the fact that fate has left you in serious need of a bright blue and red outfit with a cape and underwear on the outside, you're still human." Her gaze wandered the space before returning to meet mine. "And look. Everything is fine. Even Rosemary is taking five."

"But—"

"You're not going to do anyone any good if you're exhausted all the time." She climbed up my body inch by tantalizing inch. "And, between you and me, I'd like you to be in peak shape the next time we truly have a moment alone."

The blood rushed to my cheeks at that last comment.

And possibly some other parts of my body.

"Sorry about everything back in Denver." My eyes dropped. "I'd like nothing more than for it to be just the two of us tonight, but if there were an attack, and I wasn't able to stop them alone, I'd—"

"It's okay, Ethan. I wasn't playing around before. I get it." She finally arrived at the finish line of her slow shimmy up my chest: our eyes locked, our noses nearly touching, our lips less than an inch apart. "You're the kind of guy who always does the right thing. Don't see too many of those these days. It's one of the things I like best about you." She closed the scant distance between us and kissed me, her lips soft and warm and her breath like fresh raspberries. "Even if it can be a bit infuriating."

"Oh?" I answered, returning the kiss and doing my best to give as good as I got. "I'm the one who's infuriating now?"

She quirked her lips to one side and shot me a raised eyebrow of faux surprise. "And what is that supposed to mean, Mr. Harkreader?" she asked, delivering my name in a gross exaggeration of my Tennessee accent. "Are you trying to say that I'm somehow..." She leaned back like a fainting Southern belle and splayed her fingers across her heart. "*Difficult?*"

"Perish the thought, Miss Snow." I laughed a quiet belly laugh, and leaned into my hometown drawl as well. "A *true* gentleman would *never* say such things to a *lady*."

Somewhere, Mel Blanc rolled over in his grave as I did my level best to channel the most famous rooster in cartoon history.

"Why, Mr. Harkreader," her voice shifting from irate to sultry on a dime, "I never knew you thought of me as such." She shot me a knowing stare. "A lady, that is."

"To be honest," I whispered, dropping out of character, "it's really hard to know what to think."

Seph downshifted as well, meeting me at this new crossroads of flirtation and real talk. "Tell me."

"Up until that night in Albuquerque, I was nothing to you." I shook my head. "And that night in particular, less than nothing."

She nodded. "Go on."

"It's just, going from that experience to seeing that sparkle in your eye every time I come around—I guess I'm just suffering from a bit of whiplash."

"I'm sorry, Ethan. I really am." She pulled away, her expression suddenly sad. "I try to stay grounded with all of this, but it's really hard."

"I can only imagine."

"It's so easy to get swept up in everything and forget that I used to be..."

After several long seconds, I finished her sentence. "Nobody." I sighed. "You used to be a nobody, just like me."

"You're anything but a nobody, Ethan." She encircled my chest with her arms. "Like I said before, you're the best man I've ever met."

"But you *just* met me." I squeezed her back and brought our faces close again. "How can you possibly know that?"

"Sometimes, Ethan, you just know." She stared deeply into my eyes. "Now, what say we table this discussion in favor of a different form of communication?" She closed her eyes and leaned in for round two when another voice pulled us from our all-too-brief tryst.

"You and Seph can play kissy-face later, Ethan." Rosemary shot from her seat and grabbed her katana. "We've got work to do."

I scanned the interior of the bus, my every sense vigilant for whatever it was that alerted Rosemary to this latest danger we faced.

In the end, however, it was the goosebumps along my flesh that gave me the necessary clue.

"Why's it so cold all of a sudden?" Seph asked, clearly detecting the sudden drop in temperature as well. "And why are we slowing down?"

I looked to the front of the bus and wished for the first time that we actually shared space with the driver.

"Hey, Gus!" I hoped my voice carried through the wall of faux wood. "What's going on? Is there a traffic jam?"

Rather than the aged bus driver's voice, it was Rosemary's harsh whisper that answered as the wheels below us ground to a quick stop.

"Look to the window, Ethan." She pointed to the large square of bulletproof glass behind my head through which Seph and I had been watching the darkened landscape earlier in the evening. "What do you see?"

We were in the middle of nowhere Colorado, or maybe we'd made Utah by that point. There were no street lamps, no lights, not even the cool silver sheen of the moon from before.

"Nothing," I answered. "Just darkness."

"Precisely." Rosemary dropped into a low martial stance, her sword before her. "Get ready."

"Wait." Seph stammered. "The stars." Her eyes grew wide as she picked up on Rosemary's meaning a split second before I did. "Dear God, where are all the stars?"

CHAPTER 17

ROAD TO NOWHERE

"Skiomancers, then." My eyes swept left and right as I rose from my seat, watching the various shadows inside the bus for the slightest movement. "But how could they have found us?"

"The tour dates have been available online for months." Rosemary held out her hand and pulled Seph up from her seat. "Doesn't take much effort to figure out the shortest distance between two points."

"They've been waiting for me." Seph's voice trembled. "In the dark."

"That's what bottom dwellers do." Rosemary eyed me and then shot a glance toward the front of the bus where her mother's paired blades lay propped in the corner. "Get ready, Ethan. If I were planning this attack, I would have staged such an ambush far from anything resembling civilization. I fear this time it will be up to you and me."

A familiar knock at the bus door preceded a most welcome voice.

"Rosemary," came Delacroix's rumbling baritone, "let me in."

Rosemary rushed to the door and, after establishing bona fides, turned the latch and allowed her father inside.

"Father," she whispered as she locked the door, "are you all right?"

"Other than the fact I had to blindly wade through several meters of ice-cold darkness to get to you, I'm fine." He shivered as if he'd traversed a mile of frozen tundra. "I hate to tell you this, but we're all alone out here."

"What about Mr. Shepherd?" Seph asked with uncharacteristic concern. "Is Gus all right?"

"I went to the cab first, feeling my way through the darkness," Delacroix said. "Couldn't see a damn thing, but I found the driver's door open." He let out a quiet sigh. "And the seat, while empty, was still warm."

"Where is he, then?" Seph asked, her eyes wide. "We have to find him."

"No idea," Delacroix answered. "He didn't answer when I called. I'm hoping he did the smart thing and headed for cover."

"What about the rest of the convoy?" I asked. "We started out somewhere in the middle. Where is everybody?"

"Probably long gone by now. I started losing visibility a few miles back. Both phone and radio connection have been pretty much non-existent for a while, and I'd know. I've been calling all of you non-stop since—"

"Since what, Father?" Rosemary fished her phone from her pocket, her brow furrowing as she stared at the screen. "This doesn't make any sense."

Seph and I followed suit, each of our phones presenting the same mystery.

No calls. No texts. No signal. Nothing.

"I didn't know what was happening at first," Delacroix continued. "Every few seconds for the last couple of miles I'd lose track of you on the road. Once that started, I stepped on the gas and followed right on your tail so we wouldn't be separated." He looked left and right. "As for the rest, it appears our shadow-dealing friends manipulated the darkness to their advantage to get us alone. As the rear truck in the caravan passed both the Commander and your bus, one thing became clear."

"They couldn't see us." A chill stole up my back as the temperature dropped another few degrees. "They don't even know we're missing."

Seph pulled close to me, shivering. "We're all alone, surrounded by darkness."

"And they've picked an area where the phones don't work." I considered for a moment. "Unless they can block cell towers as well as control shadows."

Rosemary's eyes shot up and to the left, as if she were performing a complex calculation. "That's not within skiomancer purview as I understand it."

"No," Delacroix answered, "but they might have employed a technomancer, as I suspect the elementalists did back in Denver to keep their attack off the internet and television. If that's the case, all bets are off."

"Wait," I asked, "there are technomancers?"

Rosemary nodded. "There are many classes of Ascendant, Ethan, each with their own purview and sphere of influence."

I shook my head. "Look, once we make it through all this, I'm going to need someone to give me a class in Ascendant 101."

"I like the confidence, Harkreader." Delacroix turned to address his daughter. "Any thoughts on how we get ourselves out of this mess?"

"We do what Delacroixs always do." Rosemary headed for the door. "We fight our way out." Halfway to the exit, she stopped midstride, her voice dropping to a whisper. "I know we discussed such a scenario before the tour began, but that was before we lost Mother." With sad eyes, she met her father's gaze. "What would you have me do?"

"What you've trained your whole life to do." Delacroix wrapped Rosemary in his muscular arms and hugged her tight. "As you said, fight and win."

I moved to the window and attempted to peer through the

opaque darkness outside. "It goes without saying, but if we go out there half-cocked, or worse, afraid, they'll just pick us off one-by-one like they did the rest of the convoy and take whatever or whoever they want." I locked eyes with Seph. "We need a plan if we're going to make it through this."

"Funny you should say that," Seph said before anyone else could speak, a strange smile invading her features. "Maybe I've watched one too many movies, but I think I've got an idea."

~

I stood at the door and stared into the stygian darkness, my attention captivated by the beautiful young woman on my arm. The thick tresses of platinum hair coursing down from her scalp coupled with a full-length coat and the surrounding shadow obscured her features, but the nervous energy pouring from her set the hairs of my neck on end nonetheless.

"You ready, *Seph*?" I asked, her only answer a curt nod. I turned the lock on the door and rested my fingers on the handle. "Until it's time, just keep your head down." At her second nod, I opened the door and took her hand. "All right. Here we go."

We stepped down onto the Colorado highway, the asphalt beneath our feet inscrutable in the surrounding pitch black, and then moved as quickly as possible away from the bus. With every step, I prayed our feet wouldn't find a hole; even one misstep could spell disaster.

"Stay with me," I whispered. "This darkness can't go on forever."

Half a dozen steps later, my prediction held as we stepped beyond the curtain of darkness and found ourselves beneath a starry Colorado sky. The moon, halfway through its cycle, stared down like a half-closed eye, its light making just visible the mountains to the east and the road ahead that disappeared between two hills on the western horizon. We took a few more careful steps before looking back to check out the section of road where the bus should be. There, we found only a blob of darkness the size of a small house, the area devoid of all light as if some ancient monster had simply taken a bite out of reality.

"At least we're clear of the shadow," I whispered, fighting off a shiver. "Now we—"

"*Now*, you step away from the girl and hope I'm in a generous mood." The voice of the Raven responsible for Danielle Delacroix's death broke the silence. "I haven't forgotten Albuquerque, boy." The man, again dressed all in black with his brimmed hat and raven mask in place, floated down atop a mass of semi-solid shadow. "Hand over Snow, and you can walk. Make me so much as break a sweat, and I'll ensure you never walk again."

I brought the longer of Danielle Delacroix's blades before me, the shorter sword left strapped to my back, and stepped into the space between the skiomancer and my silent companion. "I stopped you before. I'll stop you again."

"We've already dispatched the Delacroix matriarch." He landed before me, the shadows beneath his feet dissipating like so much mist at sunrise, a sunrise that at the moment seemed a million years away. "And our intel suggests, Ethan Harkreader, that the legacy of the Daughters of Neith now resides in your flesh, mind, and soul. Do you truly wish for me to repeat history so soon?"

"Where did you hear that?" I asked, continuing to buy every second I could. "And how the hell do you know my name?"

"I was there, boy." The Raven laughed. "I have eyes and ears, not to mention all the time in the world to perform extensive research on those who cross me."

"Say what you will." I directed the blade at the skiomancer's eye. "You're not taking her anywhere."

His head tilted to one side like the bird whose visage he wore. "Clearly, you have feelings for the Snow girl, and who can blame you?" He laughed. "Admittedly, I prefer my women with a bit more meat on their bones, but to each his own."

At the Raven's snide words, the warm fingers gripping my biceps squeezed until it hurt, but not a sound left the lips of the woman on my arm.

"This new 'hero' thing of yours, however, goes deeper." The Raven studied me. "Maybe something to do with your big brother who died in Afghanistan?"

My stomach tied itself into a knot. "What did you just say?"

"Jacob Harkreader, valedictorian of his high school class." The Raven's head tilted back, allowing moonlight beneath the brim of his hat to shimmer off the shadowy lenses of his strange bird-like mask. "Medal-winning track star—"

"Shut up."

"—graduated summa cum laude from Duke with a full ride from the U.S. Army, branched Armor out of college, and quickly rose from second lieutenant to captain—"

"Shut your damn mouth."

"—only to die at the hands of a suicide bomber two weeks after his boots hit ground in the Middle East, leaving his entire unit to be killed in an ambush a month later under the leadership of a replacement ill-prepared to take over command."

"Enough." I stood before the Raven, as eviscerated as if he'd impaled me on the spot. "One more word about Jacob—"

"While you, boy, dropped out of college to pursue a career that would ensure you would never sit still long enough to contemplate how much you and your family had lost and how you could never possibly measure up to such a man."

"You don't know me," I muttered through gritted teeth.

"I know more than enough to know that you cannot stop me." He directed a gloved finger toward the figure at my side. "Now, hand over the girl, Harkreader, or my blade will cut you deeper than mere words ever could." He let fly a single dismissive chuckle. "You're no hero, boy. You never were."

"He's a better man than you'll ever be, Raven." The trembling form by my side launched at the astonished Raven, a drawn katana suddenly appearing in her olive-hued hands. "Now, prepare to meet your Maker."

"What's this?" The Raven dove backward and drew his dagger, barely getting the short blade before him in time to parry the razor-sharp sword heading straight for his dark heart. "The Delacroix girl?"

"You killed my mother, you bastard." With her free hand,

Rosemary tore the platinum wig from her dark locks and hurled it aside even as she pressed the attack. "Pray to whatever gods you serve not for mercy, but to allow you safe passage to the next life, as you will find no quarter from me this day."

I shot to the left to flank our enemy as Rosemary and I had planned, but the sheer ferocity of her attack was beyond anything I could have imagined. I drew the second blade and waited for an opening, but for the moment, this was Rosemary's show.

"But if you're the Delacroix bitch," the skiomancer grunted in retreat as he parried blow after furious blow, "then where the hell is Snow?"

"Somewhere you'll never find her." Rosemary dropped into a low crouch and sprung at the cloaked skiomancer like a jungle cat. "And I would argue that you have far more pressing matters to deal with at the moment." She lifted the katana high above her head and brought it down with a lightning-fast slash. The Raven managed to parry the strike and avoid Danielle Delacroix's fate, but the blow sent his twisted dagger flying into the night. Without missing a beat, he glared down and raised his arms as if he were a minister asking his flock to rise.

And the congregation of shadow and darkness at his feet readily complied.

In the space of a breath, every shadow cast by the moon above and the headlights of the still running Commander sprang to life, flying up from the ground to surround the lone Raven like a swarm of ephemeral hornets.

"Fellow Ravens!" he shouted. "We have been deceived." He looked left and right. "Still, the Snow girl is here somewhere." Flashes of Tolkien's Ringwraiths from the Peter Jackson films echoed in my subconscious. "Reveal yourselves," came his harsh whisper, "and find her."

A large shadow to the Raven's right began to roil like boiling water in a pot beneath the half-moon, and in a blink, the solitary figure in black was joined by three others.

"I thought we ended these assholes," I shouted to Rosemary, "or at least sent them to the infirmary for a few weeks."

"As I've told you, Ethan," she answered in a quiet monotone, "Ascendant heal quickly." She shed the long coat that had obscured her form and gripped her katana with both hands. "That is, if you leave them breathing." She charged the lead skiomancer, her katana held high above her head. "A mistake I won't make twice."

As relieved as I felt to learn I'd not been a party to three murders back in Albuquerque—no matter how much the quartet of Ravens before us deserved such a fate—one simple fact filled my heart with dread: we were outnumbered two to one, and that assumed the bad guys hadn't brought reinforcements.

One thing was for certain, though: this time, neither the Greyhound nor the Driver nor anyone else was waiting in the wings to bail us out. This time, it was up to us.

As if on cue, the idling Commander dropped into gear and skirted around the gigantic blob of darkness surrounding Seph's tour bus before rocketing down the road to the west.

"There!" the chief Raven cried out. "Dmitri, Fala, after her." He commanded the two nearest the road. "Don't let her get away."

Without a word, the pair leaped atop two black motorcycles previously obscured by shadow and raced after the Commander, leaving us to face the chief Raven and the first of their quartet we'd encountered back in Albuquerque, the one Danielle Delacroix had called Rupert.

At least we now knew how they'd caught up to our caravan. The fact they needed motorcycles meant their little "floating on shadows" trick likely had its limits.

In any case, our plan was working.

Having dispatched half his complement of skiomancers west, the leader of the Ravens returned his attention to Rosemary and me. "Now, Rupert, let's teach this denied Daughter of Neith and the boy a lesson."

Rupert cracked his knuckles as half a dozen shadows rose around him. "One they can take to their grave," he added in a menacing Australian whisper, the same whisper that had sent my life hurtling down this bizarre path.

I brought Danielle Delacroix's blades before my body, crossing them as though I were fending off the Prince of Darkness from one of the old Hammer Dracula movies, and focused on summoning the Light, the only thing that might keep Rosemary and me alive another minute.

Rosemary, in turn, took a trio of steps backward to come shoulder-to-shoulder with me as each side awaited the other's attack.

We didn't have long to wait.

Rushing our left flank, the still-nameless leader of the Ravens sent dozens of shadows rushing at us as he leaped at me, his foot extended in a flying kick. Before I could so much as think, my body whirled like a tiny tornado, one glowing blade held high and the other low, dispatching the majority of the shadows as my spin delivered me from the Raven's booted heel.

On our right, Rupert sent a similar bevy of shadows at Rosemary, the resultant charge like a pack of dogs all vying for a lone hunk of raw meat. In one fluid motion, Rosemary pulled a flashbang grenade from her belt and hurled it at the oncoming stampede of darkness.

"Eyes and ears," she shouted half a second before the explosion that lit up the deserted Colorado roadside like midday for half a second. Even turning my head to one side and plugging my ears with the heels of my hands—a dodgy maneuver at best when holding a pair of razor sharp blades—did little to shield my senses from either the flash or the bang. Despite the blinding light and deafening roar, I gathered myself in an instant and charged at the Raven's nameless leader, hoping I would find him temporarily blinded or at least disoriented. My hopes were dashed, however, as he dropped into a low fighting stance and motioned for me to attack.

Apparently, we weren't the only ones who'd learned a few lessons in Albuquerque.

"Our employer insisted on a few upgrades." He tapped the side of his mask. "You and the Delacroix girl are quite clever, but you'll have to try some new tricks if you wish to defeat us a second time."

Rosemary spun in the cloaked figure's direction. "I've spent my entire life learning more tricks than you could possibly imagine, skiomancer."

"Oh, really, little girl?" His voice dropped to a low growl. "I'd like to see—"

Before he could so much as finish his thought, Rosemary lunged sidelong at the Raven, hurling her katana at him while simultaneously dropping her leading hand to the ground and sending her legs flying upward into an insanely fast cartwheel. The Raven dodged to one side to avoid the blade whirling end over end at his chest and wound up directly in Rosemary's path, no doubt precisely as she'd intended. A quick roundoff into a back handspring sent Rosemary flying over the ducking Raven. A deft grab at the beak of his avian disguise sent both mask and hat flying, revealing the face of our enemy despite the low light of the Colorado roadside. Short-cropped blond hair framed a broad forehead, square jaw, and aquiline nose. His eyes, barely visible in the dim, brimmed with anger, much like the pair of thin lips twisted into a snarl.

"You'll pay for that, you little—"

"Ethan, your blades," Rosemary cried out, "cross them! Touch steel to steel!"

Instinct had already brought both blades before me anew, and no sooner had Rosemary called the play than I executed the plan. As the two lengths of razor-sharp steel met just above their respective cross guards with a satisfying clang, the pale light of the paired blades flashed like a magnesium flare and night turned to day a second time. Rupert, still protected by the dark lenses of his birdlike mask, wasn't affected, but his nameless leader cried out, as both his eyes and the shadows at his command were pounded with purging, blinding, unstoppable light.

"Krage!" Rupert rushed to his blinded leader's side, the Raven drawing his own blade as he summoned another squad of shadows from the surrounding dark. "Stay back, both of you."

Rosemary took advantage of the momentary distraction to retrieve her katana, employing yet another impressive gymnastic maneuver barely visible in the night before springing back to her feet, armed anew.

"Step away from my mother's killer, Rupert, if you know what's good for you."

In answer, the Raven sent another wave of shadows flying at Rosemary, but a second clang of Danielle Delacroix's blades dispatched them all with another flash of blinding brilliance.

"Kill them, Rupert," the blinded Krage shouted. "Kill them both."

"I can keep this up all night, little girl." Another dozen shadows rose around Rupert's cloaked form and orbited him like dark moons. "My shadows and the boy's stolen Light seem evenly matched. Care to try out your swordsmanship skills against one who knows you're coming?"

"You bet I do." She raised her sword to shoulder height and stepped toward the taunting Raven. "Do you care to die defending a brazen murderer?"

"Rosemary," I shouted. "Wait."

"What, Ethan?" She stopped midstride. "I'm a little busy at the moment."

"I get that, but the other two are after the Commander." And if they managed to stop Delacroix's house on wheels, I didn't want to think about what might happen. "I know you have unfinished business here, but we've got to go."

Rosemary shot me a rage-filled snarl. "We'll go when I've avenged Mother's death."

"I understand what you're going through, but—"

"Do you, Ethan?" she snarled. "Do you really?"

"Seph is counting on us," I continued, hoping I could force-feed a little logic through the red haze that had clearly overtaken Rosemary's every thought. "And so is your father."

Rosemary's shoulders rose in defiant anger, and then fell. She directed her katana at Krage's chest.

"This isn't over, Raven. Not by a longshot."

"Agreed, little Delacroix." Krage stepped forward, his vision recovering and his naked face reflecting the moon's dim light. "I suggest you watch your back."

"And I suggest you watch yours." Rosemary retreated a step and turned her head to look in my direction. "A request, Ethan. One last flash of Neith's Light before we go?" She gestured to a bank of swirling darkness I hadn't noticed not thirty feet away. "I'd like to see what Krage and Rupert here are so keen on hiding."

I spared but a thought on how I could have missed something so obvious, and then, for the third time that evening, touched steel to steel and briefly transformed night into day. The dissipated darkness revealed a black sports car, low to the ground, its engine purring quietly in the still night. Rosemary reached for her boot and hurled two angular objects at the car in one fluid motion, the pair of throwing knives piercing the front and rear driver's side tires, one with a loud bang and the other with a protracted hiss.

"Keep the shadows off us until we're away from here." Rosemary moved for the bus in sidestep fashion, never letting the two skiomancers in our presence out of her sight. "I'll drive."

CHAPTER 18

RUNNING WITH THE NIGHT

"How far ahead do you think they are?" I stared out the bus windshield at the highway that stretched west to the horizon. "Your dad hauled ass out of here like the devil was on his heels."

"Two devils," Rosemary muttered as she dropped the bus into gear and stepped on the gas, "lest we forget."

As we spun onto the highway, I started with the calculations. Mr. Delacroix had at most a five-minute head start, but it might as well have been an hour as we were stuck following his armored land yacht and the pair of pursuing motorcycles in what was basically a studio apartment on wheels. We'd all topped off our tanks before leaving Denver, so gas wasn't going to be a problem. Still, regardless of how impenetrable his vehicle was, Luc Delacroix was just one man with a lone sidearm against two shadow-wielding maniacs with nothing to lose.

"What about Gus?" When we'd arrived back at the tour bus no longer obscured by shadow, we'd found the driver's door standing open and Gus's seat empty just as Delacroix had said. "They wouldn't kill him, would they?"

"Not unless he gets in their way." Rosemary gripped the steering wheel with both hands as we hurtled down the highway. "Assuming he left the bus voluntarily, he should be fine as long as he avoids our friends in black and stays out of sight until morning." She cleared her throat. "The next motorist to hit that stretch of highway, however, is going to be in a world of hurt."

Rosemary's stunt with the knives had left our skiomancer friends with two flat tires, but that would only hold them until the next car came along. Whoever that might be was in for a rude surprise. A part of me felt guilty about not taking care of Krage and Rupert more definitively, but every second we spent fighting was another Mr. Delacroix was facing their counterparts alone.

"Do you think your dad can hold them off until reinforcements arrive?" I squinted at the highway ahead as Rosemary stepped on the already punched accelerator. "And by reinforcements, I mean us?"

"Father has seen more combat than most, and while he may not be the best equipped to handle two super-powered assassins, he can more than hold his own until we catch up."

"Will we, though? You know, catch up?" I glanced at the speedometer. "You've got this thing floored and we're barely pushing eighty. For a house on wheels, your dad's ride is way faster, and those motorcycles the Ravens took off on? They're likely flying circles around him."

"I'm painfully aware." Rosemary's hands trembled at ten and two, her knuckles white. "Do you have anything to add to the discussion besides pointing out the painfully obvious?"

Ouch. "I still don't get it, though." I leaned back in the passenger seat, willing my muscles to relax. "Three attacks in, and we still don't have the first clue." We sped past a sign that showed we were still fifteen miles outside Grand Junction. "Why are all these people after Seph? What could they possibly want with her?"

"I don't know, Ethan. I'm sorry." Rosemary shook her head. "We could have interrogated Krage and Rupert once we had them at our mercy, but you were right. There was no time." She clenched her jaw and stared straight ahead. "Not with Father's life on the line."

"We had to go." I rested a hand at her shoulder. "Don't second guess that."

"I'm betting that bastard, Krage, knows at least part of the answer." Her chin dropped. "Given time, Mother could have made him or his lieutenant talk."

"Like you said, there wasn't time."

"Doesn't change the fact that even had the Transference come to me instead of you, I'm not sure I'll ever measure up to the kind of woman Mother was." Her lip trembled despite her best efforts. "She was perfect."

"Are you kidding me? I only met her once, Rosemary, but trust me when I say you *are* your mother's daughter."

She glanced my way, my fingers still resting at her deltoid.

"I miss her, Ethan. I don't know if you could possibly understand, but she was my whole world." She swallowed back the emotion, clearly unwilling to let me hear the quivering in her voice. "As far back as I can remember, it was me and her. Dad too, but like you said, I am my mother's daughter. All that I am and all that I'm supposed to be is literally summed up in all that she was."

"I've seen you in action, Rosemary." I pulled my hand away and let it drop to the seat between us. "In Albuquerque, in Denver, just minutes ago. Your mother would be proud."

"All I've ever wanted was to live up to her example."

"I know how you feel."

Rosemary looked over at me, her usually cool eyes warm with compassion. "Is this about your brother?"

"Jacob's been gone three years, but it feels like yesterday." I shook my head. "You heard the Raven. Talk about an impossible act to follow."

Rosemary considered my words, keeping her eyes on the road. "So you do understand."

"Jacob was born eight years before I came along. He was straight As all the way and could run like an antelope. He blew college out of the water, and once he hit the Army, he was promoted ahead of his peers every time. We always half-joked that they were going to pin a star on him before it was done." My own eyes watered up a bit. "Now he's gone, and I'm left to pick up the pieces of our family. I barely talk to my sister these days, and the only time I see Mom is when I head home for the holidays. That's about all I can handle, to be honest."

"A sentiment I understand all too well." She shot me a sarcastic grin. "At least Jacob didn't leave you with the responsibility of saving the world every other week."

I answered with an amused smile of my own. "And yet, look where I ended up."

"Touché." She rested her hand atop mine on the seat. "Thank you, Ethan. It's nice to talk to someone who understands."

"Of course."

"Now, we just need to catch up with Father." Her eyes narrowed as any levity left her features. "By whatever gods look down from above, I will not lose both my parents the same week."

"We'll get to him in time. We have to."

Rosemary bit her bottom lip. "If anything were to happen to him, I don't know what I'd do." She looked over at me, her features drawn in a masque of fear. "I'd be all alone."

"You're not alone, Rosemary." I turned my hand beneath hers to squeeze her supple fingers. "For better or for worse, we're in this thing together."

$\sim$

M r. Delacroix hadn't made it as far as I'd hoped. Five miles from where we'd left a half-blinded Krage and a furious Rupert, we found the Commander spun out on the road, its tail resting on the shoulder and the front half obstructing the far-right westbound lane of I-70. The driver's door stood open as did every other door and hatch on the massive vehicle, but Delacroix was nowhere to be seen. A pair of jet-black motorcycles, barely visible in the dim, rested together a hundred feet or so from the road.

"Looks like the skiomancers didn't find who they were looking for." Rosemary pulled the bus to a stop on the shoulder mere feet from her armored mobile home.

"Surprise, surprise." I glanced toward the back of the bus. "So far, the plan is working."

"Except now Father is all alone against those bastards."

"Like you said, your dad is pretty resourceful." My hand went to the door handle. "I'm sure he's all right."

"Your optimism knows no bounds." In one fluid motion, Rosemary was out of the bus and on the pavement, her body assuming a low martial stance as natural to her as standing was to the rest of the world. "Let's go."

I pushed open the passenger side door and made my way to the concrete shoulder with I hoped at least half the grace of my de facto partner in crime. With one last look back to ensure the bus was secure, I rounded the right front corner of our ride and headed for the shoulder. With a deep breath, I raised before me the paired blades Rosemary's mother once wielded with an expertise I feared I'd never possess. Rosemary brandished her katana, and then, with a shared nod, we moved for the wooded incline not ten feet from the pavement's edge with her in the lead.

"How do you know he went this way?" I squinted at the ground at my feet. Even in broad daylight, tracking someone over hard-packed sand and rock wouldn't have been easy, but now?

"He'd seek cover immediately." Rosemary answered in a low whisper as she scanned the rocks and bushes for any sign of movement. "Facing skiomancers out in the open is suicide, at least for those of us without the power to thwart their shadows." She pointed up the incline. "Come on." With that, she scaled the boulder before us like Peter Parker on steroids and disappeared between a pair of low shrubs, leaving me wondering whether her words were a subtle dig or simply a statement of fact.

Knowing Rosemary, it was likely a bit of both.

I grabbed the nearest sapling at its base and pulled myself up the boulder. Though my ascent was awkward compared to Rosemary's effortless climbing prowess, my upper body strength more than made up for any lack of grace. Still, she was going to teach me all her parkour tricks of the trade if and when we made it through all of this.

I busted through a row of bushes and found Rosemary studying a pair of barely visible parallel ruts in the dirt, the two lines about shoulder width apart.

"Someone was dragged that way." She pointed east. "And farther up the hill."

"Your father?"

"Who else?" Rosemary took off at a dead sprint. "Come on."

As I raced after her, I kept one eye on the ground and the other on my desperate partner. The twin ruts in the dirt occasionally blurred with signs of a scuffle, though even in those spots, the only tracks belonged to whoever was being dragged.

Then it occurred to me. Shadows don't leave footprints.

I picked up my pace, as I didn't want to lose Rosemary in the darkness. We hadn't gone much farther, though, before she stopped cold in her tracks. From behind the trunk of a massive oak, her entire body shook with adrenaline, fear, and rage as she peered into the clearing just past the tree. I caught up to her a moment later, winded and with a cramp forming beneath my ribs on the right. I didn't have to ask what had left her so upset.

At the center of the clearing and hovering in the sky some fifty feet in the air, Delacroix groaned in agony, his arms stretched between two swirling spheres of shadow, crucified by darkness itself. Below him, the pair of skiomancers Krage had called Fala and Dmitri stood staring up at their quarry as dozens of shadows of every size danced about their feet. A good thirty yards of uneven ground separated us from our enemy. Even Rosemary at peak speed wouldn't be able to get to the shadow-dealing assassins before they ripped her father limb from limb.

"For the last time," the massive Russian shouted, "where is Snow?" Dmitri raised a fist in the air and the shadows surrounding one of Delacroix's fists answered, twisting his entire arm until a loud pop shattered the relative silence and elicited a pained grunt from the massive Frenchman.

"Dmitri just dislocated your shoulder, Mr. Delacroix," Fala added. "Unless you'd prefer me to do the same to your opposite arm, I suggest you tell us what we want to know."

"Otherwise," Dmitri said, "this process will continue, and I can guarantee it will hurt you far more than it hurts us."

"What do we do?" I pulled close to Rosemary's hunched form. "I'm not close enough to dispel the shadows, and even if I were, that would leave your dad dropping five stories onto Colorado granite. If we charge, they'll tear him apart before we make it halfway there." A thought skittered across my consciousness. "Hey, do you have any more of those flashbangs on you?"

"My stash is back at the Commander." She looked up at me. "And like you said, we can't risk disrupting shadows when Father's life literally hangs in the balance."

"Then what do we do?" I asked as another agonized cry from Delacroix split the night.

"The only thing we can do." Rosemary rose from her hiding place and stepped into the clearing. "We give them what they want."

"What?" I brought my two blades before me and summoned the Light of Neith to their steel even as Rosemary sheathed her own blade across her back and stepped into the moonlight, her bare hands raised in surrender.

"Skiomancers!" she shouted. "A trade. My father's life for the information you seek."

Fala and Dmitri spun around as one, the latter sending a dozen shadows flying at us out of instinct. A simple crossing of my blades dismissed them before they'd halved the distance between us, the Light continuing its undefeated streak against the two-dimensional emissaries of darkness.

"Don't come any closer." Fala released her hold on Delacroix, leaving him hanging by only Dmitri's swirling sphere of black, and brought her entire complement of shadows about her body. Delacroix screamed in agony as the sudden drop put his full weight on his dislocated shoulder. "We're not falling for any of your tricks."

"No tricks." Rosemary continued her slow walk forward. "You

SHADOWS OF THE NIGHT

want Snow, you've got her. I've already lost one parent this week defending her. I won't lose another."

"Rosemary?" I shouted after her, my voice cracking at the sudden betrayal. "What the hell are you doing?"

"Sometimes life gives you options." Step after step, she continued her slow march into darkness. "And sometimes there is no other option."

"But Seph is counting on us."

"Stop your mewling, boy." Dmitri twisted a finger in the air and Delacroix spun slowly like a ball on a tether. "We trust neither this powerless Daughter of Neith nor the unwitting usurper of her power." His attention shifted to Rosemary. "Still, I would hear her offer, be it genuine or simply an ill-advised ruse." Moonlight glinted off the smoked glass lenses of his avian mask. "Try to pull a fast one, girl, and not only will your father die, but I'll make sure to make his suffering last."

"Do you want Snow or not?" Rosemary's tone remained calm regardless of Dmitri's efforts to get under her skin. "My father's life for hers. Is it a deal?"

"You are in no position to make demands, little Delacroix." Fala stepped forward, leaving mere feet between her and Rosemary. "Tell us where Snow is, and then Dmitri will return your precious father to you."

"Not good enough. My father is in agony fifty feet in the air. Bring him to earth and—"

"So he can do his trick with the swords?" Fala pointed in my direction. "Not a chance."

Clearly, my confusion at how they could possibly know about a skill I'd learned less than an hour before registered all over my face as Fala reached into her pocket and produced a rectangle of glass and metal.

"We may work with shadows, boy, but we have phones just like everyone else."

Of course the skiomancers had good reception. Neither Rosemary nor I had been able to get a call out to anyone as we raced west to face our current predicament, but that was evidently intentional and almost certainly courtesy of our shadow-dealing friends.

"Fine." Rosemary removed her katana, rested it within its scabbard on the ground before her, and took two steps back. "Ethan?"

"What?" I knew what she was about to ask. That didn't change the fact I thought she'd lost her mind. "You can't be serious."

"Mother's swords. Put them on the ground and step away."

"But—"

"Do it."

"Don't, Rosemary," Delacroix shouted down from above. "Don't let them—"

"I will not watch you die, Father." She returned her attention to me. "Mother's swords, Ethan. Now."

I trembled with anger and shock and adrenalin. After all this, we were going to give up?

And that's when it hit me. Rosemary doesn't give up. Ever. She had something up her sleeve, literally or figuratively, and was asking me to trust her. And if there was one person on this planet I trusted to get me through the next five minutes alive, it was Rosemary Delacroix.

I knelt beside Rosemary and placed the shorter of her mother's two blades on the ground, never taking my eyes off the two skiomancers before us.

"You're sure about this?"

"They have my father," she whispered, her voice never more grim. "I've never been more certain about anything in my life."

"If you don't put that other weapon on the ground in the next five seconds, boy, little Miss Delacroix's daddy is going to be missing an arm." Dmitri glanced up, and with a simple spin of a finger, brought another cry of agony from their dangling hostage. "Like the girl said, Harkreader. Do it. Now."

As Rosemary had taught me, I pulled in a deep cleansing breath, released the air from my lungs, and placed the curved sword on the cool stone before me. Rising from the ground, I took two steps back and positioned myself to Rosemary's right.

"Now what?" I asked

"Now," Fala said, siccing her collection of swirling shadows on us like a pack of rabid dogs, "you will bring us Snow, or I'll end all three of you." She drew close to my face, one of her dozens of shadows acting as an ephemeral gag as I fought to breathe. "And I'll save you, boy, for last."

CHAPTER 19

NEVER SURRENDER

Rosemary and I stood there, as helpless as her father, at the mercy of the skiomancers. Wisps of darkness that were only as solid as they needed to be encircled our arms, our legs, and our necks, holding us immobile before their dark-clad master and mistress.

I'd seen what the shadows had done to Delacroix's arm and shoulder and shuddered knowing one of Fala's rested across my windpipe like a phantom garrote. Whatever Rosemary's change of plan was, it needed to kick off pretty quick.

"So," Dmitri whispered, drawing close to Rosemary, "where is the Snow girl?"

A shadowy gag similar to mine filled Rosemary's mouth. With an insistent grunt and a jerk of her head, she convinced Fala to allow her to speak.

"I'll tell you where she is," Rosemary got out between panted breaths, "once my father is safely on the ground."

"You are in no position to make demands, little Delacroix," Fala said.

"And you have no idea where Persephone Snow is." Rosemary inclined her head in my direction. "And truth be told, neither does Harkreader."

My eyes grew wide. What kind of game was Rosemary playing? I knew exactly where we'd hidden Seph.

Or did I?

"We've relinquished our weapons," Rosemary continued, "and offered up our bare necks. You have us at your mercy, do you not?"

Fala and Dmitri shared a glance, their emotions hidden behind their avian masks.

"I'm not asking you to release my father. Just bring him to me so I can ascertain whether you've lived up to your end of the bargain." Rosemary's eyes narrowed in the cool silver light of the moon. "Once I see that he's all right, I'll tell you exactly where Snow is."

"What's stopping us from simply torturing you until you tell us?" Fala asked.

Rosemary laughed. "Eighteen solid years of training learning how to withstand pain."

Dmitri shifted his gaze skyward. "We could always torture your father instead."

"As if you're not doing that right now."

"Then what about your little friend?" Fala drew close to me and the serpentine shadow encircling my neck constricted ever so slightly. "You two seem to have grown rather close in the last few days."

"He is but a vessel containing that which is rightly mine. While I tolerate his presence, his life means nothing to me." Rosemary ground her teeth. "And if anything happens to him, you will grant me the power I've awaited since I was old enough to walk. Trust me when I say you wouldn't want to be in the same time zone with me were I to acquire Mother's Light right now."

Fala and Dmitri both took a half step back and shared a masked glance of concern.

"Very well." Fala gestured to an area on the ground between her and Rosemary. "Dmitri, bring the Delacroix girl's father to ground."

A subtle shift of the larger Raven's head suggested he was less than sure of his partner's plan, but at her insistent nod, he complied.

Delacroix tumbled from the sky, his form buffeted by shadow after shadow as he made his descent, and fell graceless before his daughter. As he'd been held aloft by only his injured arm and shoulder, he landed on his opposite side, his uninjured hip and shoulder taking the brunt of the rough landing. Though the impact forced the air from his lungs, I was never so glad to hear someone take another breath in my entire life.

No sooner had Delacroix hit ground than Rosemary glanced back at the wood line where we'd hidden minutes before and tipped her head forward in a quick nod. In answer, a sound like a soda can popping open echoed across the darkened clearing followed by a gentle whoosh of air.

"Eyes shut, Ethan," Rosemary whispered half a second before something metallic landed at our feet. "Now."

My few days with Rosemary had left me intimately familiar with all three sounds. Someone had just tossed one of her flashbang grenades at us. But who?

Shit. You've got to be kidding me.

I tilted my head back to look up at the silver half-moon and squeezed my eyes tightly shut. Blinding light and deafening sound exploded up from our feet, dissipating the myriad shadows holding us and freeing both Rosemary and me to go on the offensive. Obscured by the smoke of the flashbang—which could have only been thrown by one person—Rosemary dove on her discarded katana, rolled between the two surprised skiomancers, shot up onto the balls of her feet, and spun around to bury her blade in Dmitri's thigh.

The Russian's guttural roar did nothing to slow the whirling dervish in their midst. Yanking her sword from Dmitri's leg, Rosemary feinted at Fala with the tip of the curved blade, sending the lone female among the Ravens diving to her right and directly into the path of a throwing knife Rosemary had hidden in her boot. The perfectly balanced blade flipped end over end, its razor tip finding Fala's unprotected shoulder. The skiomancer's shrill cry provided a screeching counterpoint to her fellow Raven's low bellow.

"Not so easy to concentrate when you're bleeding, is it?" Rosemary leaped into the air and sent her feet flying in opposite directions. The toe of one boot caught Dmitri to one side of his windpipe while the other clocked Fala in the chin, sending her beaked mask and hat flying, revealing a Native American woman in her thirties, her dark hair pulled back in a braided ponytail. Dmitri dropped to his knees, struggling to pull air into his lungs, while Fala grabbed the knife protruding from her shoulder and tried to yank it out.

I'm not sure if the sound of tearing flesh or the scream that welled up from the pit of the woman's soul was the bigger clue that she'd made a colossal mistake.

"I don't typically throw the ones with barbs," Rosemary pulled close to Fala, and grabbed the protruding knife handle herself, giving it a not-too-subtle twist that sent the unmasked woman to her knees like Dmitri. "But you and your brood of murderers took something very precious from me. You had me at your mercy, and could easily have saved yourself the pain to come, and still you failed."

"Rosemary." I touched her shoulder, half afraid she might attack me as well.

"Now, you will suffer as I have suffered."

"Rosemary," I whispered, "stop."

"Stay out of this, Ethan."

"No, Rosemary." Delacroix pulled himself up from the ground with his one good arm, the other hanging at his side like a hunk of meat. "Ethan is right. You were at their mercy. Now they are at ours." He gritted his teeth together to keep his composure, though I suspect his every instinct screamed at him to cry out in pain. "The difference is the Delacroix family knows the meaning of the word."

"These animals killed your wife and my mother, and you expect me to show them mercy?" Rosemary twisted the knife in Fala's shoulder again, and the woman's entire body shook, though she didn't scream again. "Is that what Mother would have wanted?"

"Your mother taught you to fight for what is right, to defend those who cannot defend themselves, and to bring justice to a world that is often lacking in such a concept." He took a step toward Rosemary and rested a hand on her fingers, her trembling fist still twisted around the knife in Fala's shoulder. "She taught you nothing about vengeance, and certainly nothing about cruelty."

As Rosemary pondered her father's words, Dmitri finally caught his breath and worked to return to his feet, the shadows surrounding him remaining notably still. I knelt quickly and retrieved Danielle Delacroix's blades and crossed them before me, summoning the Light of Neith to their steel.

"Fair warning." I brought the blade of the longer weapon to the brim of his hat and sent it flying. "I see a single shadow move so much as an inch and I'll light this place up like midday and make sure you and this magic-infused blade get much better acquainted. Is that clear?"

"Crystal." Dmitri's voice came out as a hoarse whisper, courtesy of Rosemary's blow.

The two of us returned our attention to the drama between Rosemary, her father, and Fala. A war played out on the younger Delacroix's barely visible features, and I shuddered as I realized I had no idea which side was going to win.

"They are murderers, Father."

"And we, Rosemary, are not."

Her eyes narrowed in a look I'd never seen her direct at her own blood. "They've brought us so much pain."

"And inflicting more pain will not bring your mother back."

"What would you have me do then, Father?"

"Walk away. We've won this fight."

"They will come again. For us, for Ethan, for Persephone."

"Let them."

This new voice, one I'd been awaiting since the flashbang grenade landed at our feet, came from behind us. I spun around to find Seph, who wasn't supposed to be within a quarter mile of the two shadow assassins before us, walking toward us, a tiny flashlight in one hand and a strip of flashbang grenades across the opposite shoulder.

"I knew it was you." I'd never been so happy and so absolutely furious to see a person in my entire life. "Last I checked, you were supposed to be back on the bus."

"That's the strangest thank you I've ever heard." She tipped her head forward with a hint of a smile. "You're welcome, all the same."

The plan, as the four of had discussed it, had been for Seph to hide in the back of the tour bus—with very specific instructions not to as much as poke her head out until the coast was clear—with Delacroix leading one or more of the skiomancers away so Rosemary and I could take care of the rest. The fact that we all owed Seph our lives did little to quench my anger at the apparent change of plans on which neither I nor Delacroix had been consulted.

Only two options made any sense. Either Seph had taken it upon herself to grab Rosemary's belt of grenades and follow us through the Colorado night on the off chance we got in trouble, or the two of them had had a little tête-à-tête on the side about how things should go.

I'm not sure which version had my blood boiling hotter.

"You wanted Snow?" Rosemary asked. "Well, here she is."

"The girl." Fala's eyes, previously fastened on the leather-wrapped handle protruding from her shoulder, now sat riveted on Seph. "It was the girl."

"Just little old me." Seph held one loose flashbang in her hand, the pin already removed and dangling from the pinky finger of the hand holding the flashlight. "Sorry I had to send all your shadows packing, but I've got a show in less than forty-eight hours, and there will be thousands of people pretty upset if I don't show up on time."

"Stupid child. You have hunters dogging your every step, and yet you prattle on about your silly performance." Dmitri glared up at her, his eyes invisible behind the smoked lenses of his Raven mask. "Do you have any idea the danger you're in? The kind of individual with the resources to send such as us to collect you?"

"I don't, actually." Seph knelt before the larger Raven. "But I'm all ears." With the business end of the flashlight, she tipped the beaked mask up and onto his forehead, revealing the broad-faced Russian's features. "You and the others have made it clear that whoever is after me needs me alive. If you know who or why, then spill it."

"Whether we succeed or fail this night, those pursuing you will continue to come, and while you and your protectors have proven most fortunate three times running, I would not count on your lucky streak lasting much longer, girl."

"Maybe now isn't the best time for you to be handing out threats." Putting aside my feelings about being left out of the plan, I knelt by Seph's side and looked Dmitri square in the eyes, bringing the shorter of Danielle Delacroix's blades up under his chin. "Just because we've decided you get to live doesn't mean—"

"Oh, please." Dmitri's face twisted into a mocking sneer. "The Delacroix girl has shown that she's not afraid to inflict a little pain, and even your little girlfriend here has enough of a mean streak for me to take her seriously, but you, Boy Scout? I bet you pick up the spiders in your house and let them outside instead of squashing them as is your God-given right as a man."

Every fiber of my being tensed, and yet I didn't move a muscle. I was angry at the skiomancers, at Rosemary, at Seph. The only person I didn't want to tell off in that moment was Delacroix who, despite his injuries, looked like he was about to go off any minute as well.

"Who is it?" Persephone Snow punched the Raven right in the nose, sending his head rocking backward with a jolt. "Who is it that's after me? Give me a name, or I'll take that sword and jam it straight up your ass."

"The client is right." Fala laughed despite the pain. "The girl has fire."

"The client?" Rosemary continued to hold tight to the knife embedded in Fala's shoulder. "My father has yet to convince me that mercy is the better play this evening, so you'd best start talking if you want to retain the function of this arm."

Before anyone could say another word, movement at the periphery of my vision caught my attention. I'd hoped it was just a deer or some other animal stealing by in the near darkness, but as I lowered my weapons to my sides and allowed my eyes to readjust to the low light, I discovered a river of shadows flying at us from the east and south where we'd left both the Commander and Seph's tour bus. Neither Fala nor Dmitri appeared to be in any shape to command their own limbs, much less the shadows normally at their beck and call. That meant only one thing: Krage and Rupert had managed to catch up to us.

And this time, the Ravens had the drop on us rather than the other way around.

"We've got company!" I shouted, bringing my blades together and dissipating the first few ranks of the shadowy onslaught with a blast of white brilliance.

I glanced over at Rosemary, her eyes darting between the unmasked Raven before her and her injured father.

"Come on." She pushed Fala to the ground and grabbed Delacroix's good arm. "Let's get you out of here."

I clanged the two blades together and sent another ripple of radiance through the encroaching army of darkness. Krage and Rupert were clearly practicing new tactics, as the packs of encroaching shadows attacked one at a time rather than en masse as they had previously. Banishing each shadowy attacker individually forced me to expend way more effort and energy. I'd never tested the limits of the Light of Neith that lived within me, but I had to imagine the power I'd inherited was far from limitless.

Meanwhile, a Colorado night contained an infinite number of shadows at the disposal of a man who'd already demonstrated no compunction whatsoever about taking a life in the cruelest manner possible.

"Seph?" Despite this newest danger, she continued to kneel before Dmitri as if attempting to wrest the information from his mind. "We need to get out of here."

"Not until this big ox tells me what I want to know." She spared me the shortest of glances. "Keep the shadows off me."

"Keep the shadows off you?" Not the right time for the pop star I'd met that first night to reappear and dig in her heels. "Seph, the others will be here any minute. We have to go." I summoned another burst of blinding white light, but the shadows and their masters continued to learn, as the majority of our ephemeral attackers stayed out of range. "Now."

She shot me another glare, the frustration burning in its intensity despite the fact I wasn't necessarily the target of her ire. "Dammit." She shot to her feet and turned to follow Rosemary and the injured Mr. Delacroix. "Now, what? We just wait for them to come for me again?"

"And come we will, little girl." Dmitri smiled despite the blood trickling down his face from a likely broken nose. "And trust that your luck will not hold out a third—"

Seph let fly a roundhouse kick that caught the larger Raven square across the cheekbone and sent him to the ground. Fala's eyes grew wide, but the lone female Raven had seen enough pain that evening and wisely held her tongue.

"Wow," I said, pulling Seph in the direction of Delacroix's armored home on wheels and her own tour bus. "That was impressive."

"I may not have been ninja trained since I was in diapers," Seph grumbled, "but sixteen years of dance and eighteen months of stage combat training have left me with at least a few skills worth writing home about."

We sprinted away, hand in hand, and quickly caught up to Rosemary and her father who were hobbling along as best they could, given his injuries.

"Watch our backs, Ethan." Rosemary shot Seph an impressed wink I could barely make out in the low light. "And Seph? That was some kick."

"You saw?" Seph asked.

"Saw? I heard." Rosemary laughed. "Nice throw on the grenade as well." She looked back at the two of us with almost a grin. "Maybe I'm training the wrong one of you."

"Hey, you two." I spun around and sent the longer of the two blades through a trio of shadows, dispatching all of them back into the night that spawned them. "In case you hadn't noticed, I'm right here."

"Don't let her push your buttons, Ethan. You're still my hero."

Seph flew up the trail beside me, barely winded despite the darkness and the increasing incline. I wasn't sure why her boundless endurance surprised me. I'd seen the cardiovascular workout she'd put on in front of thousands every couple of nights for months.

I smiled, vindicated. "Still, I hate to say it, but I think the red cape and boots for the evening go to you."

Two confluences of shadow converged on us from either side and a third from above, the inky blackness blocking out the stars as the three blobs of black surrounded us. I dispatched each in turn with a few deft spins of Danielle Delacroix's blades, all the while scanning our rear for the skiomancer responsible for our shadowy assailants. Whoever it was, be it Krage or Rupert or, God forbid, a skiomancer we hadn't met yet, they were making a point of staying out of sight.

"Rosemary?" I caught up to her and Delacroix, the latter limping along with his daughter acting as a walking crutch. "Can I help?"

"We'll manage." Delacroix was doing his best to maintain a brave face, but the pain in his voice came through loud and clear. "Thank you all for coming to my rescue."

"Of course, Father." Rosemary whispered.

"As if we wouldn't come running," I added.

"Especially after all you've done for me," Seph finished the thought.

"Still, Rosemary," Delacroix said, his voice strained with pain, "you and Ethan put your lives at risk to save me, you exposed the client to the very people we're trying to protect her from, and apparently failed to incapacitate the remaining skiomancers at the original ambush site as evidenced by the fact that we are currently being chased by shadows along a western Colorado trail in the middle of the night." He snorted something, likely a gob of congealed blood, from his nostril. "While I truly appreciate all our efforts, once we make it back to the Commander and get on the road, we're all going to have a long talk about operational security."

CHAPTER 20

PAPA DON'T PREACH

"What were you thinking, Rosemary?" Delacroix groaned from the passenger seat of the Commander, a seat I suspected he rarely occupied. As Rosemary was caring for her father and Seph had never sat behind the wheel of such a big vehicle, it had fallen to me to drive, and we'd kept everyone together in the cab in case the other shoe decided to drop. "Those maniacs could have killed you both. Hell, all three of you, since you brought Miss Snow into it as well."

"I was *not* going to watch you die, Father." Rosemary sat next to Delacroix, the pair sharing a seat so that Seph could have the middle seat to herself. "Not after losing Mother." She turned her eyes from him and back onto the highway rocketing at us through the Commander's windshield. "If I had to do it again, I would." Her chin dropped. "Without hesitation."

"And we didn't die, Mr. Delacroix." Seph as well kept her eyes straight ahead, not willing to meet either my or Delacroix's gaze. "We all made it through, including you."

"As I said, I appreciate your efforts more than you know." Delacroix, who sat between the two young women, patted Seph's knee with his good hand. "It doesn't change the fact that you all wagered three lives to save one."

"You'd rather I be an orphan, Father?" The shadows around Rosemary's face couldn't have gone darker had she been a skiomancer herself.

"I'd rather you be alive and safe, Rosemary."

"Mother didn't train me my entire life in every form of combat ever devised so I could cower on a bus," Rosemary grumbled. "She trained me to fight, and that is exactly what I did."

"You laid your weapons on the ground and left yourself vulnerable. I don't think your mother ever taught you that."

"In case you've forgotten, she did the exact same thing when your life was on the line back in Albuquerque."

"Yes," Delacroix muttered, "and that was the night she died."

Rosemary's entire body trembled. "Mother taught me to do whatever was necessary to win, as did you."

"They had me," Seph chimed in. "Doesn't that count for something?"

That's when I finally spoke. "You were supposed to stay on the bus."

"Rosemary said you might need me and told me to follow and stay out of sight. Even left me the flashbangs in case the skiomancers came for me."

"Or in case things went south with our negotiations," Rosemary added.

"And when exactly did this conversation occur?" I asked.

"When I was getting her the wig and the clothes." Seph studied me, simultaneously indignant and contrite. "Rosemary said that if the two of you got in trouble with the shadow people that I was to shed a little light on the subject."

"You could have been hurt." I kept both eyes on the road, but a quick glance Seph's way revealed she was not happy. "Or worse."

"So, now you're siding with Mr. Delacroix. Look, Ethan. I'd never thrown a grenade before, much less at another human being. I was scared shitless, but I did it for you." She looked away. "I did it for us." Her voice dropped to a whisper. "I swear, can't everyone just be happy that we're all alive and made it through one hell of a night by working together?"

I let out a sigh. "I just don't know why you both kept me in the dark."

"Because, Ethan," Rosemary countered, "you would have thought it was too dangerous, told Seph to stay put, and we would all be dead with Seph in our enemy's clutches." Her eyes danced between me and her father. "Honestly, if the shoe had been on the other foot and you two brave men had saved the day, would we even be having this discussion?"

Delacroix cleared his throat. "Point taken. Despite everything else I've said tonight, what you did tonight, Rosemary, was very brave. Your mother would be proud of your courage, intuition, and ingenuity."

"And roundhouse kicking a skiomancer in the jaw?" I added with a smile for Seph. "I already knew you were a badass in pretty much every way, but after tonight, you've proven it beyond a shadow of a doubt, pardon the pun." I reached over and gave her knee a gentle squeeze, keeping my other hand firmly on the wheel. "Thank you for saving my life." I looked over at Rosemary and Delacroix who both looked on Seph with admiration. "All our lives."

"It was the least I could do for my own personal Clark Kent." She pulled in close and nuzzled her head on my shoulder. "Sometimes it's Lois Lane's turn to save the day."

~

I was getting really tired of hospitals.

We hit Grand Junction, Colorado less than half an hour after our grand escape from Krage and his crew. Rosemary and I wanted to stop there to get her father medical attention, but Delacroix insisted we keep going as we hadn't put enough distance between us and the quartet of skiomancers on our tail, especially with morning still several hours away. Continuing our westward trajectory, we took the risk of stopping for gas in Green River, Utah. With miles of national park straight ahead, the idea of running out of gas in the middle of the wilderness with shadow-dealing assassins and possibly elementalist mercenaries not far behind seemed like a bad idea.

Delacroix winced with every bump in the road as we crossed Utah, his likely dislocated shoulder leaving his dominant arm a worthless hunk of meat. Rosemary and I had done our best to get it back into its socket a few hundred miles back, but even with Seph's assistance, we'd met with no success. My brief EMT training led me to check the pulse in his wrist and the feeling in his fingers, and with both of those apparently intact, we opted to wait until we hit the other side of the state before stopping again, which led us to the emergency department at St. George Regional Hospital, right on the Utah/Arizona border.

We reached the small city not long after daybreak with Seph using her Google-Fu to guide us the last few miles, the techno embargo finally letting up just as mysteriously as it had started. Five and a half hours across rough terrain with a man with a dislocated shoulder and likely internal injuries was difficult both to watch and listen to, but Delacroix remained as stoic as possible despite the curvy mountain roads at Utah's heart.

We arrived at the hospital during a lull before the morning rush, thank God, and they were able to get Mr. Delacroix back almost immediately. Rosemary disappeared into the bowels of the hospital with her father, leaving me and a disguised Seph together in the waiting room. The morning sun pouring through the east windows remained a constant reassurance that the skiomancers at the moment were anything but a threat, yet I couldn't help but look across my shoulder every few seconds after the night we'd had.

"They're not coming for us, Ethan." Seph reappeared from the opposite end of the waiting room where she'd gone to make a few calls after we determined that whoever or whatever had kept our mobile phones from working on the road thankfully didn't seem able to block landlines as well. "You can relax for a second." She rested a hand on my thigh. "Right?"

"I'm not sure I'll ever relax again." I took her hand in mine. "I already feel like I've cheated death half a dozen times, and we're not even a week into this insanity."

"Once we get to L.A., maybe I can help with that." She squeezed my fingers gently as a yawn escaped her lips. "Ha. I just came onto you and yawned in the same breath. Sorry."

"We're all running on fumes, Seph."

She glanced at the door leading back to the treatment area. "Mr. Delacroix has been back there for over an hour. Do you think he's all right?"

"He was pretty banged up. I guess we'll have to wait and see."

"Right." She bit her lip in that way she does when she was wondering about something. "Why is all this happening, Ethan?" She pulled her hand away and rested crossed arms on her lap. "We've already lost Rosemary's mother and nearly her father over me. Me, you, and Rosemary: we've all been hurt, not to mention we've been fighting for our lives at every turn, and for what? What could these people possibly want with me?"

"If I could answer that, we'd be well on our way to knowing how to resolve this whole mess. Meanwhile, I'm sitting here glad the sun is up and keeping the shadows at bay while wondering non-stop if we're about to get an encore performance from Earth, Wind, and Fire."

"If either group knew where we were, they would already have come for me." Seph peered around the room. "I may be a bit naive, but I think, at least for the moment, we're safe."

"There's still tomorrow night's show." An image of Seph on stage, surrounded in light and sound and suddenly swallowed up by darkness, sent a shiver up my spine. "Are you up for it?"

"Do I have any choice?"

"You always have a choice. Rock stars cancel shows all the time. Vocal cord stuff, injuries, because they've had a bad day. I've seen it all."

"I couldn't do that, Ethan." She looked at me, her expression the epitome of innocence. "What about all my fans? I can't let them down when it's the last show of the tour."

I flushed with admiration at such commitment and work ethic while simultaneously swallowing back my retort that she wouldn't be there for her fans at all if the bad guys managed to accomplish their goal.

"At this point, I guess, we just have to do our best to get there." I looked down at the phone in her lap. "Any luck getting through to your manager or anyone with the rest of the convoy? They must have freaked out when your whole damn bus ended up missing."

"My manager is on vacation in Europe, of course, but I was able to get through to Mr. Reid."

"What did he have to say?" I had a feeling Jerry was going to have a few choice words for me the next time we saw each other. "Everything all right?"

"He said they were halfway through Utah before they realized we were missing. They did everything in their power to get through to us, but they were meeting the same interference we were." She held her phone up before her. Five bars, just like it had been the hundred times she tried to make a call over the preceding few hours, and yet not a single text, call, or message had gotten through. "More than shadows or fire and water, the people after me seriously have someone who can block cell signal across an entire state?"

"Assuming their theory is right, neither Rosemary nor Mr. Delacroix have ever actually met one of these technomancers they're talking about. In this day and age, you can imagine that someone with power like that would be an asset like none other." I gestured to the waiting room television where the morning news went forward without one mention of a statewide communication blackout disaster. "I'm just glad to find out that even their abilities apparently have limits."

"Great." Seph looked away. "God only knows what comes next."

I brought my opposite hand across and stroked the back of hers with my fingertips, the electricity between us palpable, despite our shared exhaustion. "Whatever comes, we'll beat that too." The wheels in my mind continued to turn. "So, where are they now?"

"They made it to Las Vegas, per the original plan." A sarcastic laugh escaped Seph's lips. "They're all having breakfast in the City of Lights, and we're stuck here in Backwater, Utah." She shook her head. "Not exactly how I imagined the next to last day of this leg of the tour."

"Europe is supposed to be next, right?"

"Yeah." She bit her lower lip. "As if that's going to happen now."

I had looked into traveling overseas with the tour a few months back. It had been looking pretty good for me to go, but with everything that had gone down the last few days, I wasn't sure if Jerry placed me in the "dependable" column anymore.

If only he knew.

"It's only three months, right? Then back to the U.S. a few weeks later to finish up the last month and a half?"

"That's the plan." She sighed. "Or at least it was."

Rosemary appeared from around a corner, and before I knew what was happening, Seph rose and wrapped her in a warm embrace.

"How's your dad?" Seph asked.

"He's fine." Rosemary shot me a quizzical look at the unexpected gesture, and I answered with a quick shrug. "The doctors say he has a torn rotator cuff and a bad sprain of his right shoulder. He's going to be in a sling for a while and will likely need surgery and a few months of physical therapy to fully recover, but he should be fine."

"Thank God." Seph disengaged from the hug and stepped back. "I owe him, you, and Ethan so much." She shot me a worried smile. "Who knows where I'd have ended up if it weren't for you three."

"At this point, we're all in this together." I rose and joined the pair. "So, he's going to be okay?"

"He's injured, doesn't like doctors, and doesn't like to take medication." Rosemary's lip quivered. "Without Mother around to get him to take so much as an aspirin, I suppose that task will now fall to me."

"He can't be as stubborn as my mom." Seph responded. "I think she'd have to see bone sticking out before you could get Wynter Snow to the emergency room."

"Then you understand. I have little doubt that a man who stays in shape the way Father does will already exceed any physical therapist's recommended regimen. Still, I do not wish to see him in pain."

"Your dad is made of pretty tough stuff." I gave Rosemary as convincing a nod as I could manage. "He's going to bounce back."

"This time." Rosemary sat, and Seph and I joined her on either side. "After seeing Mother cut down in cold blood, all I can think about is what would happen if something were to happen to him. Mother always said that connections were both strength and weakness. Sharing a battlefield with someone you love can bring both incredible courage but also lethal distraction."

I kept my eyes straight ahead, not willing to so much as look at Seph after that.

"You are stronger than you give yourself credit for." Seph draped an arm around Rosemary's shoulder. "It's like when I saw you and Ethan with the shadowmancers last night. I thought I was going to pee my pants, and yet, I knew I didn't have any choice but to come through, for both of you. You did the same for your father, and like you said, both you and I would do it again in a hot second."

"Then you do understand." Rosemary smiled. "I've said it already Seph, but you showed real fortitude last night. Not everyone would have been able to come through the way you did."

"Thank you." Seph blushed. "That means a lot coming from you." She looked away. "Back when I was doing *Teen Spies*, a lot of people wanted to be around me, you know, be part of my entourage, despite the fact that I was just a kid. Then, when I switched gears into singing, that whole thing went ballistic. But you two, you don't like me because I'm 'Persephone Snow.' Hell, if I were Ethan, I wouldn't like me at all based on the way I treated him the first time we met."

"You don't need to keep apologizing." I shook my head with a forgiving laugh. "It's all water under the bridge."

"I know, and I'm so grateful for that." She took each of our hands and squeezed them tight. "I guess I'm just grateful to *have* actual friends."

"More than friends." Rosemary allowed herself a subtle smile. "My own mother died defending you from these rogues, and I would die before allowing them to achieve their goal and disgrace her memory." She gave Seph's palm a gentle squeeze. "We are bound together, you and I, Persephone Snow."

"I'm nowhere near as eloquent as Rosemary." My fingers interlaced with Seph's in a way that would have seemed a pleasant if not impossible dream just a week ago. "Just know that from here on out, I will always have your back."

"Thank you both." Seph pursed her lips, the emotion of the moment threatening to overtake her. "What an honor and privilege to have two such incredible people like you in my corner."

"We aren't simply in your corner, Miss Snow." Mr. Delacroix, his right arm in a sling and his suit jacket only half-draped around him, emerged from the back of the emergency department. "We're fighting right alongside you."

Delacroix joined our circle and used his good arm to pull Seph into a fatherly hug.

"Thank you, Mr. Delacroix." Seph wrapped her arms around Delacroix's chest and gave him a gentle squeeze. "For everything."

"It is our honor, Seph." Even Rosemary joined in the group hug. "And our privilege."

I drew close and joined the spontaneous huddle, feeling for the first time in a long time like I actually had a family. For all the cuts and bruises, the moment was worth it.

"So," I said as we broke and headed for the Commander, "Vegas anyone?"

CHAPTER 21

HIGHWAY TO HELL

According to the maps app on my phone, Saint George, Utah to Las Vegas, Nevada was supposed to be just shy of a two-hour drive, though I suspected the fine folks at Google and Apple didn't figure in the extra time necessary when the literal elements were doing their level best to end you.

The first hour went by without incident as we got the hell out of Utah and crossed the northwest corner of Arizona, but no sooner had we made it past the first couple of towns in Nevada along I-15 than everything went south.

Well, southwest, if you want to be precise.

A good five minutes had passed since we'd seen a car on the northbound side of the interstate, a fact that hadn't sat well with me, and yet with no exits for several more miles, we'd had no choice but to continue to forge ahead. Then, at the midpoint of the thirty miles of empty Las Vegas Freeway on the map between Bunkerville and

Glendale, Nevada, the old Irish blessing Mom loves to give at weddings tried to kill us.

"May the road rise up to meet you" sounds nice until the highway in front of you flies up in a tidal wave of rock and earth and rockets at you almost as fast as you're already traveling.

"May the wind be always at your back" comes across as a pleasant wish until gale force gusts hit your vehicle from behind and send you flying at the gigantic mass of asphalt and concrete rolling your way.

"May the sun shine warm upon your face," takes on a new meaning when giant fireballs descend all around from a previously blue sky, a scene straight out of every disaster movie I've ever seen.

And the rain fell anything but "soft upon our fields" as a sudden deluge reduced visibility to zero and forced me from the road.

Or, at least, what was left of it.

In that moment, I hoped the final line of the blessing somehow held true and that God truly did hold us in the palm of his hand, because otherwise, we were totally screwed.

"What the hell do we do now?" I barked at Delacroix, who still shared a seat with his daughter while Seph stayed belted in the center of the Commander's cab. "They've got us dead to rights, and I can't even see to drive, much less fight."

"Cowards," Rosemary muttered under her breath. "The skiomancer ambush seemed all but a foregone conclusion, but I expected better of Ada and her crew."

"Seriously?" I asked. "You think they're following some kind of superior moral compass after the way they tried to take Seph back in Denver?"

"Last I checked," Rosemary answered, "they haven't killed anyone."

"Not for lack of trying." I peered through the windshield, the wipers at full speed doing little to clear the glass enough to see for more than a split second at a time. Before us, the enormous mound of earth, concrete, and asphalt loomed but held fast as if awaiting further instructions. No tornado, inferno, or tsunami hit the vehicle either, suggesting that our friends from Denver still needed Seph alive, though I was relatively certain that caveat, regardless of Rosemary's assertion, didn't apply to the rest of us.

"These elementalists certainly don't seem to mind leaving behind serious property damage." Seph noted. "Tell me, how have these Ascendant been operating for all this time and nobody has ever noticed?"

"Disasters happen every day, Miss Snow." Delacroix rolled his injured shoulder and winced. "If you control the very elements or other forces of nature, then all it takes to make anything look like an accident is a little planning and decent timing."

"And people do notice," Rosemary added. "But they are often dismissed as paranoid or conspiracy theorists."

One of Dad's favorite sayings popped into my head. "Just because you're paranoid, it doesn't mean they aren't out to get you."

"Fantastic." Seph cleared her throat. "So, like Ethan asked, what do we do now? If we wait here for them to come for me, I can think of a dozen ways off the top of my head they can take us out, each worse than the one before."

"But if we go out there and literally face the elements," I added, "we play right into their hands."

"As powerful and dangerous as the skiomancers have proven to be," Delacroix rumbled, "they are nothing compared to such a coordinated attack as we face now."

"And I don't think the 'old switcheroo,' like Seph called it, is going to work this time." Rosemary dropped her chin to her chest. "I'm afraid I don't see a clear path forward."

Rain and hail continued to pelt the Commander as gust after gust of wind whistled around its angular framework. Occasionally a tremor would shake the entire vehicle, the master of earth letting us know he was still around. And though no further fireballs fell from the sky, I guessed that Ada was merely biding her time and conserving her energy.

"The way I see it, our options are limited." I caught everyone's gaze one by one. "Seph already said it. If we just stay here, we're basically fish in a barrel, and if we go out there and fight, they have the upper hand in every way. We're at the midpoint of thirty-five miles of nothing with no cover to speak of, so even if we make it off the highway, there's nowhere to run and nowhere to hide."

"What do you suggest, then, Mr. Harkreader?" Delacroix studied me with an oddly amused gaze. "That we give up and surrender Miss Snow to her would-be abductors?"

"Our goal is to protect Seph, and it's pretty clear they're holding back to avoid hurting her." I locked gazes with Seph. "I don't like it either, but the alternative involves some or all of us getting hurt or worse, and that's no good."

"You'd have us concede, Ethan?" Rosemary looked upon me with more disappointment than I'd ever seen in those dark eyes. "After everything we've already overcome?"

"Do you have a better idea?" My cheeks grew hot with a potent mix of anger and embarrassment. "Because I'm all ears."

"No fighting." Seph unbuckled her seatbelt and directed her gaze at the driver's door handle. "Let me out."

"But—" Rosemary started.

Seph's gaze dropped to her lap. "You and Ethan have both already laid your lives on the line for mine in the last few hours. Mr. Delacroix was nearly torn in half defending my freedom. We're outgunned and outmanned, and yes, I'm scared, but Ethan's right. They need me alive. If I go out there, I think they'll leave the rest of you alone. Otherwise," she choked on the word, "I get to watch them do whatever they're going to do and then take me anyway." She raised her eyes again and pointed to the handle. "Ethan, open the door."

"Okay." I grasped the handle. "But I'm coming with you."

"No, Ethan—" Seph started.

"Not to fight." I opened the door a crack, the wind whistling through the cab a reminder that its master could suck the air from my lungs at any instant should he wish me dead. "Simply for emotional support." I motioned to the paired blades resting on the floorboard at her feet. "I'll even leave the swords behind."

"You would face them defenseless?" Rosemary asked.

"With all due respect to the power and skill imparted me by your mother, I'm not certain how much good one man with two swords would do against four pissed off elementalists in a micro-hurricane."

I pushed the door open another inch against the gusting wind. "Now. Seph isn't the only one nervous about the next five minutes. Let's do this before I lose my nerve."

"What about me, Ethan?" Rosemary asked. "You plan to surrender yourself with Seph. What would you have me do?"

"Guard your father's life with your own." I put my shoulder to the door and pushed it open, the pounding rain outside drenching me in seconds. "As I will Seph's." I took Seph's shaking hand in mine. "Ready?" I asked the trembling pop star.

"Not even close, though that changes nothing." She drew close, a waterlogged smile on her face, and planted a kiss on my cheek. "Shall we?"

Together, we climbed down onto the drenched pavement, our shoes soaked through in seconds. Gale force winds and pounding rain hammered at us from above while a warm fog billowed up from below our feet, the not-quite-solid asphalt warm through our soles.

All four of our quartet of adversaries brought their powers to bear, though each remained hidden from view. As our unseen enemy collectively demonstrated patience beyond what I'd expected, I was painfully aware that any of the four could kill all of us at any moment.

"We surrender!" I shouted, the words ripped from my mouth and lungs by yet another blast of wind. "Now call off the deluge so we can discuss terms."

In the space of a breath, both wind and rain ceased, though the sky remained grey and overcast. The road beneath us was both warm and spongy, making clear that both fire and earth were in play, and I understood all too well that wind and water could be brought to bear again in an instant.

But still, I had their attention.

"Mr. Harkreader," came a German voice from above, "have you not already used this particular ploy to your advantage in the last few hours?" Dietrich Falco floated down from above our heads, his new white suit pristine and dry despite the previous torrential rains. "Such pretense may have served you well against Krage and his shadowy underlings, but you deal with professionals now."

"How could you possibly know what went down with the skiomancers last night?"

Ada appeared from around the rear of the Commander. "The number of things you fail to perceive or understand, little man, is impressive." She advanced a trio of steps, but stopped a respectful distance away. "We've monitored Miss Snow's activities undetected for weeks. After tracking her from Albuquerque to Denver, your rooftop rendezvous seemed the opportune time to obtain our target with minimal risk of collateral or property damage."

"You're kidding, right?" I scoffed. "They'll be fixing that block for years."

"Thanks to you and Miss Snow's bodyguard." Ada's head tilted to one side, a mocking smile flashing across her features. "How is his arm doing after last night, by the way?" Not waiting for an answer, she continued, the amusement in her features shifting to frustrated irritation. "Your involvement led to Miss Snow nearly being killed and millions of dollars of property damage, not to mention poor Dietrich's shoulder may never be quite the same."

I whistled and shook my head in mock sadness. "I'm devastated."

"We did get to see the Greyhound, though." Violeta in her purple bodysuit, black leggings, and teal boots came around from the front of the Commander, leaving us surrounded on three sides with the massive vehicle blocking our only escape. "I'd only ever heard the legends, Mr. Harkreader, so I suppose I must thank you for that." Her brown fingers toyed with her waist-length braid. "He, unlike you, proved quite a worthy opponent."

"Indeed he did." A different emotion briefly occupied Ada's features before she again narrowed her eyes at me. "In any case, we are more than aware of all that has transpired over the preceding hours." She laughed. "In fact, we'd hoped that the Angel's shadow-dealers might succeed in taking Miss Snow off your hands, as we have far less issue with ridding the world of those cockroaches than being intertwined with anyone associated with a Daughter of Neith."

"Thanks," I scrunched up my nose, "I think."

"Enough!" Seph spat out, no longer willing to be silent. "You all are posturing like a bunch of stupid kids on the playground, but I'm the one who decided to step out of that RV and face the music."

"Then what is he doing out here?" Falco asked.

"He insisted." She shot me a sidelong glance. "Please don't hurt him. He stands before you unarmed."

"I can see that." Ada advanced another step in our direction. "Such a move strikes me somehow as simultaneously wise and foolish."

"Admitting defeat and facing us alone took courage," Falco added. "I'll give you both that."

"So," Violeta asked, "if you don't plan to fight us, Mr. Harkreader, then what are you doing out here?"

"Standing by a woman I care deeply for." I glanced in Seph's direction. "You've made it clear that whoever is paying your fee needs her alive. All I ask is that you let me come with her, so she isn't alone."

Ada and Falco exchanged glances and a quiet laugh.

"You attempt to barter when you have nothing," the pyromancer said. "We have no desire to snuff out your life, Mr. Harkreader, if for no other reason than such action would reunify the power living at your core with an individual who actually knows how to use it. Regardless, in what reality do you believe we would bring you along when at any time you could attempt in vain to turn on us?"

"You have my word that I'd only be there to keep her safe." I searched desperately for anything that would get them to agree. "I may not seem much of a threat to you elemental types, but I've proven pretty effective against our skiomancer friends."

"The Light of Neith is a powerful weapon indeed," Violeta said, "but please understand that our little foursome has never had a problem dealing with the Midnight Angel's dark emissaries."

"Then bring me along as extra collateral." My entire body tensed despite my efforts to maintain my cool. "Look, I'm not letting you take her without me."

"The line between bravery and foolishness is narrow indeed, boy." Falco smiled in my direction, his eyes hidden behind those mirrored shades. "You'd do well to stay firmly on one side unless you'd like another sample of what I can do."

A shudder started at the base of my spine at the thought of having the very air taken from my lungs, but I refused to let him see me sweat.

Not that that was much of a problem, as I was already soaking wet.

At the brief pause in conversation, I looked over at Seph. She stood, red-faced with pursed lips, her arms crossed and her foot tapping a quick beat. "Are you done?" she asked.

"What?"

"You shouted 'We surrender!' as if it was your idea." She looked around at each of the three elementalists, leaving me wondering where their geomancer, the one called Daichi, was hidden, as he had clearly made his presence known. "I'm the one they want, and I'm the one standing here offering myself up. Not to mention, last I checked, I'm the only one standing here without the benefit of superhuman powers like I just stepped out of a fucking Avengers movie." Her eyes narrowed at all of us and at me in particular. "And all of you are ignoring me as if I'm not even here."

"My apologies, milady." Falco, still floating on a constant upward current of air to one side, drew close to Seph and slid into a wicked grin. "We shall ignore you no longer." He cast his mirrored gaze at the raised mound of earth and asphalt that had blocked our path minutes before. "Daichi? A moment?"

The miniature mountain of shattered pavement shuddered as if hit by an earthquake, and then, at its center, the pile of broken rock shifted as if alive. Rising from the rubble, a familiar form began to draw together. Hands and arms and feet and legs around an enormous torso and oblong head, the sumo wrestler Daichi chose as his earthen avatar pulled itself together from the disparate hunks of ruined highway. Eight feet high and growing by the minute, he trundled in our direction, his every step probably setting off seismic monitors for miles around.

"Are you all done chatting?" The shambling mound of earth and rock asked, the rumbling voice like a rockslide. "Let's get this done."

"Patience, Daichi," Ada said. "We've got nothing but time."

"You'd think we have all the time in the world, the way all of you have been going on." The sumo of rock and concrete glared at me, or at least I think he did. Its eyes appeared to be fashioned of the same shattered asphalt as the rest of him. "Some of us have plans this evening."

"Work comes first," Violeta drew closer. "Isn't that right, Ada?"

As the quartet of Ascendant moved to surround us, a sound hit my ears from the northeast: the roar of a distant engine. I scanned the road in the direction we'd come, fully expecting to find a black limousine with a mysterious man in a black suit and tie behind the wheel racing to our rescue.

But that wasn't it.

Far louder than any car, the alternating rev and whine of the vehicle headed our way reminded me more of the big semi-trucks that rule the highways of America.

But that wasn't it either.

The earthbound rocket of steel, glass, rubber, and gasoline that hurtled down the shoulder in our direction was a strikingly familiar bus, the lone driver homing in on us like a guided missile. As one, the four elementalists turned to follow my gaze at this latest addition to our impromptu mid-highway gathering, their shared expression evidence that this was the first event of the day that had caught them the least bit by surprise.

When the bus finally got close enough that I could make out the driver, I wondered briefly if I was hallucinating or if one of our opponents had knocked me unconscious and left me delirious in the world of dream.

Behind the wheel of none other than Seph's own tour bus, his steady gaze peering out from beneath the curved L of the "SPARKLE" logo emblazoned across the vehicle's massive windshield, sat Gus Shepherd, a man of few words and apparently even fewer fucks.

CHAPTER 22

DANGER ZONE

"Mr. Shepherd?" Seph muttered under her breath. "But we left him—"

"Somewhere right off the highway, about five miles from a bus he knows like the back of his hand."

"They're going to kill him." Seph's lower lip trembled. "Right in front of us."

"I don't know." I grabbed her arm and pulled her to the side of the Commander. "He's the one sitting behind the wheel of twenty tons of steel."

"Daichi," Ada said, rolling her neck in exasperation, "end this."

The sumo of shattered rock and concrete raised an arm, but before he could exercise his influence over the earth, two grenades the size of soda cans landed between his gigantic feet and filled the air around him with impenetrable green smoke.

"Not so easy when you can't see." Rosemary stood atop the Commander and hurled another smoke grenade at the feet of the remaining three elementalists. "On the other hand, I suspect the driver of that bus can easily aim for a big blob of smoke."

"Scatter!" came Ada's cry from within the mass of billowing green. "Reconverge on my command!"

The bus hurtled at us like a silver meteor, cleaving the large cloud of thick green vapor with a horrific crunch before sliding to a screeching stop in the highway median. A hunk of arm-shaped concrete went flying end over end from the opaque cloud, and I stepped in front of Seph to shield her from any shrapnel. As the cloud of green smoke cleared, I noted that the right front corner of the bus had taken a serious hit colliding with the giant sumo of stone and concrete. The driver's side, however, as well as Gus behind the wheel, appeared intact.

The trained professionals they were, our adversaries were in motion before I could process another thought. Falco took off straight upward, a sudden gust of wind sending him hundreds of feet into the sky while Violeta leaped from within the quickly dissipating smoke and landed at our feet, guessing correctly the bus wouldn't be aimed at us.

Ada, on the other hand, had vanished without a trace.

Gus, spryer than I'd ever seen the man, popped his head out the bus's driver's side. "Come on, you two." His voice maintained a preternatural calm. "Time to get you out of here."

He didn't have to tell me twice.

Without a second thought, I took Seph's arm, and the two of us sprinted across the two lanes of broken pavement to the rocky highway median where the bus awaited. When just a few feet remained, a powerful gust threatened to send us tumbling, but somehow we navigated the whipping wind and made it to our destination. Gus pushed the driver's side door open and dragged Seph up and into the front seat, a section of her home on wheels I was almost certain she'd never seen.

Once Seph was safely inside, I tried to pull myself inside as well, only to find my foot firmly embedded in what had previously been solid road. A glance across my shoulder revealed Daichi fully recovered, his rocky arm reattached and directed at the ground beneath my feet.

"You're not going anywhere, Harkreader." The rumbling tone of his words shook my bones. "At least not with your foot still attached."

"Ethan!" came Rosemary's frantic voice as stony tendrils began to snake up my calf. "Catch!"

My eyes flicked to the left where Rosemary still stood atop the Commander, her arm held high at the apex of a throw. Both my and Daichi's gazes went skyward where shining metal caught the rays of the sun as one of Danielle Delacroix's paired blades flipped end over end at the height of its arc.

"No, no, no." Falco shot down from the sky and with a wave of his arm, summoned a blast of wind that sent the sword flying eastward in the direction we'd come. "We won't be having any of that."

No sooner had the last word passed his lips than a loud clang of metal sounded as something struck the bus. A glance down revealed the longer of Rosemary's mother's blades protruding from the bus's steel exterior like the proverbial sword in the stone no more than a foot from my thigh, the hilt all but screaming for my touch. Centuries of passed-down reflexes led my hand to the weapon in an instant, and the space of a breath, I'd yanked the sword from the punctured side of the bus, summoned the Light of Neith, and brought the tip of the blade down upon my stony shackle.

As bright as any of Rosemary's flashbangs and easily as loud, the strike shattered the jagged stone encircling my foot. I'd never stepped on a land mine before, but the flash of pain that went up my leg had to be somewhere in the same ballpark. Half afraid I'd blown my foot off along with the rocky snare, I peered through the dust and found my foot intact and miraculously unharmed.

Apparently the elementalists weren't the only ones with a little magic on their side.

No sooner was my leg freed than Seph dragged me inside the cab and pulled the door closed.

"Mr. Shepherd," she shouted, "hit it!"

The usually reserved Gus hit the gas of Seph's mobile studio apartment as if he sat in a Formula One race car with the Devil himself coming for his backside, and the motor answered in kind.

The bus had taken a serious hit colliding with the giant sumo of stone and concrete, the right side of the windshield a spiderweb of shattered glass and crumpled steel, but the engine in the rear under Seph's sleeping compartment seemed to be doing just fine.

We took off down the highway's rough median, just skirting the barrier formed from Daichi's will and several tons of what used to be I-15, and shot into the left lane. Gus, usually the definition of chill, maintained a white-knuckled grip on the wheel, which served him well as the right lane of the highway erupted upward like a tiny Vesuvius. Countless smoking fragments of rock struck the side of the bus, nearly sending us back into the rocky median.

"Hang on," Gus said, "this thing isn't the most maneuverable vehicle on the planet."

His last word barely registered as a blast of wind from the opposite side sent us careening across the right lane and onto the shoulder.

"Well, that's not fair," he muttered, yanking the wheel to the left and aiming the bus at the dotted line down the road's center. "What's that song? Clowns to the left of me, jokers to the right?"

And here we were, stuck in the middle with earth, wind, fire, and air all jockeying to be the one to knock us from the road. Before us, one after another, hunks of rock sprang out of the road as if we were watching the world's largest game of Whack-A-Mole. Somehow, Gus managed to dodge each of them like an Olympic slalom skier going for the gold.

"Where the hell did you learn to drive like this?" I asked.

"Explanations later," Seph screamed as Gus accelerated straight through a not-so-spontaneous downpour and around another barely visible mound of broken highway. "Just get us the hell out of here."

"Yes, ma'am."

Gus continued his daring run down the highway, dodging fireballs, jagged rock, and micro-squalls every few feet and plowing straight through hurricane-force gusts like a sailboat tacking straight into a brutal gale. One by one, the attacks eventually fell away, the gusts of unnatural wind the last to go as we settled into the steady whistle of air whipping past the bus's crumpled right front corner.

That made sense, I guess. Dietrich Falco, the aeromancer of the group, was the only one who could fly as far as we'd seen, and Rosemary had established with the smoke grenade that at least Daichi, the geomancer, required line of sight to do his thing. If any of them had followed us, it would have been Falco. Even his reserves, it would appear, had limits.

"Is it possible?" Seph asked. "Did we get away?"

"For now." Gus pointed across the median at what appeared to be a gigantic pile of boulders that blocked all the eastbound lanes and extended well past both the shoulder and completely across the median. "Huh. I guess that answers that question."

"What question?" No sooner had the words left my mouth than I knew exactly what he meant. "That's why there were no cars on the other side."

Boy were there cars on the other side now. Backed up for miles, the opposite side of I-15 was a parking lot. A few of the braver drivers were forging an off-road path into the rocky desert in an effort to circumvent the roadblock, but most were just standing by and waiting. Folks all along the highway were out of their vehicles walking around, picnicking on the hoods of their cars, and sunbathing in the median.

"Huh. They had their geomancer block northbound traffic." It suddenly occurred to me that not a single vehicle had come from behind as we faced the elemental assault minutes before. "Southbound too."

"Property damage aside," Gus said, "it does seem like these people who are after Miss Snow are going out of their way to avoid unnecessary loss of life."

"But why?" Seph asked. "You'd think that a bunch of soulless mercenaries would just consider that—what do they always call it in the movies—collateral damage?"

"Like Rosemary said before..." I pondered for a moment. "Unlike the skiomancers, they haven't actually killed anybody."

"Humpf," Gus grunted. "Doesn't mean they're not trouble."

"Clearly." I peered over at Gus, the old man continuing to drive as if he hadn't just successfully navigated an attack by a quartet with the powers of gods just hours after narrowly escaping the onslaught of a foursome of shadow-dealing murderers on two quite abandoned stretches of highway in the middle of the night. "How the hell do you know what's going on anyway?"

Gus shot me a sidelong glance. "Just because I don't say much doesn't mean I don't keep my eyes and ears open." He smiled, the upturn of his lips at play against the thick bush of white hair below his nose and his saggy cheeks. "I listen. I watch. Sometimes I comment, though most times I don't."

"So, you've known this whole time what was going on?"

"I know you, Miss Snow, and the Delacroix family, God bless Ms. Delacroix's soul, have been in deep shit since Albuquerque." Gus shifted into the right lane and accelerated. "I know all about the shadow-freaks and the elemental weirdos we just left in the dust. I know that Miss Rosemary and her dad are stuck back there with the bad guys, and that there's not a damn thing any of us can do to help them. And I know, despite everything you've got going for you since Ms. Delacroix passed on her mojo to you instead of her daughter, that you, Mr. Harkreader, are in way over your head."

"Now, hold on there. I—"

"I wasn't finished." Gus silenced me with a raised hand. "I didn't say you weren't capable. I'm just saying that even the best juggler in the world can have too many balls in the air at once, and without Miss Rosemary to back you up, you're juggling with one arm tied behind your back."

"Hey," Seph said, "in case you missed it, I'm the one that bailed us out back in Colorado." She puffed up her chest. "A little credit?"

"You are braver than I'd ever imagined, Miss Snow." Gus's eyes flicked in her direction. "It's one thing to face a crowd of thousands who adores you and another thing altogether to face monsters that would as soon see you dead."

"Oh." Seph swallowed hard. "Thanks?"

"Now don't get all freaked out. Just letting you know that I recognize you've got some serious gumption." He shot her a wink before returning his attention to the road. "There's clearly a lot more to you, Miss Snow, than meets the eye."

~

The rest of the trip to Vegas passed with nothing but the occasional pothole. With all interstate traffic stopped both ways for miles, I-15 remained anemic for a long time, though the number of cars picked up considerably a few miles out of the city where the interstate ran into Highway 93.

Seph had made it through uninjured but no closer to figuring out why both the Midnight Angel's Ravens and Ada's clutch of elementalists had been hired to bring her in alive. Surprisingly, other than the scattered bruises, aches, and pains along my back and the dull ache from nearly having my right foot wrenched from my leg, I had pulled through reasonably intact as well.

And Gus? Usually tight-lipped, we learned that once the quiet bus driver got going, he proved to be quite the chatterbox.

Twenty-five years of prior service in the U.S. Army working with the Transportation Corps got to the root of why retired Master Sergeant Gustavo Shepherd not only knew how to keep a bus in tiptop condition all by himself but could navigate a vehicle of such size like a NASCAR driver at Talladega. Out of the Army just shy of two decades, he'd driven buses for everyone from Adele to ZZ Top and had initially been hesitant to take on Persephone Snow's Sparkle Tour, but had reconsidered the day he met her.

"You reminded me of my granddaughter," he'd said, "and I figured somewhere, your actual grandpa would appreciate it if I kept you safe on the road."

And kept her safe, he had, using skills he'd learned from over a quarter century of training and deployments to pretty much every corner of the world.

And Seph thinks *I'm* a superhero.

Back in Albuquerque, he'd stuck to the shadows, as it were, as the ride Jerry had called for him hadn't shown up when the skiomancers first made their presence known.

"If I'd had my AR-15 from back in the day," he'd said, "there'd be a few less shadow-people walking around, I'll tell you that."

He'd stayed out of sight through the entire fight, knowing "damn well" how little good an unarmed sixty-year-old man with three herniated discs would have done in the fight and watched as the tiny battle unfolded. He'd looked on from mere feet away as Danielle fought first Rupert then the trio of skiomancers while we dealt with their leader and rescued Seph at the far end of the darkened parking lot. He'd almost come forward to help when Dmitri held the blade to Mr. Delacroix's throat, but had remained silent as Dino approached from behind and took out the enormous Raven in likely the bravest and stupidest moment of his life.

"And then," he said, his voice going quiet, "what happened with poor Ms. Delacroix." He shot me another glance. "You did what you could, but I've seen wounds like that before. There was nothing you could have done to save her." He reached over and patted my knee, a move my dad used to do when I'd had a bad day. "I know you must feel like a lot has been laid in your lap, Mr. Harkreader, but I've seen your heart. You can do this."

"Thanks. That means a lot."

"Still, just because you've been handed a powerful weapon doesn't mean you know what to do with it." He inclined his head in Seph's direction. "Miss Snow there is counting on you, so be careful out there and don't let her down."

"Oh, he won't, Mr. Shepherd." Seph had remained uncharacteristically quiet through most of the conversation. "He hasn't so far."

As for how he'd managed to arrive in the nick of time to save the day against Ada and her crew, that was "a little luck, not all of it good, and a lot of persistence."

As the shadows had descended around the tour bus back in Colorado, Gus had known instinctively what was happening, having witnessed the attack in Albuquerque. Not satisfied to wait on the sidelines this time, he'd left the cab to help us all to safety.

"I overestimated my ability to navigate the pitch black of those damned shadows, though." He pointed to the back of his head where a goose egg I hadn't previously noticed was crowned with dark dried blood. "Knocked my noggin real good."

"Are you all right?" Seph asked.

"Tripped over a rock in the median, fell and hit my head. Balance ain't quite what it used to be." He cracked his neck. "When I came to, both the bus and the Delacroix's RV were long gone, so I did what anybody would do in the middle of the night." He stuck out his thumb in demonstration. "After a couple dozen cars blew by, a nice couple eloping from Kansas took pity on a poor old man and let me hitch a ride." He laughed. "Imagine my surprise when I found my very own bus waiting for me on the side of the road, keys in the ignition and everything."

"Yeah." I let out a chuckle of my own as I remembered cursing myself for leaving the keys behind. "Lucky for us."

"Once I was back on the road, I tried to call, but there was no signal."

"Courtesy of our friends in black, I imagine." Seph shook her head. "This deck was definitely stacked against us."

"I made it a few more miles down the road and took a minute back in St. George to hit a gas station and doctor on my head a bit." He switched lanes to pass a slow-moving Subaru laden with luggage. "And then, about an hour into the last leg to Vegas, traffic came to a halt about half a mile ahead." He cracked his neck. "Something told me to hightail it up the shoulder."

"Traffic jams happen all the time, Gus. How'd you know it was us?"

"Seen a lot of rockslides in two decades of driving, kid." He punched the gas as we got off the highway at the exit for the Las Vegas Motor Speedway, our prearranged meetup point with Delacroix if things went sour. "This was the first time I ever saw rocks flying up instead of falling down."

CHAPTER 23

QUEEN OF LAS VEGAS

"Do you think they're going to show?" Seph leaned against the side of her disfigured tour bus just below the dented R of the "SPARKLE" logo, taking full advantage of the tiny bit of shade to escape the brutal Nevada sun. "We've been waiting here for hours, and nothing."

"I wish I knew, Seph."

We'd planned to rendezvous with Rosemary and Mr. Delacroix at the periphery of the Speedway's gigantic parking lot. It hadn't occurred to me the lot would be basically empty; roadside and out in the open had been anything but the plan. The skiomancers were likely out of commission until nightfall, but Ada's team had a person who could literally fly. With no cover and no other vehicles to mask our presence, we were basically sitting ducks. However, with all our mobile phones still on the blink, despite the fact that I could see a cellular tower from where we stood, we didn't really have any other choice. This was where Team Delacroix said they would head, and there we would stay until they arrived.

Stick to the plan Ethan, Rosemary had said, *no matter what.*

"And what," I muttered, "if said plan goes belly up?"

"In my experience," Gus offered, "the *best* plans leave room for a bit of improvisation." He chuckled. "Though that old saying about adjusting the sails because you can't direct the wind takes on new meaning in this case, I guess."

"That's actually funny," I laughed despite myself, "in a morbid sort of way."

"The way I see it, it's way past lunchtime"—Seph's stomach growled as if to emphasize the point—"and though the bus is pretty well stocked, I'm just not feeling microwave cuisiney at the moment. Not to mention we have to find a landline to let everyone know our most recent whereabouts. The L.A. show is tomorrow night, and a lot of people have got to be freaking out by now." She fished a tiny wallet out of her back pocket and held up a trio of credit cards, one platinum, one jet black, and the last a metallic blue. "Any chance I could talk you into escorting me into town so we can get something real to eat and make a couple of calls?" She flashed that world-famous Persephone Snow smile. "My treat."

"Like you'd have to pay for anything once they figure out who you are."

"Au contraire, Mr. Harkreader." She stepped inside the bus and returned with a pink scarf across her long platinum locks and a pair of sunglasses that took up nearly half her face. "With skiomancer assassins and elemental mercenaries hot on my tail, I plan to remain incognito to the rest of the world."

Good idea, though unless she were going to put on a radiation suit, her midriff-showing tank, skintight jeans, and boots were still going to attract a lot of attention.

Still, it was a start.

"Look, I'm starving too, but if we leave the bus, I'm not sure how Rosemary and Mr. Delacroix will track us down when they finally arrive."

The unspoken "if" hung in the air between the three of us.

"Promise to bring me something back," Gus said after a few moments of uncomfortable silence, "and I'll stick around here and wait for the Delacroixs to show up." He inclined his head in the direction of Vegas proper. "Just so you know, I've driven this section of road more times than I care to remember. I know the sign there says 'Vegas,' but we're still about twenty-five miles from the center of town."

"Gus has a point. He's got the only wheels in sight other than the couple of cars at the far end of the parking lot, and I'm not leaving him next to an abandoned speedway in the sun to die of heatstroke." I crossed my arms and studied Seph, my eyebrow raised in curiosity. "Exactly how do you propose we get downtown?"

Seph tilted her head to one side in consideration and then spun on one heel and made a beeline for the highway exit we'd taken, making a point to hypnotically sway those million-dollar hips of hers with every step. At the end of her brief sashay, she rested one hand at her waist, raised her opposite arm in the universal sign of hitchhikers coast-to-coast and shot a wicked grin across her shoulder. "I've got a thumb, don't I?"

∼

"So." There I was at the heart of the Entertainment Capital of the World—no offense, Los Angeles—holding hands with one of the most beautiful women on the planet and wondering for the hundredth time that week if I were dreaming. "This is Vegas."

"Everything here is so much bigger than I could ever have imagined." Seph peered up and down the busy Strip at the multitude of people and cars. "How is it that I've never been here before?"

"Finally," I smiled, "a first for both of us that doesn't involve someone trying to kill, maim, or kidnap us."

"The day is young," she muttered with no small amount of sarcasm.

We'd been roadside along I-15 less than five minutes when a stretch Hummer full of dudes my age on a bachelor party weekend pulled over. I'm sure Seph's toned arm, arched back, and tilted hips

215

had absolutely nothing to do with the driver slamming the brakes on the interstate. They were all a bit disappointed that it was a package deal, but it turned out one of the guys was from Knoxville like me, so the ensuing twenty minutes ended up okay. Only one of the eight, the groom's younger brother, seemed to clue in on exactly who it was they'd picked up in their rented land yacht, but his discreetly raised eyebrow and subtle wink let me know that he wouldn't spill the secret until we were long gone.

Seph handled the adoration like a pro, somehow deflecting five different offers to exchange numbers—fortunately none of those from the groom-to-be—and yet kept the party alive with her effervescent laugh and unstoppable smile. And with each passing minute, her eyes returned to me like a pair of moths to the proverbial flame. The quiet assurance that at the end of the day she'd still choose me, even in a car full of guys buff enough that any of them could have walked off the cover of *Men's Fitness*, was enough to make me fall in love all over again.

Love.

Well, now I've said it for sure, if not out loud.

Though, to be honest, as many times as I caught Seph smiling in my direction over the short ride into Vegas despite the fact that she was being chatted up by dudes who make me look like last week's lunch, I got the feeling the L-word was a two-way street.

I'm pretty sure Rosemary wouldn't approve of us moving so fast emotionally, regardless of us hitting the brakes from a physical standpoint back in Denver.

The funny thing is, I wasn't sure I understood exactly why I thought that or why Rosemary's feelings on the matter weighed on my mind in the first place.

Anyway, after seven stories of debauchery, three rounds of shots of which both Seph and I kept our involvement to a sip or two—though I could have seriously used a drink even that early in the day—and one drunken and graciously rejected proposal later, the micro-mob of party animals dropped us off at the Bellagio.

Like the rest of the world, I'd seen the place on television dozens of times, but nothing prepared me for the sheer scale of Vegas. Even

Seph, who had stood centerstage in front of thousands every other night for weeks, found herself overwhelmed by the immensity of it all.

As if on cue, the fountains in the lake before the enormous hotel came to life, sending hundreds of jets of water several stories into the air, the unbelievably precise aquatic bursts in time with Ol' Blue Eyes piped in singing "Luck Be A Lady."

Seph looked on in wonder at the fantastic display of music, light, and engineering, the little girl who still lived somewhere inside the fledgling star coming to the forefront, her lips wide in a jubilant grin and her cheeks flushed with excitement.

Her eyes were on the fountain, and mine were on her.

"Here." Seph fished her phone out of her back pocket and held it out to me. "Take my picture. Despite everything else that's been going on, I'd like to commemorate the moment."

"Our phones still aren't getting any signal." I snapped a picture of the gorgeous woman before me, those crystal blue eyes smiling at me from shades pulled halfway down her nose and her perfectly painted lips turned up in a half-smirk. "You won't be able to post this on social media until we get out of 5G Purgatory." I shot a couple more, as I learned a long time ago from my sister that one picture is simply never enough. "Not to mention, probably not a great idea to announce to the world that we are standing in front of one of the most recognizable landmarks in the Northern Hemisphere."

"Oh, sweetie, I'm anything but Instagram-ready." She pulled close, took her phone back, and examined the picture. "This one is for my personal collection." She motioned in the direction of the fountains. "Now you, Superboy. Go flex your muscles in front of the pretty water for me."

I raised an eyebrow. "You're serious?"

"Never more." She flicked her hand at me. "Now, get over there so I can get a decent picture of my own personal superhero."

I'd never been the biggest fan of having photos taken of me, but this was not a hill worth dying on. I walked over to the water's edge as Frank Sinatra's disembodied voice headed into the song's chorus a second time.

Luck be a lady tonight, indeed.

I dropped into as manly a pose as I could muster, caring for the first time in recent memory about how the picture might look. As I saw it, Seph didn't know how to take a bad photo, while I couldn't remember the last one of me I hadn't wanted to toss in a shredder.

Not that Seph seemed to care. She took a good two dozen shots, having me try on two or three different poses before she was done. I walked over to take a look at the results of my impromptu photoshoot when the sound of a clearing throat behind us caught both of our attention.

"How about I take one of you two together?"

Seph and I spun around to find a Paul Rudd look-alike dressed in full Ant-Man regalia from the Marvel movies.

"Pardon me?" I asked.

The celebrity impersonator held out his hand. "Would you like me to take your picture together?" He asked the question very slowly, a beaming grin across his face.

"That would be great." Seph held out her camera. "Thanks."

She pulled me over to the edge of the fountain and turned her body into mine. Considering the circumstances, I wasn't too keen on dealing with strangers, but a guy wearing nothing but a goofy grin and superhero cosplay—and a pretty convincing one at that—was likely okay.

For the next couple of minutes, "Ant-Man" put on a frenetic show of enthusiasm, leaving Seph giggling and even coaxing a legit smile or two out of yours truly before returning Seph's camera.

"You two have a nice day."

I fumbled with my wallet, working to find a ten-spot to tip the man.

"That won't be necessary." He smiled. "This one's on me."

"Seriously?" I asked.

He nodded. "All of us out here hiding in plain sight have to stick together, right?"

His comment raised the hairs on my neck. "What do you mean by—"

"Thank you, Mr. Rudd," Seph whispered before I could get another word out. "You and your daughter have a great day."

Our snap photographer gave us both a jaunty salute and then walked over and took the hand of a little girl in a Wasp costume and the two of them proceeded down the strip.

"Huh," I muttered. "I figured he was one of the cosplayers who takes pictures for tips."

Seph laughed. "That was no cosplayer, Ethan."

Just a few steps down the street, the man in red, blue, and silver stopped for a photo himself, shot the pair of giggling girls who took his picture a wink, and put his finger to his lips before taking his daughter's hand and disappearing into the crowd.

"Thank God," I groaned as I bit down on the first delectable bite of prime rib. "I was starting to see black spots."

Seph and I had made our way across the street to Caesars Palace and taken full advantage of the Bacchanal Buffet, a hedonistic hoard of every food imaginable. With plates piled high with beef, chicken, seafood, potatoes, and more, we'd picked a table in as dark a corner as we could find and kept our heads down as we devoured our first food since the previous evening. We'd hit Caesars during the magic hour after lunch and before the dinner rush, so the lines had been relatively short. Still, even the scant wait time had left me feeling a bit weak in the knees.

"So," Seph said after swallowing back a particularly jumbo shrimp, "I guess as soon as we're done, we should get a box for Mr. Shepherd and grab a cab back out to the Speedway. He's got to be starving too."

"Sounds like a plan." I wolfed down a hunk of baked potato slathered in butter and sour cream. "God willing, Rosemary and Mr. Delacroix will be there by the time we return."

Our table grew quiet as the two of us filled our bellies, partly a side effect of the delicious meal, but mostly because neither of us wanted to face the question of what we'd do if the Delacroixs weren't there when we got back.

On a different note, Seph's trainer would likely have had a heart attack if she'd seen the calories our favorite pop star was putting away, though after the night and morning we'd shared, I suspected Seph couldn't care less. And seeing Seph tear into a steak like a lioness on the Serengeti? Pretty damn sexy.

"Should we take some extra with us for the Delacroixs?" she asked. "Just in case?"

"Of course."

"Miss Snow?"

We both looked up to find a bearded man in a dark suit and silk tie smiling down at us from a respectful distance.

"Who's asking?" I asked, my muscles tensing in preparation for the worst.

"My name is Bryan Murcin. I'm the general manager of this hotel." His already beaming smile brightened a couple megawatts. "One of my associates let me know that Miss Snow was enjoying our buffet, and I wanted to come down and—"

"Look," I pointed to the empty chair before Mr. Murcin. "We're trying to stay kind of low-key here. Would you mind sitting down?"

"It would be my pleasure." With practiced grace, he slid into the chair, never taking his eyes off Seph. "Miss Snow," he kept his voice down, "Caesars Palace is honored by your presence in our hotel, but wouldn't you prefer our formal dining room? We can have our chef whip you up anything your heart desires."

"That won't be necessary. We're just grabbing a bite."

"Of course." He nodded, a hint of nervousness in his features. "Can we at least get you a private room, your own server, and whatever else you might need?"

"I very much appreciate your offer, Mr. Murcin." Seph considered for a moment. "My friend and I have already availed ourselves of your fantastic buffet, but might your chef be able to put together a surf and turf for two and an exquisite vegetarian plate for one?" She put on a smile bright enough to match Murcin's. "I have some friends on the road with me who could certainly use a quality meal."

SHADOWS OF THE NIGHT

"Of course, Miss Snow." He bowed his head slightly. "It would be our pleasure."

"And, like my friend here said," Seph added, "we're trying to keep everything pretty low-key. Can we keep everything on the DL until we leave?"

"Of course." Murcin stood. "I'll do my best to—"

"OMG!" came a whispered voice that traveled well with the room's acoustics. "It's her!"

All three of us turned in the direction of the voice. Across the space, a trio of Asian young women in school uniforms stared in our direction. Though likely at the end of their high school career, they giggled like middle schoolers.

Pink flashed in Murcin's cheeks, his eyes rolling subtly as he offered us a quick shrug. "Like I said, I'll do my best."

As Murcin scurried away to relay our order as well as to quell the likely impending rush of Persephone Snow fans, I shot Seph an amused grin and raised an eyebrow in question.

"Incognito, eh?"

"Hey, you try hiding all this with just a pair of sunglasses and a scarf," she answered without missing a beat, passing an open hand down the front of her body. "Might as well try to hide the midday sun."

I laughed. "And here I was worried you might have self-esteem problems."

"More than you might know, Ethan." She squinched up her nose. "Everybody's got insecurities, and those of us at the quote-unquote top sometimes have more than most."

"I can believe that. I remember when—"

"Good afternoon, Miss Snow." For the second time in as many minutes, a voice interrupted my and Seph's conversation. "If you would, please come with us."

Their approach eerily silent, a trio of men in short-waisted tuxedos now waited patiently by our table. In the lead stood a grey-bearded hulk of a man, his features Slavic and his expression cold. To his right waited a man of Asian descent, short and compact with lean musculature, his gaze wandering the room as if in anticipation. To

Grey Beard's left leered a dark-skinned man with immaculately braided cornrows and a wicked grin that showed off a grill of gold teeth.

"Thank you," Seph said with a pleasant lilt, "but we've already talked with Mr. Murcin, and we're fine finishing our meal right here."

"Yeah," I added, "we're trying not to make too big a splash." I smiled to the front man of the trio despite his discomfiting stare. "We'll be out of your hair as soon as we get our order."

"I don't think you understand." The Asian man stepped forward to address us, his pupils narrowing like a cat's into vertical ellipses within his green irises. "Miss Snow, you *are* coming with us."

The man with the golden grill let out a breathy chuckle. "Whether you like it or not."

Grey Beard bared his teeth, his canines as prominent as a wild animal's. "Do not be confused. Though we are working to maintain a semblance of civility, given the public nature of our current discussion, this is not a request."

CHAPTER 24

WELCOME TO THE JUNGLE

As difficult as it would've been to walk around the Las Vegas Strip with a three-foot sword slung across my back, I immediately regretted leaving Danielle Delacroix's remaining blade on the bus with Gus.

"Who are you?" I asked, standing and inserting myself between the three men and the suddenly pale Seph. "What do you want?"

"What we want," Golden Grill said with a wheezy laugh, "should be obvious."

"And who we are," Grey Beard added, his yellow irises enlarging to envelop the white of his eyes as his pupils shrank to pinpoints, "is none of your business, pretender."

"Pretender? You don't even know me."

"We know enough." The leader of the pack sniffed the air. "I've only crossed swords with the Daughter of Neith a handful of times in my life, and each left its own share of scars, I assure you. The electric tang that hung in the air in her presence, however, is one I will never forget." His golden eyes narrowed at me. "You harbor power within you, boy, that few outside the Ascendant have ever known, and yet you reek of fear." His lupine gaze flicked past me to study Seph. "Not to mention, you and the Snow bitch are out here in broad view of the world, flirting like animals in heat when any man with his head on straight would have kept her hidden safely away rather than letting his hormones rule his decisions."

"Snow bitch?" Seph grumbled under her breath.

"If it makes you feel any better, she'll be safer with us," the third muttered, unable to take his green cat eyes off Seph. "You don't have what it takes to protect her alone."

"She's not going anywhere with you." I balled up my fists, praying that whatever strength, reflexes, and skills I'd inherited from Rosemary's mother would pull me through a three-on-one fight with Ascendant straight out of *The Island of Dr. Moreau*. "I've already stood up to the Midnight Angel's skiomancers and a quartet of elementalists who all wanted Miss Snow, and here I am, still swinging." I swept up a steak knife from the table and wished again that I had an actual sword in my hand. "Now, step away from the table and leave us be."

"Leave you be?" Grey Beard looked back at his dark-skinned second and joined him in a growling lupine laugh. "You think this is some sort of a negotiation?"

I brandished the few inches of steel before me. "I won't let you take her without a fight."

"How fascinating." Golden Grill took a solitary step in my direction. "We'd heard whispers that the Daughter of Neith met an untimely end earlier this week. While we've always worked to stay off her radar over the years, our pack has significant experience with her only offspring. In fact, we were just discussing what we'd do when we eventually crossed paths with young Rosemary again."

"And now, pretender, here you are, flush with stolen power that you have no idea how to utilize. It's simply tragic." Grey Beard straightened himself to his full height and offered me what I'm guessing was supposed to pass for a congenial smile rather than a baring of teeth. "As a courtesy to one so clearly out of his depth, we offer one last opportunity to bow out of a fight that, despite your recently purloined inheritance, is not yours."

"Ethan?" Seph whispered.

"Persephone Snow is with me." I stepped forward, coming nose-to-nose with the Big Bad Wolf. "I've made this my fight."

"Very well." Grey Beard's lips parted in a low growl. "Do remember when all this is over that you were warned."

Faster than my eye could follow, he shot out a hand, grabbed me just above the elbow, and flung me across the room as if I weighed nothing. My flailing body landed atop a table shared by an elderly couple several buffet trips ahead of Seph and me and sent their stack of plates flying, the cacophony of shattering dishes deafening.

Oh well. I guess "low-key" just flew out the window.

I'd barely gotten back to my feet when our other two tuxedo-clad assailants moved on Seph. Each grabbing one of her arms, they lifted her from the ground as her feet worked like pistons beneath her.

"Stand down, pretender." Grey Beard bristled, every bit a wolf in human clothing. "I bear you no ill will and have no desire to end either your life or your most-likely-brief time in the spotlight." As I took an angry step forward, he raised a finger and added, "Understand, however, that I have no problem whatsoever removing obstacles from my path."

"Well, I hope you brought a bulldozer, because this 'obstacle' isn't going anywhere." I rushed the man and hurled myself into the air. My foot shot out in a flying kick that came as naturally as if I'd thrown it a thousand times. Instincts I'd never earned prepared me for the sudden stop of my heel impacting his chin.

Unfortunately, the man's reflexes more than equaled what I brought to the table. Dodging beneath my roundhouse kick, he shot up an arm and batted me into a nearby column like an errant ping pong ball. I managed to twist my body around midair so that my back bore the brunt of the hit. Still, regardless of how you slice it, getting body slammed into solid concrete hurts like hell. Though winded from the impact, I executed some catlike reflexes of my own to land on both feet and one hand in a move that would have made Scarlett Johansson proud.

Felix the Cat and Golden Grill sprinted away through the crowd, carrying a kicking and screaming Seph between them while their lupine leader ran interference. Following them in a zigzag pattern, he kept pace with his subordinates, dodging folks left and right without taking his unnerving yellow gaze off me for even a second as the trio made their strategic withdrawal. I raced after them at a dead sprint, knowing full well that if I lost them in the crowd at Caesars, I'd never find them or see Seph again.

The three raced past a circular establishment called Apostrophe Bar and down a hallway to the left that led to a replica of the famed Statue of David as they did their best to lose me. The trio of animalistic marauders clearly knew this place far better than I ever would, a fact I guessed they'd soon be turning to their advantage. They ran past a restaurant called Nobu and the trendy looking Numb Bar, all the while leaving the Big Bad Wolf in the rear to keep me from their prize. We'd just passed Gordon Ramsay's place and the ubiquitous Starbucks when my stomach began to cramp. Not eating for nearly twenty-four hours, gorging myself on more calories than I normally eat in two days, and then running a 400 was likely not the best idea I'd ever had.

Seph was counting on me, however, and come hell or high water, I wasn't going to let her down. Not that Seph herself wasn't a player in all this. Our attackers clearly thought they had this whole thing wrapped up, but they didn't know Seph like I did. The woman had way more grit than most people gave her credit for.

As they sprinted for the entrance to The Colosseum, a legendary arena I'd never worked but heard was something to behold, the pair took a hard right beneath a sign that directed tourists toward the buses outside. A brief pause as Golden Grill tried to zig while Felix the Cat attempted to zag allowed Seph to finally land a kick. In true movie fashion, her size eight sneaker ended up squarely between Golden Grill's legs.

With an unnerving screech, he released her arm, allowing Seph's feet to touch the floor. Not wasting a moment, she shot out with the heel of her hand and caught Felix the Cat beneath his chin, driving his teeth up into his lolling tongue and eliciting the shriek of a wounded animal.

Wolfman Jack cursed under his breath and took his attention off me for the first time since our chase began in favor of pursuing their prize. Closing the distance between him and Seph in an instant, he lunged at her faster than my eye could follow and caught her by the wrist. He immediately paid the price, however, as she slashed out with her opposite hand and raked her manicured nails across his right eye. Another growl sounded from his drawn lips as he flung Seph in the direction of a large columned arch, the Romanesque letters above the doorway proclaiming the entrance to The Forum Shops.

"You'll pay for that, little girl." He ran his sleeve across his face to wipe the blood from his eye. "Those who desire your capture have instructed that you are to be delivered intact." He flashed his sharp canines in Seph's direction. "No one said anything about pretty."

Her eyes wide with fear, Seph turned and fled into the shops.

"After her!" The lupine Ascendant shouted to Felix the Cat as he tried unsuccessfully to pull his wheezy friend up from the ground. Golden Grill, however, was still nursing the assault on his favorite pair of dice. "Fine. I will deal with this nuisance."

"Who are you calling nuisance?" I brandished the steak knife before me and channeled every ounce of brooding badass I had into my stare. In answer, the wolf cracked his neck and bared his pearly whites, the four canines prominent along his two even rows of teeth. He held one hand before his face, and though only well-trimmed fingernails graced each digit, I had little doubt he could tear out my throat without trying.

"You should've cut and run when we gave you the chance," he said with a growl. "Last mistake you'll ever make."

"I've been hearing that a lot lately." I fought to keep any hint of fear from my voice. "Can we get on with this? I've got a gorgeous pop star to save."

"Oh, so brave." His body shook with an odd convulsion, and though his form remained human, his entire demeanor and stance shifted into something unmistakably canine. "Answer me this, Little

Pig. Are you really planning on facing the Big Bad Wolf with nothing but a dull steak knife?"

"I've done more with less since taking on this gig." I dropped into a low martial stance, my left hand stretched before me and the knife held tight in my right, blade down in a power grip like Rosemary had beaten into my head half a dozen times already. "Let's do this."

Despite the confident swagger, his eyes on the makeshift dagger at my side let me know the self-proclaimed Big Bad Wolf hadn't written me off completely. As the six inches of serrated steel began to glow with an inner light, those yellow wolf eyes of his grew cold and narrow.

Without warning, Wolfman Jack charged headlong at me, more like a bull than any canine I'd met. I brought the knife around to defend myself, but he was on me before my mad slash made it halfway through its arc. A quick block saved me from the nails of one hand, but the opposite tore into the front of my shirt and left four parallel lines of scarlet across my left pec. The quartet of cuts across my chest brought a cry of agony cut short as I crashed into the floor, the impact forcing the air from my lungs. Half-blind from the pain and gasping for air, I brought the knife down on the only part of the man I could reach. As the glowing blade penetrated the top of his black boot like a chef's knife through filet mignon, he howled anew, a sound that will haunt me until the day I die.

Yet again, reflexes I'd never earned came to the fore, sending me rolling backward and onto my feet in one nimble maneuver. Winded and bleeding, I raised my fists for the next round.

The good news? I was no longer flat on my back with whatever passes for a werewolf in this strange new world standing over me and ready to gut me without a second thought.

The bad news? The only weapon I had besides my brain, fists, and feet was currently stuck somewhere south of my new enemy's shin, and boy was he pissed about it.

"I'm going to filet you, pretender." He reached down and yanked the knife from his foot, the serrated blade exiting the wound with a sickening rip and a spurt of crimson. "And I'm going to do it nice and slow."

228

"Hands in the air!" A pair of security guards appeared around the corner, pistols leveled at both of us. I couldn't really blame them, I guess. The way they saw it, I was the one running loose in Caesars Palace stabbing people. "Now!"

"Take it easy, okay?" I followed their instructions and put my hands above my head. "We can talk this—"

Before I could finish my sentence, the wolf in human clothing rushed the two men in grey and black uniforms, sending one careening into a column across the way while grabbing the other by his gun arm, holding him aloft as easily as one might a newborn child.

"You should have fired when you had the chance, little man." He squeezed the man's wrist until he dropped his gun, the ominous clatter of metal on marble sending a chill up my spine. "Now, skitter away before I am forced to bloody my hands further this day." He hurled the man in the direction of his unconscious partner. "And tell the rest of your worthless associates to stay clear of me and mine unless they want their wives to start cashing in their life insurance."

The shorter of the two guards stared at his bloodied partner lying sprawled on the floor for all of two seconds before high-tailing it out of the room like his hair was on fire.

"Just you and me now." The two of us circled, man and beast straight out of a fairy tale, each taking the other's measure. "You got in one fortuitous strike, but I wouldn't count on rolling seven twice in a row. This is Vegas, after all, and Lady Luck can be a real bitch sometimes."

"You call yourself the Big Bad Wolf?" I motioned for him to come at me, hoping my attempt at bravado didn't end up being the last thing I ever did. "Why don't you stop all your huffing and puffing, and let's get on with this."

Without wasting a breath, he charged me again, but this time I was ready. As he dove at my midsection, I leaped into the air and somersaulted over him, using his shoulder blades as a springboard, and landed feet first on the fine marble floor. He spun around and rushed me again, watching my body language in case I tried to repeat the move. This time, I employed the opposite tactic, waiting for the last possible instant before shooting out a leg to trip him. He tumbled away from me into one of the columns in the direction Seph had fled, but shot back up in an instant, the rage in his features doubling every second. His third pass was a blur as he nearly ripped out my throat with those claw-like fingers of his. Fortunately, a quick backpedal and a couple evasive maneuvers—that a voice deep inside suggested I'd learned in East Asia two hundred years before I was born—somehow kept me alive.

"You fight well for one with no training or skill." Wolfman Jack studied me, his rage-filled gaze shifting into mock sympathy. "But your run of luck, pretender, has ended."

Before I could respond, a pair of rough hands grabbed me from behind, their grip on my upper arms like steel. A phlegmy laugh sounded in my ear.

"Like Linus said, you fight well." The wheezy tones were those of the third of their crew whose testicles had apparently recovered from their encounter with Seph's foot. "That being said, your situational awareness could use some work."

The wolf, who apparently shared a name with Charlie Brown's blanket-toting buddy, drew close. "Where is all your bluster and boasting now?" His yellow lupine eyes narrowed at me. "I will admit that you are not without skill, and perhaps one day might prove worthy of your ill-gotten inheritance of power, but it would appear that your career as Bane of the Ascendant will soon be coming to a premature end." He lashed out with one curved finger and slashed open my cheek. "That's for my foot." He brought the bloodied nail to his flaring nostrils, sniffing at the scarlet dripping down his fingertip before lapping up the tiny sample of my lifeblood. "It's funny. Before we approached you and Snow, the three of us had decided simply to take her and let you live, more out of professional curiosity than anything else, as your existence remains a unique happenstance in our strange history, but between her crude assault on poor Harold and your unwillingness to stand down when facing your betters—"

This time, it was Linus's turn to have his thought interrupted, as the high whine of an engine filled the spacious atrium and captured our shared attention.

"What now?" came a wheezy grumble at my right ear, the vise-like grip on both my arms slackening ever so slightly.

In seconds, my wildest hope was confirmed as around the Colosseum box office rocketed a black motorcycle carrying an olive-skinned beauty wielding a katana held high above her head.

"Ethan!" Rosemary screamed as she popped a wheelie and leaped from the back of the bike in a move straight out of *The Matrix*. "Duck!"

As the motorcycle flew end-over-end at me and my captor, I stopped struggling against the hyena's iron grip and instead let my entire body go limp. My full body mass suddenly became dead weight, the last thing Harold expected, and my resultant drop to the floor freed me from his grasp.

And then, as I curled into a fetal position at the hyena's feet, a second thing he hadn't expected hit him, namely a quarter ton of jet-black motorcycle we'd shoved in the back of the Commander after our most recent escape from Krage's skiomancers.

The engine still revving as it hit Harold square in the chest, the impact of the sleek black machine sent him soaring along with the bike into the far wall of the atrium. Though the rear wheel of my savior's stolen ride continued to spin, neither motorcycle nor man moved again.

"Well, what do you know?" Rosemary rose from a low crouch, smiling with faux congeniality. "It appears you've found my missing partner, wolf." Danielle Delacroix's daughter strode toward us in black boots, skin-tight leather pants, and a torn red tank top, her katana held before her in a way that left zero doubt that she knew exactly what to do with such a weapon. "Thank you, Linus."

CHAPTER 25

EYE OF THE TIGER

"Rosemary!" I pulled myself up from the ground, trying to determine which of my bones or joints ached the worst. "You're okay."

"We can catch up later." She returned her attention to Linus, whose canny gaze revealed that he recognized the two-on-one advantage was now on the other foot. "Though I am curious how you managed to attract the attention of this particular pack of theriodans."

"Theriodans?" I asked.

"Ascendant," she lowered her voice, "in touch with their more bestial natures."

"You'd know." The lupine Linus proved her point, pacing back and forth between us like a caged animal. "What do you want, Rosemary?" he growled. "There is no bad blood between Delacroix and theriodan. I suspect you don't want to change that."

Rosemary studied him for a moment before sheathing her sword. "True."

"What are you doing?" I asked. "This guy and his friend were about to disembowel me a minute ago."

"And now they're not." She inclined her head in the direction of the pile of chrome and flesh at the far end of the room. "Is that Harold?"

"Of course it is." Linus shook his head in disgust. "Did you have to hit him with a motorcycle?"

"You two were threatening my friend. You both understand that's not something I would ever take lightly."

"*You*?" Linus growled. "We're used to dealing with your mother, Rosemary."

"And now you're dealing with me."

"Then the rumors are true." Linus shot a look in my direction. "Golden Boy there has the Light now—we've seen it, smelled it, in fact —which leaves you just another one of…these." He gestured around at the growing crowd of rubberneckers, each holding their phone aloft hoping to catch a piece of mortgage-paying footage. "You sure you want to be talking so tough when you don't have the *oomph* to back it up?"

"What you don't know about what I'm capable of would fill a library, wolf." She inclined her head in the direction of the exit. "Look, I've already left Harold there with wounds he'll be licking for weeks. You have one minute to vanish from my sight, or you will be joining him." Any hint of smile left her features. "The choice is yours."

Linus considered for a moment.

"Fifty-nine."

"But we were just—"

"Fifty-eight."

Linus hung his head. "Fine." He stalked over to the crashed motorcycle, extricated his friend's limp form from the wreckage, and headed for the nearest exit. "You get a bye this time, Delacroix."

Rosemary laughed. "I would argue that you're the receiver of this particular moment of benevolence, but if it makes you feel better, you can consider our ledgers balanced as of this moment." She narrowed her eyes at him. "A fresh start?"

With one last frustrated look in my direction, Linus nodded and then strode away with a still-unconscious Harold slung across his shoulder.

Once the Big Bad Wolf had finally vacated the area, Rosemary turned to me and asked simply, "Where is Seph?"

"She ran into the shops." I pointed in the direction Seph and Felix the Cat had gone. "The third member of the Beastie Boys was after her."

"Wait. Green cat eyes? Not quite as nasty as the rest?"

"That's the one."

"Neko." Rosemary strode over to the wrecked motorcycle and knelt by the still-spinning back wheel. "This should be interesting."

"So," I asked, "how do you know all these theriodans?"

"I'll fill you in later." She killed the motor and slid her hands beneath the seat. "Help me flip this thing?"

I got my own fingers underneath the leather of the seat and then, together, we righted the motorcycle. There, lashed to the side, rested both of Danielle Delacroix's blades, waiting for me.

No. More than that.

Calling for me.

"You obviously caught up with Gus," I said as she cut loose the longer of the two swords and handed it to me. "But the other blade? Last I saw, a hurricane gust blew it into the middle of the desert."

"Falco's winds, no matter how powerful, can only carry a hunk of metal so far." She handed me the shorter blade, the scabbard in my grip as familiar as if I'd been born holding the ancient weapon. "These swords have been in my family longer than anyone knows. Their steel will not be left in the desert to rust while I'm alive. Took me a while, but I found it."

"A needle in a sandbox, I guess." I crossed the weapons before me. "And you trust me with your mother's blades?"

Rosemary's face broke into one of her rare smiles. "Surprises me almost as much as it does you." The focused Delacroix stare I first saw in her mother overtook her features anew. "Now, let's go find Seph."

Rosemary turned in the direction of the crowd that had gathered between us and the mouth of the shops and parted the mob faster than Moses did the Red Sea. Staffs that turn into snakes are cool and all, but a katana held before you as you sprint at a throng of panicked tourists apparently works just as well.

"Curious," I asked as I raced to keep up with Rosemary, "how'd you find us anyway?"

"Gus said we missed you by about fifteen minutes. I left Father with the bus and headed into town to find you." Rosemary spun around a slow-moving couple in their sixties and then sprinted past a statue of Athena on a pedestal beneath a large dome supported by six brown marble columns. "I was cruising up and down the strip looking for a clue when a flood of people ran from Caesars Palace screaming about terrorists." We skirted either side of an enormous Chinese dragon statue built from what appeared thousands of blinking Christmas lights. "Say what you want about us, but subtlety hasn't been either of our strong suits lately."

The crowd grew thicker as we raced forward, every set of eyes focused on something just beyond our field of vision. Rosemary ran straight up the middle of the crowded hall, leaping parkour-style onto the marble banister surrounding an escalator leading down, and slid to the other end and out of sight.

Despite the confidence I had in my newfound abilities, I opted for the slower path, making my way through the crowd as quickly as I could along the left side of the concourse. As I stepped between another pair of enormous marble columns and around the last few onlookers, the hall opened up on a faux European city: street lamps every few steps, second-story windows lit up as if people lived there, and flooring like black slate. Any sense I remained inside what was basically a glorified shopping mall evaporated as the ceiling transformed into an artificial blue sky with clouds overhead and the floor beneath my feet into an Italian city street.

Straight ahead, a fountain straight out of ancient Rome with marble representations of Jupiter, Neptune, Mars, Diana, and Venus with multiple Pegasi among their number grew bigger in my vision with my every step. Seated on the floor beneath the statue of Neptune holding his mighty trident, Persephone Snow seemed right at home, though the ancient Romans would have called her Proserpina, as I recalled from my middle school obsession with mythology.

A similar song to the one she sang for me in the shower back in Denver filled the air, and the crowd listened, entranced by the beauty of her voice. And more than just the crowd, the feline theriodan Rosemary had called Neko, whether tiger, panther, or lion to his compatriots' wolf and hyena, sat beside Seph, his head resting on her thigh as she stroked his lustrous black hair. Seeing a woman in a tank top, jeans, and boots with a tuxedo-clad supermodel of a man lying in her lap before a Roman fountain seemed a bad cliché of pretty much every perfume ad I'd ever seen on television. Tears welled in his green cat eyes and trailed down to the dark denim covering Seph's leg, and yet his expression suggested they were not tears of sorrow, but of joy.

Even Rosemary stood as if in rapture, taking in the entire curious scene, her body swaying side-to-side, katana held loose at her side.

"I've watched Seph perform," Rosemary whispered as I drew near, "sing song after song that can hold an entire arena under her spell." She dropped to one knee as if her legs would no longer hold her upright. "But this moment?" She looked up and met my gaze with tears forming at the corners of her own eyes. "This is magic."

In the moment, I wasn't sure if Rosemary's words were hyperbole or just straight truth, but one thing I understood was that the man resting in Seph's lap like a well-fed pussycat could attack her at any moment, and lullaby or not, he had to be dealt with.

I strode over, the longer of Danielle Delacroix's swords brandished before me and the shorter held close at my side in reserve, both blades glowing with the Light in case I needed the extra juice.

"Please," Neko said as I came into his field of vision, "I beg of you, don't ruin what may be the most perfect moment of my life."

"Dude"—I took another step toward Seph and Neko—"in case

you've forgotten, your buddies were doing their level best to gut me like ten minutes ago."

"Bygones." His eyes left mine and dreamily wandered to Seph's all but glowing face, her own eyes resting closed as she continued to sing, her body swaying in time with the tune that sprang from her as if a living thing. "All I ask is that you let her finish, and then you and your friends may go with my blessing."

"I don't think you understand how this works, Tony the Tiger. You're outnumbered two-to-one, and last I checked, your friends—"

A hand at my bicep stopped me mid-sentence. Rosemary stood to my right, a strange half-grin plastered across her face as she gave my upper arm a gentle squeeze.

"Just let her finish, Ethan." She rested her head on my shoulder. "Mother always said that some moments should be savored rather than severed."

I n one of the strangest reversals of my couple decades on this planet, Seph, Rosemary, Neko, and I had adjourned the whole "attempted kidnapping/fight to the death/impromptu concert out of a Disney movie" to having drinks at the Caesars Palace sports bar like we were old college buddies. We sat around a circular table beneath an enormous bank of televisions showing pretty much every sporting event occurring that day, half a dozen movies, and at least three syndicated runs of *The Office*. Neko and Rosemary sat next to each other across from Seph and me, Rosemary doing her best to avoid the curious gaze of the jungle cat in our midst, while Seph and I held hands beneath our side of the table, her grip not nearly as insistent as I'd have expected after the events of the preceding hour.

Though I appreciated the wisdom of staying sober in a public place where we'd just narrowly avoided yet another attempted abduction—not to mention the fact that at latest count, there were at least three different groups of Ascendant after Seph—my patience was at an end.

Come hell or high water, a stiff drink was in my immediate future.

A tiny Asian woman in a slinky black cocktail dress came and took our order. Neko asked for a whiskey neat and I followed suit. Seph ordered tequila, a Don Julio Reposada neat with a slice of lime to be exact. Even Rosemary, ever the responsible one, skipped her usual ice water in favor of a Coke Zero, though she did ask Seph for a sip of her drink when our server returned.

Neko, whose eyes appeared human again, had undergone an even more miraculous transformation: from vicious would-be kidnapper to the guy buying rounds to make up for the previous "misunderstanding." And the strangest thing? I actually kind of liked him.

"So, now that we've all sat down to talk like adults"—I stared around at my three tablemates during a lull in what was some of the most surreal small talk of my entire life—"is someone going to explain to me what the hell happened earlier?"

Neko blew off the question with a shrug and a laugh while Rosemary's eyebrows rose as she studied Seph like an entomologist might a strange new beetle discovered in their own back yard. Seph, in turn, kept her eyes in her lap, avoiding all our gazes, mine in particular.

"Well?" I asked. "One second we're fighting for our lives against yet another team of rogue Ascendant out for blood; the next, the entire damn mall stops what they're doing to sing 'Kum Ba Yah' with Seph and Tiger Boy here." I matched gazes with Neko and raised my hands before me in a friendly gesture. "No offense, of course."

"None taken." Neko smirked. "Though I did catch that 'Tony the Tiger' joke." He shook his head with a quiet growl. "Never heard that one before."

"Sorry. Still working on the witty battle repartee." I turned to the silent pop star sitting next to me, and all eyes at the table followed mine. "And now for the elephant in the room. Your singing, Seph. That was amazing, spellbinding even, but how did you know to do that?"

She pulled her fingers from mine and returned her hand to her lap, a place from which her eyes had yet to deviate since we'd all sat at the table.

"What do you want me to say, Ethan?" Her entire body shook, whether from fear, anger, or sadness, I wasn't sure. "I was terrified for my life, and I didn't know what else to do. I don't have superpowers like you, and I can't fight like Rosemary." She finally met my gaze. "So, I sang." She took a sip of her tequila. "It's what I do."

"But how did you know that would work?" I stared at her, incredulous.

"I have no idea." She glared at me, her eyes filled with both emotion and tears. "How do you know how to make solid steel glow just by thinking about it?"

"We're not talking about me, here," I grumbled. "I mean, Neko had you at his mercy. He could just as easily have ripped out your throat on the spot as listen to you."

"As if I would ever damage so perfect an instrument, not to mention a neck so flawless." Neko's lips spread in a smarmy smile. "I'd as soon take a razor to the Mona Lisa."

Color rose in Seph's cheeks at the gruesome compliment.

"Fine, Neko. Let me ask you, then." I locked gazes with the tiger sitting across from me. "What was it in Seph's little lullaby that made you stand down? Why are we all sitting here together like we're on the last day of a college road trip?"

"I just said it." Neko gave Seph an appraising up and down. "I've heard her on the radio, seen her on TV, but to experience a Persephone Snow serenade up close and personal is another thing altogether, wouldn't you agree?"

"What's the old saying," Rosemary asked, "about music having charms to soothe the savage beast?"

"It's 'savage breast,' actually," Seph answered with a faint smile, "but yeah, I think it's something like that. When I'm on stage, I can feel the song, the music, like electricity flowing through me. The band feels it. The crowd feels it." Her eyes slid closed, her grin growing wider by the second. "When I really get in the zone, I don't have to think about the words or the melody or harmony. I just sing. It's like...magic."

"Magic?" I asked. "Like—"

"Look," Neko interrupted, "I'm not stupid. I know that there's a bounty out for the one and only Persephone Snow—to be honest, for reasons I don't understand—but we weren't stalking her or anything. Admittedly, the boys and I were quick to take advantage of the situation presented, but it's not like we're one of the squads hunting her down."

"Squads?" I asked. "And how many of these squads are there?"

"Who knows?" Neko took a sip of his whisky. "You do know you're in way over your head, don't you?"

"That's what everyone keeps telling me." I sucked in a frustrated breath. "So, you and your buddies were just walking along, spotted us at the buffet, and figured you'd go for whatever bounty is on Seph's head?"

"Not our finest day, I must admit. We're usually a bit more circumspect in our activities. Linus doesn't like losing face." He glanced Rosemary's way. "And if you hit Harold as hard as it sounds like you did with that motorcycle, he's going to have a pretty rough recovery."

"Come on, Neko." Rosemary scoffed. "You seriously expect me to believe you three just happened to be on the Vegas strip as we were passing through?"

"Maybe you lot are just passing through." Neko snorted a chuckle. "But me, Harold, and Linus? Hell, we practically call Sin City home these days." He peered around the room. "Wine, women, and song? Everyone having the time of their lives? Where else would we want to be?"

"And you're not afraid you're going to get booted by the authorities if you lower yourselves to public kidnapping?" Rosemary asked.

"First, I already said I was sorry." He scrunched up his nose, the feline in his features making an appearance. "And second, you'd be shocked if you had any idea how many times we've ended up helping out the Vegas PD over the years." His voice dropped to an ironic whisper. "Whether we meant to or not."

"Wait," I asked. "You guys help the police?"

"What, you think Ascendant all sit in underground lairs and plot overthrowing the world? We're not all bad, Harkreader, and we've got lives too."

"But separate from the rest of humanity, I guess?"

Neko considered the question. "My kind survive by avoiding the notice of the majority of people who walk this world. Even with the wonders Ascendant can perform, normal human beings outnumber us by many hundreds of thousands to one. If the populace at large ever learned of us, they would do what humans have always done."

"Hmm." I hadn't thought of it that way. "Makes sense."

"Our society is separate by necessity, and has been for longer than anyone truly knows." Neko met my gaze. "Despite all of us having to fly beneath the radar to stay alive, however, most aspire to rise above the necessary secrecy and covert existence thrust upon us by our shared birthright." He smiled, a sad laugh parting his lips. "What the hell do you think we're Ascending from, anyway?"

CHAPTER 26

TAKE IT ON THE RUN

"Absolutely not." Luc Delacroix, his gravitas diminished not one iota by the makeshift sling supporting his injured arm, glared at his daughter and me. "You can't seriously want to bring someone like him with us." His eyes shot briefly to Neko, still in his tuxedo, albeit a bit frayed around the edges, who stood a safe distance away on the dusty shoulder by the Vegas Speedway. "I mean, he and his associates attempted to kidnap Miss Snow just hours ago, and now he wants to ride along to help keep an eye on her?"

"He did say he was sorry." I suddenly felt like my five-year-old self explaining a broken cookie jar to my mother. A glance through the intact half of the bus windshield revealed Gus watching me, his head shaking slowly from side to side. "I don't know. He seems sincere."

"You don't understand theriodans like I do, Mr. Harkreader." Delacroix turned his attention to Rosemary. "And you, young lady, should know better."

Young lady. Wow. Never heard Delacroix talk to Rosemary like that before.

"He made a mistake, Father."

"A mistake that could have cost Miss Snow her life." Delacroix shot a nasty look in Neko's direction. "Or worse."

"Now, Father." Rosemary's eyes narrowed. "Neko may not exactly be innocent in all this, but he is no—well, he's not like that."

"Just a kidnapper, then?" Delacroix grunted. "And what of his friends? The hyena?" His own eyes drew down to slits as he met his daughter's gaze. "And the wolf?" He let out a disappointed sigh. "They're animals, Rosemary. Beasts of the wild, as untamable as the wind."

"The plan was to turn her in unharmed as the contract requires," Neko half-shouted from across the way. "We weren't going to hurt her. I swear."

Rosemary shot Neko a look that said in unequivocal terms that he wasn't helping.

"Did you learn nothing two years ago?" Delacroix continued to rail at his daughter. "Did the burn from your dalliance with the trickster coyote not leave deep enough of a scar?"

Rosemary deflated like a torn parade balloon. "I can't believe you'd bring that up in front of Neko." Her voice descended into a sharp whisper. "Or Ethan."

So there's a coyote too, huh? Probably best if I pretended I didn't hear that.

"Tell me, Rosemary," Delacroix asked, "what reason could you possibly give that would make me even consider this?"

"He can come." Seph stepped out of the bus where she had gone to clean up, her torn tank and jeans replaced with a sweatshirt and cargo pants that she somehow made look not only fashionable, but sexy. "But I'd like to talk with him first."

She walked across the street to where Neko stood. All of us, Gus included, looked on as they held a private conversation that lasted two minutes but seemed to take a month. When they were done, Seph returned to our circle.

"My decision stands."

"But, Miss Snow," Delacroix groaned, "you can't seriously be considering—"

"Mr. Delacroix, with all due respect, you're injured." Seph shifted her gaze to Rosemary. "Your daughter, for all her skill, is up against shadow-dealing assassins and elemental mercenaries, and now these theriodan people are in the picture." She looked to me, her eyes filling with both care and concern as her voice dropped to a whisper. "And Ethan, even with the power he inherited from your dearly departed wife, is still learning the ropes." She inclined her head in Neko's direction. "Would it be so wrong to have a tiger in our corner?"

Delacroix raised an eyebrow. "The tiger that just tried to kidnap you in broad daylight?"

"Neko didn't hurt me in any way, has humbly apologized, and assures me that going forward, he will have my back."

Delacroix ground his teeth. "Please, Miss Snow. You've hired me to keep you safe. I ask that you simply allow me to do my job."

"And I ask, Mr. Delacroix, that you trust my judgment." Her hands went to her hips in a move I already recognized as Seph digging in her heels. "With all due respect, my life has been in danger for far longer than since I learned about skiomancers and elementalists and theriodans, longer even than you've been in my employ. The threats may have escalated recently in power and influence, and I appreciate all you've done to keep me safe through it all, but I am still Persephone Snow. There will always be someone who wants to take advantage of my position or wishes me ill as long as I'm in the public eye." She glanced back at the tiger waiting across the street. "Neko may hang with the wrong crowd, but best as I can tell, he isn't any danger to me."

Delacroix stood dumbfounded, studying the woman in his charge before looking for support from me and finally from his daughter. Then, with a defeated wave of his hand, he gestured for Neko to join our circle.

"You are taking a tiger by the tail, Miss Snow," he muttered as he gestured for Gus to start the engine. "I suggest you hold on tight."

~

"How much longer until we hit L.A.?" I checked my watch. "We've been on the road for over an hour."

For years, I'd been using the maps app on my phone for anything but the shortest trips, but whatever magic or computer virus or technomancer crap was keeping our tech from working had basically turned my smartphone into a glass and metal brick that could play solitaire but apparently not much else.

Neko, who had remained quietly curled up in one of the bus seats opposite Seph and me since we left Vegas, stretched and yawned like a house cat, and set his face in a quizzical expression, his eyes going up and to the left in calculation. "We're likely coming up on the California border." He licked his lips. "Probably four or so hours to go."

"Thanks." Though far less threatening in the too tight t-shirt and baggy sweatpants he'd borrowed from Seph, I never forgot the tiger stripes that hid beneath Neko's tawny skin.

Outvoted three to one on Neko joining us, mostly due to Seph's insistence, Delacroix had moved to the front of the bus for this leg of the trip. I'd asked if he really wanted to sit behind a half-shattered windshield the five hours to L.A., and he'd made it clear he had no interest in riding in the back with Neko or the rest of us until he'd had a few hours to cool down.

It was as mad as I'd seen him, and I'd been with the man the morning after his wife was killed before his eyes. Rosemary had vouched for the tiger, Seph had spoken, and I, for once, kept my mouth shut and hoped Delacroix's instincts would not be proven right.

I sat with Seph opposite Rosemary and Neko, not only out of a sense of protection for the woman of the hour, but also because Rosemary clearly knew Neko best—God knows what that story was —and would be best equipped to deal with him if he decided to pull a heel turn en route to Los Angeles.

An hour of barely interrupted silence left me a lot of time to think.

For some reason, the tiger in our midst left me wondering nonstop about this "coyote" from Rosemary's past. Her father had called him—or, I suppose, possibly, *her*—a trickster. Maybe that relationship had been strictly professional, another aspect of the role the Daughter of Neith held among the Ascendant, but it certainly didn't seem that way.

"So, Neko, you're the first Ascendant who has stopped trying to kill me long enough that we could have a conversation."

He raised an eyebrow. "What do you want to know?"

"I was just curious. How does it happen?" I shifted in my seat, a bit uncomfortable. "I mean, how did you find out that you were...different?"

"Wow." Neko pulled himself straight in his seat. "Never been asked that before."

Flat and matter of fact, I couldn't tell if the statement was legit, dripping with sarcasm, or somewhere in between.

"Let's see." Neko's nose scrunched in an already familiar expression of thought. "I guess I always knew something was different. A lot of kids I grew up with liked climbing on jungle gyms, stealing into places they weren't supposed to go, getting back into nature—you know, normal kid stuff. But even doing parkour on some of the taller buildings in Cleveland as a teen, the occasional breaking and entering—I was never caught, by the way—and a hunting trip or two with my dad when he was still around didn't quite scratch a certain little itch."

"Itch?"

"I'm a tiger, Harkreader, stuck in a human body. I was supposed to be an orange-and-white, black-striped killing machine roaming the jungle for fresh meat. Instead, I wound up stuck as a ninth grader doing algebra and world history in a room full of adolescents so musky even humans could smell their stink."

"Wow," I chuckled, "and I thought my high school experience sucked."

"What about the eyes?" Seph asked. "And the moves and reflexes and all that?"

Neko graced Seph's question with a far more positive response, his face lighting up at her words like the countless other fans we'd encountered over the preceding months.

"Some of it started when I was a kid. The whole 'cats always land on their feet' thing? That's me. Any normal person would've been dead or at least hospitalized taking some of the falls I've walked away from without a scratch." He puffed out his chest in pride. "The other stuff started around middle school. Everybody else was freaking out over getting pubes. Meanwhile, I was fighting the instinct to pounce on anything that moved. Tigers are naturally nocturnal, did you know that? You know what's not? The rest of the whole damn world."

"You mentioned your mom and dad." I studied his expression, the war raging in his features. "How did they deal with all your...stuff?"

"*Mom* did fine, like any decent mother with a kid going through puberty." Neko shook his head. "Some of the changes I went through were beyond anything she had the capacity to understand." A vibratory sigh, all but a purr, filled the space. "But God bless her soul, she did her best." His eyes dropped. "*Dad*, not so much."

"Your mother," Rosemary asked, the first words she'd said in quite a while, "is she still with us?"

"Mom?" Neko asked, the curtain of years parting on a teen boy who still loved his mother very much. "Yeah, she's fine. Back in Cleveland with my stepfather. Her first marriage didn't exactly survive...me." He gazed out the window at the passing "Welcome to California" sign. "I don't make it back there much, but we email, and I sneak a peek at her Facebook from time to time. She's got my brothers and sisters and her grandkids to keep her busy." His shoulders dropped. "I just try to stay out of the way."

"You should go see her." Rosemary's gaze dropped to her lap. "You never know when you might never have the chance again."

Neko was quiet for a moment. "Sorry about being so crass back at Caesars. The boys and I always thought very highly of your mom despite the times she kicked our collective asses over the years. Please understand I meant no disrespect toward you or your mother, God rest her soul."

"Your apology, Neko," Rosemary said with a quiet nod, "is noted and appreciated."

I'm not sure which surprised me the most, the reverence in the theriodan's voice, the all-but-royal status Danielle Delacroix and her line held among many of the Ascendant I'd already met, or Rosemary's kind, if not formal, response.

In any case, Neko was behaving, and at least so far, Delacroix's concerns seemed to be misplaced.

But the words "tiger by the tail" captivated my thoughts, and I continued my internal exercise of every few seconds mentally unsheathing the sword resting at my feet.

"Hey, Rosemary, if it's not too delicate a subject," Neko asked, his face a mask of contrition, "have you heard from Maddox?"

Rosemary stiffened. "Are we seriously going to discuss him?"

Maddox? Must be the coyote Delacroix mentioned.

"We haven't heard from him in ages," Neko continued. "None of us have since, well, you know."

"Perhaps that is for the best," Rosemary answered. "May I suggest we focus on the present instead of dredging up the past?"

"Message received." Neko curled back into his chair, admonished, though for reasons that continued to be unclear.

One thing was for certain, though: "Maddox" and "Coyote" were two words that would remain out of my lexicon for the time being.

"So, everything's all lined up in L.A., right, Seph?" I did my best to shift the conversation back on track. "Your tour manager has got to be freaking out with you missing."

"Everything is full steam ahead, as far as I know." Seph and I had already covered this ground hours before, but she was picking up what I was putting down and answered the question as if the topic were brand new. "Whatever ailment has hit our phones and the rest of our communication equipment apparently can't hit every landline west of the Mississippi. I finally got through to Trish back at Caesars and let her know we should be there by tonight. Fortunately, the stage is all set up at the venue, and all they're waiting on is me for rehearsals and sound checks."

"Did she buy the story we came up with?" I asked. "I mean, it's pretty far-fetched."

"I told her we had an accident that crunched the front of the bus and injured Mr. Delacroix and that we had to stop overnight in town for repairs and to get him medical attention." She shrugged. "Honestly, that's barely a lie." A quiet sigh escaped her lips. "In any case, she's just glad to know I'm all right and that the show is still a go."

"From your mouth to God's ears." Rosemary shook her head. "As I see it, we have yet to make it to Los Angeles." She peered out the window. "And as we've learned the hard way, a lot can happen along four hours of highway."

"So, four hours to go." Neko murmured from his seat with a mischievous laugh. "Whatever shall we do between here and there?" He eyed Seph. "Anybody up for cards?" He raised an eyebrow. "We could play a little strip poker to keep it interesting."

"In your dreams, tiger boy." Rosemary rolled her eyes.

"Like it's you that's on my mind." His furtive gaze passed from Seph to me before returning to Rosemary. "Then how about a few rounds of Truth or Dare?" His already devilish grin grew wider. "I'm just bursting with questions about what's going on with you three."

"I just bet you are." Rosemary was taking no prisoners. "You've been invited along on a trip because we needed a little extra muscle. Don't pretend that we're all buddies now."

Neko crossed his arms, his lips in a subtle pout. "Well, I suppose we could all just sit here and stare at each other until we get to Los Angeles."

"Two truths and a lie." Seph perked up. "For each one of us, the other three can guess which statement isn't true. That way, we can all get to know each other better, but no one has to reveal anything they'd rather leave unsaid."

"I'm in," Neko said, a strange eagerness coloring his words. "Harkreader?"

"Sure," I said with a hesitant smile, "I'll play."

With my answer, only Rosemary remained without comment.

"Fine," she muttered eventually. "If we have to play some sort of game, that one sounds harmless enough."

"Great!" Neko's gaze wandered around the room, landing briefly on each of us. "Now, who wants to go first?"

"I'll go, I guess." I considered for a moment. "Let's see. Okay. I once got stuck on an elevator with Lady Gaga for half an hour when she was on tour; back in high school, I played Kenickie in our school's production of Grease; and I've never been outside the U.S." I peered around at all of them. "Which is the lie? What have you got?"

"The Kenickie one, right?" Seph asked. "Because you are totally my Danny."

"Nope." My cheeks flushed. "It was me and Rizzo for three straight weeks."

"Lady Gaga?" Rosemary asked. "She's another performer, like Seph, right?"

"Wrong again."

"Really?" Seph asked. "What's she like?"

"As delightful as you might think. I was admittedly a bit starstruck, but..." Seph's expression twisted almost imperceptibly as I began to explain further, prompting me to shift the topic of conversation. "Anyway, I hit most of Europe last year working tech for a band out of Ireland and that's when I met—"

"*Boring.*" Neko answered in sing-song tones as his eyes drifted closed. "Wake me up when you all want to play a game with some teeth."

"All right." Seph stepped up, a mischievous smirk etched across her features. "First kiss was behind the piano in first grade with Brad Durden; first time was with the son of one of the producers on *Teen Spies*, totally legit and legal, by the way; and the strangest place I've ever, you know, was backstage at a show in Seattle on top of a couple of—"

"That's enough detail," I interrupted before Seph could finish.

"Now we're talking." Neko sat up straight and leaned forward on his elbows. "I'm guessing you've done it in way kinkier places than that, Miss Persephone Snow."

"Perhaps." She looked to Rosemary. "What do you think, Rosemary?"

"The boy from first grade?" Rosemary answered. "You were so young."

"Maybe." She patted my knee. "Ethan?"

"Oh, I'm pleading the Fifth on this one." I took her hand, a move that caught Neko's attention and, strangely, Rosemary's as well. "But, do tell."

"This round goes to Rosemary." Seph offered her a friendly grin. "I may have been a child star, but I was a bit of a late bloomer when it came to matters of kissing, et cetera. First kiss was Brad Durden all right, but that was my ninth-grade spring dance. Mom was chaperoning and broke that up real quick."

"Yet again," Rosemary pulled in a breath, "our mothers sound a lot alike."

"Your turn, Rosemary." Seph raised an eyebrow. "Tell us something we don't know about you."

"Yes, Rosemary," Neko rested his chin atop steepled fingers. "I'm all ears."

"Hmm." Rosemary's cheeks pinkened a bit. "Mother never let me date, so I was a bit of a 'late bloomer' myself."

"Well," Neko said, "we know that one's true."

Rosemary and Seph both shot Neko a sharp glance, quieting him instantly.

"Ummm…" Rosemary's face continued to flush. "That wasn't one of mine, but okay." She considered for a moment. "My first kiss was at the age of nineteen, and—"

"That's two truths." Neko fell to one side, chuckling to himself. "She may not know it, but I was there and can confirm."

"Shut it!" I shouted, quieting Neko's laughter.

"Let her talk," Seph added.

"I'm not very good at this, I guess." Rosemary's already pink features ran full scarlet. "Mother always taught me never to lie."

Seph moved to Rosemary's side. "It's just a game. You don't have to say anything else." She glared in Neko's direction. "This was about getting to know each other, not leaving you mortified."

"No," Rosemary said, "it's fine." She peered around at each of us. "Since my turn has been ruined—thanks so much, Neko—I suppose, by the rules, my final statement must be a falsehood." Her eyes locked with mine. "And since all of you know that already, my words will clearly reveal a third truth."

"Rosemary," I whispered, "don't."

"It's okay." She quieted me with a subtle nod and a raised palm. "Somehow, it would seem I've made it to twenty-one years of age," she cleared her throat, "and I, Rosemary Delacroix, have never been in love."

CHAPTER 27

BROKEN WINGS

Gus pulled off I-15 in Victorville, California for gas, a little over an hour from our hotel. Rosemary and I stood guard by the bus while Gus pumped, Delacroix escorted a fully incognito Seph inside, and our feline friend skittered off to do God knows what.

"You never told me." I steeled myself for the blowback. "How is it exactly that you know Neko? You know, if it's okay to ask."

"Neko and me?" she answered without looking up. "We go way back."

"You're twenty-one years old, Rosemary." I studied her, trying to parse what could have happened to leave a woman who charged headlong into danger against living shadows, man-beasts, and the elements themselves so skittish over what sounded like a bad breakup. "How 'way back' can you and he really go?"

"Understand something, Ethan. I fought off my first skiomancer when I was nine and Mother was sick. I may be young, but I've been at this for quite a while."

"Sorry" I stepped back. "Sometimes I forget who I'm talking to."

"It's all right." Her foot kicked back against the side of the bus, she tilted her head back so that her crown just kissed the cool metal beneath the "SPARKLE" logo. "Why are you asking about Neko?"

"I don't know. I've only known you a few days while you and Neko have known each other for what? A couple of years?"

Rosemary studied me through narrowed eyes. "You're fishing, Ethan. What is it you really want to know?" A sharp intake of air shifted her inquisitive gaze to one of understanding. "Oh, of course. You want to know about Maddox."

"Maddox?"

"And I thought I was a bad liar." She shook her head. "You're perceptive, Ethan. You clearly picked up on my conversations with Father and Neko before, and you're sensitive enough to figure out that talking about Maddox is the last thing I want."

"Three for three." I took a step back. "Sorry. Didn't mean to pry."

"It's okay." She kicked off from the side of the bus and began to pace. "It's been two years. I really shouldn't let him get to me anymore."

"Was Maddox a boyfriend?"

"My first and only," she answered quietly. "First infatuation, first kiss, first love, first..." A shudder overtook her body. "The best six months of my life, followed by the worst year."

"What happened?"

"As Mother told me when it was all said and done, 'What almost always happens.' In the grand scheme, it's not that big of a deal, I guess. I may not be the most well-versed individual in matters beyond what Mother taught me of my family's place among the Ascendant, but I've seen, read, and experienced enough to know I'm not the first or even the million-and-first to suffer a broken heart."

"What did he do to you?" The myriad of potential offenses a coyote in human form might have committed flitted through my mind. "Did he...hurt you?"

"Nothing like that." She shook her head. "One day he was there, and everything was good. The next, he was gone, and everything was...not so good." She let out a long sigh. "Promises were broken, trusts violated, assurances abandoned. Devastated, I didn't sleep a full night for three months, and I lost anything approaching an appetite for way longer than I care to remember. I lost over twenty pounds by the end of the whole thing, if you can believe it."

"Twenty pounds?" I gave her a quick up and down. Her body remained as lean as any magazine cover model's. "From where?"

"It wasn't pretty." Her eyes shifted left and right. "I was virtually a skeleton for weeks. My clothes just hung on me, and still I couldn't eat. Nothing Mother or Father said or did could break me out of my downward spiral. I thought I was going to die." Rosemary's poker face, usually on point regardless of the situation, broke as the emotions welling within her soul played out across her features.

"What did you do? How did you make it back to...this?" I motioned up and down at her general badassedness. "I mean, have you seen you lately?"

"Thanks." She huffed out a single laugh. "You'd think it would have been Mother, but in the end, it was Father who got through to me and brought me back from the brink. After that, I focused on my training, forced myself to eat, figured out that weighted blankets and heating pads helped with the various aches that kept me from sleeping, and slowly but surely, I clawed my way out of the hole." She nodded, biting her bottom lip as if convincing herself as much as me. "Some days are easy and some days are hard, but I'm back now, and I'm not going anywhere."

"I certainly hope not." Seph rounded the corner of the bus with a stuffed plastic bag in her hand and Delacroix in tow. "I don't know what I'd do without my new ninja-bodyguard-BFF to hang with."

Startled at the interruption, Rosemary and I both instinctively took a step away from each other. Our shared moment had been innocent, but the undeniable pangs of guilt bubbled up anyway. I'd done nothing but listen as Rosemary shared a painful secret from her past, but the connection between us, for those few moments, had been palpable.

Had Rosemary felt what I had? And, if so, what did that mean?

"Ready to go." Gus popped around the opposite corner of the bus with a thumbs up and headed for his vehicle's driver's seat.

"We restocked on drinks and snacks for the last leg of this trip." Seph handed Rosemary a Mocha Frappuccino, her new favorite. "Everyone ready?"

"Where's Neko?" Delacroix rumbled, his voice like thunder from a gunmetal grey sky. "Already decided to venture off on his own?"

"To the contrary, daddio," came a voice from above. From atop the gas station's canopy, Neko leaped down, executing a complex dismount on par with some of Rosemary's best moves. "I was just keeping watch while you all did your thing."

"You were up there the whole time?" I asked, my cheeks suddenly hot. "What? Were you listening in on our conversation?"

"First, Harkreader, I have more important things to do than listen in on private chats. Second, the next time someone pulls guard duty while everybody else takes five and gets snacks, you could just say thank you. And third?" He pointed into the distance to the east. "He probably doesn't know I spotted him since he's hovering a mile out observing us with binoculars, but does anyone know a guy in a white suit who can fly?"

"Falco." I shook my head. Here we'd been, sitting ducks out in the open, and the only person paying enough attention to keep us safe was someone who'd only been invited along by the skin of his tiger's teeth. "What do we do?"

"Nothing else to do." Delacroix's lips became a straight line. "We head out."

"But they know where we are," Seph said. "Is it safe?"

"All Neko has done is confirm what I've suspected for hours. The whereabouts of Krage and his skiomancers notwithstanding, I'd have been legitimately surprised to learn Ada and her people had lost track of us after our most recent confrontation. They do, after all, command the forces of nature itself."

"Not to mention the tour schedule has been online for months," Seph whispered, visibly shaken. "The question is, if they know where we are, why haven't they attacked us again?"

"They're biding their time." Rosemary cracked her neck as if preparing for a fight. "We've managed twice to prevent them from abducting you, Seph, and both times cost them more than they likely anticipated. Unless I'm way off base, I suspect they're simply waiting for the right opportunity."

"Let's not give them one, then." Neko motioned to the doors leading into Seph's studio apartment on wheels. "Shall we hit the road?"

~

"Back in L.A." Neko snorted. "Swore I'd never set foot in this town again, and yet, here I am."

All of us stared at the lean, mean, self-reputed killing machine in our midst. After forty-five minutes of silence as we headed west into Los Angeles while the rest of us discussed plans for what we'd do if attacked, he finally spoke up.

It hadn't escaped my attention that at the end of our game earlier, he'd failed to volunteer any information about himself.

I wasn't sure if I was happy or worried that he'd decided to rectify the situation.

"There's a story there, and we're still like an hour from the hotel." I motioned for him to continue. "Spill."

Neko stared out the window, clearly uncomfortable. "What Rosemary said before, you know, got me thinking, remembering." He shifted in the seat to face me. "Not to mention, Harkreader, how you asked earlier about my being different. How I knew."

None of us said a word. For my part, I was still a bit wary of our resident tiger by the tail, and yet, I was curious about what could leave someone so brash at a loss for words.

"Imagine discovering you're a tiger at the tender age of twelve. Cleveland is only about two percent Asian, so you're already the odd kid out in seventh grade, and then your eyes go all weird, everything starts to smell funny, and you have to keep yourself from chasing after every bird and squirrel that crosses your path."

We all listened. Rosemary kept an air of cool detachment—not surprising as I suspected she already knew a lot of what he planned to say—while Seph leaned in, giving Neko her full attention, her inner therapist coming out to say hi.

"By sixteen, I'd made it to L.A. The City of Angels was going to be my new home, my fresh start, my reset." His eyes slid closed. "I found my people, a new place to hang my proverbial hat, and my first love." The way he whispered that last word made it clear the story wasn't going to have a happy ending.

"It was all good for the first year. I got work washing dishes at a diner along with a few side gigs, made some connections, and found a place to stay with a few other recent transplants from all over. Then, some dude at work told me one day I should try out for a commercial that was casting a few blocks over. One of the big chain pharmacies, as I remember. Went the next day, gave it my best shot, and got told I just wasn't right for the part." He snorted out a chuckle. "But I didn't really care all that much because that was where I met Quinn."

"Quinn?" Rosemary asked.

I wasn't sure which surprised me more, that Rosemary hadn't already heard this story, or that she seemed to actually care.

"Preacher's kid from West Virginia. We were auditioning for the same commercial, and both got told unequivocally that we would not be getting a call back. Too Asian and too Black, I suspected, though they didn't come right out and say it." Neko grumbled something under his breath and then continued. "Quinn had moved to California a year before me and was a year or two older, which suited me just fine. When we met, it was all fire and lightning like you see in the movies. Less than a month later, we moved in together, a studio apartment over a restaurant in Inglewood. The owners let us work in the kitchen to keep rent down, and for a while, things were perfect."

"Nothing gold can stay," Seph murmured, the Robert Frost sentiment the theme of one of her first hits. "What happened?"

"Inglewood, Compton, that whole area of L.A. has come a long way, but a decade ago? Not exactly the safest place to be." His eyes drifted to one side as if deep in thought. "Quinn and I were walking home from the corner grocery one night when a couple of gangbangers decided to jump the wrong people." His lips drew down to a thin line, his eyes squinted in ten-year-old anger and frustration.

"Seeing Quinn lying there bleeding, not knowing whether he was going to survive the night—"

"Wait," I asked before my brain caught up with my mouth, "Quinn is a man?"

"Careful, Harkreader." Neko shot me a raised eyebrow. "Your Knoxville is showing."

"No, it's cool." I mentally backpedaled, my cheeks getting hotter by the second. "It's just...the tux and all the muscles, not to mention the way you looked at Seph, and—" I quickly figured out my every word was not only proving his point but digging the hole deeper. "Never mind," I whispered, "please, continue your story."

Neko shook his head and laughed. "First, thanks for noticing. The soul of a mighty tiger may reside within my flesh and bones, but it's not like biceps and pecs like these just happen." A full-body flex inside Seph's t-shirt which fit him like a second skin showed off his compact physique. "Second, it's all good. No harm, no foul." He smiled. "And third, I've got a much thicker skin than I did back then."

"What happened?" Rosemary asked, no longer disengaged. "Did Quinn make it?"

"I made damn sure of it." Neko fumed. "Let's just say the men who attacked us learned real quick not to harm the partner of someone who harbors an untamed animal lurking just behind their eyes."

"Did you kill them?" Seph asked, her voice low and eyes downcast.

"It was close, but no." Neko shook his head. "They'll both be explaining those scars for the rest of their lives, though."

"So, you saved Quinn." Seph leaned in, clearly moved by the story. "He must have been grateful."

"Oh, I saved him, all right. And not just that. I let him see the tiger within for the very first time." He looked away. "In all its glory, for what it's worth."

"And he didn't like what he saw, I'm guessing." Rosemary lowered her head.

"I thought he looked terrified when those assholes jumped us." Neko's voice grew quiet. "It was nothing compared to when I reached out a hand to help him up from the ground." He ground his teeth, his canines flashing in the low light of the bus's interior. "He never looked at me with anything but fear ever again, and within a week, he was gone. Didn't even leave a note."

"All you did was defend him." Rosemary's cool tone had warmed considerably. "I can't imagine how that must have hurt."

"Quinn and my dad, the two most important men in my life." He paused, his voice cracking. "Both threw me out of their lives for pretty much the same reason."

"Go ahead." I tilted my head forward. "It's okay."

"Dad didn't want a 'sissy boy' for a son, and Quinn couldn't handle the tiger inside me. Each of them in their own way made it quite clear I wasn't *man* enough to be in their lives." Neko cleared his throat, forcing away the emotion that threatened to choke him up. "Anyway, I left L.A. as soon as I got my shit together. Traveled the country from one end to the other. Made ends meet and kept my head down. Eventually found out what I was, met some other theriodans, and found a group that accepted me for who I am."

"You mean Linus and Harold?" Rosemary's eyes filled with warmth. "How many times have I told you, Neko? You're different from them. Better than them. You do know that, right?"

Neko fixed Rosemary with a fierce glare. "Neither of them have ever once looked down on me for being exactly who and what I am. Acceptance is a powerful motivator when everyone else looks at you as if you're lesser than."

"Lesser than?" I asked. "You're Ascendant."

"Tell that to Quinn." Neko muttered. "Or my dad."

"They were wrong." Rosemary pulled close to Neko and, in a surprising show of compassion, wrapped an arm around his shoulders. "So, prove them wrong. Turn it all around." Her voice dropped low. "I told you two years ago that continuing to run in the wrong circles was never going to get you anywhere. Agreeing to help us is a start, but no matter how much you feel accepted with Linus and Harold, that path is only going to lead to pain."

"And you would know." Neko locked gazes with Rosemary. "If I haven't said it enough, I'm really sorry about everything that went down back then."

"Water under the bridge." Rosemary smiled.

"Good to know." Neko leaned back in his chair and stretched the lean muscles of his arms and torso like the jungle cat that hid just beneath the surface. "So, what now?"

"We get Seph to the hotel, to rehearsals on time, and through the next thirty-six hours." I took Seph's hand. "After that, I guess we all sit and talk with Rosemary's dad and bring in whoever along the tour we can trust. Los Angeles may be the last stop on this leg, but the European leg is just a few weeks away. We've been lucky so far, but we've made it to this point by only the skin of our teeth."

"Something's got to give." Seph shook her head. "I get the whole 'the show must go on' thing, but it feels like this is never going to end."

"My earlier misbehavior aside, Miss Snow," Neko bowed his head, "rest assured that if those nasty shadowmancers come for you, they'll have to get through me first."

"God help them if they show their ugly faces again," Rosemary added, patting the sheathed sword at her hip.

"We've got this." I gave Seph's fingers a gentle squeeze. "Whatever it takes."

CHAPTER 28

FEELS LIKE THE FIRST TIME

"And you're sure you two are going to be all right?" Dino had kept his mouth shut all through the thankfully uneventful rehearsal that evening, doing his job with the same overenthusiastic diligence which he applied to every aspect of his life, but once we arrived back at the hotel and were away from the rest of the crew, he'd demanded the play-by-play of the various assaults we'd fended off since we'd last seen him in Denver. "If I'd known all that was going to go down, I'd have come along with you guys. I'd have been there and—"

"And probably got yourself killed." I clasped his shoulder. "You've already come through for us more than once when the chips were down, and thanks to you running interference with all the questions flying around from the crew and everybody, not only is the show still a go for tomorrow night, but we've managed to keep at least some of what's happening under wraps."

"It wasn't easy, Ethan." Dino bobbed his head left and right. "I'm not the world's greatest liar, but it was important, and I gave it my best shot."

"And for that, Dino," Seph touched his cheek, "I am eternally grateful."

"No problem, Miss Snow." Dino's cheeks flushed crimson, and I could practically feel the heat radiating off them. I totally got it. It wasn't every day the biggest pop star of the decade addressed you by name. "You just let me know if there's anything else I can do to help."

"Just keep up whatever plausible deniability you can about the weird goings-on with Ethan, Rosemary, Mr. Delacroix, and me." Seph shot me a sidelong glance. "Once tomorrow night is behind us, we can discuss what happens next."

Another knock came at the door to the bus, this one the familiar signal Delacroix used to announce his presence.

"Miss Snow." Delacroix popped his head inside. "Hotel security has swept your entire floor along with the rest of the hotel. No one meeting the description of any of your would-be abductors has been seen by any of the current staff on duty nor on any of the security footage of the last twenty-four hours." He stepped onto the bus and gave Seph a self-satisfied half-smile. "You'll be pleased to know the most suspicious activity was a gathering of half a dozen tweens in the lobby hoping to sneak a peek as you checked in."

"Good to hear." Seph looked past Delacroix at Rosemary waiting outside with Neko. "And what about you two? Anything to worry about?"

"Nothing we can see from the highest vantage points in the area. No way of knowing if Krage and his skiomancers, Ada's group, or Neko's theriodan friends are nearby, but—"

"But everything looks, sounds, and smells kosher at the moment." Neko cracked his neck. "It's funny. All this time, and it never occurred to me how well personal security service aligns with my particular skill set."

"Don't dislocate your shoulder patting yourself on the back just yet," Delacroix said. "We still have to keep Miss Snow safe tonight, all day tomorrow, and out the other end of tomorrow evening's show before we can breathe."

"I'll keep watch over Seph tonight and make sure everything is okay." No sooner had I inserted myself in the conversation than I wished I'd remained silent.

"Don't stay up too late, Harkreader." Neko studied me with a smirk. "Tomorrow has the potential to be a big day. Wouldn't want you showing up all worn out. "

"I'm not certain what you're trying to insinuate, Neko," Seph countered, perturbed, "but Ethan has been nothing but a perfect gentleman since our very first meeting." She crossed her arms before her chest and narrowed her eyes. "You and your friends could learn a thing or two from him."

"Oh, please," Neko snickered. "Never forget that the pheromones that pour off people tell a story all their own, and lately, it's been like a perfume store around here." He studied each of us in turn. "The only thing I can't quite figure out is whose hormones are running the hottest."

"Stand down, Neko." Rosemary stepped between me and the theriodan, shooting him a no-nonsense glare. "Playful banter is all fine and good, but talk like this is—"

"Playful?" he said with a sneer. "Hey, I just call it like I smell it." He tapped the side of his right nostril. "The nose knows, as they say."

"Just because a series of words pops into your head doesn't mean you have to say them." Delacroix scowled at Neko. "Are we clear?"

"Clear as clear can be, daddio." He turned toward Seph. "My apologies, Miss Snow, if I spoke out of turn. May your evening be filled with virtue and your honor continue unsmirched."

Rosemary rolled her eyes in exasperation. "That wagging tongue of yours is going to get you in trouble someday."

"Someday?" Neko laughed. "There I was, hanging with my buds in Vegas, minding my own business. A couple rounds of drinks later, I'm on the side being hunted by not only those very friends, but two Ascendant mercenary squads, any of which could end us all in a New York minute if the cards fall right." He surveyed us all with a devilish grin. "How much more trouble do you think I can get into?"

No one said a word as we pondered Neko's words. In the end, the least likely of us broke the silence.

"Well, if that's it for the day," Dino said as he moved for the door, "I'm going to grab a bite and crash for the night."

"A good idea. We should all turn in early." Delacroix shot me a not-so-subtle raised eyebrow. "We've got a long day tomorrow. Miss Snow has to perform, and the rest of us will have to be at our absolute best in case any of the groups who have already made a play for her make another attempt or, God forbid, yet another Ascendant faction decides to throw their hat in the ring."

"And this hotel is the best we can do?" I asked, peering out the bus window at the building's sheer facade of glass. "Nothing but windows straight up. What keeps Falco from getting her room number and tornadoing a bowling ball right through the building to get to her? Any of Ada's people could make short work of this place if they put their mind to it. Hell, if Neko's theriodan friends got inside, they could literally go room to room, sniff her out, and take down the door. And God only knows what Krage and his skiomancers might have up their sleeve if they decide to make another play."

"All the more reason that the only people who will know exactly where Miss Snow is to be sequestered overnight are on this bus."

"Sequestered?" Seph groaned. "Not exactly the word a woman wants to hear the night before the final stop of her second U.S. tour."

"Don't worry," Neko purred. "I'm sure you and Harkreader can find something to occupy yourselves with until morning."

"*Neko.*" Rosemary grabbed the tiger by the ear and gave it a good twist. "Have you ever in your life simply let a thought continue to ricochet around in that demented mind of yours instead of loosing it upon the world?"

Neko inhaled to let fly another scathing insinuation, but the twin glares of Team Delacroix convinced him to keep quiet. Regardless, his eyes spoke loudly enough.

Backing Seph's call that we bring Neko along had seemed the right thing to do at the time, but as I studied his feline smirk from the corner of my vision, I saw things Delacroix's way far more than I had before. The extra muscle had seemed smart, and keeping a possible problem close at hand had also appeared to be a good idea. But now, when secrecy rather than brute force was paramount to surviving the next twenty-four hours, I found myself wishing for one less set of eyes and ears on the bus.

"We've randomized several rooms on five floors, most of which will be empty, to make guessing Miss Snow's location a gamble. As long as we keep our senses about us, I feel we've done all we can do, outside of checking her in with the local police, and I don't think any of us want to do that."

"Still, it's just the first night of thousands." Seph's lip trembled with trepidation. "What do we do tomorrow night after the concert? And the night after that?"

"Whatever comes, we'll face it." I took Seph's hand and pulled her gently into me.

"Once we get you through tonight," Rosemary added, "we have several weeks to play with before the European leg of your tour begins." She forced a half-smile. "Father knows of safe houses the world over where we can—"

"Thanks, Rosemary, but I can't think of safe houses or danger or any of this for another moment." She turned to her mountain of a bodyguard. "Mr. Delacroix, take me to my room, please. I need to rest."

"Of course, Miss Snow."

"You'll still stay with me, won't you, Ethan?" Not that there was any question about my answer, but I doubt any man alive could have resisted her doe-eyed stare in that moment of vulnerability. "Please?"

"Nowhere else I'd rather be."

I waited for the inevitable snark from our resident feline in human flesh, but when Neko not only held his tongue but instead offered me a nod of affirmation, I had no idea what to do but answer in kind.

"Father and I will be next door, Seph," Rosemary offered, "should anyone be foolish enough to come for you in the night."

"And I, fair maiden," Neko said with a deep bow, "will scour the rooftops for any of my ilk or anyone else who might wish you ill." He shot Delacroix a minimally penitent glance. "I can sleep tomorrow when the rest of you are awake."

And now, the moment of truth. With Neko off doing his own

thing, we either had an ace in the hole against our enemies or an inside job in the making.

I hoped we'd all awake the next morning to the former and prayed that allowing a tiger into our midst didn't end up being as bad an idea as my gut suggested.

~

"Can it be?" Seph turned all the locks on her hotel door. "Alone? Just the two of us? And nobody bleeding for once?"

"Until some crazed lunatic comes flying through that plate glass window, at least."

At her cross glance, I immediately wished the words back into my mouth.

"Hey, I've been dying to have you all to myself again for the better part of two days. Don't spoil it for me." Her eyes studied me through those long dark lashes of hers. "For us."

"Of course not." I breathed a quiet laugh. "It just seems like the quickest way to make things start exploding is to put the two of us alone in the same space."

"Oh, I'm predicting some fireworks, Mr. Harkreader." She flashed a furtive smile. "Contrary to popular belief, explosions aren't always a bad thing."

I swallowed so hard, my Adam's apple practically bounced inside my neck. "Mr. Delacroix said we needed to keep our guard up tonight. God only knows if—"

"Mr. Delacroix is on the other side of that wall and more than capable of doing his job." She gestured with exasperation. "I swear, it's like he's the father I never had, he's chaperoning me at prom, and my date is texting with him instead of looking at me."

"I'm sorry, Seph, but I've had to watch no less than three different groups of superpowered mercenaries try to steal you away and take you from me, and no matter what I've done, they just keep coming. What if I can't stop them next time? What if I lose you forever?"

"What if you just let the world down off your shoulders for five minutes and actually live?" Seph sat on the end of the bed and cradled her chin in her hands. "Look, I appreciate everything everyone has done for me since all this began, and no one more than you. Having my own personal knight in shining armor step into the breach every time danger rears its ugly head has been quite the heady experience. But King Arthur isn't who I need right now." She patted the bed by her hip. "On the other hand, an hour or so with Lancelot would go a long way toward making me feel better."

Wow. I'd never really given that name a lot of thought before.

"The last few days have been the most exciting and simultaneously the worst of my entire life," Seph continued. "Would it be so bad to get lost in each other for just a little while? Forget about skiomancers and theriodans and elementalists and just be young and in love?"

The word escaped her lips before she could stop it.

"I mean," she stammered, "you know what I mean, right?"

"No need to wish the words back, Seph. I love you too." A nervous tingle worked its way down my spine. "I know it's quick and everything, but—"

"Don't qualify, Ethan. I heard you just fine." She squeezed my knee. "And sorry about the backpedaling. Wearing my heart on my sleeve has left me bleeding more than once, and way more recently than I care to remember."

"Spencer Cole?"

"I don't want to discuss anyone else right now except you and me."

My heart skipped a beat. "Got it."

A furtive smile peeked through her solemn expression. "In case no one's ever told you, Ethan, independent of whatever abilities you've suddenly inherited that let you fight off all that's bad in the world, *you* are a good man. With you, I feel safer than I've ever felt with anyone in my entire life." She laughed. "Funny. The fact that I can have a conversation on this level with someone I've known less than a week tells me everything I need to know about you." Her eyes slid closed. "About us."

"I have to tell you, Seph." I studied her flawless features, my heart pounding. "This all still seems so surreal."

"And yet, here we are." She scooted closer to me until our hips touched. The room filled with electricity. "Just you and me." She curled into me and rested her temple against my chest. "Whatever shall we do?"

"But you have to perform tomorrow. I don't want to—"

She placed her finger to my lips. "I certainly hope you're not worried about tiring me out. You may be one cape short of Kryptonian these days, but I've been dancing and singing for three straight hours several nights a week for months."

"It's not that." I looked askance, not quite willing to meet her eyes. "I just don't want to hurt you."

"Hurt me?" She raised an eyebrow. "What kind of weaponry are we packing, Mr. Harkreader?"

My cheeks flushed. "No, no, no. It's not that. I just—"

"Stop." She turned her body to mine, bringing her thigh up and over my lap to straddle me at the end of the bed. "You're not going to hurt me. You're not going to mess up the show. None of the million other things that you're worried about are going to happen." She nuzzled my neck, running a series of kisses from my collarbone up to my ear, ending with a gentle nibble at my earlobe. "I've been running for my life for days, barely escaping one horrible fate after another, and the only thing that's kept me sane through all of it is you. You've been there for me every time without question, even when the world was falling down around our ears." Her crystal blue eyes gleamed despite the dim light of the hotel room. "Now that everything is okay, even if it's just for a moment, just be with me, please."

"Are you sure?" My body responded to her nearness, though my mind still reeled in disbelief. "I mean, really sure?"

"Ethan Harkreader." She brought her lips to mine, and with them a potent mix of passion and peace the likes of which I'd never felt before. "I've never been surer of anything in my entire life."

269

CHAPTER 29

IN THE AIR TONIGHT

"I can feel it." The ozone smell, the tension in the air, the palpable electricity: the potent combination raised the hair on my neck. "Something's coming," I shouted at Seph, the roar of the crowd scant feet away deafening. For all my trepidation, the woman before me had never looked more radiant or more in her element. "I don't know what it is, but—"

"It's gonna be great?" Seph shouted back at me with an amused wink on her face. "I couldn't agree more."

"No." I wondered if this was what Peter Parker felt when those little squiggles appeared above his head in the comics. "Something bad." I pulled close to her so I could speak to Seph and only Seph. "Are you sure you should go on?"

"First, Ethan," she spoke into my ear, just loud enough to be heard over the din, "we did this back in Denver, and everything went okay." She brushed my cheek with her lips. "Second, it's a little late to back out now, don't you think?"

270

The roar of the crowd rose a few decibels as the pre-show music kicked into the lead up to Seph's opening number.

"It's never too late"—I returned her kiss, pulling her lips to mine for a sweet couple of seconds before completing my thought—"until it is."

"Then I'll just have to trust that you, Rosemary, Neko, and Mr. Delacroix can keep me safe for the next three hours." Her eyes went to a tape-marked X at center stage. "I've got to go."

"I know." I stared through the thick curtain at the invisible crowd of thousands. "Be careful out there. You see something dangerous, you run, understand?"

With a quick smile and a confident nod, she headed for her mark. I returned to the wings where Rosemary and Mr. Delacroix waited, reviewing every event of the day.

Seph and I had enjoyed breakfast in bed courtesy of the hotel, though after Delacroix's shakedown of the poor attendant who brought our omelets, waffles, and coffee to the room, I felt obligated to offer the kid a pretty fat tip.

Seeing Mr. Delacroix's face first thing the next morning had brought new meaning to the word "awkward." Seph and I had kept things as quiet as possible out of respect for our across-the-wall neighbors, but Delacroix was a trained bodyguard, and Rosemary was, well, Rosemary.

Delacroix hadn't said as much, but his expression at our door revealed he understood fully that Seph and I had crossed a significant rubicon in our relationship. In the set of his features, I found neither approval nor disapproval, merely the tacit understanding that things were different now, not to mention the clear understanding that I had stepped into another realm of responsibility.

She'd called Delacroix the father she never had, and now I was feeling it too.

Funny, I don't know what I'd have done if Rosemary had been standing at the door with her father in that moment.

Something to chew on later.

From there it had been sound checks and hair and makeup and

the rest. We'd all had a strangely quiet lunch together, Neko included, with Dino running interference midday with the rest of the crew. I'd stood personal guard as Seph took a much-needed and well-deserved afternoon nap and made sure she'd made it to the venue for makeup and costume well ahead of schedule. Honestly, the day couldn't have gone better.

Why, then, couldn't I shake the feeling of unmistakable dread that it was our last day together? Not just me and Seph, but all of us. Something was coming, and unless my gut was way off, nothing would ever be the same again.

I settled in the wings between Delacroix and Rosemary as the pre-show music headed for the bombastic moment when all sound and light would cut out, leaving the frenzied crowd ready for the moment they'd all been waiting for.

"Seph okay?" Rosemary asked, two of the maybe three dozen words she'd said to me that day.

"She's fine." I shook my head in exasperation. "Everything's fine." I ground my teeth. "Why do I feel like everything's not fine, then?"

"We feel it too, Mr. Harkreader." Delacroix motioned in Seph's direction. "And I'm certain Miss Snow does as well."

"And yet, she's just going to go on like nothing is wrong?"

"She's a professional, Ethan." Rosemary studied me, those big brown eyes of hers touched with a hint of sadness. "It's what professionals do."

All at once, the entire place went dark and the music pounding from hundreds of speakers went silent. The crowd did its best to fill the gap with a cacophony of claps, stomps, cheers, and whistles. And then, the crystal tinkling that had started every concert throughout the months-long tour began in earnest.

Time for Seph to "Sparkle."

As the four-count drumbeat I'd heard dozens of times over the preceding months sounded and the curtains parted on the number one pop star in the country, if not the world, I peered around backstage, amazed at how the rest of the planet continued on as if we weren't all potentially at ground zero of an attack by men and women who walked the world as gods.

In the far corner, Jerry Reid worked with the crew to ensure that the show went off without a hitch. He hadn't had much use for me upon my arrival earlier in the day. He was smart in the same way Delacroix was, and he believed my status as Seph's "personal assistant" about as much as he believed in Santa Claus or the Tooth Fairy. Still, since Dino was shouldering all my responsibilities and, quite frankly, doing them at least as well as I could've, Jerry seemed to be dealing okay.

It was funny how Dino's constant earnestness seemed way less annoying when it came down to brass tacks and his ride-or-die mentality became an asset. After all the rolled eyes and behind-the-back snickers, I desperately owed the man an apology. More, I owed him respect and friendship, both of which he'd earned in spades.

More things to chew on, if we all survived the night.

Gus sat in the wings. He'd decided to come in and actually catch the show for once rather than his usual practice of waiting on the bus. Well-deserved after all he'd gone through to ensure Seph made it to L.A. in one piece, she'd gotten him his own director's chair and seated him next to a couple of teens who'd won backstage passes in a radio contest. I'd questioned Delacroix on the wisdom of having teens backstage when an attack seemed imminent, and he'd shrugged. His world-weary wisdom about the benefits of "knowing which things are under your control and which ones aren't" still rattled at the back of my brain.

Seph launched into the second verse of "Sparkle," bringing my attention back to the woman of the hour, the woman who'd come to mean everything to me in just a few short days. I could still feel her skin on mine, experience her scent, her taste on my tongue, and the potent electricity that rested behind those crystal blue eyes.

My heart and mind warred as I watched Seph enchant the audience in her first costume of the night. As it had every night since the tour began, the white tank, miniskirt, tiara ensconced within her platinum locks, and those knee-high platform boots boosted her sex appeal into the stratosphere. Tonight, however, seeing her strut about the stage hit me a bit differently. Suddenly jealous of her connection with the thousands beyond the stage, the memory of our hearts beating out their own intertwined rhythm the night before helped quell my insecurity.

She'd said she loved me, and I'd told her I loved her as well. Simple as that.

Still, being in love with an international superstar was going to take some getting used to.

"If we both survive the night," I muttered, as the doom cycling through my mind began another spin.

Delacroix, Rosemary, and I looked on with bated breath as Seph belted out "Sparkle's" final chorus, her opening song drawing to a close without event.

One down, two dozen to go.

As had been the case at every show since the first, the spiderweb of spotlights that met centerstage at Seph's feet went black at once, plunging the entire arena again into darkness. My heart froze in the interminable five seconds before the drummer kicked into the opening syncopation of "Kiss Me at Midnight," and I'd never been so glad to see stage lights come back up in my life.

Once you've fought actual shadows, being in a pitch-black room becomes a very different experience.

At the end of yet another unmistakable John Hart run across the drum kit, the band took the stage as they had at dozens of shows over the tour. Jimmy Katz stared out from beneath his dark curls as he made his bright red Gibson guitar sing, Peter Freund answered with a few bone-crushing tones from his big black bass, and Missy MacArthur filled the spaces in-between with lush tones from her bank of keyboards. Seconds later, Seph's pair of backup singers appeared from the dim, the dark-skinned Mandy King and blonde and freckled Joelle Reece elevating the pure tones of Seph's crystal-clear vocals into rich three-part harmony.

Each of the seven on stage reveled, as they had every night of the tour, in the adoration of the pure white spotlights that poured light down from every corner of the enormous arena.

That is, until the shadows cast by those very same lights, one by one, began to rise from the stage. At first, the audience was into it. I guess the appearance of a shadowy entourage for "Kiss Me At

Midnight" seemed like a pretty cool stage stunt to the uninitiated. The illusion fell away, however, as Seph's backup singers belted out a pair of amplified shrieks and dropped their mikes. The music ground to a screeching halt in seconds, the sonic void soon filled by screams from stage and audience alike.

"Shit."

I was out of my chair in an instant, Danielle Delacroix's blades in my hands already glowing with Neith's Light. With Rosemary close on my left flank, we charged the pentad of ephemeral silhouettes that surrounded Seph. Though the shadows encircling Seph kept their distance, isolating her from the others while not harming or attacking her, the dark phantoms assaulting the remaining members of the band proved far less congenial.

"You go high," I shouted to Rosemary, hearing her mother's words come from my own lips, "I go low."

Her only answer a nod, Rosemary was in the air half a second after I'd spoken. She hurled one of her two remaining flashbang grenades at the feet of Seph's guitarist, the resultant flash and bang dispatching back to darkness the trio of shadows tearing at Jimmy Katz's clothes and pulling at his dark curls. Meanwhile, I slid across the stage, one glowing blade slashing through the pair of shadowy forms rising around Peter Freund's legs as I hurled the shorter of the two blades into the air, its bright blade flipping end over end straight at the spotlit drum kit besieged with shadows.

"John," I shouted to the terrified drummer, "catch!"

John Hart's bearded face shifted instantly from confused fear to crystal clarity.

I prayed that a man who routinely caught thrown drumsticks midair on a darkened stage while keeping a double bass drum kicking and maintaining the beat for an entire band night after night could catch one lone blade without difficulty. Still, I'd never been so relieved as when the sword ended up in John's massive hand and not the center of his chest.

With a flourish only a professional drummer could execute, John swept the still-glowing blade through five shadows in one intricate maneuver, held the sword before him behind his massive kit in a pose right out of *Mortal Kombat,* and with a quick salute, hurled the blade back at me. No sooner had I snatched the sword from the air, yet again using reflexes downloaded into my brain just days before, than he shot me an impressed nod and fled backstage. Without missing a beat, I shifted to rescue Seph's beleaguered keyboard player as Rosemary raced at the pair of screaming backup singers, both of whom writhed on the stage as a confluence of darkness tortured them both.

As I impaled the pair of shadows attacking Missy MacArthur with a coordinated scissor-slash of both blades, Rosemary hurled the last of her flashbangs into the air. The grenade rose and fell in a high parabolic arc, and then, not to be outdone by a mere expert percussionist, Rosemary flung one of her throwing knives. The compact blade struck the flashbang mere feet above the backup singers and their shadowy attackers, the burst of brilliance annihilating the swarming black shapes and allowing the two women to escape backstage.

The floor and seats in front of the stage cleared as the crowd rushed the exits. Here and there, a person limped away having been trampled by the fleeing crowd, but everyone I could see seemed to still be on their own two feet. I hoped the trend continued, especially considering that this particular boxing match was about to enter Round Two, and all bets were off.

That left me and Rosemary on opposite ends of the stage with a beleaguered Seph still at its center. Surrounded within a pentagon of shadowy figures, the wispy arms of each silhouette stretched to either side as if engaged in some sort of ritual, Seph stared wide-eyed off the stage. As the woman I'd professed my love to less than a day before somehow kept herself from screaming, the focus of her panicked gape became clear.

The void left by the fleeing mob of Persephone Snow fans now held four dark forms in full length black cloaks, brimmed hats, and masks like the corvids that were their namesake. No smokescreens or subterfuge this time—the Ravens had come knocking.

Krage, Rupert, Fala, and Dmitri in all their skiomancer glory glared at us with renewed confidence through their avian masks.

Krage stood at the center with his three subordinates standing to his left, right, and rear, forming a diamond of cloaked forms.

"We made short work of your shadows as always, Krage." I moved in Seph's direction. "Call off the ones surrounding Seph and walk away."

"While you still can." Rosemary took a step forward. "Trust that I've already learned a hard lesson about showing mercy to a skiomancer."

"You pathetic children," Krage said, his thick accent lending menace to his words, "so full of yourselves and your perceived superiority." He pointed at Rosemary. "You, girl, have proven quite formidable, but you haven't your mother's power to back up your skills." He turned his attention on me. "And you, boy? You have simply proven more fortunate than I'd dreamed possible."

I crossed the paired blades before my chest. "I've got a lot more where that came from."

"I'm quite certain you do," Krage whispered, "but the time for play is over."

The other three Ravens raised their arms in concert, and shadows from one end of the arena to the other rose from every surface, blocking exits as far as the eye could see and sending the screams of the already terrified crowd into a frenzied cacophony of panic-stricken wails. Nobody else in the crowd, it seemed, was going anywhere. Then, at a twirl of Krage's index finger, the five shadows encircling Seph converged on her and lifted her struggling form high into the air above the stage.

"Let her go!" I shouted.

"End this, Krage," Rosemary directed her katana at the Raven leader. "So far, I've left you and your associates alive at every encounter, but if you force my hand—"

"Quiet, girl." Krage shook his head confidently. "Regardless of what I said before, we won't be underestimating you this time." He again flicked his gaze in my direction. "Either of you." He crossed his arms as he regarded me with simultaneous contempt and concern. "No surprises this time, Harkreader? No aces in the hole to bring out now that the chips are down?"

"Well," came a voice from above, "perhaps one."

Unleashing the tiger whose heart beat within his chest, Neko dropped from a catwalk above the gathered skiomancers to land before Krage, a matching pair of daggers from Rosemary's personal stock gripped in his clenched fists. Before anyone could so much as take a breath, the tiger slashed with his borrowed claws, tearing open both the front of the Raven leader's cloak as well as the flesh of his chest, leaving a pair of crossed slashes in a bloody X.

As Krage dropped to one knee, the shadows holding Seph aloft dissipated, sending her plummeting toward the stage.

"No!" I screamed, running to catch her knowing I'd never make it across the stage in time. "Seph!"

I'd barely made it three steps when a hurricane blast of wind shot upward from the floor, knocking me on my ass while catching Seph mid-fall and depositing her safely back on the stage.

Next, a burst of flame high above the floor seats set off sprinklers across the entire arena, turning the entire place into a gigantic sauna.

In seconds, the falling water began to pelt sideways, hammering me with hail that stung like bullets.

Just visible through the impossible deluge, a tongue of concrete rose from the floor and grabbed Neko before he could make another move, encircling his legs and waist like a boa constrictor of stone.

"You'll pay for this, you filthy animal." An infuriated Krage glared at Neko who struggled to free himself from his concrete snare. "But first," he said, cracking his neck, "to complete our business." He looked past the captured tiger and again met my gaze. "I certainly hope you've brought more than a lone theriodan to aid your cause, Mr. Harkreader, for as you can see, you aren't the only one who has discovered the wisdom in forming unconventional alliances."

CHAPTER 30

CROSSFIRE

As if on cue, the other quartet of Ascendant who'd plagued us since Denver came out of the woodwork, though each had already made their presence known.

First came Falco, their aeromancer, who dropped from the topmost reaches of the arena like a bird of prey only to stop twenty feet off the floor to hover above the gathered skiomancers. He'd taken the time to acquire a fresh white suit, and his dark sunglasses remained firmly in place above his permanent half-grin.

Next came their leader and pyromancer, Ada, who literally burst onto the scene in an orange ball of fire. The waves of heat radiating off her form evaporated the water pouring down from the sprinklers above before so much as a drop could touch her fiery robe.

At the far corner of the stage beyond where Rosemary stood, a whirlwind of water and ice brought the purple-and-turquoise-clad Violeta back into our midst, her long dark locks no longer braided but cascading down her back like a dark waterfall, the visual befitting the group's hydromancer.

And lastly, a hunk of concrete the size of a small car sent chairs flying as it erupted from the center of the floor, twisting and churning like dough in a blender until achieving the rocky sumo form preferred by their geomancer, Daichi.

A quartet of pissed off shadow assassins and all four forces of nature versus a rookie representative of Neith, a college-age ninja who was fresh out of flashbang grenades, a theriodan wrestling without success against living concrete, and a terrified pop star who'd nearly fallen to her death seconds before and who only still lived by the grace of the very individuals standing against us.

At every corner of the giant arena, people scurried for the doors like cockroaches with the lights flipped on. The falling water and flying shades had spread terror and confusion, leaving injured and trampled forms in every direction, and the appearance of the elementalists at the center of the space did little to improve the situation. With terror after terror at its core and every exit blocked by shadow, the entire arena soon devolved into a pressure cooker of panic, and the main course had yet to be served.

"Interesting, I must say." Rosemary sauntered to the lip of the stage soaked to the bone, keeping one eye on the hydromancer in the wings as she addressed Ada. "Until a few seconds ago, I got the distinct impression that you and Krage's skiomancers were each other's competition." Her face twisted into one of scorn. "I never dreamed any of you would stoop so low as to work with their ilk."

"Strength in numbers, little Delacroix." Ada stepped forward, a ball of fire coruscating with orange shimmer a foot above her outstretched palm. "Something your own side seems to be lacking by my estimation."

"Indeed," Krage added, turning his beaked mask my way. "Admittedly, what becomes of Miss Snow once our combined forces are finally rid of you lot is a bit up in the air, but to never hear your stupid name again, Harkreader? Worth it."

"But why her?" I motioned to a drenched and shivering Seph who stood petrified centerstage as the artificial deluge continued to rain down. "Who is this person who is so hellbent on taking Persephone Snow? What do they want with her?"

"As if that is any of your concern, boy." Falco sneered down at me. "You're in no position to be making demands. Forget not that it is only by my good grace your lungs still reside within your chest," he chuckled, "or that your new lady love doesn't lie there on the stage bleeding this very moment."

"If it weren't for me, she'd have died back in Denver, or have you forgotten you threw her off a building?"

"To be fair, I'd been shot." Falco offered a half-apologetic shrug. "You try and maintain control over the wind itself when you've been winged by hot lead." He shifted his attention to Rosemary, his brow furrowing. "And speaking of broad-shouldered Frenchmen with more firepower than brains, where exactly is your father, Miss Delacroix? We've already taken out the vast majority of this place's security, but dear old Dad was nowhere to be found."

Without a word, Delacroix emerged from behind a curtain, his tread stealthy for a man his size. Grabbing Violeta from behind, he shoved the barrel of his pistol hard into her back. His arm about her waist, he forced her forward toward the front of the stage, his eyes narrowed in concentration at Ada and Krage. "Listen up. You Ascendant may be long-lived and heal fast, but you're not invincible. I suggest that all of you consider your next action carefully."

"Advice you'd best follow yourself, Luc Delacroix." Falco laughed. "Truly pathetic. Consort to a Daughter of Neith for over two decades and you don't know any better than this?" He motioned to the pyromancer below him. "While Ada and I may simply bend our respective elements to our will"—he inclined his head toward the gigantic sumo of concrete—"and Daichi there cocoons himself within his"—he tilted his head forward to stare at Delacroix above his dark sunglasses—"Violeta simply *is* water."

In an instant, the woman in Delacroix's arms disintegrated into a puddle at his feet only to shoot up behind him as a spout of water that quickly resumed human shape, if not substance. In an instant, the hydromancer's index finger elongated into a six-inch icicle which she positioned at the vestibule of her captive's ear canal. "Hold very still, Mr. Delacroix. I'd hate to have to show you what I can do with my little finger of ice."

"You all have proven most fortunate thus far," Falco continued, "but from the beginning you've been woefully out of your league, and none more so than a man whose only power over the world rests within a gun." With a wave of his hand, the aeromancer summoned a blast of wind that sent Delacroix's pistol flying end over end into the darkness at the rear of the stage. "Now, do yourself a favor and keep your tongue while I and my compatriots make very clear how the next few minutes are going to go."

"Release him!" Rosemary dropped into a low fighting stance, her katana at the ready. "Or I swear I'll—"

"Rosemary," Seph said, breaking her silence, "stop."

"But—"

Seph raised her hand, quieting Rosemary, and turned to face Krage and Ada who stood side by side, fire and darkness personified. "You've proven your point. You have us outmanned, outflanked, and outgunned." Tears formed at the corners of her eyes. "No one else will be hurt today over me." She bowed her head as if in prayer. "We will hear your terms."

"Our terms?" Krage laughed. "Our terms are simply this. You come with us without another word while the rest of your bunch of junior league wannabe superheroes looks on in defeat."

"Personally"—Rupert stepped forward, obviously still furious from his team's previous two defeats—"I'd have preferred the version of the plan where we leave you all in pools of your own entrails, but I was outvoted."

Ada looked to the skiomancer leader. "I thought, Krage, we agreed that your subordinates would remain silent during our negotiations."

"First, these aren't negotiations, and second, all of your people have had opportunity to get in their digs." He studied her through the lenses of his Raven mask. "You must admit that my team has faced at least as many frustrations as yours at the hands of our shared adversaries." He surveyed the room. "But your point is well taken. The time for grandstanding is over. Let us take our prize and be gone."

Before anyone could take a breath, the roar of a gun sounded from darkness at the back of the stage. An instant later, Falco dropped from the air and landed atop Rupert, sending the two men tumbling to the floor in a knot of arms and legs. As crimson spurted from his thigh, a bloody rose blossomed along the otherwise pristine white of what I guessed were extremely expensive slacks.

"Dammit," Falco grunted as he pulled himself up from the ground. "What do you people have against new suits?"

A second gunshot sent a bullet flying at Ada, the tiny projectile burning up in the corona of heat around her body like a meteor hitting the stratosphere. In answer, she sent a fireball hurtling at the spot from where the mysterious gunman had fired, but only managed to destroy John's beautiful and quite expensive drum kit in an explosive conflagration.

As Ada scanned the stage for any sign of movement, a third shot thundered from a different part of the stage, the bullet sending Violeta's unprotected shoulder rocking backward.

Despite the hydromancer's ability to shift into water at the drop of a hat, I was strangely relieved to discover her human form could still bleed.

For the second time in as many minutes, Violeta's form devolved into a turbid column of semisolid liquid, allowing the bullet to drop to the floor with a metallic clink and enabling Delacroix to break free. Wasting no time, he made his way to Seph's side and quickly positioned himself between his charge and her would-be abductors.

"Enough!" Krage raised a fist, and a dozen shadows, at least one of them my own, rose from the floor and flew to the rear of the stage. "We haven't come this far to be picked off by some wannabe hero with a gun."

A loud crash just beyond the massive curtain followed by a series of shouts and another pair of gunshots led to a brief moment of silence. Then, the squad of shadows returned, holding aloft not one, but three men, the last remaining of our quickly growing inner circle.

With Delacroix's pistol clutched in one fist, Gus struggled against his shadowy captors. Dangling by one leg, Dino swatted ineffectually at a pair of smaller shadows that flitted around his inverted head.

And then, the last person I expected to see: Jerry Reid, my boss, his arms crossed before him and held in place as if the shadows had formed a straitjacket about his torso.

"Jerry!" I shouted. "What are you doing?"

"Trying to save your tail, kid."

"You okay?"

"I will be once you kick that shadow guy's ass and get me down from here."

Shadow guy. Jerry knew. How he knew and how much he knew, I hadn't the foggiest idea, but he knew

Because of course he did.

"You wretched people." Ada glared at each of us in turn. "You dare to cast us as the purveyors of violence, and yet you've shot poor Dietrich a second time, ruining yet another of his fine suits, and worse, you have injured my dear Violeta." Her baleful stare came to rest on me. "Stand down, all of you, or you shall see exactly what we are capable of when we throw restraint to the wind."

And...they'd been holding back. This just kept getting better.

"What precisely did you think would happen when you all started this?" Delacroix, still catching his breath, raised his arms out to his sides. "You and Krage's people have come for someone under the direct protection of the Daughter of Neith."

"Not to mention," I added, "one of the most famous people on the planet."

Ada crossed her arms, defiant. "Once word spread that Krage and his Ravens had met with difficulty in Albuquerque on what should have been a relatively simple extraction—"

"Don't you mean abduction?" Rosemary interrupted.

"Semantics," Ada growled. "In any case, we'd planned Denver as a minimally invasive operation."

"Minimally invasive?" It was my turn to laugh. "That entire block is going to be closed for months."

"Not to mention the number your earth mover did on the interstate on the way here," Neko quipped, still held aloft by the tongue of concrete protruding from the floor.

Ada's lips drew down to a tight circle. "Daichi can be a bit... enthusiastic at times."

"Well," Neko said, "if we're all going to sit and chat for a while, can he enthusiastically let me down from here?"

Ada considered for a moment before directing a quick nod in Daichi's direction. At a wave of the earthen sumo's hand, the protrusion of concrete retreated into the floor, leaving Neko uninjured in the midst of our gathered adversaries. Ada shot Krage a sidelong glance, and with a frustrated grunt, the head skiomancer ordered his shadows to lower Gus, Dino, and Jerry to the ground. A lone wisp of darkness delivered a pair of pistols, one of them Delacroix's Glock, to the floor at the skiomancer's feet.

"Violeta." Ada directed her attention to the amorphous blob of liquid that swirled at the far end of the stage. "If you have had sufficient time to get yourself together, would you be so kind as to tend to poor Dietrich?"

The five-foot column of murky water shifted into a quasi-humanoid form for a moment, and then, like some gigantic amoeba, flowed off the stage and went to Falco's side. Resuming her flesh and blood form, Violeta knelt by her compatriot and willed her arm alone to resume its liquid state. The tentacle of cloudy liquid curled in the direction of Falco's thigh and invaded the wound there, bringing an anguished groan to the aeromancer's lips.

"Quiet, Dietrich." Ada looked on, impassive. "Let Violeta do her work."

In one of the strangest moments of my life, all present disengaged for the roughly ninety seconds the delicate procedure required. At least twice, I would've sworn Falco was about to burst into a fit of pained screaming, but he kept what composure he had until a strangely satisfying metallic thunk sounded amid the still constant shower of sprinkler water.

"I have the bullet out, Ada," Violeta said after shifting back into flesh and blood, "but there is still some bleeding." She stepped away from Falco's supine form and gestured to his leg. "Care to do the honors?"

Ada stepped to Falco's side. "My apologies, old friend." A six-inch finger of fire leaped from her outstretched palm. "As always, I'm afraid this is going to hurt." She knelt by the aeromancer's wounded thigh and with a surgeon's precision, cauterized the wound. Again, Falco managed to keep from bellowing in pain, but the large drops of sweat coursing down his grimacing face told the story well enough.

When she was done, Ada helped Falco to his feet. "Now," she murmured, "where were we?"

"I can't believe any of this." I lowered the blades crossed before me an inch. "One second we're all fighting for our lives and the next we're all watching you two play combat medic."

"We're not savages, Harkreader," Ada replied, "despite what you may think of us."

"Perhaps your people, Ada"—Rosemary directed her blade at Krage's heart—"but the same cannot be said for those with whom you've allied yourselves."

"Do tell, girl." Krage chuckled, his face hidden behind his dark avian mask.

"You killed my mother, you bastard, as we tried to care for my injured father." Rosemary took a step in Krage's direction. "There was no professional courtesy, no allowance for the wounded, only heartless brutality." Another step. "Allow me to make one thing very clear, Krage. Should you live to see the morning, know that you will spend the rest of your days looking over your shoulder and praying you don't find me standing there."

"Big talk," Krage said, "from a half-orphaned girl with only a little sword to back it up."

"Now, now, Johan," came a new voice, this one like a whisper through a megaphone from another universe that cut through the pitter-patter of the sprinkler's false rain, "no need to stoop to name-calling."

From above our heads and held aloft by countless wispy slashes of darkness floated down a woman covered head-to-toe in black, though whether her clothing was dark or she was literally draped in shadow, I couldn't tell. Not one drop of water touched her, the artificial deluge rolling off her as if she were surrounded by a force field straight out of a comic book.

The various elementalists maintained respectful silence as the woman lit before Krage, while the remaining three skiomancers knelt before this strange newcomer as if she were royalty.

The Midnight Angel, it seemed, had decided to make a personal appearance.

"Can it be?" Fala pulled close to Dmitri, and despite the manmade torrent of sprinkler water, her whispered questions came through loud and clear. "Is that really her?"

Violeta helped Falco sit up, and both of them looked on, gobsmacked. Ada lowered her head in deference and quietly motioned for an alarmed Daichi across the way to stand down.

Rosemary went to her father's side and placed herself between Seph and the shadowy stranger, her face filled with a potent mix of trepidation and wonder.

Seph, on the other hand, had seen and heard more than enough.

"So," she pushed between Rosemary and Delacroix and stormed toward the woman in black, "you clearly know what the hell is going on."

"Seph!" Rosemary and I shouted as one. "Don't!"

"Miss Snow!" Delacroix yelled as she approached the front of the stage. "Come back!"

Seph ignored us all completely, leaping from the lip of the stage and hurdling the security fence in her quest for answers. "Who are you?" she asked as she stalked straight for Ada, Krage, and the strange new arrival. "Did you send all these people after me? What do you want?"

The woman clothed in darkness turned to face the reigning Princess of Pop, an amused cast to what little of her face remained visible despite the shadows and continued deluge.

"Who am I?" her harsh whisper hit my ears like a voice from another realm, sending my heart racing faster than it already sped. "I, my dear Miss Snow, am the Midnight Angel, and you'd do well to maintain a respectful tongue in my presence."

"Excuse me, lady, but I've heard just about enough—"

A complement of shadows leaped from the woman's dark form and secured Seph's arms, legs, and neck while another encircled her head and covered her mouth, preventing her from speaking further.

"Seph!" I screamed.

"She is unharmed, Mr. Harkreader." The Midnight Angel returned her attention to Seph. "Little girl, trust that I will answer all your questions with the understanding that you will show proper manners from this point on. Are we clear?"

From my vantage atop the stage, I could just make out Seph's quick nod.

"Good." With a wave of her hand, the various shadows binding Seph dissipated. "Now, shall we start again?"

Another nod.

"Better." She studied Seph from behind her veil of shadows. "Now, my dear, what do you know of why we're all here this evening?" she asked, gesturing for Seph to speak.

"Someone wants me, for reasons I don't understand at all."

"Oh, someone wants you indeed, girl."

Seph bristled at the Angel's tone. "And both Krage's shadow-dealers and Ada's elementalists are under orders to take me alive, for whoever it is they're working for."

"As I understand it, that is correct."

"As you understand it? Don't these people, or at least the skiomancers, work for you?"

"They did." The Midnight Angel cast one weary look in Krage's direction. "Once."

"But I thought you sent them to take me."

The woman clothed in shadow crossed her arms and sighed. "Truth be told, though we are all of the Shadow, I did not in fact send them, Miss Snow. Regardless, I am glad indeed to have made your acquaintance."

"Then why are you here? Who *is* responsible for all of this? What could they possibly want with me?"

"The last of your questions is the most obvious, though I'd have thought you'd have figured it out for yourself by now." Her head tilted to one side. "As for who is responsible for your current misery, it could be one of several people, but alas, I do not have that information." She pulled in a long breath, the sound an unnerving hiss. "As for why I am here..." She took Seph's hand. "Simply, it has been quite some time since I've been present for an Ascension."

"An Ascension?" Seph asked. "What the hell are you talking about?"

"Three different groups of Ascendant have come for you over the last few days, Miss Snow, each attempting in their own way to sever your ties with your old life and welcome you to a new world." The Midnight Angel studied Seph with a pitying gaze. "Have you truly not yet discerned the reason why?"

CHAPTER 31

SONGBIRD

"I'm...one of them?" Seph asked. "I mean, one of...you?"

"You were closer the first time, dear, but yes." The Midnight Angel released Seph's hand and took her by both shoulders. "You are Ascendant."

"Or at least you will be."

All present swung about as yet another unfamiliar voice, this one with a Spanish accent, entered the fray. If the Midnight Angel's words hit the ears like an angry snake's hiss, this new voice possessed the finely tuned timbre and musicality of an opera singer.

A woman with ageless tawny features and long dark tresses that flowed to her calves approached. Clothed in opulence, her fitted dress covered one arm and left the other bare, the shimmering fabric hugging her flawless form from a deep red at her shoulder to a bright gold at her feet as if she wore a sunrise. Even to my untrained eye, there was no doubt the golden triangles and diamond clusters that made up the belt encircling her waist were the real deal, and I suspected the matching shoes cost more than I make in a year. More than anything she wore, however, the aspect of this woman that captured my imagination most was her gaze: eyes green like emeralds and keen like a hawk's.

"El Ángel del Alba." Rosemary dropped to one knee as did Ada and all her brood.

The difference in reverence given this second Angel to enter the space brought a frustrated sigh from the first.

"Alba," she whispered, the word as much warning as greeting.

"Midnight," the woman answered in kind.

As the two women took each other's measure as if neither had laid eyes on the other in years, a connection formed in my mind: Los Angeles truly was the City of Angels.

I pulled close to Rosemary. "Didn't your father say there were three of them?"

"Yes. Three Sisters, though none related by blood. Two share the same city, while the third has chosen the opposite coast as her home for longer than most who walk this world have been alive." Rosemary's voice, already a whisper, dropped a few more decibels. "I've never met her, but if rumors serve, she makes her shadowy sister there seem positively effervescent."

"Careful, girl." The Midnight Angel shifted her dark eyes in our direction. "I may have walked this world for longer than you can imagine, but my ears work just fine."

The color stole from Rosemary's cheeks. "My apologies, Madame Midnight."

"Better." Midnight turned her attention back to her estranged Sister and we all wisely held our tongues as the two women squared off. "I see you've sent your latest collection of hired guns to collect our fledgling Ascendant."

"And I, Sister, see your little team of mercenaries gathered here as well."

Madame Midnight forced a laugh. "Krage was indeed once one of mine, but in this sequence of events, he and his band of skiomancers acted alone." The shadows clothing her all shifted at once, and her dark attire transformed into a jet-black counterpoint to Alba's dress.

Her revealed face pale as the full moon in a cloudless night sky, she studied us with dark eyes that peered from beneath immaculately groomed eyebrows and a pixie cut of deep brown hair with just a hint of curl. "My agents comprise a worldwide Conspiracy of Ravens far beyond anything this Murder of Crows might aspire to be."

Krage stepped back, as if physically wounded, but still didn't mutter a syllable.

"You expect me to believe that you're not the mind behind their malfeasance?" Alba asked. "I know you better than anyone still walking this world. Such boldness would seem your trademark."

"Believe what you will, Sister. It matters not to me." A faint smile returned to Midnight's eyes. "Though I note that, as I understand it, your own people have lowered themselves to ally with Krage and his underlings." She raised a manicured brow. "It would seem that you rather than me, dear Sister, are the Angel working with Crows."

Fire flashed in Alba's eyes. "An oversight I will deal with at a later date."

Midnight glanced in Krage's direction. "I have little doubt of that."

"So," Alba said, her eyes narrowing at her Sister, "with a few words, you hope to absolve yourself of all responsibility for this epic travesty?"

"Your people are not without fault in this either, Alba." Midnight waved a hand at Ada and the others. "Did they not destroy an entire city block in Denver in their quest to claim the Snow girl? Have they not left a major stretch of interstate in ruin, crippling travel for months to come and drawing more undue attention than these misguided skiomancers could ever attempt? Far from a shining example of discretion, I would argue."

"It is true the actions of my emissaries have indeed caused some regrettable property damage. Your agents, however, ended the life of a Daughter of Neith, and a particularly good one at that." Alba gestured to Rosemary. "Not to mention, left this girl without a mother."

"And for that, I am truly sorry, though, as I've already said, I am not responsible for the actions of former acolytes."

"Aren't you?" Alba asked.

"Former?" Krage grumbled simultaneously.

"How dare you come to this place and attempt to pass yourself off as better than me." Midnight made a wide pass with her arm as she peered around the immense arena. Everywhere you looked, unconscious forms littered the space, and cries filled the air from one end to the other as the massive crowd still fought to escape their shadowy prison. "Your people started this havoc while I and mine sought only to contain it."

"You keep this multitude here against their will." Alba's lips drew down to a thin line. "This escalating panic is all your doing."

"You'd rather I release them into the world, Alba? Let them wag their tongues about what they saw here today? Our web of technomancers may be quite effective at keeping all of us off the collective radar of society, but people still have lips and ears. Would you have us live through another Inquisition? Another Dark Age?"

"Excuse me." Seph took advantage of the moment of quiet that followed Midnight's question and forced her way between the arguing Angels. "This is all very interesting, but last I checked you were both here for me. If it's not too much trouble, can we get to the part where you all tell me exactly what it is you want?" Every word louder than the one before, she shouted at the women, either oblivious to or ignoring the fact that each was a force of nature incarnate.

If either of them had unhinged their jaws in that moment and bitten her head off, I'm not sure it would have surprised me in the slightest.

Before Seph could say another word, I rushed to her side with Rosemary on one flank and Delacroix on my other.

"Well?" Seph's eyes danced angrily between the two, the shared shock on their faces at Seph's sheer audacity quickly fading into amusement. "Is someone going to talk, or are we just going to stand here gawking at each other?"

"Of course, dear." Midnight studied Seph with an inquisitive, if not kind, gaze. "This is, after all, your day."

"In more ways than one," Alba added, her expression similarly vague.

"Each of us have come to offer you a taste of our power so that we might kindle that which has laid dormant inside you since the moment of your birth." A half-smile spread across Midnight's features, even if the expression didn't quite make its way to her eyes. "It is time for you to embrace your destiny."

"My destiny?" Seph gestured back at the stage. "*This* is my destiny." She stepped back. "This was supposed to be the final night of the U.S. leg of my tour, and you and your people have ruined it." She swept her arm to indicate the fleeing crowd. "These people have waited months to see this performance, and now dozens of them have been trampled, injured, or worse. And for what? So you two can prove who's higher on the Ascendant totem pole?"

"You have fire, indeed," Alba said with a laugh. "Far be it from me to shatter the illusions of one who has managed to actually catch one of her dreams, however transitory, in her dainty little fingers, but you are meant for far more than even this grand fate, Miss Snow."

Seph's entire body shook, not in fear but with rage. "You two don't know anything about me."

"Oh, dear girl, but we do." Alba rested a hand on Seph's shoulder. "In some ways, more than you yourself know."

"You are a true beauty, my dear, and I would know." Midnight studied Seph as if looking upon a fine painting, "I once had tea with Helen herself."

"Ever with the name dropping, Sister." Alba returned her attention to Seph, her smile like a sunbeam. "Though she's not wrong." She stepped closer to Seph, who didn't shrink away one inch. "Everything about you is beauty. Your features, your hair, your form." She paused, her gaze dropping to Seph's parted lips. "Your voice."

"To be honest, child, I enjoy your music." Midnight crinkled her nose. "Catchy indeed, though your every song was written by committee. Not an original melody, harmony, or lyric there, but simply rehashing of songs and themes that were old when even I was young." Midnight drew close to Seph as well. "That voice, though? Now, that is something indeed."

"My voice?" Seph's hand went absently to her throat. "Is that what makes me different?"

"Many can sing, child." Alba smiled. "Not many can sing like you."

"There are those in history whose voices have lived on in legend." Midnight cleared her throat as if trying to improve the timbre of her whispered speech. "The sirens of ancient myth, the banshee of Ireland, a young man named Orpheus who storytellers swore could make the very stones weep."

"Once in a generation, one such as you might come along," Alba continued. "The last was taken from us all too soon, long before his time."

"He refused the Ascension," Midnight spat, "and he paid the price."

Alba silenced her Sister with a glance. "Do not speak ill of the dead." She returned her attention to Seph. "Like you, he had risen through the ranks of humanity and literally became musical royalty. Yet, despite the potential for greatness beyond his wildest dreams, he made it clear that he had absolutely no desire for *our* world."

"What if *I* refuse, then?" Seph asked. "What if I don't want whatever it is you have to offer?"

"Times are different now." Alba crossed her arms. "Many Ascendant who once remained in the shadows—no offense, dear Sister—now feel more than comfortable making their presence known. You've already been publicly sought out by Krage and his quartet of shadow-dealers as well as the pack of theriodans that haunts the Vegas casinos."

Midnight cleared her throat with an audible hiss. "Don't forget your own little quartet, dear Sister."

"Of course." Alba growled, the sound deep and guttural. "I fear, Miss Snow, that if you continue to leave your power and destiny unclaimed, others will continue to seek you out, others who will force your hand. Would you not rather Ascend here and now, at least somewhat on your own terms?"

"You call *this* 'on my own terms'?" Seph laughed aloud. "You've ruined the end of my tour, hurt hundreds of people, wrecked this place, and dare to tell me it's all for my own good?"

"Compared to what others might do to secure your talents,"

Midnight grumbled, "what has transpired thus far these last few days pales in comparison."

"So, now we're down to brass tacks." Seph's face twisted into a frustrated frown. "You do want something from me."

"Of course we do, dear." Alba's smile began to show some strain.

"No favor comes without a price." Midnight drew close. "Have you not learned that already in your short but oh-so-successful career?"

"That's it." Seph stepped back, her cheeks burning with crimson heat. "I have worked and trained and fought for years to get to this point. I don't care who you are. No one is going to wreck what should have been one of the best nights of my life and then tell me I don't deserve every ounce of success that's come my way." She raised a hand. "Whatever it is you're selling, I'm not buying."

"It seems we haven't made ourselves clear." Alba stepped into the space Seph had vacated. "You will Ascend, girl, here and now."

"And yes," Midnight added, "it *is* for your own good." Her dark eyes narrowed at Seph like a serpent about to strike. "Whether you struggle against us or merely accept the inevitable, the outcome will remain the same."

"You may choose to side with the Angel of the Morning," Alba started, holding out a hand surrounded in golden fire.

"Or the Angel of Midnight." Midnight extended her own hand, her outstretched fingers surrounded in a swarm of tiny shadows. "But you will choose."

"You heard the woman." Rosemary stepped forward, katana brandished before her and any of the previous deference gone from her voice. "She's opting out. Leave her be."

Both Sister Angels turned as one to regard Rosemary.

"How disappointing." Midnight's whisper raised the hairs on my neck. "I would have thought your mother would have trained you better than to raise your voice to such as us, Rosemary Delacroix."

"You haven't the power to back up your moment of bravado, little girl." Alba stretched out her bare arm at Rosemary, waves of shimmering energy radiating between her splayed fingers. "Let this serve as your first and final warning."

"If it's power you want," I focused, channeling the full force of the

Light into Danielle Delacroix's paired blades, "you've come to the right place."

Both Angels paused an instant before laughing in my face.

"If there is one individual present less intimidating than an impotent Daughter of Neith, boy," Alba sneered, "it is you."

"Since it seems the three of you need to be taught a lesson"— Midnight drew her arms up on either side, the complement of shadows covering her body lifting her into the air—"then I shan't leave you waiting another instant." She glanced down at her former lieutenant. "Johan, care to take advantage of a rare chance at redemption?"

"Of course, my lady." Krage grabbed at Seph's arm. "You're coming with us, Miss Snow."

Rosemary swatted his hand away with the flat of her blade. "Hands off, Krage. The woman said no."

"And she meant it." I pulled the longer of Danielle Delacroix's two blades beneath Krage's chin, the steel shining with inner Light. "Back off, while you still can."

"So," Alba whispered, "it has come to this." She sighed. "Dearest Ada, do remove these obstacles from our path and prepare the Snow girl for Ascension."

"With pleasure." The waves of heat radiating off the pyromancer flared. "Dietrich, Violeta, Daichi, restrain your targets."

Violeta returned yet again to her liquid state and rushed at Delacroix, encircling his arms and legs with spirals of turbid water before solidifying into ice. Simultaneously, Daichi trundled in our direction, each step of his rocky outer shell shaking the concrete floor that quickly flowed Neko's way. With a mighty gust, Falco flew straight upward, and before Rosemary could so much as look my way, the aeromancer literally swept her off her feet and into the air before him, spinning her at dizzying speed.

And that left me, once again, to face Ada, the woman who could melt my face off with no more than a glance.

I'd hoped there would be no Round Two; I'd barely escaped our first match, and that on a technicality.

"Well, boy," Ada said as shimmering waves of heat cascaded down her body, "would you prefer to surrender now, or are you truly hellbent on going home with a few third-degree burns?"

"And that's if I don't get a chance to filet you alive first." Dmitri, the biggest of the skiomancers stepped to her side, dagger in hand. Silent for the entire interchange, it was clear he was itching for a fight. "Your choice."

My entire body trembled as a flood of instincts both mine and not mine told me simultaneously to attack and defend, charge and retreat, go out in a blaze of glory and surrender completely.

And then, cutting through the psychic static came an unmistakable voice I'd only ever heard once in my life, a voice I never dreamed I'd hear again.

The voice of Danielle Delacroix.

The elements of your victory lie before you, came the whispered words. *Do what you must and know that the Light of Neith will protect you.*

I looked to Rosemary to see if she'd heard her mother's voice as plainly as I had, but not a hint of emotion played on her face.

Then, another voice murmured across my psyche, this one much older.

While not every weakness is a strength, every strength of your enemy can be exploited as a potential weakness.

Just once, couldn't someone offer some straightforward non-cryptic advice?

At least in this case, I was able to put the pieces together.

"You know what, matchstick? I've learned a thing or two since we last met."

"Oh, really?" Ada's efforts at keeping the vexation from her face failed miserably. "Do tell, Mr. Harkreader."

"First things first. Whatever this thing is that lives inside me now? It's left me more powerful than you." I swept the shorter blade in an arc, directing its tip at all present. "More powerful than all of you."

"The boy suffers from delusions of grandeur." The Midnight Angel crossed her arms before her midair. "A pity."

"A pity, indeed." Shaking her head sadly, Alba looked to Ada. "Bring him down."

"You can try," I said, "but as long as I hold these blades, you can't hurt me. I know that now."

"Ethan," Seph whispered, "you don't have to—"

"Too late, girl." Ada stepped forward. "While I take no joy in this, your lover has crossed the fine line that separates bravery from stupidity." Waves of heat shimmered around her form. "Now, unfortunately, he must pay the piper." Her eyes narrowed at Seph. "Step aside."

Seph pulled closer to me. "If you kill him, you're going to have to kill me too."

Dammit. "Seph," I whispered, "I've got this. Just do as she says."

"But—"

"Trust me."

Seph hesitated but a moment longer, and then leaned in to plant a kiss on my cheek.

"I don't just trust you, Ethan." She pulled away, those crystal blue eyes of hers filled with equal parts hope and terror. "I love you."

My heart swelled at the words, but I kept my tongue regarding my own feelings, not daring to give the other side even one more piece of ammunition.

"Give us some room," I spoke instead of the words I truly wanted to say. "I have to know you're safe."

"Oh, she'll be perfectly safe in a moment, Mr. Harkreader." The pyromancer raised her arms at me, palms out and fingers splayed. "Now, prepare to take your medicine."

"Bring it."

With an almost imperceptible shift in her features, Ada let fly a burst of orange flame. Praying that the voices in my head had spoken the truth, I brought both blades around, crossed them before me, and summoned the Light. For half an instant, I feared that all my problems were over as the hairs on my forearms singed and my face burned in the heat of her ironically cold stare.

And then, something inside my head clicked.

"No," I whispered.

A silver shimmer passed from one blade to the other and back, followed by another and then another until the Light surrounding the paired swords glowed brighter than the column of flame that threatened to immolate me on the spot. The heat remained sweltering as I sheltered behind the shield formed by the interplay of the Light of Neith and Danielle Delacroix's two weapons of choice, but other than a healthy sheen of sweat, I remained unharmed.

Ada, barely visible beyond the flames flowing around me, continued to escalate her attack, but regardless of what she threw at me, the protection afforded by the Light more than rose to the challenge.

"My dear Ada," came Alba's flat tones, "I would never have imagined that dispatching a lone boy who barely understands even the couple of tricks at his disposal would test your finely honed abilities."

"My apologies, Mistress." The flames shooting past me like a river of fire doubled in intensity. Despite the shield of Neith's Light, my clothing, hair, and even my flesh began to smolder in the heat.

Fortunately, I only needed her to bring the fire for another few seconds.

"Is that all you've got, fire-witch?" I shouted, my lips and throat drier than desert sand. "And here I thought you were the strongest of your little quartet."

Ada scowled. "You truly have a death wish, Mr. Harkreader."

Here it comes.

"And since you asked, I'll show you exactly what I'm capable of."

Three. Two. One.

As Ada redoubled her attack, I pivoted to one side and shifted the blades and the shield of Light to direct the flood of flame rather than simply block it.

My target? The seven-foot living block of ice that had encased Delacroix, holding him immobile to the point of suffocation.

Or, as her friends called her, Violeta.

I'd never imagined what an iceberg's scream would sound like.

I wish I'd never learned.

The frozen monolith shattered into dozens of hunks that flew in every direction. One striking Dmitri center chest, and another nearly knocked Falco from midair. The countless shards of ice all fell to the ground and melted into a smattering of puddles, the ones nearest Ada evaporating before they'd even hit concrete. I wasn't sure if I'd just killed my first hydromancer or not, and I have to admit, the bigger part of me didn't care.

Freed from his icy prison only to find himself in an open blast furnace, Delacroix stumbled backward, blinded by the inferno surrounding him.

"Get down!" I shouted as I pulled both swords close to my chest and rushed at Delacroix's massive frame. As I buried my shoulder in his chest, I prayed my weight and momentum were sufficient to knock him out of Ada's lethal corona. Though the experience felt very much like trying to tackle a marble statue sitting atop an active volcano, I managed to push him out of harm's way, and the two of us went tumbling across a nearby row of still-upright folding chairs. Not the most glamorous of rescues, but alive and not skewered by my own swords was going to have to do.

"Harkreader." His voice came out a pained rasp, the superheated air clearly already having done some damage to his lungs and throat. "Save Rosemary."

Delacroix's every word and action since I'd met him had revolved around "the client" and whatever it took to keep Seph out of danger and safe. Good to know that when the shit hit the fan, though, his priority remained his own flesh and blood.

Unless, of course, his ever-tactical mind was still working, and the daughter who'd been training for this moment since before she could talk was indeed the only way we all walked away at the end of this.

I spun around and scanned the battlefield.

Dino, Jerry, and Gus had wisely chosen the better part of valor and vanished backstage with the band and crew. That was for the best as it was three fewer people I had to keep track of.

Ada appeared to be powering down, her devastated expression shifting to one of relief as the various puddles that comprised Violeta all began to flow together once more. Daichi worked at keeping Neko under wraps, though this time the theriodan had been prepared for his particular mode of attack. Having escaped the earth elementalist's rocky assault, he now dodged snare after snare of animated concrete shooting up from the floor. That left Falco, who hovered twenty feet above us with an incapacitated Rosemary stuck in the aeromancer's prolonged spin cycle, the quartet of skiomancers converging on me and Delacroix, and the Angels of Midnight and Morning respectively biding their time: a pair of queens watching their pawns, to return to a metaphor we'd entertained in the backseat of the Driver's limo.

There in the middle of it all stood Seph, trembling with a potent mix of fear and rage and adrenalin. She was counting on me. They were all counting on me.

"All right, Neith, whoever or whatever you are." I dropped into a low fighting stance and once again crossed the paired blades before me. "Don't let me down."

CHAPTER 32

WHEN IT'S OVER

"First things first," I muttered under my breath, "Rosemary."

With a spin like a discus thrower, I let fly the shorter blade, praying the shining steel would find its mark and my wild throw wouldn't hit Rosemary instead.

Falco, who'd already been shot twice in the last couple of days, had kept an eye on me. With a quick gust of wind, he easily dodged the short sword that flipped end over end past him and clattered in the distance.

"Harkreader!" Neko shouted through the artificial downpour. "Need a hand?"

I wasn't sure what it was in his tone and body language, but something deep inside knew exactly what the theriodan was proposing. I rushed at Neko, avoiding the encroaching skiomancers, as the tiger spun out of the way of a trio of concrete tentacles that burst from the floor beneath his feet. With only a few steps before I was on top of him, he knelt, getting into position for a maneuver I'd never have dared a week ago. With his fingers interlaced below one knee, Neko risked being bludgeoned by Daichi's myriad of concrete tendrils, so I did my best not to keep him waiting.

With one last running step, I leaped, planted my foot in his joined palms, and kicked off as the theriodan hurled me into the air. Both surprised and yet unfazed, I quickly discovered this predator clothed in human flesh was far stronger than his compact form would suggest.

I flew at Falco, knowing I'd only get one shot before he either hit me with a hurricane or sucked the very air from my lungs. I directed the longer sword still in my grasp for the center of his chest and, predictably, he dodged to one side.

Just as I'd hoped.

Instead of slashing with the blade, I tucked and rolled, and then shot out a foot aimed directly at the side of Falco's head. The blow landed, sending his mirrored sunglasses flying along with a spray of scarlet. In an instant, the winds holding both him and Rosemary aloft cut out, the air becoming perfectly still.

And then, the part I hadn't prepared for.

Getting twenty feet in the air wasn't so hard, but getting back to the ground without breaking every bone in your body was Neko's specialty. As I'd hoped, our tiger friend ducked past another pair of stony tentacles and rushed to catch Rosemary, his every step as sure and fluid as you'd expect from a jungle cat in human form.

That was all I saw before I hit the top of my arc and gravity took over at 9.8 meters per second squared, straight down.

This was going to hurt.

Except, I didn't fall.

I just hung there midair.

For a moment, I almost allowed myself to believe I'd been saved.

That is until I tried to move and found my form bound tight by a dozen shadows, the bonds ephemeral enough that I couldn't strike at them, but more than solid enough to hold me fast.

My remaining weapon, the steel of the blade still glowing as bright as a newborn star, fell from my grasp as the shadowy forms constricted around me, stealing the blood from my limbs, the warmth from my body, the very breath from my lungs. Around me, inside me, through me they coursed, leaving me without so much as the ability to scream. Everything began to go dark as fear gripped my racing heart and the gut-wrenching panic shifted into mind-numbing despair.

My last thought before everything went black? I didn't even care anymore.

"Let him go." The words, spoken with the authority of someone not only with power but someone who knew how to use it, echoed through the arena, channeled at top volume through every speaker in the house. "Now."

"Stop her," came Krage's suddenly desperate voice, his words hitting my ears as if spoken a thousand miles away. "She's—"

Silence held sway for a long moment as Krage, just visible at the corner of my fading vision, pulled himself up to his full height as if presenting for inspection.

"Now, at last," came Midnight's hiss, just audible above the continued rain of the sprinklers, "she understands."

"Or she will soon enough," followed Alba's rich tones.

"I said," came the voice both familiar and foreign that filled my senses, "Let. Him. Go."

And then, any doubt as to the speaker's identity fled my mind as a lone sung note, as crystal clear as a cloudless sky, pierced the darkness that clouded my eyes, my body, my soul.

The song previously interrupted by the skiomancer attack, "Kiss Me At Midnight," filled the arena, but this time without accompaniment. No riffing guitar, no teeth-shaking bass, no pounding drums. No rich chords from the bank of keyboards or harmonies from the pair of backup singers.

Just Persephone Snow, the lone microphone held before her perfect lips every bit as much a weapon as the blades I'd carried since Danielle's Delacroix's death.

"The poets say it's always darkest just before the dawn..."

Every other sound and all the pain and worry and care were washed away by the beauty of Seph's song.

"*But the shadows of the night are for us a beginning, not a denouement...*"

Before, utter despair had left me apathetic as to whether I lived or died, and now, utter beauty had done the same.

"*For in the blackest of nights, you found me...*"

The shades lowered me to the ground, leaving me with Rosemary and Delacroix to one side, the two Angels to the other, and the remainder of the gathered Ascendant scattered in every direction.

And I didn't care.

"*With arms of steel, you surround me...*"

The entire arena, including each of us embroiled in our latest life-or-death struggle between light and darkness, had stopped to bear witness to a miracle.

And I didn't care.

"*With your tender words, you unbound me...*"

The sprinklers that had rained down on us for the better part of half an hour suddenly ceased as if commanded by only the power of a song.

And I didn't care.

"*Kiss...kiss me at midnight...*"

The only consideration in that moment as Seph broke into the chorus, be it of mind, heart, or soul, was waiting for the next note, the next word, even the precious rests between Seph's vocals as the living instrument of such perfect song stopped occasionally to take a breath.

Joy and sorrow and guilt and redemption and a thousand other emotions played across my consciousness for what seemed an eternity as Seph sang. Verse and chorus and bridge, all expertly woven together, led to the final heartbreaking lyric, ending the most perfect moment I'd ever experienced.

When the last note was sung and Seph lowered her head, I wept.

I wasn't alone.

Krage and his skiomancers. Ada and her elementalists. Dino, Gus, and Jerry who had come out of hiding along with the entire band, backup singers, dancers, and crew. Not to mention the thousands trapped inside the arena with us.

Even the two Sisters, one Angel who presided over the world of day and one who ruled the night, were moved to tears.

"Now..." This voice, a deep bass counterpoint to Seph's sweeping soprano from seconds before, filled the silence. "That's the stuff."

Dressed as always in his black suit, starched white button-down, black silk tie, and black leather shoes that shone like mirrors, all of which were somehow miraculously still dry, the Driver strode toward Seph.

Even the Midnight Angel and El Ángel del Alba held their respective tongues in his presence.

He swept the space with those dark brown eyes of his, taking in everything as he had when we'd first met days before.

"Midnight." He gave the woman clothed in darkness a quick nod. "Alba."

"Driver," they said in unison, almost in prayer.

Every Ascendant present looked on in wonder and awe as the Driver approached Seph: the newest Ascendant on the planet and one who numbered among the oldest.

"Miss Snow." The Driver stopped more than an arm's breadth from Seph, clearly a decision borne of respect, both of her as a person but likely more so of the moment. "A word?"

"Mr. Driver?" Seph stared into his eyes terrified, her gaze flicking around the room at the legions who had stopped everything they were doing save taking breath to listen to her song. "What are you doing here? What is happening to me?"

"Not happening, Miss Snow," the Driver answered, "but what has happened." He scanned the arena, the teeming thousands all looking on at what to them must have appeared a gathering of the gods. "You have them all in your thrall. May I suggest you let these people go with a quick adjustment of their memory of the evening?"

"How is she supposed to—" I began, but before I could complete the thought, Seph brought the microphone again to her lips.

"*All of you, go in peace,*" she sang, her voice pouring like honey from speakers throughout the massive arena, "*and remember...none of this.*"

"Krage?" the Driver intoned.

Without further prompting, the leader of the skiomancers silently ordered his foot soldiers to lower their shadowy guard on the massive arena.

As the crowd of thousands rose as one and began to exit in a far more orderly fashion than I would have imagined possible ten minutes earlier, I moved to join Seph only to find my way blocked by skiomancer and elementalist alike.

"Stay back, Harkreader," Krage glared at me from behind his dark avian mask, "if you know what's good for you."

"Driver's shown up twice now, three times if the rumors about Albuquerque are correct." Ada shot me a sidelong glance. "This is bigger than any of us thought."

The Driver motioned for both the Midnight Angel and El Ángel del Alba to join his conversation with Seph. The four gathered close, their voices dropping to barely audible whispers so low I couldn't make out what was being said other than the occasional word or two.

Then, without warning, the Driver disengaged rather abruptly from the discussion and motioned for the three women to continue without him.

"As has been made clear by a disinterested third party who understands the rules better than anyone—" Midnight started, her eyes narrow in disgust.

Alba pulled in a deep breath before completing the thought. "It is clear that you, Persephone Snow, set in motion your own Ascension, and neither my nor my Sister's efforts or energies played any part."

"And therefore?" The Driver waved his hand in a circular motion that indicated the two women should skip to the good part.

"You owe us nothing." Midnight looked away. "No debt. No obligation."

"Nothing." Alba's eyes dropped to the ground. "You are, in the parlance of this country's professional athletes, a free agent."

"But, Mistress." Ada stepped forward. "After all this—"

"Miss Snow is free to go." Alba stared down her nose at Ada. "Do I make myself perfectly clear?"

"Yes, Mistress."

"None of you will stand in her way," Midnight whispered, then, noting Krage's obvious fury, repeated, "*none* of you."

"But, Mistress, what of us?" Krage sputtered. "We—"

"You and your Murder of Crows are a disgrace. You pursued the Snow girl without my approval in the employ of an individual you clearly fear more than me—an unwise shift in allegiance if ever one was—and in the process, have opened me up to scorn and ridicule. You slew the Daughter of Neith without a single thought regarding the repercussions of removing such a powerful piece from the board." She directed her attention to Rosemary. "Not to mention, you left this promising young woman without a mother during some of her most formative years." Midnight drew close to her former lieutenant. "And in the end, what do you or I have to show for it? Nothing."

"Snow stands before you, Ascendant, and ripe for the plucking," Krage grunted in frustration, his masked face turning almost imperceptibly in the direction of the Driver. "Is it our fault that your unfounded fear of one you consider your better keeps you from taking what could be your prize?"

"What you understand about the situation before you would scarcely fill a thimble." She turned her back on him and strode away into the darkness. "Begone from my sight, all of you." Midstride, she cast a quick look back in Rosemary's direction. "Know, Miss Delacroix, that I shall be keeping a close watch on you. I see a lot of myself in those dark eyes of yours." And with that, she disappeared in a swirl of shadow.

Rosemary stepped back as if struck as Krage turned on me, ripping away his mask so he could stare me down eye to eye and man to man.

"Don't get too smug, Harkreader. A time will come when you're all alone and neither of your girlfriends will be there to watch your back. When all the Angels and Drivers and Greyhounds of the world are otherwise occupied with their own business, that's when I will come for you." He gestured at the myriad of dark reflections of my form stretching out from my feet onto the shattered concrete floor. "My sincerest hope is that from this day forward you live in fear of your own shadow." He turned and stalked away in the opposite direction that the Midnight Angel had gone with Rupert, Fala, and Dmitri silently following.

"Good kick, by the way." Falco walked up, massaging his jaw. "You're lucky we all heal pretty fast."

I picked up on his almost jovial tone. "So...no hard feelings?"

Falco actually smiled. "No hard feelings." He turned to Seph and offered a low bow. "My apologies for the rooftop incident back in Denver."

"Incident?" The more bitey side of Seph's personality rose to the surface, and then, with obvious effort, she tamped down her anger and returned the man's oddly pleasant smile. "Apology accepted, Mr. Falco."

"Please, call me Dietrich."

Ada, who'd busied herself nursing Violeta back to both human form and something approaching consciousness, sauntered over, a similar conciliatory smile across her face. "My apologies as well, Miss Snow. We won't be bothering you again."

"Thank you." Seph's brow furrowed. "Why do I get the feeling your assurance doesn't mean I'm completely off the hook?"

"Wisdom, indeed." Ada took a breath. "You have achieved Ascension all on your own, without a spark from another Ascendant, and therefore owe no obligation to anyone. That doesn't mean you won't be actively recruited."

"Recruited?"

"Ascendant may be few and far between, but as the saying goes, there is safety in numbers. In general, it is not a matter of whether you form alliances, but with whom."

El Ángel del Alba strode over. "Enjoy your respite from this madness, Miss Snow, however long or brief it may be." Her eyes filled with compassion, even kindness. "Know this, however. That which you are, not to mention what a voice such as yours brings to the world, has been seen only one other time in the last century. I sought you out, admittedly, to bring you to my side, but with no obligation, you are free to align with whomever you choose. Understand that my door is always open to you, Persephone Snow, though as Ada suggested, you needn't worry that my agents will be showing up on your doorstep without invitation."

"But someone will be coming for me." Seph shivered. "I'm guessing whoever hired Krage and his goons?"

"Or perhaps another." She let out a pained sigh. "Do not underestimate who you are or what you represent." Her face broke into a smile like a sunbeam. "If and when you are ready to ally with someone who truly has your best interests at heart, you have but to call." Whether by parlor trick or legit magic, a golden business card appeared in Alba's hand. "Don't wait too long, however. For all the drama of the past few days, know that I have only ever wished the best for you and your future." She set her jaw and handed me the card. "Others may not prove to be so magnanimous."

And with that, El Ángel del Alba retreated as well, with Falco on one flank, Ada supporting a still-recovering Violeta on the other, and Daichi's enormous concrete sumo bringing up the rear.

That left me, Seph, Rosemary, Delacroix, and Neko alone with the mysterious man known only as the Driver.

"Welcome, Miss Snow," the Driver spoke with utter gravitas and just a hint of sadness, "to the ranks of the Ascendant."

Seph raised an eyebrow. "So, you're the one who's supposed to teach me the secret handshake?"

"No, nothing like that." The Driver ignored Seph's attempt at joviality. "I came here today to ensure that your transition was equitable and that you were treated fairly." He sighed. "Many of those you fought against today are still repaying their initial obligation, a regrettable state of affairs, but simply the way things are."

"I don't understand." Seph crossed her arms before her, her lips quivering.

"And I hope you never will." The Driver directed his attention to me and Rosemary. "Keep friends such as these close. There are none you should trust as much as those who loved you before they knew what you could do for them." He shook his head sadly. "I know you must be thinking that you already had the world at your fingertips, Persephone Snow, but what you are now compared to what you were yesterday is, to quote Mark Twain, the difference between the lightning bug and the lightning."

With that, the Driver pulled Rosemary aside with Delacroix, leaving me alone with Seph. Rosemary hadn't said a word since I'd rescued her from Falco's cyclonic attack. Shaken by the ordeal, she trembled before the Driver who in turn adopted a strangely paternal bearing, made doubly odd by the presence of Rosemary's actual father.

"Hey." I grasped Seph's trembling fingers, taking advantage of our first moment alone since before the show. "Are you okay?"

"I don't know if the word really applies anymore, but yeah." She squeezed my hand. "I'm okay."

"What does it feel like?" I barely knew what questions to ask. "You know…"

"I'm still me, if that's what you're asking."

My mind wandered through the dialogue of countless comic books I'd read as a kid and the dozens of shows and movies about people who suddenly became more than human, and a strange fact occurred to me: we hadn't gotten there by the same path, but Seph and I were now the same.

"Can you feel it?" I asked. "Like I do? At the back of your skull, something just sitting there waiting?"

"Yes and no." She rested her fingers on her chest. "I feel it here." Her fingertips moved up to her windpipe. "And here." And then, to her lips, her voice adopting a subtle singsong quality. *"And here."* A subtle smile pulled at the corners of her mouth. *"Funny, it may not be midnight yet, but I was wondering…"*

A compulsion filled me to taste those lips, to feel their velvet softness on my own. I didn't care that hundreds of the recently terrified audience still waking up from Seph's hypnotic song looked on in a stupor. I didn't care that a mysterious stranger was telling God knows what to Rosemary and Delacroix mere feet away or that Neko was watching us with a smirk.

All I cared about was Seph. I wanted her, to have her, to possess her, to—

"I'm sorry." Seph's eyes dropped. "I think that was me."

For a moment, I'd felt drunk yet clear-minded, ravenous yet fulfilled, confused yet more lucid than I'd ever felt, and the next, everything returned to normal.

"Not that I'd need much coaxing," I answered quietly, "but yeah. That's some powerful stuff."

The Driver finished his quiet chat with the Delacroixs and joined us. Rosemary watched me out of the corner of her eye but remained quiet, choosing to observe without offering her thoughts, at least for the time being

"Be advised, Miss Snow. You are endowed with an ability that only one other in many generations has possessed. Given your chosen career, I assumed your Ascension would not only involve but incorporate your already impressive talents. No one, however, including me, dared dream what you have already achieved with your very first expression of power."

"And that is?" As vulnerable as I'd seen her, Seph waited expectantly for the Driver's next words. "Don't keep me waiting."

"You, my dear, are a siren, straight out of a storybook, and more powerful than you or anyone could have imagined." The Driver stroked his chin. "Other than, perhaps, whoever hired Krage's cadre of skiomancers to come for you." He thumbed in the direction the Midnight Angel had gone. "Our Lady of Darkness there may be many things, but a liar she is not. Whoever sent Krage and his people for you may have information that I am not privy to, and that's a bit on the frightening side."

"And why is that?" I asked.

"Because, Mr. Harkreader, I pride myself on knowing everything." He gave Seph one final appraising up and down and turned to walk away. "Trust that I will be keeping a close eye on you, Miss Snow."

"Excuse me, Mr. Driver." Seph reached out a trembling hand for his jacketed shoulder. "If you truly take such pride in knowing everything, I can only assume that you knew I was Ascendant back in Denver."

"I suspected, yes."

"And you didn't tell me?"

"Would it have helped if I did? Would it have given you peace, or only added another onus to your already burdened heart?"

"All these people injured because of me." Seph swept an arm wide, encompassing the entire arena. "Could this have then been avoided?"

"Had you understood who and what you were, or at least what you might become, would you have then canceled your performance this evening? You knew another attack was imminent. Would knowing your ultimate fate have changed your decision?"

Seph didn't answer, but instead asked another question.

"The one Angel, the nicer one, she left me her card. What should I do with it?"

"First, as to who in the world of Ascendant is more or less trustworthy or dangerous, always remember that appearances can be deceiving, as I'm sure you already understand." The Driver considered for a moment. "As for Alba, I'd keep that card very safe, for it isn't offered to many. Understand, though, that any help from one of her stature would almost certainly involve an obligation you might not wish to incur."

"Understood." Seph's gaze dropped to the floor. "And you, Mr. Driver? If I need you down the road, how would I get in touch?"

"First, Miss Snow, if it ever comes down to you truly requiring my services, chances are I'll already know." He glanced across his shoulder, his face a mask of resignation. "And second, if that comes to pass, then God help us all." His hint of a smile returned. "As I said before, however, I will be keeping an eye on you for the foreseeable future."

Seph shivered anew at that last bit. I attempted to pull her closer into me, hoping to provide a little solace as the realization that her life going forward would never be the same continued to soak in, but she resisted, refusing to yield to anyone in the moment, even me.

"Seph?"

"It's all right." Her chin dropped to her chest. "I just need some time."

"Please, Mr. Harkreader, give her a moment." The Driver

considered for a moment. "In fact, may I have a word with you before I go?"

"Yes, sir," I said, unsure exactly how to address someone who commanded total respect and possibly even fear from the pantheon of earthbound gods who had walked away at his merest suggestion. Just as he had with Rosemary and Delacroix, the Driver pulled me aside, though what he possibly needed to tell me, I hadn't the first clue.

"Stand down, Harkreader. Believe it or not, you can relax." A lone chuckle parted his lips. "Likely for the first time in days, in fact."

Funny. I didn't feel relaxed. Not one bit.

"Do you understand what a unique position you now occupy in the world?" he asked.

"Truthfully?" I answered. "I don't understand any of this."

"Let me shed some light, then, if you will pardon the turn of phrase." The Driver rested a fatherly hand on my shoulder, his demeanor reminiscent of how he'd been moments before with Rosemary. "You now embody a force that has walked the earth for centuries. Generations of Daughters of Neith speak through you and fill you with their gathered knowledge, skill, and power, and yet, you are a man. That has never happened." He studied me for a long moment. "For all you've already experienced, I suspect you've barely scratched the surface of the power that now lies within you."

"Your point?"

"Do not squander such a gift." He locked gazes with me, the twin dark pools of brown as unnerving as any Ascendant I'd faced that week. "I fully understand that with the mantle of Neith comes responsibility beyond anything you ever imagined, Mr. Harkreader, but you have inherited far more than duty. Live up to the obligation, but embrace the opportunity."

"The opportunity?" I asked. "To carry around a dead champion's swords and slice and dice bad guys until one of them gets me like they did her?"

"While there is truth in what you say, the doors that have opened for you go far beyond mere combat. You are an agent of change, as the entire line of Neith has been before you. You walk among the

Ascendant—though you are not of them—and command their respect whether they admit it or not." He brought his hand up between us. Gripped there and previously somehow concealed, rested the shorter of the two blades I'd inherited along with my newfound abilities. "And let me make one thing clear. These blades were Danielle Delacroix's for her time on this Earth, but now, for as long as you live, they are yours."

"Anything else?" I asked.

"Only an observation." He scanned the room, his eyes lighting briefly on Seph and then on Rosemary. "I am aware that Miss Snow has taken you as a lover."

"What?"

"Don't act so shocked, Mr. Harkreader. Like I said, I make it my business to know things." He studied me, a mix of admiration and sympathy playing in his steady gaze. "A lot of men would envy your position, your days spent in training with Rosemary Delacroix, as perfect a woman and warrior as I've seen, and your nights spent in the arms of the first siren born in generations, both of whom I can assure you think very highly of the man you are."

"Envy, huh?" My cheeks burned at what seemed a compliment from a god among men. "Thanks, I think."

He squeezed my shoulder one last time, his smile fading as he turned to walk away. "I did not say, Mr. Harkreader, that I was one of them."

CODA
IT'S NOT OVER ('TIL IT'S OVER)

Atop a West Hollywood parking deck that looked out upon the mid-afternoon Los Angeles skyline stood two men. The first, an unmasked Krage dressed in a simple black button-down, jeans, and combat boots spoke to a man who wore an expensive-looking dark suit with a scarlet tie, his features obscured by a bizarre helmet of deep crimson, black, and orange that resembled an impressionist's interpretation of a cardinal's feathered head.

"What do you mean you had to let her go?" The suited man's words, amplified and distorted by the electroacoustic equipment within his helmet, hit Krage's ears as emotionless, almost robotic, and yet the seething anger behind every syllable was undeniable.

"Both the Angels who call this city home as well as the Driver himself became involved before the evening was over. Snow Ascended without obligation, and therefore was deemed free to go."

"On the say-so of your previous employer?"

"And the Angel of the Morning."

"Remind me, who is your current employer?"

"You, sir."

"Precisely."

"My apologies." Krage hung his head, resigned to his fate. "I am prepared for whatever punishment you deem necessary to make up for my failure."

"And what would be the point in that?" The suited man in the cardinal helmet studied Krage. "Taking out frustrations on subordinates, particularly those who have given their all, is for lesser men." He crossed his arms before his chest. "Please tell your Murder of Crows—I must say I prefer the new nomenclature—that they will be given a chance to redeem themselves, but this particular window of opportunity has, for the moment at least, closed."

"Thank you, sir. I will convey your message this evening."

"So," the man continued with a quiet chuckle, "both Angels made an appearance? And the Driver as well? Things are certainly getting interesting."

"Don't forget the Delacroix girl and her father as well as a theriodan tiger who usually runs with the lupine Linus and his pack in Vegas."

"Not to mention this interesting young man who has unintentionally usurped the legacy of the Daughters of Neith. You said his name is Harkreader?"

"That's correct." Krage lowered his head in shame. "Ethan Harkreader."

"Can't be too many of those, I guess." The man in the cardinal helmet stared off into the distance. "Formidable already, you say? And training with the Delacroix girl?

"Yes on both counts."

"And yet is also romantically involved with Snow?"

Krage nodded again. "As best we can tell."

"An interesting knot, indeed." The man lowered his head. "A knot that if not untied will simply have to be cut away."

AUTHOR'S NOTE

ANOTHER BRICK IN THE WALL

December 2022

An interesting place to find myself, at the end of yet another beginning.

For those of you not familiar with how I ended up pursuing this whole writing thing, a quick review. Like many of us writer types, I grew up on a steady diet of novels, comic books, movies, and television shows—some genre and some more mainstream—but also always had an interest in creating my own stories even when I was very young. Attempts at creative writing during middle school, high school, and definitely during college and medical school were few and far between; there are only twenty-four hours in a day and all that.

It wasn't until I was deployed to Iraq as a U.S. Army physician back in 2003 that I had time to ever pursue putting words to paper/screen. That year, I conceived and typed the first half of my first novel, *Pawn's Gambit*, on our dentist's Panasonic Toughbook between all the sick call and physical training and day-to-day stuff that goes along with being deployed to a combat zone. Those early days of creating the world of *The Pawn Stratagem* until May of 2022 when *King's Crisis* finally became available to the readers of the world covered just shy of two decades. A lot of things happened in the meantime, of course. I finished my last five years in the Army, moved to Charlotte, North Carolina, and have been a full-time family physician and faculty member of the family medicine residency there for the last fourteen years. On the author side, in addition to *The Pawn Stratagem* trilogy, I wrote and published all three books of *Fugue & Fable* and my young adult Dickens retelling, *Carol*, as well as attended a gazillion conventions, festivals, and other events in support of my writing and built a network of friends/chosen family in the Charlotte and Southeastern U.S. writer communities.

Still, twenty years is a long time to watch something go from a simple idea to "under construction" and finally to complete and ready for the world. To be back at the beginning of a brand-new project currently planned to include nine or more books is a bit daunting. On the flip side, as I write this, I've already worked through the primary writing of Books I and II of this new series and was able to knock out the first draft of each over the course of sixteen months, Book I from May to December of 2021 and Book II from January to August of 2022. I've spent the last three to four months polishing both manuscripts and making sure I'm happy with this world I've created while simultaneously working on early chapters of Book III.

It's interesting to see what can come from a seed of an idea. "Wouldn't it be cool if the game of chess came to life?" became *The Pawn Stratagem*. "I want to write a book about *Pictures at an Exhibition*!" became *Fugue & Fable*. A three a.m. wake up from a dream and an exclamation of "I'm going to write a young adult version of *A Christmas Carol*!" became *Carol*.

When I first noticed that the collected hits of Pat Benatar sounded like the titles of an awesome urban fantasy series, I had no idea what it would look like, but I knew that project was what I wanted to write next. Some ideas had been circulating in my head for years that didn't fit into any of my other stories: the Driver, the Greyhound, and my own version of the elemental super-team that popped into my adolescent head a year or two before Bill Willingham created *The Elementals* (which I still love). Some ideas are newer: the titular shadows of the night and what they represent as well as the various Angels (some to be named later) were all pulled from my love of 80s pop music. Then there are the overarching themes: destiny denied (or postponed), the not-so-chosen one, and the eternal search for true love and how that shakes out in a world full of roadblocks and danger, romantic and otherwise. Throw in a lifelong love of all things superhero, be it *X-Men, Heroes, Highlander, Buffy, Chuck*, or countless other influences, and you start to see how this particular combination of words you hold in your hands came to be.

As usual, the story has evolved from its humble beginnings at the back of my mind.

My lead character was always Ethan, though he wasn't Harkreader until I met Colleen Harkreader, one of our family medicine residents here in Charlotte, and loved the name so much I asked her and her husband if I could use it for my new story. Fortunately, they said yes.

Rosemary Delacroix was originally Kat, a name that fits her well, but not as well as her current, spicier name. As the series goes on, you'll understand why.

Persephone Snow was originally Brooke Bellini, as I needed a posh name for such a cool character, but as the ideas for the rest of the series continued to develop in my mind, her name changed as well, again for reasons that will become clearer as the series progresses.

Luc Delacroix was originally Robert Ward, whose name became much more interesting once I figured out a bit more about him and who he was.

Danielle has been Danielle since I first began this story, though I must admit even her name is borrowed—my first draft of *The Mussorgsky Riddle* starred a psychic named Danielle Escobar rather than the much more appropriately named Mira Tejedor.

Just a little insight into my creative process as well as recording the above for posterity, if not your amusement.

Now for my acknowledgements. As this series progresses, you are going to see a lot of recurring names. Writing a book takes a village almost as much as raising a child. The primary person with butt in chair, of course, has to be me, but without my network of fellow writers and readers to give critique and suggestions, the final product would have been very different and, frankly, not put together nearly as well.

To my first/alpha reader, Joelle Reizes, AKA J.D. Blackrose, thank you for forging through the first version of this manuscript and offering your invaluable insights as well as listening to my endless ramblings as I was producing the early draft. You helped make this story what it is.

To Stuart Jaffe, Venessa Giunta, and Sarah Sover, my second/beta readers, thanks to all of you for your thorough review of what was and what was not on the page and giving me a much-needed perspective from both sides of the gender divide.

To Robyn Huss, for an outstanding job on the edits, thank you for agreeing to help polish this book and series to a high shine.

To Paul Maitland, I'm so happy you were available to create this beautiful cover image. You captured exactly the look I was going for, and I'm proud to have your art on my cover. It's always such a pleasure to see you and Amy Jo at DragonCon each year. I'm glad we finally had the opportunity to work together. Credit to Annie Leibovitz for the original image from Bruce Springsteen's album, *Born in the U.S.A.*

To Natania Barron, your cover designs are always on point and beautiful, not to mention they've sold me plenty a book. Thank you for working with me to put covers on these books gorgeous enough for people to judge them by.

And now, before I close, I must thank the woman who is the muse for not just this book, but this entire series, not to mention the song that initially sent me down this new rabbit hole.

"Shadows of the Night" was composed by D.L. Byron for the 1980 film *Times Square*, but ultimately was not included in the movie or the soundtrack. Recorded first by Helen Schneider in 1980 and then Rachel Sweet in 1981, the most famous take and the one still played the world over is the 1982 recording by Pat Benatar, featured as the lead single from her fourth studio album, *Get Nervous*. The song rocked charts across the world and won Pat Benatar her third Grammy Award for Best Female Rock Vocal Performance in 1983. One of my perennial favorites, I can't tell you how many times I've listened to this 80s rocker.

As for the woman herself, what can one say about Pat Benatar that hasn't already been said? That voice. That range. The skill, the emotion, the power. When she was inducted into the Rock and Roll Hall of Fame in 2022, all I could think was that it was about time. She's been one of my favorite singers since before I was old enough to know exactly who Pat Benatar even was. We all know her songs; they're ingrained in our collective psyche and guaranteed to get your foot tapping and your blood pumping. This book and this series are my thank you to someone who has touched my life so many times in so many ways. Pat Benatar, may you continue to rock the world for years to come. This series is dedicated to you.

ABOUT THE AUTHOR

Darin Kennedy, born and raised in Winston-Salem, NC, is a graduate of Wake Forest University and Bowman Gray School of Medicine. After completing family medicine residency in the mountains of Virginia, he served eight years as a United States Army physician and wrote his first novel in the sands of northern Iraq.

His first published novel, *The Mussorgsky Riddle,* was born from a fusion of two of his lifelong loves: classical music and world mythology. *The Stravinsky Intrigue* continues those same themes, and his **Fugue & Fable** trilogy culminates in *The Tchaikovsky Finale.* **The Pawn Stratagem**, his contemporary fantasy trilogy of *Pawn's Gambit, Queen's Peril,* and *King's Crisis* combines contemporary fantasy, superheroics, and the ancient game of chess. His young adult novel is *Carol,* a modern-day retelling of *A Christmas Carol* billed as Scrooge meets *Mean Girls.*

His latest series, **Songs of the Ascendant,** falls at the intersection of *Highlander, X-Men, Buffy the Vampire Slayer,* and *Chuck,* all told through a filter of 80s pop music and specifically the oeuvre of Pat Benatar. Comprised thus far of *Shadows of the Night, All Fired Up,* and *You Better Run,* this story is just getting started.

His short stories can be found in numerous anthologies and magazines, and the best, particularly those about a certain *Necromancer for Hire,* are collected for your reading pleasure under Darin's imprint, 64Square Publishing.

Doctor-by-day and novelist-by-night, he writes and practices medicine in Charlotte, NC. When not engaged in either of the above activities, he has been known to strum the guitar, enjoy a bite of sushi, and rumor has it he even sleeps on occasion. Find him online at darinkennedy.com.

THE BAND
ETHAN HARKREADER
PERSEPHONE SNOW
DANIELLE DELACROIX – DAUGHTER OF NEITH
LUC DELACROIX
ROSEMARY DELACROIX

SKIOMANCERS
JOHAN KRAGE | RUPERT MARTIN
FALA HAWKINS | DMITRI DROZDOV

ELEMENTALISTS
DIETRICH FALCO – AEROMANCER
VIOLETA LOPEZ – HYDROMANCER
DAICHI KANDA – GEOMANCER
ADA ABEBE – PYROMANCER

THERIODANS
LINUS – WOLF
HAROLD – HYENA
NEKO – TIGER

OTHERS
THE DRIVER
THE GREYHOUND
MADAME MIDNIGHT / THE MIDNIGHT ANGEL
EL ÁNGEL DEL ALBA / THE ANGEL OF THE MORNING
THE CARDINAL

SHADOWS OF THE NIGHT - PAT BENATAR
WORKIN' FOR A LIVIN' - HUEY LEWIS & THE NEWS
THE WARRIOR - SCANDAL
HEARTBREAK BEAT - THE PSYCHEDELIC FURS
HARD TO SAY I'M SORRY - CHICAGO
SHE'S A BEAUTY - THE TUBES
MIDDLE OF THE ROAD - THE PRETENDERS
YOU'RE THE BEST - JOE ESPOSITO
TAKE MY BREATH AWAY - BERLIN
SYSTEM OF SURVIVAL - EARTH, WIND & FIRE
DANCING IN THE STREET - DAVID BOWIE/MICK JAGGER
HOT HOT HOT - BUSTER POINDEXTER
DRIVE - THE CARS
I THINK WE'RE ALONE NOW - TIFFANY
TALK TALK - TALK TALK
RHYTHM OF THE NIGHT - DEBARGE
MIXED EMOTIONS - THE ROLLING STONES
ROAD TO NOWHERE - TALKING HEADS
RUNNING WITH THE NIGHT - LIONEL RICHIE
NEVER SURRENDER - COREY HART
PAPA DON'T PREACH - MADONNA
HIGHWAY TO HELL - AC/DC
DANGER ZONE - KENNY LOGGINS
QUEEN OF LAS VEGAS - THE B-52'S
WELCOME TO THE JUNGLE - GUNS N' ROSES
EYE OF THE TIGER - SURVIVOR
TAKE IT ON THE RUN - REO SPEEDWAGON
BROKEN WINGS - MR. MISTER
FEELS LIKE THE FIRST TIME - FOREIGNER
IN THE AIR TONIGHT - PHIL COLLINS
CROSSFIRE - STEVIE RAY VAUGHAN
SONGBIRD - KENNY G
WHEN IT'S OVER - LOVERBOY
IT'S NOT OVER ('TIL IT'S OVER) - JEFFERSON STARSHIP
ANOTHER BRICK IN THE WALL - PINK FLOYD

KICKSTARTER BACKERS

A special thank you to our 227 Kickstarter Backers!
You helped make this happen, and these books are for you!

~

Sheryl R. Hayes, Kiersten Keipper, Bill Feero, Chuck Teal, Beth
Wojiski, Kerney Williams, Dino Hicks, Jessica Bay, Rowan Stone, Josh
Minchew, V. Hartman DiSanto, Hope Griffin Diaz, April Baker,
Princess Donut, Allison Charlesworth, Shanda, maileguy, Joelle
Reizes, Alexandra Corrsin, Joseph Procopio, Kevin A. Davis, Robert S.
Evans, Eric P. Kurniawan, Amber Derpinghaus, Andy Bartalone, R.
David Grimes, Patti & Joan Holland, Scott Casey, Asha Jade Goodwin,
Chuck & Colleen Parker, Jessica Nettles, Sarah J. Sover, Joe Compton,
Brendan Lonehawk, Tera, James & Hannah Fulbright, Chris
Fletemier, Carol B, A. L. Kaplan, Joey & Matt Starnes, Wanda
Harward, Dennis M. Myers, Evelyn M, Nick Crook, Bob!, Bill Bibo Jr.,
Karen Palmer, Dina Barron, Charlie "Kaiju Mapping" Kaufman,
Nancy E. Dunne, Rachel A. Brune, Noella Handley, Sara T. Bond, SM
Hillman, C Keeley, John L. French, Anthony Martin, Lynn K, Fay
Shlanda, Cristov Russell, Candice N. Carp, Samuel Montgomery-
Blinn, Susan Griffith, Vee Luvian, Randy Cantrell, Gail Z. Martin,
Tawni Muon, Caryn S, Jimmy Liang, Preacher Todd, Casey & Travis
Schilling, The King of Rhye, Ruth Brazell, Melisa Todd, Vic Chase,
Tom Sink, Nicholas Ahlhelm, Donna Berryman, Richard Novak, Liz
Lamb, Angie Ross, Jonathan Casas, Christy Wilhelm, Robert Claney,
Carol Gyzander, Ollie Oxxenfree, Ángel González, Caitlin Wright,
Michelle Botwinick, Ashley & Cody, Amelia Sides, Nicole Rich,
Ardinzul, Scott Valeri, Richard Dansky, Josh Bluestein, K.H. DeNeen,
David Price, Mair Clan, Leonard Rosenthol, Vikki Perry, RHR,
Jennifer & Benjamin Adelman, Everette Beach, Charlie Hawkins, Zeb
Berryman, Julia Benson-Slaughter, Jesse Adams, Ash Peeples, Susan

Ragsdale, Tina Hoffmann, Robert Osborne, A.M. Giddings, Michelle LeBlanc, Amanda, Ken St Clair, J. T. Arralle, Alec Christensen, hemisphire, Marian Gosling, Zack Keedy, Dee Kennedy, Andrea Fornero, Allison Finch, Sandy Reece, Maya Barb, Shirley Kohl, Ronald H. Miller, Adrianne McDonald, James Ball III, Louise K, Elyse M Grasso, Steve Ryder, Debbie Yerkes, Brendon Towle, LB Clark, Jenn Huerta, Emily L, Eric Guy, Reverend Trevor Curtis, Jim Reader, Shauna Kantes, Stephanie Taylor, Kyla M, Micah Cash, Eric R. Asher, Cindy & Scott Kuntzelman, Avery Wild, Wes "nothing clever to say" Smith, Tamsin Silver, Steve Saffel, phoenix17, Mike Dubost, M.C. Jordan, Sarah Thompson, Cursed Dragon Ship Publishing, Venessa Giunta, Drew Bailey, Sue Phillips, LaZrus66, Scott M. Williams, William C. Tracy, Larissa Lichty, David Scoggins, Mari Mancusi, Jim Ryan, Seth Keipper, Marc Alan Edelheit, Dr. William Alexander Graham IV, Perry Harward, Liam Fisher, Jessica Glanville, Susan Roddey, Regina Kirby, Jeremy Bredeson & Leon Moses, Misty Massey, Janet Iannantuono, Regis Murphy, "Yes That Mark" Wilcox, Berta Platas, Kristen Clark, Matt, B. Y., Theresa Glover, Carol Malcolm, Dr. Keith Hunter Nelson, Adam, Leigh A. Boros & Robert A. Hilliard Jr., Aysha Rehm, Gary Phillips, Tom Savola, Audrey Hackett, Michael J. Sullivan, Annarose Mitchell, Karen M, Patrick J. Blanchard, Kayleigh Osborne, Chris Oakley, Andrea Judy, Casey, Helen Gassaway, J. Matthew Saunders, Carol Mammano, Danielle Ackley-McPhail & eSpec Books, Jared Nelson, and The Creative Fund by BackerKit

SONGS OF THE ASCENDANT

Shadows of the Night

All Fired Up

You Better Run

ALSO BY DARIN KENNEDY

FUGUE & FABLE

The Mussorgsky Riddle

The Stravinsky Intrigue

The Tchaikovsky Finale

THE PAWN STRATAGEM

Pawn's Gambit

Queen's Peril

King's Crisis

Carol: Being a Ghost Story of Christmas

The April Sullivan Chronicles: Necromancer for Hire

Printed in the USA
CPSIA information can be obtained
at www.ICGtesting.com
CBHW021249060624
9643CB00005B/18

9 781943 748044